THE FEY HOTEL

BOOK ONE IN THE HAUNTED CREATURES, HAUNTED PLACES STANDALONE SERIES

VERMILION H BAINE

THE FEY HOTEL

VERMILION H BAINE

For information contact: www.authorvermilionhbaine.com

Formatting and Interior Design by Vermilion H Baine
Cover Illustration by Rashed AlAroka
Cover Design by Safeer Ahmed
Title Font by Balibilly Design
Interior Title Illustration by A.B. Fominaya

Developmental Editing by Jessica Stowe
Copy/Line Editing by Belle Manuel
Proofreading by Jessica Hay

Paperback ISBN: 979-8-9888144-0-5
Ebook ISBN: 979-8-9888144-1-2

First Edition: January 2024
10 9 8 7 6 5 4 3 2 1

The Fey Hotel is the first book in the *Haunted Creatures, Haunted Places* series.

The *Haunted Creatures, Haunted Places* series comprises multiple books, all set in the same modern, magical world and all contain elements of enemies to lovers within them. Each book is a standalone novel and can be read on its own.

Books in the *Haunted Creatures, Haunted Places* series (in order of publication)

The Fey Hotel

The Academy of the Dead

CONTENT WARNINGS

While The Fey Hotel is a dark, adult (18+) modern fantasy, it is rather lighthearted. That being said, I would like to warn the reader of some darker content.

Warnings: harsh language, dealing with loss of a parent, physical violence, swordplay, torture, tooth extraction, characters with anxiety, animals in precarious situations (that they survive!), brief mention of fertility issues, on-page romance between consenting adults

THE FEY HOTEL PLAYLIST

Hotel California
Eagles

Surface Pressure
Jessica Darrow

Sound of Silence
Disturbed

Monster
Dodie

Free
Florence + The Machine

Run
Daughter

Last One Standing
Zoe Clark

Cold Arms
Mumford & Sons

Blood Upon The Snow
Hozier and Bear McCreary

The View From Here
Octavia Spencer and Will Ferrel

I'm Not Calling You A Liar
Florence + The Machine

What's Wrong With Me
Zoe Clark

The Night We Met
Lord Huron

Oceans Away
Barlow & Bear

Into The Unknown
Idina Menzel and AURORA

Northern Attitude (with Hozier)
Noah Kahan and Hozier

—because angry girls deserve cozy love stories, too—

CHAPTER 1
AVALON

Avalon's eyelids ached so heavily that she had to fight the persistent, masochistic urge to gouge out her own eyes. As if she could dig past those gelatinous orbs and up into the grey matter that sat behind them, clawing out the traitorous parts of her brain that made her an anxious, sleep-deprived mess.

All she wanted was sleep—dreamless, boring sleep. She shook her bottle of melatonin, the empty silence mocking her. Exhaustion tickled her synapses, eliciting an unwelcome, hysterical giggle that echoed throughout her drafty, one-bedroom apartment in Seattle. An apartment she shared with her younger sister.

The anticipation of her little sister's night terrors, real and deadly, was what kept her up at night. For a banshee like Odele, living in such an overpopulated city was unbearable. Death was constant, cyclical. It was killing Odele. More than anything, they needed to leave. If only the accident hadn't depleted their meager stash of getaway money.

Avalon's resume blinked at her from her computer screen, the name *Avalon Golightly* changing fonts as she fussed over tiny details that mattered little. Not that she *wanted* to change careers. Their boss was a huge pushover—that wasn't something one should give up willingly. But the hotel management service she worked for couldn't control where they sent her. And that stint in Chicago had nearly killed her sister. Where Odele had foreseen a murder so bloody, so wrong, that she'd screamed her vocal cords raw and had fled their hotel room before Avalon could stop her.

Odele had run into the street, half-awake and searching for the future victim to warn them of their fate and—

The dull, wet thud of her sister's body hitting the hood of a car was not something Avalon wished to relive. It would be a long time before they'd recover from that hospital bill or the associated trauma Odele had dreamt that night.

Emergency surgery left a hole in one's pocket. A sucking, parasitic black hole. And they were both suffering the consequences of that forced down payment.

"I still can't believe they even paid it," Avalon muttered, her parents' motives still unknown to her. "Even if it had been to save face." Perhaps it would have been better to remain in debt to the hospital, rather than the mercurial Bruce and Valerie.

Thrusting away from her crowded work desk, away from the piles of unanswered invitations to various fundraisers for their father's reelection campaign, gilded and unfeeling, Avalon headed to the bedroom she split with her sister.

Odele lay sleeping, still as a corpse and nearly the same shade as one. Her pale hair curled and waved, loose and undoubtedly going to be a giant tangle when she awoke. There was a time in their childhood when Avalon would watch Odele sleep for hours, waiting to soothe any fussing before their father heard and quieted her down in his own way.

The urge was still there—to watch, to guard. Avalon forced her heels to turn and kicked off her house slippers before sliding into bed. Her eyes had barely fluttered closed when the premonition appeared.

Odele, her kind face twisted painfully into a scream, obscured her vision. Avalon hauled herself out of bed, her comforter flying across the room. She didn't need to see past the image of Odele in agony to reach her sister's side, finding her place beside Odele's bed by memory alone. Their hands clasped together in the dark, and Odele's sharp intake of breath was a warning for what would come next.

The wailing.

Her sight clearing from her vision, Avalon snatched the hearing protection off the wall where it hung, waiting, and threw it over her ears. Odele had already found her mouth guard and ground her teeth on it, her scream escaping in shrill, but hushed tones. Ignoring the neighbors banging on their shared wall, Avalon let her sister dig her nails into the back of her hand. The sisters had done their best to soundproof the tiny room, attaching foam panels to the walls, but it was impossible to muffle a banshee's scream entirely.

"I'm here! I'm here, Odd." Avalon's words became lost in her sister's tearful shriek—but she didn't let up. Avalon muttered her reassurances, anyway, and ran her thumb along Odele's knuckles.

Avalon was not gentle, but here, in the dark, with her little sister clutching desperately to her hand, Avalon could be as soft and as soothing as Odele needed her to be.

Her skin bore crescents, red and deep, after Odele's fit

passed, and her grip slackened. Avalon slipped the protection off her ears, the faint chime of her tinnitus perhaps more obvious now that she was listening for it. She never mentioned the constant ringing in her head—Odele was responsible for it, and Avalon hated to remind her sister of that fact.

Odele slipped back into sleep, though fitfully, and Avalon made no noise as she returned to her own bed.

She thought back to the first few nights Odele's powers had awakened. Bruce thought such outbursts required physical solutions—physical *consequences.*

"I can quiet her down! Let me try!" The plea of a desperate child forced to protect another echoed throughout their high society household. Someone pulled Avalon out of her younger sister's room, some maid or one of her father's security team. Her heels dug into the spotless white carpet, failing to halt her forced retreat.

Odele's wails increased in volume as their father entered her room and shut the door.

Avalon hated that her Sight sometimes threw her back into the past, rather than into the future. It didn't matter how many times she had prevented Bruce's violence. Avalon would always remember the times that she wasn't enough.

Things would seem less dire in the daylight. It wouldn't make them any less so, but she'd be able to shove aside her fears for a time.

She wished her sister could have such a reprieve.

"What was it this time? Was there anyone you recognize?" Avalon couldn't wait another minute, not even for her sister to finish chewing the sugary cereal Avalon thought she had hidden from her.

Odele's golden eyes, the only feature the girls coincidentally shared, peered sleepily over her rainbow children's cereal at her anxiety-ridden sister. Their round kitchen table barely fit the pair of them. Odele leaned back in her chair and stretched her back out—the car accident had left her with a few stiff joints and aches. "It was a mugging gone bad. And I didn't recognize anyone. As usual."

It was worse when Odele recognized the victim in her premonitions. Her unlucky banshee sister. Avalon couldn't imagine being unable to stop such dark visions. Not that Avalon's own Sight always let her control what she saw.

Avalon almost poured her own bowl of cereal, something bran-filled and boring, before she set it back down and opted for coffee. Living here was unbearable for Odele. People died in Seattle every day, and when it was violent, Odele got a front-row seat to every gory detail.

Avalon took over the conversation, knowing Odele's distaste for discussing her deathly foreshadowing. Avalon was the type to dive too deeply into things, to obsess. So, she let the matter rest entirely, clenching her jaw and willing the need to over-analyze to vanish. "What does Thompson have you doing today?" The sisters worked together, and though they worked in different departments, it eased Avalon's anxiety greatly.

"I have to renovate a B&B on a shoestring budget," Odele beamed. For anyone else, those types of jobs were nightmares—giving an entire inn a makeover while pinching pennies. But Odele loved it. Her sister continued eating her already too soggy breakfast. "And what about you?"

"New client, I think." Avalon thought back to their boss's

email before she'd gone down a late-night rabbit hole of job searching and resume editing. "I have to go in person. Thompson said the client isn't even sure what he needs."

"Oh, it's one of those. Don't get impatient!" Odele ordered, her utensil now stabbing in Avalon's direction like a spear. "I know how you get when you have to deal with someone who can't make decisions. Not everyone can cheat and see the future like you can."

She didn't appreciate the accusation in her sister's tone. Avalon was well aware of her problem. Having anxiety and slight paranoia was bad enough without having the ability to ease her worries by peeking into the near future. Avalon looked into the future so often, and for such silly reasons, that she went to bed every night exhausted past the point of functioning.

"Odd, If I were trying to cheat at life, we'd have won the lottery ten times by now." Avalon sighed, her coffee leaving an unpleasant taste in her mouth. "Though the Commission wards against that, anyway. Takes the fun out of being a Seer." She was, of course, referring to the North American branch of the global *Commission of Magic Management.* It was previously named the *Commission of Unnatural Threats,* which, after an abbreviation issue, had been quickly changed.

The all-seeing, ever-annoying Commission kept all beings with the tiniest crumb of magical abilities in line. And Seers were no exception.

"Eat something without sugar," Avalon advised, taking away her sister's bowl of multi-colored sludge.

Odele leaned back, brushing crumbs off her fuzzy blue pajamas. "I don't think I will."

On the way to the office, Avalon dropped off Odele at her B&B job site, promising to return before it grew dark. Odele was spared the traffic that soured Avalon's mood as she drove the rest of the way. She parked her deteriorating car, gathered her laptop and half-finished coffee, and stepped out. Once exposed to the outdoor wind, Avalon's wild hair, somewhat tamed into a loose, braided bun, tugged ruthlessly at her temples. Feeling a headache coming on, Avalon wanted nothing more than to pull her hair—a bright blonde and strawberry mess—free and arrive at her meeting looking like she was coming from an audition for *The Taming of the Shrew*. But she avoided the urge, smoothing her dark green silk shirt before stepping out of her car.

Thompson Hotel Management Solutions was housed in a small brick corner building. The front of the building was all glass, their logo bright and clean against windows that were washed daily. Thompson kept the place spotless and so minimalist that it hurt Odd's soul (or so she had claimed). Avalon visited the building rarely, as she did most of her work on her computer and through frustrating virtual meetings.

Thompson's helped hotels with a multitude of things—training new managers, exploring new technology, interior design (Odele's side of things), and web design (Avalon's expertise). If Avalon was attending this new client meeting in person, there must have been major problems with the hotel's website. Though Avalon had her certification in management as well. Thompson might have been trying to hit two birds with one stone.

As Avalon strode inside, the secretary, Miss Pike, waved a hand in greeting and never glanced away from her well-read bodice ripper. Miss Pike was a witch (though a weak one), mainly skilled in aura reading.

Avalon cleared her throat. "Is the client here, Miss Pike?"

Miss Pike smiled, placing her book and its shirtless cover down. "Oh, yes. He arrived as soon as we opened."

Avalon decided she may as well learn a little about what she was about to walk into. She could cheat and peer into the near future, but she was curious to get Miss Pike's opinion. She saw things Avalon overlooked. Not to mention that Avalon's Sight exhausted her, and she needed to learn to work without it.

"What was the client like?"

"Dressed casually. And..." Miss Pike paused, readjusting her glasses. "This may sound odd, but he's one of those men that look out of place in this century. Like he should have 'the conqueror' after his name."

"I meant what kind of mood was he in..."

The secretary hesitated. "His aura is compatible with yours."

Avalon raised a brow and hummed, unsure of what Miss Pike wanted her to do with that. Luckily, her boss made a distressed groan and Avalon pushed further into the office.

Thompson was in the hallway, nervously picking at a soon to be dead plant. He brightened when he saw her, even as she smacked his hand away from the suffering fern. Thompson was completely human and believed, naively, that those touched with magic, however faint, were good luck.

It was a belief Avalon found difficult to share. Most witches she had met were fine, but the *Folk*... She knew from personal experience what they were capable of.

"Thank the gods you're here," Thompson whispered, eyes darting about as if they were being followed. "The owner of the Refuge on the Moor has already arrived. Negotiations have *not* been going well."

Facing the most demanding of clients wasn't anything to Avalon, not when one grew up in a household like she had. Her mother, Valerie, had often roped her into helping plan her very demanding father's political events. Back then, Avalon had hated it, but she had to acknowledge that the experience helped her now.

"Stop running your hands through your hair. It's making you look greasy." Avalon took the client's thin file out of Thompson's hands before he wrung it to pieces. "Refuge on the Moor?" She flipped through the file quickly. "Good name, at least. Located on the southwestern Washington coast? It's got to be hard to draw guests all the way out there."

"They have a steady stream of regulars, but they've been getting some complaints after the sudden change in owners. It's going to be an extensive project—the owner is new to the business. His, ah, his mother passed away."

Sympathy softened her features before her foot began tapping with increasing speed. Getting her hint, Thompson led her down the hall. When she stepped inside the conference room, thanking Thompson quickly for opening the door for her, Avalon became aware of two people in her periphery. Before she could even turn to greet them, one of them had already risen to his feet.

Avalon made eye contact with a broad chest and blinked, her brows already trying to meet in irritation. Someone was much too close, forcing her to crane her neck to look up and offer her waning excuse of a smile.

The client took up too much space in the bland, too white meeting room, practically looming over her. The impeccably tailored suit he wore clashed with Miss Pike's claim that he'd been taking part in casual Friday. Though the man seemed uncomfortable in such attire, pulling and pinching at his seams.

His brows were dark, angled in such a way that made him appear angry. The hair was black, nearly blue in the fluorescent light. The dark waves were thick, fighting tirelessly against whatever gel had molded them carefully into place.

Though he was a prospective client, Avalon refused to move first, her face blank and unbothered as she waited patiently for him to realize their inappropriate proximity. Grey eyes, reminding her of a winter's storm and the smoke of a house fire all at once, met hers before he took a slow step back.

Avalon wordlessly took her place at the oval conference table and began setting up her laptop. She could hear Thompson making introductions.

Thompson was always one to overreact, but for once, Avalon could understand his discomfort. The client wasn't just unsettling because of his size—his gaze settled directly on a person, unblinking and seeming to glean hidden information off their every move, breath, or eye twitch.

"Mr. Cavanaugh, this is my web developer and designer, Avalon Golightly." Avalon raised a hand in a simple, uncaring greeting. She typed Refuge on the Moor into her search engine. "She will also help you with your management, ah, issues."

Her typing paused; it was going to be an extended stay then. Her brows rose, relaxing when Thompson added, "Of course, her sister Odele will be there, too, to take care of your interiors."

"Mr. Cavanaugh, who did you bring with you today?" Thompson indicated the small, kind faced woman that sat poised next to him. The blonde, with grey peppered in, was probably in her sixties, though she seemed to be the most energetic person in the room. She offered them a genuine smile.

Slowly moving his focus away from Avalon's computer

screen, Mr. Cavanaugh's head swung like a predator who was carefully deciding between two equally annoying prey. He spoke with a light accent, the ghost of a brogue emerging as he made introductions.

"This is Nora Lee. She's our head of housekeeping and is helping me get the books in order." The man stared in Avalon's direction until she met his eyes. "I suppose you'll be the one helping us transition over to electronic bookkeeping." Not a question. Nothing he said had an ounce of uncertainty in his rumbling, steady voice.

"I'm going to be helping you with a lot of things." Avalon whirled her laptop around so Mr. Cavanaugh and Nora Lee could see her screen fully. She had their website on display. "This—this is *unusable*. Half of these links don't even work. It would be better for me to start from scratch. But I want to wait until I see the place in person and get an idea of your clientele."

Mr. Cavanaugh frowned, the lines somehow enhancing his handsome, angular features. He was attractive, unfairly so, and in that stoic, uncaring sort of way that both intrigued Avalon and pissed her off. "My mother's personality made up for any technological shortcomings. But I'm not gifted in the same way she was. And," he huffed, clenching his jaw, "we have several weddings to prepare for. And one that is especially important for our reputation."

"I see." Weddings were her least favorite part of the hotel business. But there was no getting around it. Odele would be busy with her own projects, so Avalon would be forced to work alone with Mr. Cavanaugh until the contract was up.

Avalon sat by while Thompson and the innkeeper hashed out every excruciating detail of the pending contract. She nodded or shook her head, depending on the context, whenever

Thompson shot her a hopeless glance. Cavanaugh was a brutal negotiator. She had to give him that.

Thompson's phone vibrated, and he stood quickly, eager for any excuse to leave. The man was absolutely drenched in sweat despite the cool, fall air. "Avalon, since we agreed upon the contract verbally, can you oversee the signing of it while I take care of this?" He waved his phone around and vanished before Avalon could muster up an answer. Or call him a coward.

Fishing the new, finished contract out of the office printer, Avalon gave it a cursory once-over before passing it to the client. He had requested ten weeks of service—that was a long time to pack for. A long time to be living out of a hotel room. *Not that our apartment is much larger than a standard suite.*

The man made no move to take the contract from her. Avalon hid her frown and meaningfully slid the papers across the table to him. She walked over, extending her hand in greeting. "I look forward to working with you, Mr. Cavanaugh."

One would have thought she was handing him a snake. Those grey eyes widened, and then narrowed suspiciously. If it wasn't crazy, Avalon would have thought she saw him lean physically away from her.

She stood there like an idiot while he sneered distastefully at her hand. But if he was determined to make this awkward, Avalon would gladly play along. She thrust her hand further forward, and her smile was fake and aggressive.

"Elden." Nora Lee tapped Mr. Cavanaugh's arm. But whatever the head housekeeper was going to say was lost. Mr. Cavanaugh, *Elden*, left the room, brushing past her hand without another glance back.

Avalon curled her hand into a fist, searching for her calm while Nora Lee finished up the paperwork herself. Nora Lee cringed as she said, "You'll have to deal with me, I'm afraid." Her pen danced hurriedly across the lines, the only messy thing about the woman. "Elden told me to handle this part. I should have told you." An apology from someone Avalon doubted should ever have to apologize for anything.

"Oh, that's completely fine," Avalon chirped, her tone almost believable. She instead focused on stretching out her fisted hand, willing the tension and anger to leave her bones. "I'm sure we'll get along better once we get to work."

Nora Lee's smile faded.

"I see why you were nervous." Avalon passed the finished contract to her boss, pointing to Nora Lee's signature, which was illegible, but still there. Thompson's office was cavernous and filled with only essentials. "Cavanaugh looks like he should be waving a sword and shouting, 'There can only be one!'"

When Thompson didn't laugh, she rolled her eyes. "I've told you to see that movie a dozen times. If you can't understand my references by now, that is on you."

"I think he's a vampire."

"I think he's a jackass. And it's an uncommonly sunny day in Seattle." Thompson suspected anyone and everyone of possessing some sort of supernatural ability or background. It was odd, or a miracle, that he remained oblivious to what *she* was.

Thompson jumped as if the client might hear them. "He's a well-paying one, at least. You can work with him, right?"

Her smile showed too many teeth. "You know I can work with anyone. He just might not like it."

CHAPTER 2
ELDEN

It was not a relaxing process, driving a manual transmission through the traffic and sudden uphill starts riddled throughout the Seattle streets. Again, as Elden had done plenty of times while he was replacing, rewiring, and rebuilding his mother's old Ford, he questioned her aggravating choice in vehicles. He had worked the math, and he spent more time repairing the damned thing than driving it.

A jaywalker strode right into the side of his truck and had the nerve to curse *him* out. Elden grimaced. "I pray we don't need to come back here. Ever." His white-knuckled grip on the steering wheel didn't relax until they reached Highway 101.

Nora Lee was unusually quiet. That meant she was about to launch into a lecture he'd currently be powerless to escape. "I understand your avoidance of handshakes and promises, but I thought that girl was about to murder you with her fountain pen when you turned your nose up at her hand."

He scowled, checking his mirrors to buy him some time to think. "If you know the why, what's the point of bringing this up?"

"We have to work with that girl, and you have a habit of not making things as easy as they should be." Suspicion clouded her clear, kind eyes. "At least you were well-dressed. *Unusually* well-dressed."

That unhelpful statement was ignored. Nora Lee continued, never having needed a response to carry a conversation. "She was dressed rather nice, too, wasn't she?"

The only sign that he gave he heard her was a brief grunt.

"Skirt was a little tight in the back, I'm sure you noticed."

"I regret making you head of HR," Elden snapped.

When he had refused Avalon's handshake, brushing past her extended offer of friendship (who was he kidding, *acquaintanceship*), there had been a spark of something uncontrolled and dark in the woman. Something that was meant for the wild, and not for a boardroom.

Or meant for the bedroom, some ignored part of him snickered. Elden gritted his teeth and refocused on the memory, recalling how swiftly her eyes had narrowed and that customer service demeanor had been stripped away.

It was fury he read in her, fury bloody and raw, and directed so fiercely at him that it was hard to believe such a tiny human could boil up such animosity for so small a slight.

And quickly it had been tapped down, something he knew personally took years of practice and willpower. Fighting one's nature would never become habit—it would always be work, tremendous, unrewarding work.

Still, Elden was unbothered. Solutions came to him easily— all of them quick, logical, and efficient. "She won't be training me, anyway. She'll have her hands full with Tahoma and Kenan." Especially Kenan. The man could accomplish many things, but Elden still wasn't sure if hotel management was one of them. It was unavoidable—he didn't wish to promote one twin and neglect the other. Neither of them had the right qualities for the job as it was.

"Handshakes and signatures won't turn you into your father. It would take more than that to strike a true deal," Nora Lee said, her lecture ongoing. "And you're nothing like him. Ashling made sure of it, and I need you to understand that."

Sure, he wouldn't purposely strike a bargain, but if the human said the wrong thing at the wrong time...and humans themselves were untrustworthy. He knew what a bad deal could lead to, and it was not worth the risk.

"I know—"

"And yet guilt hangs over you like a storm's shadow," she scoffed. "You hold shame so close to your heart that I'm afraid you'll turn Catholic."

"Sounds like a good way to find myself the center of an exorcism."

The sight of his mother's—no, *his* inn failed to lift Elden's spirits. The edges of the hotel drive needed trimming, leaves needed to be raked, and branches picked up. And Elden couldn't even think about the *mud.* Autumn always left the inn a mess, turning the Refuge on the Moor into a beautiful fall landscape—for about two weeks. After that, the inn needed more maintenance than he could do himself.

"Your mother loved the inn during the fall. The air's so crisp." Nora Lee stared dreamily out her car window as they hit the inn's gravel driveway. "And, of course, you were home."

They parked the truck in the inn's garage, walking together inside the Refuge. Nora Lee had been his mother's truest friend, and privy to most of her secrets. Perhaps even more than Elden was. But the frequency that the head of housekeeping brought up his late mother sometimes made him flinch.

Lucky for Elden, as the pair entered the inn, a regularly scheduled interruption arrived. Elden batted the air in front of his face, nearly smacking the utensil to the ground. "What," he seethed, "have I said about shoving food into my face?"

"Well, every time I do it, you say it's delicious." Lyra, the over-enthusiastic chef that she was, tried again with her current weapon of choice—the spoon. He ought to keep her locked up inside the kitchens so she could no longer hide behind the front desk to attack him with food. "How am I supposed to learn a lesson when I get exactly what I want?"

Elden took a bite of whatever soup she was force-feeding him this time. He raised one brow, forcing a blank look as he said, monotone, "Did you add enough salt?"

"I ought to kill you for even suggesting that I did not." They weren't related, but Lyra had so many cousins that she told him he may as well be added to the list. "I'm placing this on Maetta and Sabella's wedding menu. Ricotta dumplings in onion broth."

"Maetta's been calling for days. I was hoping I could hold off and have Thompson's Hotel Management deal with it."

"Not looking forward to telling her the previous event planner is, ah, no longer available?" Lyra danced from one foot to the other, bouncing with nervous energy. "That's not a bomb I'd care to drop. And you, I wouldn't exactly call you sil-ver-tongued."

"Yes, save that word for the rest of my damned family," he

griped, not wanting Lyra to see that barb stung more than it should.

"Call Maetta. Say *something* and let these experts handle the more sensitive parts. Otherwise, what are we paying them for?"

A miracle. Elden walked behind the front desk and into the inn's main office, ignored the mess that the past year had left, and picked up the phone.

Maetta clicked her tongue when she recognized his rough, unemotional voice and let him know precisely how many calls he'd missed. "I heard about your mother," she began. "I'm so sorry, Elden. You know I hate to even bring this up, but I want to know how this is going to affect our wedding."

Perhaps now was not the time to inform her that Ashling's binder and contact list were gone, lost in the mess Ashling had called the main office.

Elden made assurances and mentioned the hiring of a temporary manager (who actually knew what she was doing). It might be cruel, throwing Avalon to the mercies of Maetta and her goal of a "perfect wedding", but he was sure he'd get over the guilt. If he needed help doing so, he'd just look at the bill Thompson sent him.

Next on Elden's agenda was inspecting the surrounding gardens and the grassy hill that lay directly in the center of the hedge maze. Nothing seemed out of place, but that guaranteed nothing. During his inspection, one of the managers-in-training appeared to help him finish up.

Kenan was overly friendly, something that benefited his new managerial duties, but he also had a bad habit of laughing at anyone who was upset with him. Less than ideal for someone who had to deal with needy customers all day. Not that Elden, his patience at his young age already spent, was any better suited for it.

"This came through for you," Kenan said, thrusting a paper that had spent too much time in his pocket, judging by how wrinkled it was. "I'll be reading over your shoulder, so if you could crouch down a smidge and make that possible for me, I'd appreciate it."

Kenan was shorter than Elden, but the man was much broader and walked around in a way that annoyingly and perfectly accentuated this trait. Elden hunched over and skimmed the note.

My dear, mysterious nephew,

Congratulations and condolences! Losing my sister was sudden, and I'm sure the new title of warden weighs heavy on your naïve, little head.

I cannot wait to meet you, nephew! We have much in common, as I am a warden myself. I'm sure you'll be pleased to meet with me since you've yet to introduce yourself to any of your mother's family. No, we're not upset. We're disappointed.

Surely this was solely Ashling's wish, to keep family apart, and you'll be keen to correct it.

Patiently waiting,
Uncle Evander

Elden shut his eyes. What would the universe shit on him with next?

"Ah," Kenan read, sobering. "That doesn't seem good."

It was fine. He could ignore his uncle for now. The

additional help would allow him the time to focus on his *other* job. Even if Elden had pissed the woman off, Avalon would have to deal with him very little if he had his way. Once she arrived, Avalon Golightly would make his life infinitely easier.

CHAPTER 3
AVALON

Odele was way too excited for 5am on a Friday. She had an entire vacation planned for their west coast stay. Among the activities were gems such as cranberry picking.

Avalon shoved down on the lid of the tiny trunk of their car until it somewhat clicked into place. Their apartment's parking lot was deserted, triggering Avalon's paranoia and putting her on guard. Odele's tools and paint brushes took up the entire trunk of their aging sedan, and she had dumped their clothes and toiletries unceremoniously into the backseat.

Avalon couldn't keep herself from being a grouch. "I don't think we're going to get a lot of time off, Odd. This guy, to put it poetically, *sucks.*"

"Maybe he has a germ thing?" Odele tried. Which was useless. Once Avalon formed a grudge, however small, it wasn't going anywhere. "One missed handshake shouldn't—"

"It wasn't missed," Avalon argued, feeling her face flush. "He deliberately ignored me. *He looked down on me.*" How was she going to handle ten weeks answering to this guy? She would have told Thompson to find someone else if it hadn't been for her sister. The inn hugged the western coast of Washington, and the single nearby town had a population of mere hundreds. Odele would finally get a break from wailing and warning Seattle about its many, *many* oncoming deaths.

"He can't help it when he's that tall, can he?"

"Odd!" Avalon started the car, ignoring any new sounds coming from under the hood, and took off, leaving Odele to frantically pull up directions on her phone. She already regretted telling Odele so much about Cavanaugh. "Pick a podcast and stop looking up things for us to do that involve me wading in freezing water. I don't think it's even cranberry harvesting season, anyway." Avalon glanced out the driver's side window at the passing blurred, deciduous trees that were dulled to shades of muddy brown.

"Don't worry," Odele grinned, choosing a podcast about Pacific Northwest mushroom foraging. "I'm sure I'll be able to find something that you'll hate just as much."

The drive to the inn was long, filled with podcasts, and Odele played the same five songs on repeat for an hour. The sisters skipped lunch, not satisfied with the local gas station's rotating hot dogs that Avalon suspected had been spinning for about a week prior to their arrival. Avalon hoped her stomach wouldn't rumble in front of the client—she hated to show weakness in front of her enemies.

Yes, Elden Cavanaugh had upgraded to "mortal nemesis" status after Avalon had hours trapped in a car to sit and steam, playing their last interaction over and over in her mind until Lucifer sat higher in her favor.

As their car approached an empty hollow in the steady line of thick trees, a sign for the inn swung from an arch. The words *Refuge on the Moor* were made of twisted, welded metal. Avalon squinted at the tall iron gate that blocked their path. While they parked and Odele called the inn, requesting to be let in, Avalon kept an eye out for her new adversary.

Fortunately, they were not greeted by Cavanaugh. Nora Lee met them instead at the gate. Nora Lee also arrived flanked by two tan, dark-haired siblings. Those two looked more like bodyguards than hotel employees. It was easy to see that the pair were twins. The brother's hair was shoulder-length, and scattered with small braids, while the sister wore her hair shaved on one side with a long, thick braid down the other. Both were stocky and well-muscled—and were whispering to each other.

The gate swung open, though Avalon failed to see a keypad or remote to actuate that movement. Nora Lee approached their car and waited for Avalon to lower her window.

"Welcome to Refuge on the Moor," Nora Lee smiled, gesturing behind her fruitlessly as the inn was hiding behind groves of giant, old trees. "I'll show you where to park." The older woman turned and hopped on a turquoise bicycle. Nora Lee rode ahead of them slowly down the inn's impressively long driveway, giving Avalon and Odele time to take in the grounds while they followed in their car.

The trees here had succumbed to autumn's kiss, but the leaves were still bright and vibrant in shades of red, yellow, and orange. Small cabins, clean, though Odele pointed out that they could use a little maintenance on the roofing, rested on both sides of the white gravel drive. The tiny homes were spaced far enough apart to give the occupants a genuine sense of solitude, something Avalon appreciated. Most hotels with cabins built them on top of each other—it was easier and cheaper, but less picturesque.

Odele's sudden gasp caused Avalon's foot to stomp on the brakes. Her fingers curled around the steering wheel, squeezing hard as she spat, "What the hell was that for?"

Her sister pinched her arm, pointing off to the left. Past the forest and woven brambles, the inn was finally visible. They had seen pictures, of course. A few images had been posted on that joke of a website, and though most of them were blurry and one even had part of a finger obscuring the shot, Avalon *thought* she had at least an idea of what they were about to walk into.

Coastal inns usually kept up with the seaside motif, but not Refuge on the Moor.

"A castle," Avalon said without enthusiasm.

"A castle!" Odele grabbed her sister's arm and shook her until Avalon swatted her away. "How incredible!"

"How ridiculous."

Avalon was ignored.

"Nanny Blair would have loved this place."

It surprised Avalon that Odele even remembered the woman—the memories of children were untrustworthy and fleeting, and the nanny had left while Odele was still young. She was fired, if one wanted to be technical about it. *But* Odd was right. Nanny Blair had a love for the uncanny, the odd, and the ridiculous for the mad sake of it. It had been a miracle she lasted as long as she did in the rigid Golightly household.

Odele consulted a travel blog from ten years ago. "They're known for their bird watching. And there's even a forge."

"A *what?*"

"Like for a blacksmith. The former owner used to teach classes on forging weapons. Isn't that cool?"

"It is cool," Avalon agreed, searching for such a building. "It's also very weird."

Odele prattled on, planning renovations before she had even seen the inside. Tuning out plans that were sure to change in a minute, Avalon pulled into a parking lot and Nora Lee circled back on her bike to stop at her window.

"You can park in the front." Nora Lee pointed to the first row of empty spaces. "Most of our guests don't use the lot."

"Huh?" Avalon startled at the remark. Refuge on the Moor was more than out of the way—while trying to find the place she had expected Bugs Bunny to pop out of the ground, yakking about wrong turns. How were people getting here if not by car?

"There's a bus service," Nora Lee offered, a little too loudly. "The nearest town, Fair Harbor, is only a two-mile hike. There," she continued, pointing out a small dirt path that vanished into another grove of trees. "It's a lovely walk."

Before Avalon could question this oddity more, Odele had jumped out of the car, skipping to the inn with her sketchpad already in hand. Not wanting to get left behind, or have Odele run into Cavanaugh without her, Avalon settled into a parking space, tossed the car keys to the twins who had followed behind in a golf cart to unload their luggage, and ran to catch up.

Avalon's nose itched as she studied the building before her. The inn was two floors, all white and grey stone on the outside, and ivy trailed lazily down the walls. Large windows with blue stained glass eyed her approach. Such an imperious structure wouldn't be the architectural style Avalon would have chosen for a seaside inn, but it somehow, amongst the golden foliage, didn't seem out of place.

A creek encircled the inn, a small footbridge the only crossing Avalon could find. She knew from her research there was also a lake somewhere, but she failed to see it from her current position. Avalon raced over the creek's bridge, though its bubbling, musical sound drew her in and made her wonder if she'd be able to hear the happy brook from her hotel room.

Once she stepped inside the Refuge on the Moor, Avalon discovered things weren't so bright and cheery. Avalon watched Odele's eyes wander to the low lighting, knowing that would be the first update Odele would make. Though the inn's interior was dated even to Avalon's amateur taste, she felt an overwhelming sense of being cared for once she stepped inside. It was a foreign feeling and made her skin prickle.

The front desk was a huge wooden bench with a dried lavender wreath attached to the front. A golden bell sat next to a vase of dying flowers. The bell was an obvious replacement for an electric bell that sat right next to it. Avalon pushed the button a few times to verify what she already knew—it was broken. The inn appeared to be in mourning; the shades drawn too far closed and faint specks of dust floating in what little light remained. But Avalon could see what it had been, despite all of that. This was once an inn full of choices, full of hope.

"Someone cared about this place. It was someone's heart." The words, too flowery for her tongue, escaped without warning. Odele shot her a teasing grin.

"My mother wanted this place to bring people, however different, together."

Elden Cavanaugh appeared in the foyer, dressed impeccably even at his home field, and an unwelcome heat rushed to Avalon's cheeks. She hadn't wanted to start this business venture by complimenting him—the snub against her was too fresh in her mind. Perhaps he had not heard her?

Luckily, Odele took the opportunity to introduce herself and kept Avalon from saying something vaguely rude. "I'm Odele Golightly. I'll be giving your rooms some maintenance and freshening up. We'll have to go over the scope of my work later. If I could roam the grounds for today, to get a full picture? I don't want to make this place unrecognizable."

Elden's shoulders relaxed at Odele's words; the emotion barely readable. Avalon thought she might have been the only one to catch it, thanks to years of bottling up her own feelings. "Call me Elden. And that's fine. I understand some changes will need to be made. I appreciate that you both can see what this place meant to my mother."

Avalon squirmed under the man's attention. There was no denying it—he *had* heard her. Damn it. She disliked how Elden towered over her little sister, though Odele was tall herself in her willowy way, and, unthinking, Avalon stepped between them. Time to change topics, and quickly. "Since I'm here to fix the website and help with management, I would like to take a look at the guest book. And you had in the contract that you don't need assistance with accounting? Other than the transfer from paper to electronic?"

"Math, I can do," Elden sniped, but his annoyance did not seem to be directed at anyone present. "It's the guests that I could do without."

That would defeat the purpose of owning an inn, Avalon thought. "Also, your electric bell isn't working."

Elden huffed, the tired exhalation of an overworked man. "It is on the list."

Ah, the famous, never-ending list. Avalon doubted the bell was anywhere near the top—it would be years before that particular line item was touched if she didn't step in.

A woman, young and vibrant in bright green clothes, with a heaping amount of black, curly hair, sprinted into the lobby. She was short, tan, and impossibly curvy. A mid-size bombshell. Avalon gave Odele a quick glance to make sure she wasn't drooling.

"When my cousin said he was going to welcome you, I knew I had to get over here." The woman beamed, attempting to wipe a streak of flour off her face and failing. "I'm Lyra, head chef at the Refuge. Would have been here sooner, but I had to get the bread dough kneaded for dinner service. We're renowned for my restaurant here."

"We are the only restaurant for thirty miles." Elden's dry response shocked Avalon, who had assumed humor was beneath him.

Lyra revealed she had seats in the dining room reserved for the sisters. "We'd love to have you join us!"

"We get a meal allowance from the company," Avalon politely returned. "It's not your responsibility to feed us." She didn't want to incur extra charges that she'd have to answer to Thompson for.

"I feed *everyone* here." Lyra smiled aggressively. Not even Avalon felt the need to argue. "I'll see you at seven. Don't be late!"

"I can show you to your rooms," Elden offered. "I'll email you a copy of the guest book, Avalon."

She itched to correct him, to make him call her by her surname. But he had introduced himself as 'Elden' today. It would be immature and petty to make such a demand when she wouldn't make it of anyone else.

Instead, Avalon muttered some thanks, and the sisters

followed him away from the front desk and up a winding staircase. It was then that Avalon learned that there was a third
floor. Well, *nearly* a third floor.

It was a turret, a small tower she didn't see from the outside,
and the stairs leading to it were barely wide enough for one person. It was comical watching Elden walk up that tiny, cramped
staircase. He filled the space, wall to wall, and almost from ceiling to floor.

Someone had painted the door at the end of the stairs a dark
green, and it possessed a single word brushed on it in gold.
Whimsy.

Elden unlocked the door and passed her the key. He entered
the room with her, setting down a basket of lovely smelling
soaps and white towels on the bedside table. A switch flicked,
and the attic was illuminated—strands of feyrie lights hung
across the sloped ceiling. There was a bed, larger than she would
have expected, and a few pieces of furniture—a desk, a
nightstand, and a wardrobe. There was even a bathroom on one
end, tiny, but with all the necessities.

Elden opened some curtains, revealing an arched window
that threw even more light into the room. Avalon took it all in,
noting the color scheme of green, gold, and white scattered
throughout. A pair of books sat on the bed frame, and she inspected them, feeling the pages' soft, worn edges.

Gods, she loved it all.

How infuriating. She was a constant outsider—no place,
not even from her childhood, had ever felt so homey. Avalon
hated to feel this way now. *You love what his mother has accomplished. That has nothing to do with him.*

But there was one thing she could nitpick.

"My sister and I asked for adjoining rooms," she sniffed,

replacing the books in their resting place. "So, this won't work."

"I apologize." Elden sounded stiff, unsure. And then his voice became certain. "Your sister called and requested a cabin for her own use. We had one left, so I was happy to provide." A pause. Then, "I'll see you at dinner."

CHAPTER 4
AVALON

Elden's threat to "see them at dinner" barely registered. Avalon returned Odele's gaze, the truth stinging and swelling under her skin. Odele really *had* called and requested to be roomed separately.

Odele slunk away to be led to her own room, stepping on Elden's heels in her haste to escape. *Of course,* Odd needed space. They practically lived on top of each other.

It would be safe, Avalon assured herself. The population was sparse out here. Nothing but old farm families and tourists, and even the tourists were nothing to worry about. The people who came out here loved hiking and peace and quiet. It was doubtful Odele would have a deathly premonition in such a secluded area. Avalon had looked up the crime statistics. Mathematically, they were in the clear.

But different floors hadn't even been enough. They weren't even in the same building. She didn't care that Odele needed that much space. But she had hidden it from her. And, though this hardly compared to the fact her sister was afraid to tell her how much solitude she needed, *Elden* had witnessed Avalon being blind-sided.

It's fine. It is fine. Fine. FINE.

Rummaging in the small backpack that acted as her purse, Avalon retrieved her headphones and turned the volume up, overlooking the damage she was causing her already injured eardrums. She let her favorite metal music distract her while she angrily jammed her clothes into the wardrobe until dinner.

Avalon waited outside the inn's noisy dining hall. Odele arrived exactly on time for dinner, leaving no time for Avalon to confront her privately. Avalon resorted to scowling openly at her sibling as they were quickly seated at a large ten-person table.

The restaurant was filled with loud, happy guests, and every wall bore photographs of the inn's different stages of existence. The tables were heavy and formed from thick wooden planks. Avalon might have noticed more, but she had too many questions for her sister on her mind.

"Did you forget to tell me you called the client to ask for a different room?" Avalon knew the answer before Odele could muster up the courage to even give it. When she grew this impatient, this desperate, Avalon had the bad habit of throwing her gift out, scanning the future for answers.

A vision of Odele, eyes downcast, whispering, "I was afraid that you would talk me out of it," appeared in her mind's eye. Her sister looked small, so broken. Odele twisted a strand of nearly white hair around one finger until it cut off the circulation of the appendage. It was a nervous habit of hers. "You do that without even meaning to, and I feel like I'm being erased."

Avalon stiffened; her gold eyes impossibly wide. "Shit. Odd, I am so sorry—"

Odele slammed down her water glass. "Don't do that. Don't look ahead without giving me the chance to say it." There was more; Avalon could envision it without even trying this time. But their table was being occupied.

Sinking into a cushioned chair, Nora Lee seemed to shake all her worries and the workday from her shoulders. "I should find something that requires less time on my feet," she sighed, though the woman was smiling fondly around the dining room. "Did you two get a good look around? Ashling, Elden's mother, was incredibly proud of this place. She oversaw everything, even the construction."

There was a twitch of Odele's head, and Avalon recalled the architectural rundown she had been forced to listen to in the car. "I thought this place was a hundred years old."

"Reconstruction, I said," Nora Lee corrected, sipping her iced tea politely.

Avalon nodded. It must have been her own damaged hearing.

Two others, the twins who had taken their luggage, joined them. Kenan and Tahoma were both slated for management. Elden, Nora Lee explained, had his own career that took up most of his time, so they had hired the twins. They had worked for the inn before, as foragers and hunters for Lyra's Pacific Northwest themed menu. They still did that, but now they had to learn to run an inn as well.

It explained why Elden was so ill-prepared to handle the inn's responsibilities, and why he had purchased such a long contract with Thompson. Elden had never been meant to take over, and now everyone was treading water, waiting to see if he could step up.

Odele chatted easily with everyone at the table. Her banshee curse must have been silent today, being so removed from the violence of over-population. Normally she acted reserved around anyone that wasn't Avalon—it hadn't yet been a day, and already she was blooming.

Perhaps Odele wouldn't need Avalon at all for this trip. Perhaps, if they ever had the money to move out of Seattle, Odele wouldn't need her ever again.

No one at the inn expected the sisters to start work until Monday, but Avalon and Odele were given the go ahead to order supplies and expense it to the inn as needed. The sisters had seen the budget for each of them, and Elden's inexperience was brutally obvious. It had been quickly decided that they would take pity on him and stick to a much, *much* smaller number.

Prior to their arrival, Avalon had advised Elden, via email, to order a pair of desktop computers and he had purchased the first example she had listed. Nora Lee, at her request, let Avalon into the tiny office behind the front desk so she could verify he had ordered everything she would need to transition them into the modern world.

One glance inside and Avalon politely asked Nora Lee to leave her there and go on home for the night.

Midnight had approached quietly, and despite Avalon's third cup of terrible coffee, she fought off a yawn that seemed to last forever. Cleaning the office's coffee station had been her top priority, though the entire room was in such a state of disarray that she couldn't tap down the twinge of sympathy she was beginning to feel for the new innkeeper. Avalon would have preferred tea, but after checking that one blend with the crushed purple bits, she had quickly lost any appetite for the stuff. One sniff and she had received the flash of an image of her vomiting onto the floor. Had the tea molded? Avalon threw the tin away to be safe.

Avalon sat cross-legged on the floor, having cleared enough room for her to work without causing an avalanche. There were stacks of papers everywhere, which was absolutely no way to run an inn. It might take the entire contract to organize this monstrosity of an office, but she had managed to diminish a few unnecessary piles of papers.

She snapped a picture of the mess on her phone, saving it for justifying her overtime to Thompson. Avalon juggled downloading programs and anti-virus software on the new, put together computers while throwing away papers that no logical business owner would have kept.

The pressure changed drastically in her head, forcing her eyes shut tight in pain as that high-pitched bell, like wind chimes in a tornado, tore through her ears.

She could barely hear her own thoughts. Finally, the noise, the *pain*, subsided, and she relaxed. Avalon opened her eyes to the glint of an axe blade, sharp and clear in the dim office light.

Avalon shrieked, falling backwards on her rear and stretching until her fingers grasped the handle of her mostly empty, borrowed coffee mug. She hurled it at the presence, but the head of the axe blocked it faster than humanly possible. Shards of porcelain and drops of coffee flew everywhere as the mug disintegrated before her eyes.

"What the fuck?"

That expletive was uttered in a loud whisper that only someone who spent time working at a hotel would be able to manage in such a tense and sudden situation.

Gone was Elden's usual fancy suit of navy blue. Instead, he dressed casually in work clothes—jeans, boots, flannel, and, what was the most distracting, a red baseball cap that did not suit him at all. It almost made her forget about the axe.

"What are you doing here?"

A stupid question and it earned her a stupid answer. "What am I doing in *my* office?" Elden said dryly, staring down at the fragments of the cup. The room smelled like pine and smoke— with an edge of stale coffee.

"*With an axe*," Avalon clarified, her face now tinged with red.

"I'm hiding this in here," he replied and followed that with a long pause.

Avalon raised her eyebrows.

Elden sighed. "Cabin Three, the Solace cabin. Somehow, they burned through months of cut wood and needed more chopped. And, conveniently, my axe was already at their cabin."

Cabin Three was visible from her room's window. Avalon had spotted the middle-aged trio of women earlier, passing around bottles of wine. How many bottles of cheap chardonnay had it taken to come up with that ridiculous plan?

Elden set the axe down on the cleanest available desk. "I suspect they took some perverse pleasure in it."

Avalon pursed her lips, fighting her first childish instinct to laugh. But if the genders had been reversed, she may not have found the situation so endearingly funny. She offered, "Next time they try that, send me over. I can take the fun out of any-thing."

He didn't respond, pushing the brim of his hat up to scratch at his dark hair underneath. It wasn't until the computer made a quiet sound, notifying her of another completed download, that he spoke again. "The inn wasn't always like this." Elden nudged an overflowing file cabinet with his boot. "It was a slow downturn, but somehow still too fast."

The inn or what happened to his mother?

Elden looked around, pulling a set of keys off a line of hooks beside the door. "Take this," he offered, holding out some keys. "If you're going to be working late like this, you'll need it."

She was cautious, ensuring she wouldn't accidentally touch his hand as she took the keys from him. "Thanks."

Elden left quickly and for a moment Avalon was nearly convinced that Odele had been right, that she had imagined the animosity she had witnessed pouring from him during that failed handshake.

Perhaps he knows what you are. No one would take your hand if they knew what you're hiding.

Her paranoia had ensured they made it past childhood and had saved Odele in more ways than one. Trusting Elden's change of attitude while on his home turf would be a misstep she couldn't afford to take. She *knew* what had been in his eyes the first time she had offered him her hand. *Suspicion.*

It was familiar, the pulsing wariness. She hadn't made an error, hadn't miscalculated. She and Odele, what they were, what they were hiding...there could be no mistakes.

CHAPTER 5
AVALON

The bedside phone in Avalon's hotel room rang, the tone bright and competing with the morning birdsong in volume.

Half-asleep, she ignored the first call and the second, opting to cover her face with her pillow. On the third call, she knocked the phone off the receiver, silencing it for good.

Her dreams had been riddled with teasing glimpses of the future. When her sleep consisted of such constant, brief visions, she never woke feeling rested. This time, what she recalled most clearly had been multitudes of black, coiling tentacles. Crawling like snakes toward her until that warm, living arm coiled around her throat—

Shivering, she tried to replace that nightmare with a more pleasant dream, but whoever she had hung up on was undeterred. The insistent banging on her door, battering the already chipped paint, was not so easily dealt with.

Hold on. Odele would never be so inconsiderate with other

guests around. It had to be someone else.

Though, Odele still could have something to do with this early morning interruption. Had her sister screamed throughout the night? Had Odele torn at her throat again, begging for an end to the bloody images in her foresight?

Avalon hardly had time to leap from bed and throw open the door before a miniature Greek goddess bowled her over. "Breakfast is ready, and you're late." Lyra stormed inside, her curls a defiant pile atop her head.

The only excuse Avalon could utter was, "Like I said before, you don't need to provide us with our meals." *And definitely not at this hour.* The analog clock at her bedside informed her it was worse than Avalon thought.

"Sorry, but we're the only game in town. I'll give you time to brush your teeth," Lyra warned her, taking in the sight of Avalon's sleep shirt and lack of pants. "And time to change. But that bedhead...you'll have to figure out something because you have six minutes before your food gets cold." The way Lyra spoke about food turning even a degree less than optimal was strangely terrifying.

Lyra was gone as quickly as she had appeared, her flour smeared apron swishing as she stomped back down the stairs, surely waking anyone unfortunate to be sleeping below her.

After breakfast with the inn's staff, with their day free, Odele suggested taking a hike to work off the pancakes. The walk from the inn to the adjacent town took an hour. If Odele hadn't stopped every ten paces to snap a dozen photos of rocks and weeds, it would have been much more efficient.

Fair Harbor. The village had more than it should have—though all of it was miniscule. The grocery was a one-roomed building with only a handful of aisles, more product crammed on its shelves than looked feasible. Antique shops were dotted down the main square. Locals strolled or biked, stopping often to speak with their neighbors. Avalon didn't think towns like this existed anymore.

A hardware store was the busiest among them, several farmers hanging around the front and watching the sisters with mild, unconcerned interest. There really wasn't another restaurant besides the Refuge on the Moor's kitchen, to Avalon's dismay.

But there was coffee. And a place to sit, and while it was just a few white patio chairs and tables outside a storage container turned coffee shop, it gave Avalon a moment's peace while she sipped lavender-infused coffee and Odele drank something that was bright pink.

"Don't you love it here?" Odele practically sang, stretching out her legs underneath the table and kicking Avalon's shins. "I slept great last night, and I could hear the crackling of a fire through my window. It was so relaxing."

"Smoke inhalation is not what I would call relaxing."

Odele stared down into her drink, her grip tense. When she spoke, it was rushed and quiet, but Avalon somehow caught every single word.

"Don't do that. Last night was the first night I've slept through in a long time." Odele looked up, eyes determined and merciless. "And you could have slept, too, but you worked. This place, it could be good for us." She held up a hand, stopping Avalon before she could begin. "I know this isn't a vacation. I am no longer the kid you had to share a bed with to keep from screaming. And Avalon, you were a kid, too."

The pair of farmers seated next to them halted their own conversation about the sudden migration of chupacabra into the area. Avalon saw the rest of their future conversation.

"We'll have to tell him about this," the older one moaned. *"I'm not the shot I was ten years ago. And those things aren't stopping at goats. They've been showing interest in the cattle."*

"I'm not letting my dogs mess with those things. My wife will kill me."

"Don't worry about it. Keep the dogs inside for a few days, and I'm sure that old, grumpy Goodfellow will get to it."

Goodfellow? Avalon observed them carefully until they took their drinks and left. She searched the near future for anything else, but the vision faded away from her grasp. Storing what little she had learned for later, she whirled on her sister.

"Are you insane?" Avalon cursed, nearly crunching her paper coffee cup out of shape. "If you talk like that, someone might guess what you are!"

Odele rolled her eyes, tossing her drink in the nearby trashcan. "If I am insane, it's because you drove me there!"

They never fought like this. They were a team. It had always been just the two of them. It had to be that way. Neither of them would even still be here without the other.

Her control of the situation was slipping away. Avalon fought what she could—the sickness in her stomach, twisting her apart, was a lost cause. The racing thoughts—she let them go. Instead, she wrangled her tongue and told Odele calmly, "Okay. *Okay.* I'll back off," she promised. "I'll relax."

After her lie, the scratching in the back of her throat didn't let up.

While Avalon knew she hadn't meant her silly promise to Odele, not truly, Avalon still made a sad, solitary go at relaxing. Back in her hotel room, she thumbed listlessly through some books she found stashed in Whimsy before tossing them all on the bed in defeat. Anger and concentrating on tiny, faded print were never a good mix.

The inn's office it was. She headed downstairs, sneaking into the office and began the boring but necessary work of personalizing the user interfaces and the computers themselves. The inn's logo was decent. There was no actual need to change that. A single thistle, drawn in clean, intricate lines above the inn's name. The flower was red, and faded, as though someone had quickly dipped it in vermilion paint. The font could use some updating. It was all a little too medieval for her taste, but it fit with the inn's architecture.

There was a knock, a quick three-part rapping, and Elden stepped inside the doorway. He was dressed simply again. Maybe the suits were the oddity, not the jeans.

"More overtime," he said, lacking any question in his words. Avalon nodded, making that face she made when someone tried to engage her in idle chit-chat in an elevator. Her breath misted, and she glanced over at the thermostat, checking to make sure the air conditioning didn't just click on.

"I want to get these computers ready before Monday. We're going to have a lot of data entry." That was the first task the twins would master—transferring their hand-recorded data into the new interface. She hadn't the patience, nor the paycheck, to incentivize her to do that for the inn.

He interrupted the dead air. Elden admitted, "I haven't

much experience with computers."

That...was not normal for what Avalon assumed was a man in his late twenties. Still, she had trained middle-aged men, men with grandchildren, on how to use spreadsheets. She was confident she could get Elden to where he needed to be.

Avalon dug down deep, mustering every ounce of her desire to keep her job, and gave a small, polite smile. "I'll make a deal with you, I—"

"No!"

He *shouted.* Her back tensed, and she clawed into the arms of her chair, straining to keep herself seated. Years of anger management flashed before her, and nothing from therapy was enough to settle the rage boiling inside her.

"What exactly is your problem with me?" She wasn't loud, just clear. Once she crossed that line, started releasing that pent-up aggression, the transition was smooth and natural.

Her employment paperwork had her listed as human. Same with Odele. But she couldn't think of any other reason for such a reaction to an attempted handshake or to the phrase "make a deal with you" than...

He knows. He KNOWS.

That buried instinct was there, to *rip* and *tear* and *bite* until there was nothing but marrow and sinew left. Her mind was so addled with rage that images clouded her vision, not of the future but of flashbacks of her father dragging her by the arm into office after office, all the same bland, cheap décor adorning the walls, and demanding that the doctors figure out what the hell was wrong with his out-of-control daughter.

But her violent, inner musings paused—when she looked up at Elden now, he seemed *frightened.* Whatever was going on with him was between that man and a qualified therapist.

"Whatever." She couldn't help but shoulder check him on her way out of the office. "I'm not going to work like this. Get some professional help."

Some stuttered explanation from Elden trailed after her, obscured by the roaring in her ears, and Avalon picked up her pace. She headed straight for Cabin Nine, Odele's cabin. Avalon stumbled through the inn's main entrance, and her feet quickly found a worn footpath that led towards the cabins.

Avalon had decided they were leaving. Now. Odele would understand once she explained. This was far too dangerous. Elden, he must have guessed what they were hiding.

Her storm out stuttered to a halt outside of Odele's cabin. *What the hell?*

Cabin Nine was having a party. Well, nothing as official as that. From her vantage point about ten feet away, Avalon could see Odele was sitting around a campfire with Lyra and Tahoma, sharing wine and listening to Lyra talk about her latest trip to Greece. Odele was laughing, louder than Avalon had ever witnessed before. A few more steps forward and Avalon would be far enough into the firelight to be seen by the other women.

Instead, Avalon turned away, retreating towards the inn. She avoided the area around the main entrance, heading into the inn's expansive gardens that sat behind the building. Avalon vanished behind the garden's first row of hedges. The garden paths between the hedges were simple stone, lit by small, round solar lights along the sides. She raced down the lighted paths quickly, silently, until she found herself in the center of the gardens—a large, green hill before her.

It was an odd central feature; a fountain would have been more expected. More photogenic. Stones were piled in a knee-height ring around the hill, discouraging guests from scaling the mound and kicking up the grass. In front of the hill was a small area for garden parties, with a stone floor and a few metal tables scattered around.

Here Avalon rested, finding a small wooden bench underneath a pair of trees with lights dangling from their branches. What a romantic place to fall apart.

She couldn't interrupt Odele and her impromptu girl's night. There was no denying that her sister was happy, already making friends and being included after a single day. In high school and college, there had never been an opportunity for any of that. For either of them.

But the only thing that had stopped Odele was her night terrors, her banshee abilities. Avalon, she could hide her powers easily. And still she had been alone, frantically clinging to the position, the responsibilities, of being the eldest sibling and using them as an excuse not to engage with anyone other than her sister.

As much as she despised the notion, Avalon *could* go back to Seattle—without Odele. No one seemed to have anything against her. Hell, Odele was roasting hotdogs and planning day trips with the girls. Not being micro-terrorized by an innkeeper.

No, Odele was as vulnerable as she was. More so. She lacked the diligence, the constant attention to detail that Avalon had been forced to learn. It was due to this vigilance, this aversion to rest, that Avalon saw the dog at all.

The canine emerged from one of the other garden paths, shrouded in darkness, until the hanging lights revealed its shaggy coat and open mouth. The dog approached her bench slowly, sniffing the air as if it didn't like what it sensed. It bared its fangs, the hair on its back raised, and those shining eyes...

This was what peasants feared when they ventured out at night. Not a black dog, a *Black Dog.* Something so big, so vicious, that the supernatural was not just suspected, but known to be the cause.

She was never good with dogs. They seemed to sense her anxiety, and it made them anxious, too, until it compounded and both of them were upset.

A door. *A door!* On the hill she had just walked past, the one with a stone circle piled around it, an entrance was almost hidden from sight and lined with crumbling stone bricks. The door was cracked open, a dim, buzzing light within. The distance between her bench and the door was worth making a break for it. Avalon didn't care if it was simply an outdoor storage closet—she'd make it work and call for a rescue later.

She broke into a run, making a beeline for that door, her one chance at safety. The dog sprinted after her, barely giving her enough time to reach the door and grasp its metal handle. Avalon felt the ice-cold burn of iron and persisted, flinging open the doorway—catching the hazardous materials warning sign at the last second—and throwing herself inside.

Avalon backed inside and slammed the door shut. She expected her back to hit a wall, and it never did. Instead, she tripped and fell on her ass.

That made little sense. The hill wasn't that large, so the storage closet shouldn't have been so deep. She shouldn't have had enough room to fall. Avalon stretched her arms above her head and reached with her fingertips to feel for a wall. There was nothing.

Leaves crunched underneath her as she rolled to her stomach and raised herself up on her elbows. She was outside—there wasn't a roof overhead, and there were no walls surrounding her. But there was *light.* Bright, undulating orbs of magical blue light that hovered above Avalon, bouncing and being carried with the wind.

CHAPTER 6
AVALON

A realization. And then denial, closely followed by fear. Avalon wasn't in some dingy, dark storage closet. And those lights? *Those are fey lights.* That simple, unlocked door had transported her into the dreaded feyrie realm, something few humans ever escaped.

Avalon laughed, scrambling to her feet and rubbing her eyes with both hands. It was no use, just a childish attempt to force her eyes to adjust to the dim light of dusk. She opened them and still was presented with the foggy watercolor world before her. Dulled by the darkness to deep burgundies and greens, she found herself to be in an old, wild forest. Glowing orbs, the fey lights, danced throughout the trees and illuminated horrible, skittering creatures that lived amongst the branches. The pine trees were thin and tall, coming together high above her, and nearly hiding the red moon from her sight.

She had read about the feylands as a child before she knew better. Before she had taken her beloved, worn copy of hand illustrated feyrie tales—a gift from Nanny Blaire, who had been fired at Avalon's twelfth birthday party when she had hugged the nanny after making her wish instead of her mother, Valerie—and tore it to pieces, leaving the shredded pages at her feet.

She was in danger. Everything in this forest meant to trick her, wanted to take everything she had and leave behind ash. And sometimes they stole that, too.

The Sight failed her here. She cast out her weak powers, searching to discover if she would ever find her way out of this. One glance behind had informed her that the door she had tumbled through was gone, the space empty and dead.

Something large moved through the trees, groaning loud enough that even the lights made to scatter.

"Wait! Help me!" she cried, and, to her shock, one of the fey lights stilled.

What will you give me?

A deal. The voice now inside her head wanted to make a bargain with her. Whatever beast was prowling those woods might come to be the safer bet.

"It consumes emotions," something half-sang. Avalon searched out the sound, blinking at a tiny man that looked formed out of wood. It danced around the roots of a tree, less than a foot tall.

"What does that *mean*?" she pleaded. The woodland feyrie laughed, tipping his small hat to her before diving into a crevice in the nearest tree and vanishing. Dammit. There went her chance to speak with something vaguely humanoid.

Defeated, Avalon turned back to the feylight, eyeing the hovering orb. Emotions? The thing craved emotional fuel, but what kind? If it was happiness, Avalon was dead where she stood.

Still, Avalon racked her brain for something harmless and still tempting. "My love for my favorite song," she offered, and from the way the light beamed ever brighter, she had given something too precious.

But it was gone. As soon as the deal was proposed, the light must have accepted. She thought of her favorite song, recalled the guitar solo and the line that made her cry when she was alone and, after a few moments, inside she was hollow, forgotten, and cold.

The woods grew tighter and tighter along the path the light led her down. A few inches of snow blanketed the ground, its wintery bite catching her through her poor footwear. Avalon tried to keep track of every turn they made from her origin, but after too many twists in the path, she gave up entirely.

The path ended and turned into overgrown bushes that were thick with thorns. But the light went through them, so Avalon hacked her way past and stumbled into a garden identical to the one at the inn. *What the hell?*

The similarities were odd, but could work in her favor. It would be easy enough to find the garden's center, and there might even be another mound. *Another feyrie mound.*

Yes, it's worthless information now, but at least I know what I literally walked into.

Something burned her—the orb was ramming into her, its heat singeing the hair on her arms. Trying to shake the light off of her, Avalon crept carefully down the pathway, despite the orb's buzzing, until she found the garden's center.

There *was* a mound. And, apparently, also a party.

She should have heard such a commotion much sooner— the drunken fey, overfilled with feyrie wine, and the over-complicated music...even her hearing wasn't bad enough to miss *that.* But once she had stepped into that garden circle, it was like someone switched on a spotlight. Like the band suddenly remembered to play, picking up their flutes and fiddles with devilish delight.

There were too many colors, too much noise layered over each other. She was going to be sick. The cacophony froze her, despite every fiber of her common sense telling her to run, screaming at her legs to work. To do something other than stand and wait to be prey.

She burned. The orb burrowed into her, into her skin, until it vanished entirely. It was enough to make her finally move, turning and colliding with a solid, overly dressed form.

"Lost, little one? Do you need my aid?"

There was honey dripping in that voice. And venom, too. This, *this* was what humans feared about the fey. The ones that preyed on humans, looking for any way to make a deal and to *take.* The lovely, fair ones were the most dangerous. They could take everything.

Avalon snapped her mouth shut, not letting herself say anything. Any word spoken to a fey was a weakness. She tried to move around him, to run back into the safety (compared to her situation now) of those creepy, deadly woods.

His hand caught her shoulder and shoved her back into place. "What a rude and silent greeting."

The feyrie was male and beautiful in that horrible way that they all were. Avalon imagined she saw him how a deer admired a mountain lion—right before it was torn apart. She'd interrupted him speaking with another fey, a woman with flowers braided throughout her hair and a green tone to her skin. The man held some sort of writhing potted plant in his hands that he quickly stuffed into the cream satchel he wore.

She avoided looking at him directly, hoping he would lose interest. He was undeterred. "I'll accept groveling if a simple 'hello' is too complicated for you."

Her blood boiled, but there was a small, frightened part that wondered if she should.

"Now," he smiled, dark and shining. He was slender, sporting long robes that were lined with silver, intricate thread. His clothing resembled a man's hanbok, a style it surprised her to see on a feyrie. A silver crown wove through his long, dark hair, and Avalon prayed that was a fashion statement and not a status symbol. "What can I do for you?"

He had her enthralled—she itched to say "yes, yes, yes!" to whatever he asked. Her sight blurred at the edges until only he, this fey, was visible. He could help her. He was *beautiful*. He could give her *anything*.

The fey forcefully gripped her face, one hand wrapped around her jaw, too long fingernails cutting into her skin. It had been the smile he gave her that finally released Avalon from his spell. The smile that accompanied the words, "*On your knees, human bitch.*"

His cold, grey eyes blinked as the bones in her face drastically changed shape, elongating. Just like her *teeth* were elongating.

Spiteful, her mother had called her. And so she was.

The fey released her, but too late. Avalon's head followed his movement, lunging and clamping down on his forearm with her teeth.

Her mouth filled with cold, thick blood—it was bitter and unlike the coppery taste she had expected, and there seemed to be too much of it. Still, she hung on, even as he grabbed her by the hair and tried to pull her off.

The fey was drawing attention, his shouts growing more and more frantic as she ground into his flesh. She remembered his previous words, and she was frenzied. He would *not* shake her off. She would gnaw through his *bone*. She would—

The fey finally pried her off of him, his inhuman strength overcoming her own rage. It was a mistake as more blood and gore left with her as she stumbled backwards. "May death find you early," the man cursed, his former smirk nowhere near his lips. Hatred took over his countenance instead.

He made to grab her again, and a frigid wind blew them both backwards. Ice filled her blood, the shock wearing on her resolve. She imagined the light inside her, that orb, was fighting back the winter chill that invaded her. But it was not enough. Her only consolation as she fell was that this spell of ice and snow was taking the fey down as well.

A man, large and apathetic, towered above her, his executioner axe silver and sharp and hovering between her eyes.

She showed her teeth and spat a mouthful of fey blood at his feet.

He knelt down, inspecting her, but nothing further. His face was fey and blurred—her eyes burned to look at him.

Until the glamour fell away and she recognized Elden Cavanaugh, eyes as unnatural as they had always been, and saw that he *knew* her.

And what she was.

"*Changeling.*"

CHAPTER 7
ELDEN

Elden watched Avalon storm out of his office, ignoring his failed attempts at an apology. He certainly knew how to royally fuck things up. Avalon had deserved none of that—his panic, his volume, his *failure*. He paced the small width of his office after she had run out, contemplating whether he should find her and explain. But how could he? There were things he could not reveal, and that left him with a worthless apology that was sure to widen the gulf between them.

Elden stepped out of his sanctuary. A few short flights, and he was at Avalon's room, knocking lightly against the painted letters of Whimsy.

No answer. That was entirely fair. Elden leaned against the door and said, "Avalon...if you're ignoring me, which I completely understand, I wanted to apologize." His words lingered in the air, and the other side of the door remained unresponsive.

"You did nothing wrong. I have unresolved issues."

Arawn help him, he sounded like a lunatic.

Though Elden doubted Arawn, a god of death, would care at all about his current situation.

Deciding Avalon either wasn't in there at all or she was packing her bags to get the hell out of there, Elden found himself back in the office, slouched in an office chair and brooding.

The brooding, he hated to admit, was not uncommon.

Avalon might have gone to her sister's cabin, though he cringed at having an audience for take two of his apology.

Perhaps it's better to leave her alone.

No, that was chickenshit, through and through. He wouldn't let himself out of this.

Memories, brought back into the light and dusted off for display, replayed in his mind. He squeezed his eyes shut and tried to first ignore them before he switched tactics and tried to force other, more pleasant, memories to take their place. Neither worked.

His parents were both seated on their thrones, and the sight of the two together was something the Winterlands hadn't seen in years. They preferred avoiding the other, preferred Ashling's self-banishment to the human realm to act as the Pacific Northwest warden. Elden wished he were back with the humans as well. None of them cared what he was or wanted anything from him. They thought him a twelve-year-old boy and nothing more. They didn't care how blue his blood ran.

He especially didn't want to be a part of this.

Taliesin, his father, the poet-king, motioned Elden to move forward.

A man clad in rags knelt on the wooden floor before his father's dais. They had banished all other servants or guards, leaving the royals to themselves. What the man in rags had done to displease the Unseelie King was unclear. It did not matter. Not to Taliesin. To Elden, it could mean everything.

"Tell him the terms of the deal, third son, Elden."

What a formal way to refer to a child. Elden finally took those few required steps forward. He'd rather execute the man than give him this impossible hope.

His elder siblings watched; Bane, eager to see him screw this up, Jin, impatient and scowling, and Hia, the Crown Princess, forced to hide her emotions.

All of his half-siblings, a century older than him, had performed this task at his age without a hitch. But they hadn't spent time among humans, hadn't been introduced to concepts like mercy and sympathy.

Was this man a thief? A murderer? Innocent?

Elden looked back at his mother. She turned away, pretending to be absorbed in the servant pouring her tea. The blend was something she kept in full supply at the inn, but to him, it tasted like medicine.

Taliesin leaned forward, snapping his ink-stained fingers at his youngest. "The two of you made this choice. Forsake your mother's magic for mine. This is the path you must take."

The king was right—Elden couldn't feel the familiar warmth of his mother's magic anymore. This cold was all he had left. Elden repeated the terms of the bargain, having practiced those terrible words in the mirror for days.

Bargains were a song he'd been taught well. Name all parties involved, lay out the stakes, and poison each word until the victim believes they can win while you have ensured they never will.

Hope sprang into the prisoner's eyes when it should not have. The fool accepted Elden's outstretched hand, overjoyed to have some small light to believe in.

Three weeks later he failed, and Elden felt the bargain snap into effect, the life leaving the prisoner's body and flowing into his.

It had happened at dinner, and Elden threw up onto his plate.

Elden rubbed his temples, willing the unpleasant memories to die and leave him be.

Nora Lee was right. Avoiding handshakes and snapping at anyone who dared utter the word "bargain" was a ridiculous way to avoid striking one.

If he didn't grovel and explain to Avalon his actions, he'd be forced to restart the search for someone to set their inn back on the right path. That meant driving back into Seattle, and there was little as unpleasant as that.

Alarm bells sounded—not literally, more of a buzzing under his skin that forced him up and sprinting toward the inn's gardens. He slipped into the hedges, the path as familiar to him as the dog that sat before him.

Hob whined, bounding to him and circling Elden's legs in frustration. "What got out, boy?" That wasn't the right question. If something got *out*, Hob wouldn't be here, pushing his face against Elden's hand—no, he'd be chasing the poor bastard down, with or without his master.

So, something got *in*. The better of the two options, but now he needed to find out exactly who. *Or what?*

The grassy hill, central to the gardens, gave him no clues, the gate now firmly shut as if feigning innocence. To all mortals, this entrance into the feyrie lands looked like a common storage closet. If something got in without his permission, they could have been deposited anywhere. The feyrie mound could control where it opened into, and there were more places one didn't want to be than the opposite. Elden raced to his home to gather supplies.

The manor he occupied was a complete waste of space. Too many bedrooms for too few people. His father had built it for his mother, made to mimic the architectural styling of her beloved inn. The building was far enough from the inn that it allowed Elden the privacy and quiet he craved. Although, lately the home had felt too quiet, sitting mostly empty, save for the ghosts of his mother and the things she had built.

The haunting things she had forged.

The door to his in-home security room creaked open, reminding him of yet another chore. Nine screens shuddered with black and white images; the night vision mode kicked on. It took him longer than it would have taken Tahoma, who was the most technologically adept out of all of them, but he was able to rewind back the security feed until he saw exactly who had entered the feyrie lands.

What was Avalon doing? That *liar.* Was she really so desperate? At best, she'd die in there. At worst, she'd actually form a bargain, and then she'd wish for the former.

The glamour he wore hid the silver-plated armor underneath. At his hip was a one-handed axe, but if he was going to have to protect a human from the dangers of the feyrie realm, he was going to have to use *that.*

That cursed thing used his mother's voice.

Finally ready to christen me in blood? An unbloodied axe is a war crime in some parts of the Unseelie lands.

He knew using the war axe would only strengthen the unwanted connection to it. That the weapon would only try to communicate with him more than it already did. But the things Elden could do with it...

Elden swore and retrieved the axe, cringing at the excited fire the weapon flooded into him as he grasped it. It wanted blood, seared flesh, and death.

"We don't know why she's there," he reminded the axe. "We can capture her without any killing."

The metal burned him until it was nearly too painful to bear.

Elden tired of his nightmares, but they had never needed him to be asleep to plague him.

He remembered how his mother had hammered her hatred into the axe, turning periodically to cough up blood. Ashling would not allow him to help her stoke the fires as she worked. She screamed at him when he begged her to rest, to see the healers his father kept sending.

"This work needs to be done." Her hammer never lost its tempo, despite her failing body. "Now leave me to it."

He turned to leave before she caught his shoulder. "Wait." His mother dragged him to the metal she was shaping, holding his palm over it while she sliced a dagger into his unprotected flesh.

Elden was too startled to react. He watched his blood pour into the metal, sinking into the blade as it drank it up thirstily.

What had she done?

"I call her, *Ember.*"

Returning to the present, Elden wanted to drop the axe, but strapped it to his back instead, cursing his dependency on it. He entered the feyrie realm with a storm in his wake.

CHAPTER 8
AVALON

Had the heavy weight of ice not already rooted Avalon to the ground, that one word would have done the trick.

Changeling.

There were a hundred other things more pressing, more troubling than that revelation. But it was all she could concentrate on. *Now, he really knows.*

Elden stared a second more before he raised a clenched fist above them and slowly uncurled his fingers. Heat hesitantly returned to Avalon's body as the ice encasing her melted. Her breath steamed as she let out a small exhale of relief.

"Bane."

A name. No, it was a command. The fey Avalon had bitten stiffened while he sat up and nursed his arm. "Well, if it isn't our *warden*," Bane sneered, saying the title as if it were some joke between them. "You let this *thing* inside. I found her trying to interrupt our celebration. And when I confronted her, like an animal, she *bit* me. I demand every one of her teeth as payment."

Bane moved toward her again, and in this world, her senses too alive and uncontrolled, Avalon knew, she could *see*, that she would tear into him again. Bane, unaware of her violent intent, announced smugly, "No need to trouble yourself, warden, though I know you love getting your hands bloody. I can defang her myself."

He could try. Avalon burned, the wildness she had struggled to smother in her youth returning to the surface. *I never left*, it seemed to taunt her. *You can't survive without me.*

That was a hard point to argue in her current situation.

Elden, unglamoured and far too tall, his presence too overbearing, stepped between them. "No." The knowledge Elden had been hiding under a glamour ate away at Avalon, forcing her senses to fully acknowledge what he was. What he truly looked like.

His face was more angular, the brows darker and more foreboding. Pointed ears sliced through his wild hair, no pretense of hair gel that wouldn't have worked on those onyx waves, anyway. Most impressive of all were his teeth, each one slightly sharpened. It wasn't the sight of them that brewed horror in her stomach—it was that she recognized her own teeth now mimicked those fangs.

Elden bore polished silver armor that was adorned with a dark blue cape. He carried a two-headed axe in one hand that Avalon knew she couldn't hold with two. He dressed like he was some sort of authority.

Bane held aloft his bleeding arm, though it had already begun to knit itself together. "You'd let her do this to a *prince* without punishment? I know you have no respect for our family, brother, but you should be ashamed enough to hide it. I even took time out of my busy schedule last year to visit your mother's crumbling little inn. This is how you treat me in return?" Bane twisted the skin around one of his fingers, as if he expected a ring to be there that was no longer present, and glared up at Elden.

Brother. Those matching grey eyes between the two fey were evidently not a coincidence, though that was where the similarities ended. *And prince?* What did that make Elden? More importantly, what was about to happen to her?

Elden laughed. The sound startled Avalon and Bane, both with its volume and its cruelty. "She did this to you? If I hadn't stepped in, she might have torn you to pieces. Imagine having to inform Father that his son, third in line to the Unseelie's unholy throne, was eviscerated by a *changeling*."

Bane bristled, smoothing his long, silken black hair down as if to make himself look more regal. "*You* let this beast in here. Don't think our father won't hear of this."

Elden hoisted Avalon up by one of her arms. "I bite back," he warned before she had a chance to say anything. In response, she spat out another mouthful of his brother's blood. He might have smirked at that—it was too dark to tell.

Iron clamped down on her wrists, conjured from the air, and she jolted, not expecting the burning pain the handcuffs caused her. She knew fey were—she couldn't think of a better word than *allergic* to the metal. But she had touched it before and it had never pained her like this.

Elden dragged her back in the direction of the feyrie party, away from Bane's protests, and toward the exit she had been searching for. Here, at this end of it, the door in and out of the fey realm was not so discreet. It was cast entirely from iron, nearly twelve feet tall and just as wide. Not to mention that the doorway on this end was also encased in a clear, thick sheet of ice.

The surrounding party stilled, watching and waiting with the anticipation of hyenas. A rare chance to break into the mortal world was about to present itself.

"I'm going to open it, and I *need* you to run. Don't look back. Don't slow down." Elden glared down at her, as if already expecting her disobedience. Like she would *want* to stay in the feylands. "Something, or someone, may try to take this opportunity to get past me, and I can't be distracted with a fool. If," he threatened, no, promised, "I find you violating my orders, I will split you in two."

One thing she could take from the situation was that she'd been right—Elden Cavanaugh *was* an asshole.

The ice began melting away, exposing the circular iron door for Elden to open with a wave of his hand. There was movement of a few beings, large and quick, but Avalon didn't dare glance back, having learned Orpheus's lesson a long time ago, to see if Elden would make it. As soon as the doorway was open enough for her to slip through, she did.

She ran through a tunnel, a tantalizing, dim light ahead. Avalon found the end of it by slamming right into a second gate. After she picked herself up and tried to shake away her disorientation, the gate creaked open just enough for her to slip through.

When she recognized herself in the garden of the Refuge on the Moor, returned to the mortal world, Avalon made a break for it. However, the Black Dog, again blocking her path, caused her to skid on her feet to a stop. Spinning around and starting her dash in the opposite direction, Avalon ran until Elden made his way through the fey entrance, black liquid dripping from his axe, and met her eyes.

"Don't."

She couldn't fight—and there was no way she could outrun that dog. It pressed against Elden's leg, looking up at him for direction.

Avalon sat down in a huff, crossing her legs underneath her. No matter how she angled her wrists, she couldn't avoid the icy burn of her iron shackles. She couldn't stop him from taking her where he wished, and she didn't dare yell for help. The last thing she could handle was Odele appearing on the scene and getting hurt.

But in no way did she have to make this easy for him. She knew what happened at "second locations". If she was going to die, she was going to make every minute of it painful—*for him*.

"What are you—" Elden stood her up by lifting underneath one of her arms. She hung limp in his hold, glaring up at him in defiance. "Do you think I won't fucking *drag* you?"

She matched his frustration. "I don't think I gave you a fucking choice."

Eyes wide, Elden stared down at her for a moment before pulling those wild, dark brows together. "How do *you* work in the hospitality business?"

He started dragging her along the ground, muttering under his breath. Avalon felt like a toddler, refusing her well-deserved time-out. That dog followed right behind them, sniffing Avalon's shoes as they moved. Her jeans were cheap; ripping out the butt of her pants was beginning to become a real concern the longer Elden pulled her along.

The sight of the inn's garage put a damper on her attitude—images of being chained in the dark, oil-filled air flooded her mind without warning. He was going to hang her from a hook, dangling from her chained hands like a side of meat.

It wasn't the first time Avalon wished she had the power of telepathy, rather than foresight. Odele was probably sleeping, unaware of the danger that hid in an unsuspecting garden.

Don't fight, she chided herself, her impulses. *You saw that blade and what was on it. If he'll kill his own kind, he'll certainly have no qualms about you.*

Her foretelling came to light—she forced herself to remain silent as Elden hooked her by her chains. An engine hoist kept her secured. Her weight tugged ruthlessly on her arms—her feet unable to touch the garage floor. The doors thankfully remained open, moonlight barely illuminating the man's—the *fey's* sharp features.

"What were you after?"

This would be an interrogation. That was better than a simple butchering. Avalon answered quickly. Odele's safety would certainly be at stake. "I wanted *nothing* from there. It was an accident. I—I was trying to hide from your dog. He chased me in there."

The dog whined as if somehow offended.

"Hob was trying to keep you *out*," Elden explained with the tone dog owners took when they were convinced their pet could do nothing wrong.

She rolled her eyes. "My apologies for mistaking the two. I was concentrating on not being eaten."

"But you took something. I can tell. Did my brother make you an offer?"

"Nothing I accepted," she snapped.

Was that relief in his strange eyes? "Fine. What did you accept?"

If Avalon wanted to avoid suspicion, she couldn't reveal she *had* made a bargain. Even if it was only with a feylight. Her mouth opened and when she tried to speak, to say she took nothing, to *lie*...she could only cough and sputter, her face turning an embarrassing shade of purple.

"Ah. You're attempting to deceive me." But Elden did not look upset—this seemed to be exactly what he had expected. "Have you never changed from your human form before? You can't be so blatantly dishonest. You have to lie without lying. Like this. *I didn't really think you were this big of an idiot.*"

She abandoned her former lie and started anew. "Fuck you."

"Fuck *me?*" Elden gave his dog an exasperated look as if to say, *can you believe this?* "You come into my employment with false records, records that say you are completely human. That's a crime, in both of our worlds, but let's continue. You're a *changeling.* Just human enough to open the iron doors to the Unseelie realm. Or you *used* to be. Looks like you fucked that up." He painfully flicked the sharp tip of one of her ears, as if to drive home his point. "You made some kind of deal while there. And what do you have to say for yourself? '*Fuck you.*'"

His sudden touch had been cold and startling. "I could elaborate on the 'fuck you' if that's the problem, but—"

He was a winter storm, emanating a frigid power around him. "How can I not think that this was deliberate? I saw you speaking with Bane. I don't know what you thought was so important, but no deal you make with an orator will ever end in your favor."

If it was even possible, Avalon's face turned whiter. *Bane was an orator?* What did that make Elden? No, no, he couldn't be an orator. If he was, she'd be spilling every secret she had to the man.

A smart man knew orators were the most dangerous of the fey—worse than goblins and boggarts and whatever other nightmares lurked in their woods. They could make you believe anything they wanted without uttering a single lie. Bane could have had anything he wanted from her—if he hadn't shaken her out of his own spell.

"Perhaps," Elden mused, true hate now flashing in his eyes. "Perhaps you crossed the boundary to take a fey child and create another changeling like yourself." His axe raised, and he leveled the blade with her throat. "If that's the case—"

The edge of his axe kissed her skin. Hatred towards her captor filled her blood with fire. The threat also sent heat down to her core, which led to an interesting, and confusing, longing.

What a terrible time to learn this about myself.

"I would never do something like that!" Avalon struggled, her toes failing to touch ground and help her escape. "How dare you, you—"

His blade lowered, and that odd wanting left her.

"Better watch that pretty mouth of yours, *changeling*. Unlike my fey brethren, I have no patience for such games."

This was the most emotion she had ever seen from Elden, and none of it was positive. What could she say in her defense? Lying was off the table and, if he didn't kill her at the end of this, Avalon would need his help. As much as it killed her to admit it, even silently. She had felt her structure change—she knew she wasn't human currently. Changelings, once they were abandoned in the mortal realm by their parents, adapted and could change their physical appearance to seem human enough to blend in. But back in the feylands something had twisted in her, reverting to her deadly roots, and Avalon had no idea how to undo it.

"Is your sister a changeling as well?"

Outwardly, she remained calm. Inwardly, she plotted his quick, yet still agonizing, death. *I'll rip out your heart if you touch her.*

"You don't need to worry about Odele," Avalon answered, finding the half-truth workaround to her own surprise. Her throat merely tickled, but she buried it with a slew of honesty. "I am the daughter of Governor Golightly. By the time my parents realized I was a changeling, when *I* realized what I was, it was too late." The memory of that revelation hurt, no matter how many years passed.

There were a lot of details she was skipping. She prayed Elden would be too overwhelmed to ask the right questions.

Elden tilted his head as he studied her. The dog lay at Elden's feet, panting, and mimicked his master's head tilt as if he was part of this. "Your father is the governor?"

Yes! She had hoped that would distract him. "And he kept my background a secret. I didn't come in disguise on purpose. If anyone discovers the truth, there'd be a political shitstorm. He built his campaign on humans and magical beings getting along. You can see how having one of his own children taken would cause issues." *And he'd make sure I'd pay for it.*

The warden was considering her words. "He must have loved you very much, to keep a child that wasn't his or even human."

She shouldn't have laughed—the hysterical bark exploded from her, ruining her chances of keeping the darker details of her family life from this fey. Avalon slumped from her restraints, exhausted physically and mentally. "That's not accurate. Bruce just didn't want the public to know how he'd been tricked. He wasn't the governor yet and didn't want this to hurt his campaign. So, when they couldn't find their actual daughter, they kept me, and kept what I am a secret."

"It's a *convenient* story."

"You said I couldn't lie," she countered. "I didn't know your stupid broom closet was a portal to hell. Did it look like I was having a good time in there? Why did I land in the middle of the forest, anyway? I saw the tunnel leads to that feyrie realm, doppelganger garden."

Elden's gaze lingered around her mouth, the blood there caked and dried, stinging and pulling as she spoke. He answered, "The mound has a mind of its own. You're lucky it didn't drop you in redcap territory. They'd have you enslaved to a smithy in an instant." His explanation was both short and terrifying. Elden sighed, relenting. "I'll let you down, but I am not my brother and my teeth are far sharper—and more experienced—than yours." There was a lazy snap of his fingers, and the iron around her wrists vanished, and she fell, graceless, to the cement floor.

Rubbing the pain away from her wrists, Avalon remarked, "I wouldn't think a fey could manipulate iron like that."

"My position as warden grants me such power over iron. It's a gift from the witches at the Commission." She blanked, his title meaning nothing to her. Luckily, Elden added, "I guard the feyrie mound and keep anything from escaping *or entering* without the proper paperwork. It's why I don't have time to deal with this damned inn or even know what to do with it. All I've ever trained to be was the warden."

Elden worked for the Commission of Magic Management? Any hope she might survive this encounter quickly died.

Elden was her worst nightmare come to life. Changelings were universally hated—there were no laws to protect them.

Any changeling reported to the Commission was returned to the feylands. Which would be a death sentence.

Would Elden turn her in? She was certain he would. It was the smart, logical choice, and the man was nothing if not brutally efficient. What could she possibly say that would save her?

"If you reveal me to the Commission, Elden, I'll *die*. I won't survive the feylands, whatever you may think. Elden..." She worried her bottom lip, rasping with her broken voice. "Elden, *please*." If Avalon wasn't tricked or enslaved the instant the Commission threw her back into the feylands, a place she didn't even remember, then that vicious prince, Bane, would surely hunt her down.

"You'd dare ask for my *mercy*," Elden scoffed, "with my family's blood on your lips? You feral creature."

But Elden didn't look angry at her request. Instead, he seemed uncomfortable and thoughtful. He mused, "My mother was no slave to the Commission. She taught me to think for myself, but I'm not sure how I want to deal with you. You *are* an illegal fey, and you crossed the border without permission, but..." Elden tentatively approached her, offering a hand to help her stand. "I'm going to have to consult someone wiser about this. Come."

Her bitterness controlled her actions—Avalon smacked his hand away and struggled to her own feet. If she had insulted him, Elden hid it well.

She was about to follow him out of the cellar, into the exposing moonlight, when she paused. "Wait."

His shoulders sagged, as if he had known she wouldn't make this so simple. "What now?"

"My face...I look like..." Her fingers grazed her cheekbones and ears, both sharper than they had been before. And her teeth...she was afraid to even touch them.

"You're a changeling," he grumped, as if the answer to her problem was obvious. "Just change back."

She scrunched her face together, endeavoring to find what mental muscle it required to return to normal.

After too long a time, Elden interrupted her. "Stop. Stop making those weird faces. It's clear you don't know what you're doing. No one would embarrass themselves that badly to prove a point." He stomped over to her and ran a hand over her face, frowning as she jerked away on instinct. "It's a glamour to conceal your fey appearance. And it will only work while you remain on my lands. So, you'll have to figure this out. Or..."

Or I can never leave without exposing myself?

He neglected to finish the sentence, but Avalon understood.

Surprisingly, Elden guided her back inside the inn and to her room instead of some secret dungeon. "I'm going to lock the door behind you," he warned. "Magically. That includes the window. Tomorrow morning, I'll collect you and we will decide how this ends."

"Fine." There wasn't any sense in arguing—even her rebellious spirit presumed that.

He patted her doorframe. "Keep her contained." Was he actually speaking to the *inn*? "Good night," Elden said awkwardly, a strange attempt to fill in the empty air between them.

Avalon shut the door in his face.

CHAPTER 9
AVALON

Whatever he had done to her room had rendered her cell phone completely useless. Avalon stared up at her ceiling fan, finding no comfort in her bed and unable to call and warn Odele. Luckily, Elden arrived to fetch her early in the morning, before any guest would logically be awake. It ended her staring contest with the ceiling before insanity could claim her for good.

She made herself ready to face him in record time, and it pleased her to see he did not appear to have slept soundly.

His storybook silver plate armor was gone—replaced with grey leathers and a sheath for a single-blade axe that was less cartoonish in size than the one he bore last night. The cape was still there, regal, and so blue it looked out of place against an earthly backdrop. Now that she knew Elden's true, terrifying form, his glamour would no longer work on her senses.

She had expected to be brought before some sort of official fey council or judge—not to be ushered into the maid's break room and greeted warmly with a cup of overly sugared coffee from Nora Lee.

The break room had a single square table and a row of lockers for the employees to use. Avalon saw another tin of that strange tea and made a note to check it for mold later. If she even made it to later.

As Elden debriefed his head of housekeeping of the night's events, Avalon squinted at the older woman. Nora Lee politely ignored her stares until Elden finished speaking.

"I am human, dear," Nora Lee chuckled. "I'm not hiding horns or feyrie wings. Neither is Elden."

"So?" Elden questioned, his tone sharp. "What do I do with her?"

"What would your mother have done with her, you mean?" Nora Lee's clarification brought a flush of heat to Elden's cheekbones—he was ashamed to have to ask, Avalon guessed.

Nora Lee looked fondly at a photograph taped on her locker—a faded picture of two young women, someone Avalon suspected to be Nora Lee and a tall, dark-haired woman wearing a cowboy hat, the white brim of it dyed slightly red. "I think," Nora Lee mused, tapping her fingers against her own mug. "I think that deciding now would be foolish."

Avalon's heart sank, a heavy stone settling in her stomach. She had wanted an answer now—to avoid prolonging her anxiety. *And to know that Odele is safe.*

Elden crossed his arms. "What. Am. I. Supposed. To. Do."

"Watch her," Nora Lee shrugged. "You have a ten-week contract with these girls, and you *are* supposed to be training with this one. I know you were trying to avoid it, but it seems to be the perfect opportunity to observe her and see if she's hiding anything. Though I can tell you she *is* the governor's daughter. I verified that last night."

Avalon wasn't the only one disappointed. Elden pinched the bridge of his nose. "But her file claims that she's human. I have a duty to the Commission. If she's dangerous—"

Nora Lee waved a hand. "I think you can judge if she's really dangerous yourself, Elden."

"About this observation period," Elden challenged. "What if I find nothing of concern?"

"Let her leave. On the grounds that she can learn to look human again."

He wasn't pleased with Nora Lee's advice. "So, *I'm* stuck with her? Grand."

Avalon covered her mouth with a hand, staring at Nora Lee. "You can see through the glamour?"

Nora Lee chuckled. "There are a few of us that *are* aware of what this inn is. The Refuge on the Moor isn't just a fancy resort. It's a place where fey in the mortal world can visit their family in the feylands. A place where they all can come together and celebrate."

Feeling like she was being read to from a fey version of the inn brochure, Avalon nodded numbly. How she acted during the next few weeks would determine whether Elden would thrust her upon the Commission's mercies.

No pressure.

Elden was staring at her, those uncomfortable silver eyes searching for something. "If you have nothing to hide, as you claim, you have nothing to fear."

Perhaps that was a sad attempt to reassure her. Still, Avalon snapped in return, "I don't think that's something that good men find themselves saying."

"Finish your coffee," Nora Lee interjected, resting a free

hand on Elden's arm. "If we're late to breakfast, Lyra will have my head. For now, let us go about the day as we normally would. As impossible as that may seem."

"Everything about this should be impossible," Avalon muttered into her cup.

But things had yet to even *begin* to test the impossible.

Avalon had not been prepared for the walk to the dining room.

Elden had mentioned that the glamour surrounding the inn and its inhabitants wouldn't work on her anymore, but he hadn't bothered to inform her that some guests hadn't just been disguised—she had been unaware of their presence entirely.

The Refuge on the Moor was no longer empty, or appearing so. The hallways were full of fey of all kinds, jostling into her as Avalon hurriedly chased Elden to the dining room. One even caught Avalon staring, and the fey morphed her face into a mimicry of Avalon's and laughed.

The fey of their world were immersed in the mythology of nearly every country. The nymphs were all over Greece, banshees were Irish, and the list went on. Avalon gave up trying to place all the fey that they walked past.

"Are *any* of the guests human?" Avalon stepped over what she could only guess was a brownie that was sweeping the entryway. The small, wizened humanoid smacked her heels with its tiny broom, urging her to move on.

"We thought you were," Elden answered.

They entered the dining room as Lyra was circling the table and taking the staff's orders. Avalon knew she was staring—way past the polite glance and leaning into stalker territory. But

Lyra was dazzling.

Lyra's olive skin now bore a light tinge of green, and her mountain of locks had several plants blooming in it. She smiled brightly at her cousin and jumped when she caught sight of Avalon.

"Oh, shit. I mean, Avalon, you look..." Lyra wrung her hands in her apron.

"She's a redcap. Like me," Elden said, his tone distant and matter of fact.

"Like you?" Avalon echoed, frowning. She searched for Odele and felt a pang of solace that she hadn't yet arrived.

Elden squinted at Lyra, studying her, before replying to Avalon's question. "Like I said, you're a redcap. Like my mother and I are. Were." He pulled out a chair, and, rather than taking a seat, motioned impatiently for Avalon to sit. "It's easy to tell us apart from other fey by the teeth."

She must look strange for Lyra to react so. But, when she eyed the chef now, Lyra was studying Elden suspiciously, and not Avalon.

Avalon begrudgingly sat, jolting as he slid her chair too close to the table for comfort. As she had expected, he took the seat next to her. *You really feel the need to keep such a close eye on me? We can't even have a table between us?*

The term "redcap" meant nothing to her. "I thought I was a changeling?"

"This is the nefarious mastermind you called to warn us about?" Kenan and Tahoma had arrived. Kenan teasingly grinned at Avalon. "Are you pretending to be stupid?" he asked.

"You know there's no way for me to answer that and come out ahead," Avalon sneered. The twins' eyes were inhumanly large and wet—the pupil entirely lost in a black void. Their dark hair shimmered, iridescent, and colorful like an oil spill bathed in light. They smelled like the sea. Avalon made a mental note to ask Elden later what they were. And then mentally puked at the thought of forcing more conversations with him upon herself.

Elden pushed a cup of coffee to her. "Changeling is what you were forced to become, not what you were born as. You were born a redcap, and we are a little unsettling to the other fey. Redcaps don't exactly have the cleanest history." He jumped topics, revealing, "Lyra's a nymph. Tahoma and Kenan are a quarter selkie."

Avalon focused on the information relevant to her, at the moment too selfish to care about the other employees' backgrounds. "All redcaps are inherently violent? It's unavoidable?" Maybe, just maybe, that wildness in her heart hadn't been entirely her fault. It had been something genetic that had doomed her from the start.

"Some more than others," Elden amended. "But it may explain why you're so aggressive and—"

"Finish that sentence."

Tahoma and Kenan giggled, while Elden took a very long pause before appealing to Lyra for help. "No, I sense that I have made some kind of mistake."

"Good morning!" Odele was certainly chipper, Avalon grumped, but she hadn't spent the witching hours fighting for her life. "I texted you last night." Odele poked Avalon under the table as she took a place next to her sister. "You could have answered, at least. I know I used the word *party*, but it was just sitting around a fire. You wouldn't have hated it."

She must have texted her after Avalon had spied their little impromptu gathering. So Avalon had been included. *As an after-thought.*

"Sorry," Avalon murmured, a reflex. "I was a little distracted." *Look at me. Can't you see what's happening to me?*

"I'm going to the beach with Tahoma and Kenan to search the tide pools. We're going to have to eat fast." Odele ordered French toast with whipped cream, powdered sugar, and huckleberries. And extra, extra maple syrup. "Do you want to tag along?"

It wouldn't matter if she did. Avalon caught Elden's slow shake of his head. A clear "no way in hell". "Next time," Avalon vowed weakly. Odele didn't seem convinced, but neither did she seem too bothered by the rejection.

Would she *ever* get alone time with her sister? Maybe she could convince Odele to return to Seattle. But she'd have to wait until her overseer was out of earshot.

"She's working with me today." Elden told Odele, startling her. "We had a *wedding emergency.*" He said the words as if he was aware of how ridiculous the phrase was. "Avalon will start a day early."

"Oh." Odele's eyes softened. "I didn't realize. Sorry, Avalon."

Avalon doubted that Elden's addition to the conversation had been done to help her. He was laying down the expectation that she would be busy with him for the remainder of the contract.

The rest of breakfast went by quickly. Avalon was too focused on learning how to chew with her tapered teeth to notice that everyone else had finished, and Odele had slipped away to get ready for her excursion with the twins.

It wasn't until Elden cleared his throat, twice, that she

bothered to glance up from her plate.

"It's not that easy," she defended herself, pushing away her plate of half-eaten food. "I'm terrified I'm going to bite off my own tongue."

"You don't need to try so hard to convince me of your ignorance." Elden glared at her; his plate was perfectly clean. "I don't understand why you're screwing with me."

Her hand curled around her fork, crunching the metal out of shape. It would have been more impressive if she didn't know this was cheap silverware. "What did you say?"

"I know you're intelligent," the warden continued while his hotel staff grimaced, "so why you insist on maintaining that you just *happened* to fall into the feylands—"

How childish would it be to throw her plate at him? "I didn't fall. Your beast of a dog chased me."

"Because you didn't tell anyone what you were! All Hob could tell was something fey was not where it should be!"

"People. *Feyries.* Whatever." Kenan groaned sleepily. "It's seven in the morning. Be quiet."

Avalon could not allow Elden to have the last word, despite Kenan's protests. She kept picking at Elden, adding, "How could I tell you? Why would I? I'd get deported back to that awful place and die in there. Sorry if I've inconvenienced you." Her life was on the line and Elden was upset about her small omission?

Elden shook his head. "I still don't believe you."

"I thought feyries couldn't lie?" Avalon countered.

"They can't. But you're a changeling—I'm sure you have some way around it. I don't have time to babysit you like this."

"Poor man," Avalon scoffed. "I'm sure it's just awful being attractive and a business owner and a feyrie prince. My heart aches for you."

Lyra replaced Avalon's plate with a bowl of oatmeal and fruit—food that would be easier to handle with her newly sharpened teeth. Lyra cocked a brow down at her. "Did you just call him attractive?"

"That wasn't the point!" *Context, Lyra!*

"Focus, cousin," Elden said, his tone uncentered. Avalon's previous statement about his looks appeared to have surprised the warden most of all. "I have the mound to deal with and this damned hotel and—" He whirled around in his seat, pointing at a couple seated a few tables back. "—if you try to send that plate back a third time, I'm shoving it up your—"

Lyra slapped a hand over his mouth just in time.

Kenan stopped sipping his coffee, shaking his head at Avalon and Elden. He looked at his sister, a wide, amused grin on his face. "Dear gods, they're the same type of insane. I can't handle *two* Eldens."

"You can't handle one," Tahoma laughed.

Elden pushed off from the table. "Changeling, meet me outside when you're done. Tahoma, watch her."

"Oh, sure. I'll make sure she doesn't do anything crazy with that oatmeal."

CHAPTER 10
AVALON

Elden's daily routine involved more walking than Avalon had imagined. A hike along the inn's grounds might have been pleasant, given time to admire the autumn beauty and with a different partner, but in her current situation, rucking through the woods was an unwelcome punishment. Hiding her exhaustion soon became impossible, and she realized she didn't even need to. Elden was doing his damnedest to ignore her very existence.

She was so busy cursing him that Avalon failed to take note when Elden opened his stride, clearing a fast and, as she would find out, ice-cold creek.

"Dammit!" she snapped, now impossible to tune out. Her socks were now soaked through.

"Pay attention," was all Elden said, shooting a quick glance down the course of the creek.

Avalon made faces at his back, doubling her pace so she could walk past him. She was tired of looking at the man and his damned wide shoulders.

When she was about to step in front of him, Elden's arm shot out in front of her chest. "Oh!" Her breath escaped as he abruptly halted her progress.

He pointed down at her feet, and Avalon paled at the sight of a large circle of fly agaric mushrooms below her.

She had nearly stepped inside a feyrie ring.

"As *amusing* as watching you dance until you drop would be, I imagine I'd get bored after a few hours." Elden repeated, all amusement gone, "*Pay attention.*"

She couldn't think of a retort, which was unusual. Instead, Avalon silently and bitterly returned to trailing behind Elden.

Avalon learned—by pestering Elden—that while Nora Lee and the twins managed the hotel, he and his dog stalked the perimeter of their territory. What he and his canine shadow were looking for, Avalon didn't care to ask. She was concentrating on keeping quiet and seeming as innocent as possible.

But everyone had their breaking point.

"Can you just tell me if you're going to kill me?"

"What?" Elden flinched, slowing his pace.

Avalon asked again, breathless, "Are you going to kill me? It's cruel to keep me in suspense like this." She mused, "I don't even have a will."

"This isn't a straightforward decision for me."

The crisp air burned her throat as she laughed sourly. "Yeah, I'm sure it kept *you* up last night."

That was sarcasm, but Elden looked as fatigued as Avalon knew she did. A purple eyed zombie had stared listlessly back at her in the mirror this morning. Elden replied, "There's no use trying to get an answer from me now. I intend to wait until I've had ample opportunity to observe your behavior to my satisfaction. But, so far," he relented, "you have done an excellent job of convincing me that you *are* indeed the luckless, wrong place, wrong time, idiot you claim to be."

She nearly slipped on a pile of wet leaves. "Comforting."

And something occurred to her that had evaded her fear-addled mind.

Odele. She would see. She would dream about it. If Elden decided to kill her, Odele would witness every gory second of it and know she would be powerless to stop someone like him.

"You can't use that axe on me."

Every muscle in his back froze. Even the dog paused, turning and staring at her with those large brown eyes, its brow quirked upward. If she had to beg Elden, had to grovel on her belly, Avalon would do it for Odele.

"Please," she implored him. "If capital punishment is the way you ultimately decide to go, can you slip something into my coffee? Smother me in my sleep? Gods, you can even *drown* me if you'd like. Anything but that axe."

Bewildered, he stammered, "You think I'm going to *kill* you?"

How was he the one shocked by his own threats? "You've said so! Back in the feylands—"

They had made it to the inn's front gate and Elden, clearly desperate for something, anything, to occupy his attention and hands, started testing the gate posts for any give. "Back there, in that place, I *have* to become that. I would have killed you then," he acknowledged it quietly, but clarified, "If it had warranted it. Our laws are different. I can take such action there as necessary. But if you stay where you are supposed to be..." His jaw was set, grim. "Then I cannot harm you. At worst, I turn you into the Commission."

The Commission of Magic Management. It had once been

a childhood dream of hers to work there, preferably in the Rescue and Return division. She had once thought she could turn her ferocity into something good. Something positive.

That had been before Avalon had realized what she was and that the Commission could single-handedly ruin her life.

They *always* sent changelings back, back to the feylands. Though, usually, the Commission knew who the changelings belonged to. Who had planted them, performing an archaic feyrie tradition that was now criminalized.

If Elden revealed her to the Commission, she was doomed. There was no human, or human adjacent being, that could survive long term in the feylands. Avalon had barely made it one night.

"How chivalrous," she sneered. "Kill me, give me to the Commission. It's all the same in the end. You work for those sadists?"

Elden possessed more control over his redcap temper than she did, but she still saw signs that his practiced patience was thinning. He ran a hand roughly through his hair before folding his arms over his chest. He clarified, "I work *with* those sadists."

A truck, red with an impeccably clean paint job, was kicking up gravel.

"Someone's coming," Avalon blurted. She waved her hands, fruitlessly urging the dog to get out of the drive and away from the open gate.

"*Hob.*" Elden whistled, watching Hob pad over to him happily. To Avalon he said, "I don't see anyone. *Or* hear anyone."

What an idiotic mistake, one she couldn't even blame on sleep deprivation if she was being honest with herself. Avalon tapped her pointed ear, flinching at the reminder of her current state. "You'll just have to trust me."

Suspicion clouded his expression. She had lost any ground she had gained with him. But after a few more uncomfortable minutes, the red truck arrived, turning a corner and coming into view.

A brunette man, grey streaked throughout his short hair, leaned out of the driver's window, slowing the truck's advance to a crawl. "Hey, elf!" Avalon recognized the driver from the coffee shop. The side of his truck had "Abernathy Farms" posted in large white letters, letters that were cradled with drawings of lavender.

He seemed to know Elden, and the fey didn't appear upset or shocked by the farmer's sudden arrival. "What do you want *this* time, Abernathy?"

The older man leaned out of his truck, his mischievous smile bright and strong. A raven, large and looming, landed on top of the truck and watched Avalon through its remaining eye. Abernathy paid no mind to the bird sitting on his hood. "To know why my stockings were empty last Christmas. The big man in red working you too hard? Didn't have time to slip some whiskey in there for me?"

Abernathy cackled at his own joke, slapping his passenger in the arm until he got an unwilling, monotone laugh out of the woman.

Avalon watched for Elden's reaction to the slight, cringing in anticipation. How did this farmer know Elden? And, more importantly, know what he *was*?

Elden approached the truck and methodically pushed Abernathy's side mirror out of position. "This is exactly the kind of behavior that's going to keep you on Santa's shit list."

This delighted Abernathy, who began unwrapping a stick of jerky he threw to Hob. "There you go, you little goblin." Ironic, as the farmer probably weighed less than Elden's massive, shaggy dog. "How are things, elf? Notice anything unnatural? And I'm not talking about what you see in your mirror."

Abernathy released another burst of laughter while the passenger moaned, "Grandad, please stop."

Avalon startled at the word. Grandad? Abernathy barely looked to be in his fifties. Was he magic, too?

Elden squinted at the man. "You forgot to shave this morning, Abernathy. What's going on?"

"You're just jealous that elves can't grow beards."

"Nothing you said was accurate. Tell me what's happening. You only make the drive over here when there's something you need." Elden sighed, rubbing the back of his neck. "And since you're being so friendly today, I imagine it will be quite tiresome. Out with it."

Abernathy's smile soured. He looked at Avalon meaningfully, and Elden nodded. Avalon knew what he was about to ask before he did, the gears finally clicking into place. Abernathy said, "Something's happening in the southwest. And it's pushing things north that shouldn't be up here. It's going to *decimate* the ecosystem. If we still had the wolves—"

"I can't get into the wolves with you again. Even when I agree with you about reintroducing them to the area, you still argue with me."

"Chupacabra," the farmer revealed, ending his dramatic buildup prematurely. "The blood-suckers are going after anything with four legs." Abernathy's chipper tone lost a beat. "I'm too old to be sitting alone in a tree stand all night, and I've been explicitly and *repeatedly* forbidden from taking my granddaughters hunting. Your mother is letting your magic go to waste," he snapped to his passenger, who only slunk further in her seat.

Ah, apparently Abernathy was some sort of witch, something nature related if Avalon was going to judge based on his profession. Did his power allow him to see past Elden's glamour and the magic that covered the inn? Or had he been let in on the secret?

But chupacabra hunting? This *couldn't* be part of Elden's duties as warden, though Avalon was honestly uncertain what that title meant, or what authority it gave him. Surely Elden would refuse. Avalon had not seen a single goat on the property.

"Is there any sign?" Elden asked.

Now what the hell would he need that information for? Avalon stared in disbelief as Abernathy got out of his truck and slapped a map on the hood. Together, he and the innkeeper traced out a few areas, marking some spots carefully in highlighter. They were too quiet for Avalon's poor hearing to catch what they said, but when Abernathy got back into his vehicle to drive off, he was looking pleased.

The map had been left behind with Elden, and he studied the markings once more before checking his watch. "I'm going to have to go to bed if I'm going to be out again tonight."

He's going to help them? Go hunting at his own expense and with no obvious benefit to himself? Her self-preserving mind could not follow his logic. "You let that farmer boss you around?"

Elden didn't address her attempt to sting him. "That farmer's the head of the local coven. And the mayor. And the chief for the volunteer fire department. If I piss Abernathy off, I'll be back to fielding all the 'cat stuck in a tree' calls. So, *yes*, I let him boss me around."

She told herself Elden's participation in the local volunteer fire department meant nothing and was not at all attractive. "What does that mean for me?" she prompted, knowing whatever it was, she wouldn't care for it.

Eyes darting away, Elden added, almost gently, "You clearly didn't sleep well, either. We should both go to bed."

His weak attempt at *appearing* nice was not appreciated. "So, you can lock me in again?" She swore through her fatigue. "What's next? Am I banned from the west wing, too?"

He looked more affected by that than by any of her earlier slights. Elden crossed those broad arms, his stance irritatingly dominating. "So, I'm to be the *beast* in this scenario?"

The fey knew some pop culture, it seemed. "If the boot fits," Avalon sneered. "And why does that man know what you are?"

That wasn't remotely her business, she realized as the words fluttered out of her mouth, like moths to a flame. Not to mention this knowledge was dangerous. The more she learned, the more likely she'd end up getting burned by it.

Either Elden didn't care what she did with the information, or he was starting to see her as less of a threat than he did before. "Abernathy's family has been here for generations, since before the inn was built. They're druids. And a pain in my ass, though not as much as they could be." He led her back toward the inn, saying over his shoulder, "Their ancestors hailed from Scotland and know the tricks to undoing a glamour. But they leave the pitchforks at home when they come to visit. So, we can't complain."

Elden led her back to the inn, pausing at the footbridge. The noise of the brook hid their conversation. "I won't have the inn lock you up again, changeling. But you have to meet me halfway."

There were a lot of rules Avalon would have to follow if she wanted to avoid being locked in her room all night.

"You cannot tell anyone about the mound, or the fact we're all fey, or anything else that a human doesn't need to know." Cutting off her protest, Elden added, "And by can't, I mean that the entire grounds are magicked and no one can say a word about our true nature to anyone that doesn't already know it. You can try it, changeling," he offered with a smirk, "but you'll find the consequences less than desirable."

Her lips, opening to tell her secrets, to expose Elden for what he was, inexplicably refused to part. Once glance in Odele's mirror, a floor length piece of glass that lay against one wall of the cabin, showed her own face, just visible over Odele's shoulder.

The skin around her lips had formed over mouth, sealing her words shut away forever.

"I can keep your secret," Avalon said without enthusiasm. Her vision caused her hands to tremble, and she tucked them in her pockets. "Just consider keeping mine."

That locked-lipped scenario can be avoided, she reminded herself, feigning confidence where she had none. *It's something that could happen, not necessarily what will happen.*

Elden continued, oblivious to her disturbing foray into the possible future. "And that includes texting or emails or whatever other forms of communication you think you might get away with. Smoke signals," he warned, "won't work, either."

"Are we done?" Avalon demanded. "And humans know about feyries. Why do you need to keep all this secret at all?"

"The locations of the feyrie mounds are all classified. There are many humans who would take advantage of such an entrance, and the fey have enough of their own to contend with. It was also the Commission's decision." Elden knelt, ruffling the dog's pointed ears. He whispered something to Hob, in a strange, rough language that was somehow foreign and familiar all at once. "Hob will keep an eye on you when I can't. I'll have to fetch him from your room later tonight when I leave to track those vermin."

My room? "He's not sleeping in my room."

Her annoyance was pleasing to him. That was all too clear. "You'll be lucky if you can keep him off the bed. And, I *hate* to mention, he snores."

CHAPTER 11
AVALON

Hob took the lead, though the dog had no idea where Avalon wanted to go, which to him seemed to be a minor inconvenience.

The dog padded jauntily ahead of her, glancing back at her every so often to verify she was still following him. This made for a rather frustrating walking partner. Every time she tripped over the dog as he took a wrong turn, Hob gave her a sharp, disgruntled bark in response.

Despite this, they did eventually make it to Avalon's intended location—Odele's cabin. It squatted low between a small grove of pine trees, with ivy snaking up one side. While it was rustic, someone had added tiny details to brighten up the dark backdrop of wood. Lavender painted planter boxes were underneath each of the two front windows, and despite the season, small flowers were still in bloom. Fey magic, she guessed. But whether it was Elden's magic or another fey's, she didn't know.

The door's color matched the planters, and it bore the same

gold, glittering letters that Avalon's room, Whimsy, sported. Odele's room had been named *Sweet Dreams* instead.

The universe was one ironic bastard.

Avalon rapped their secret five-part rhythm against the door. Hob's ears perked, alert, before settling back down. When Odele finally answered, Avalon barged inside, the dog on her heels, and she began pacing in the center of the cabin.

She had to warn Odele without breaking any of Elden's excessive rules. Avalon's fingers flew to her mouth, checking she could still open it, and she almost chewed on her fingernails before she remembered her new, razor-sharp teeth.

"What's happened to you?" Odele questioned, her fine eyebrows raising with concern. She was dressed in grey overalls and a white t-shirt. Her painting clothes. Behind her, in the small kitchenette, the white cabinets were in the process of being painted a grey-ish blue. She sensed where Avalon's focus had shifted. Odele sniffed. "I *hate* white cabinets. I figured I might as well start in here."

She must have had time to run to the hardware store after foraging with Kenan and Tahoma. Avalon smiled weakly, motioning to the fresh paint, the chemical smell harsh in her nostrils. What should she say? Avalon knew better than to try to leave. Elden would declare her vanishing an admission of guilt and hunt her down with that bloody axe of his. But Odele—if she went back to Seattle and Avalon stayed, would he allow it? It was worth trying.

The words half-formed in her head, Avalon said conversationally, "How was foraging? Find anything?"

"We found some stuff I didn't even know was edible," Odele giggled. "And the twins went for a swim!"

"It's October!" Avalon blurted.

"Yeah, I think they're half-seal."

An obvious joke, but Avalon narrowed her eyes, considering. Was there a name for that? She'd have to check.

Odele stood, waiting for any acknowledgment of her joke. She shifted her weight around, her overalls exposing her skinny ankles. Odele's model-like height made shopping for clothes impossible. They had tried men's clothing, but she was also so thin that the men's side had nothing to offer.

Next to her ethereal sister, Avalon had always felt rather plain. She was slightly above average height and the same went for her weight. Her pride was her hair, a thick blonde and strawberry halo that brushes feared.

"You're not getting homesick, are you?" A pathetic attempt on Avalon's part to switch topics.

Odele scoffed. "For our dingy, paper-thin apartment? Yes, I really miss hearing our neighbors go at it like rabbits."

"We're exposed out here," Avalon pleaded. "You should go back. Thompson can send out another designer—"

"You think that I should go back?!" Odele's volume was nearing into shouting territory. "And what, you'll stay here? I'm not the one getting into arguments with the owner, who hasn't, besides being slightly awkward and standoffish, done anything wrong."

Someone must have overheard their argument that night Avalon had stormed out of Elden's office and found herself falling into the feylands. Gossip here traveled quick, as to be expected in such a rural area.

"I want to protect you." Avalon sounded insane, even to her own ears. But she couldn't get into specifics and (her throat itched until she grew hoarse) she couldn't even lie. Not unless she could figure out how to change back to human, or at least human enough to tell a little white lie.

"Good gods, Avalon. Protect me from what? Making friends that aren't you?" Odele bit her lip as if she wanted to take her last words back. "Can you even give me a reason? You're starting to worry me."

What could she say? Not the truth, and not a lie—that left nothing. "That's how I feel, Odd. I can't explain it."

"That isn't good enough, Avalon. And, worse, it's concerning." Her sister was exasperated, pleading.

Gods, this has been such a mistake. "Then forget it." She hadn't wanted to throw in the towel this early. Though, what choice had she been given? "Forget I even mentioned anything. Just—just let me know if you want to wander the gardens or the woods. We shouldn't be out alone."

There was little Avalon could do against most fey, but if Hob was going to be following Avalon everywhere she went, then Odele would at least be safe if they stuck together. There was an unnamable, eerie force Avalon sensed emitting from the dog. She had a feeling that there was little that Hob feared.

As if the canine had sensed her attention, Hob pushed his head against Avalon's hand, his slobbery jowls rubbing against her skin. Disgusting.

"Dogs don't usually like you," Odele remarked, regarding the animal incredulously.

"It's Elden's dog. Maybe he's used to assholes?"

"Funny." Odele itched her bare ankle with the toe of her shoe. Quietly, she added, "I *want* to understand you, Avalon. I don't know what's happening with you right now."

Avalon's eyes burned, threatening more exposed emotion if she didn't get out of there now. "I want to explain it. I just can't."

After Hob had nearly scattered a gallon of paint across the cabin floor, Odele had quietly and shrewdly hinted at them to leave. Which was slightly disappointing, but welcome. Avalon was having a hard time staying awake, and she felt lingering around Odele would do more damage to their relationship.

She had seen the unspoken threat in Odele's eyes.

Maybe you should see that specialist again.

Well, *this* paranoia was justified—if Odele could just see that. And none of the therapists her mother had paid for would've been able to help Avalon deal with her issues if her blood-thirsty nature really resulted from being a redcap.

But is that just another excuse?

Back in her room, Avalon thumbed through the worn fey-rie tale books that she had found tucked in shelves and inside the nightstand. This time, she read as if her life depended on it. Avalon studied the book late into the night, fighting for bed space with Hob, who inexplicably seemed to have expanded in size once he had landed on the mattress.

Sighing as she watched Hob's drool form a small lake on her pillow, Avalon wondered if there was a more official document she should reference, rather than relying on the Brother's Grimm. The boys had done a lot of research, and yet she still found herself relying on the internet.

The search results made her feel ridiculous. As if there was a website that could tell her how to return to her human form. She scrolled through the pages, defeated, until Hob sprung from the bed, knocking her phone out of her hand and causing it to go skittering into the dark. The bedside lamp she had been using for reading was insufficient to locate her phone. So, swearing under her breath, Avalon followed Hob to the door, blindly fumbling for the light switch.

Hob scratched at the door, whimpering, and her tinnitus kicked in—a high keening. "Do you have to pee?" she asked, imagining how much damage a dog his size would do to the rug. Avalon quickly opened her door, illuminated at the top of the stairway, and still in what she wore to bed. Hob rushed past her, bounding down the stairs, and meeting up with his master at the second level landing.

Their eyes met. Avalon realized too late she was standing cloaked in the light of her room and wearing just an old t-shirt and her underwear.

Some uncharacteristic shriek escaped her, and she tugged frantically at the hem of her shirt, fruitlessly trying to cover her Fruit of the Looms. Elden slapped a hand over his eyes with enough force that Avalon heard the sound from her position at the top of the stairs.

She slammed the door shut, listening to what sounded suspiciously like Elden stumbling down the rest of the stairs. She rubbed her ears, certain she was hallucinating noises, like she did during her annual hearing test.

Hob will keep an eye on you while I can't. I'll have to fetch him from your room later tonight when I leave to track those vermin.

What was going on with her memory? Avalon groaned, raking her blunt fingernails down her face. Elden had told her he'd be coming by to collect his dog. He must think she was an idiot.

What underwear had she even been wearing—her morning routine had been too rushed for her to recall. It had better *not* be those joke underwear Odele had gifted her last Christmas.

She peeked between her legs, groaning when she found a motley of cartoon penises were eyeing her in return.

Breakfast was...uncomfortable.

Elden, the second she walked into the dining room, turned pink and ducked his head down, staring into his breakfast as if the meaning of life was hidden amongst his hash browns.

Avalon took a seat as far from him as she was able. She tried to make herself appear normal, which became more difficult as Hob, who barely fit underneath the table, started nosing her knee and begging for scraps. It seemed ludicrous now that she had once run from him, fearing for her life.

She dreaded the thought of spending another day with Elden, trudging through the woods in unbearable silence. It was impossible that he could have seen the micro, phallic print on her underwear. Not even with fey eyesight. She hoped.

Kenan nudged Elden, disrupting his breakfast meditation. "Did you find any chupacabra?"

Avalon nearly choked on her food—Odele was seated right across from him. Oblivious to the current topic of conversation, Odele, straight-faced and unaware, continued eating her waffles. Her strawberry topping had all been cut into tiny heart shapes.

Tahoma filled Avalon in, making up for her brother's bluntness. "Odele won't hear anything that would disrupt her idea that this inn is anything other than an inn where withered retirees blow their money to watch birds."

Tahoma was right. Odele didn't appear to catch any of their conversation. It felt wrong.

"I didn't find anything," Elden admitted. "I'll have to go out again tonight." He didn't look directly at Avalon, just close enough so she knew he was speaking to her. "Whatever you have planned for the inn, I won't be a part of it until the chupacabra issue is resolved."

What a relief. Avalon's face twisted into a smile that was far from a polite response to the situation. "I'll start showing the rest of the staff the new software." Having such a normal conversation with him, after all that had happened, was too surreal.

Odele was brought back into the conversation, informing everyone she'd be using one of the inn's meeting rooms to interview possible contractors to help her with repairs and redecorating.

Avalon was left wondering how she, the Schwarzenegger twins, and that behemoth dog were going to all fit into that tiny firetrap of an office.

Showing the twins the new programs and how to transfer over their handwritten data into the new interface was surprisingly easy. Even with Hob constantly trying to squeeze underneath the desk while Avalon was working.

Unfortunately, Kenan and Tahoma's adeptness left plenty of opportunity for chatting.

"So...you're a changeling, huh?" Kenan leaned back from the keyboard, stretching his back against his chair. He turned his wrists this way and that until there was a sickening "pop".

"That has already been established, Kenan." His sister kicked his chair and watched him fall off to one side. "Stop with the warmup. I don't think you need to be delicate with this one."

Avalon winced in anticipation.

"If," Kenan drawled, black eyes shining, "we are to believe your story, tell us how a changeling made it so far undocumented? They keep an eye out for that sort of thing now. Most people nowadays would love to blame their kid's bad behavior on them being fey."

Elden hadn't told them about her father? It must have slipped his mind while he was warning everyone she could be some trespassing spy or assassin. Honestly, who would want to go into the feylands? Besides the adventurous (and foolish) mushroom enthusiast, there was no logical reason for any human to dare sneak their way into feyrie territory.

Not to forget that undocumented travel between the mortal realm and the fey realm was forbidden—for humanity's safety.

What would Kenan accept and wouldn't prompt any further questions?

"I have a rich daddy," Avalon sneered, hating how she sounded. It didn't matter that Bruce and Valerie hadn't given them a cent, or any support at all, since Odele had turned eighteen and—

"Take her with you. And do something respectable." Bruce wouldn't look at them; he hadn't made eye contact with his false daughters in years. Not since the truth came out. "I don't want to see either of you in the news."

Their mother blurted, "Christmas! Remind them about Christmas!"

Bruce's tone was drastically different from their mother's. "You'll return every Christmas for the annual party. If you break these rules, I'll call the Commission myself."

It wasn't usual for her Sight to keep throwing her into the past. These throwbacks to her childhood were very unwelcome.

Kenan snorted, but Tahoma stared openly at Avalon, as if knowing there was more to her story. Something she was hiding.

Tahoma shrugged and gestured to her brother and then herself. "We're only partially selkie," she revealed casually. "Our grandmother was a full-blooded fey so our generation is more human than not. You've spent more time in the feylands than we have."

"It's not exactly a paradise. If you're looking for vacation ideas, I'd stick with something more basic and with fewer cannibals."

"I didn't believe it when he first told us," Kenan smirked. "But you are funny."

Who were they talking about? It couldn't have been *Elden*.

The following night, Avalon was fully prepared for Elden to come for his dog. But he didn't. It was *four days* before Elden went hunting again. Four days of mindless data entry, stale coffee, terrible slideshows, and avoiding each other.

At his master's whistle, Hob launched himself off her legs, where he had been sleeping peacefully while her limbs turned numb. Underneath the covers, Avalon was dressed head to toe. Still, when she opened the door to let Hob out of Whimsy, she used the door as a makeshift shield.

Hob actually paused at the doorway, looking back at her with his head cocked, as if he was waiting for her to follow.

She waved a hand at him. "Go on," she whisper-shouted,

"I'm not coming with you. And don't give me those eyes!"

Hob huffed twice before he gave up and crashed gracelessly down the stairway. Admittedly, spending a week with the beast constantly at her side had caused Hob to grow on her. Rather than chase her into the feylands, the dog now took it upon himself to protect her from *everything*—even the harmless birds that strayed too close to their path.

Avalon returned to bed, her legs kicking under the heavy comforter. Filled with nervous energy, she pulled out her phone—a surefire way to make sure she had trouble falling back to sleep, but she didn't care. She sent a few messages to Odele to see if she was awake, too, and waited for a response from her sister.

What are you doing up? I was going to call you.

Avalon typed back, *I had to let the dog out.*

The dog is sleeping in your room???

Avalon sent a few pictures of Hob, sprawled out in her bed, tongue out, and drooling. This was her way of answering Odele's question without actually providing any additional information.

If I didn't see pictures, I wouldn't have believed it. A few quiet minutes passed before Odele sent another message. *I had another bad dream.*

"Bad dream" was code for "I saw someone's possible death again". Did she dream of someone from the inn? Or were her abilities strong enough to reach its tendrils into the town that was only a few miles away?

Avalon texted, *Did you recognize anyone? Was it nearby?*

It was fuzzy. It was like I was seeing it through a veil.

The first part was a good sign. Fuzzy meant that there was a chance that it could be averted. When Odele's dreams were crystal clear...well, it was better to make some adjustments to your life insurance policy while there was still time. The second part she imagined had something to do with the protective glamour around the inn that kept outsiders from realizing the truth of it.

I heard a dog whining. There were these tattered creatures circling a man. And there were trees. The moon looked the same as it does right now. I think it's going to happen tonight.

Hob! A second later, Avalon worried for the man who was assuredly alongside the canine.

Odele's premonitions left her bed-ridden. She only told Avalon about her dreams in detail when there was any chance to circumvent it. Which was admittedly rare.

Avalon dug around for her hiking boots, a purchase Odele had demanded they both make prior to this work trip. She threw on black jeans, a dark hoodie and jacket, and a matching beanie before she headed for the front desk and called the number listed for overnight service.

Her heart sank when Nora Lee answered.

"*You're* on duty tonight?" Avalon asked, the frustration clear in her tone.

"You're not making me feel particularly wanted right now," Nora Lee huffed. "Is this an emergency?"

She nearly shouted "yes!" and asked for Tahoma or Kenan's private numbers. She had the feeling, though no one had outright said anything yet, that the twins might also act as a backup for Elden's warden duties. But how could she explain anything without revealing that Odele was a banshee and also a changeling?

"I can probably handle it," she finally said without conviction. It was the closest she could get to a "no" without lying.

"Have a good night."

Nora Lee tried to say something more, but Avalon hung up too quickly. She raced outside the inn, the night air biting at her skin, and eyed the surrounding woods with trepidation. The land around the inn was thickly forested, and Avalon was no ranger. Her phone vibrated and a quick glance informed her that Odele had sent one word. *Hurry!*

Odele would lose her mind if she knew that Avalon was trying to find the victim herself. She might have nothing to worry about, though. Avalon surveyed the thick foliage in preemptive defeat. How would she find them in that bramble? Even with her new, and unsettling, feyrie ability to see in the dark, the woods were too thick, too overgrown.

I shouldn't even be out here, Avalon told herself. The idea of leaving Elden to his death *had* occurred to her, and she would have happily fallen back asleep after Odele's revelation, all her problems about to be brutally solved for her, when she had remembered.

That damn dog.

As beneficial as Elden's death may have been for her, Avalon couldn't shake that dumb, slobbering dog's face out of her head. She *couldn't* let that creature watch his master die. She may not have been exactly a dog lover, but she had read too many clickbait articles about dogs giving up on life after their owner had passed.

The night chill lessened as her chest burned with an inner heat, a star blooming inside her rib cage. That blue feylight, the one she had met that dreadful night, fluttered out of her and hovered at eye level. It paused a moment before it zoomed off, leaving Avalon to suspiciously eye its fiery trail until the orb stopped in front of the inn's garage.

"What's in here?" Avalon touched the lock on the door and the feylight shuddered as if to say, "*do I have to do everything?*" Avalon kicked at the door once, twice, and stumbled forward as the wood caved in.

I could get used to this part of being fey, she admitted. It was strange, but the dark garage was clear as day to her. After a few steps inside, she found herself before a four-wheeled, off-road vehicle. It had two seats and a small bed, perfect for cruising the inn's expansive property. "If this was here the whole time," she angrily mused, "why the hell did Elden make me hike the whole damn acreage with him?"

The feylight pulsed, indicating a line of hooks filled with keys. Retrieving the keys and finding the button that opened the garage's car door, Avalon returned to the vehicle. She and Odele had, prior to their parents finding out their true nature, taken a family vacation where they had driven similar vehicles for a desert tour.

She wasn't an expert by any means, but soon she had the vehicle running and was crawling out of the garage. It was difficult, but she found the first wide forest path she recalled on Elden's patrol. Here Avalon stopped, looking at the feylight pleadingly. "Can you find him? The warden?"

The icy feylight dimmed. Perhaps she had asked too much of it. What was her favorite song worth, anyway?

Then the light zipped down the path and she lurched forward, chasing it down the winding forest trail.

Avalon was tense and white-knuckling the steering wheel while she squinted forward into the darkness. The orb floated back to her, flashing in and out until she stopped the vehicle. The light surged forward again, easily outpacing her, flying past the shocked, wide-eyed features of Elden Cavanaugh.

Elden swatted at the light, and Avalon saw it take an upward turn into a tall, ghostly tree.

On one of the thickest branches, a grey, lizard-skinned creature was clinging to the trunk. If demon-possessed kangaroos with a bad case of mange existed, Avalon decided they would look a lot like *that*.

The creature's body tensed, ready to leap down at the nearest target—Elden. Avalon laid on the horn and screamed, "MOVE!" before she slammed down on the gas pedal.

There was a second where it seemed Elden didn't believe she wouldn't swerve before he dove to the side. Again, the man possessed far more grace than his height and size should have allowed.

The creature had lunged from its perch, leaving her seconds to act. Avalon continued past where Elden had been standing a moment ago, crashing into the dead tree and pinning the attacking thing in the process.

Her harness caught her, digging into her chest, and prevented her from head-butting the dash. She gasped for breath—an image of several creatures, a pack or swarm or whatever, appeared in her swimming vision. Elden was at the vehicle in seconds, trying to undo her harness until she smacked him away. "There's more," she gasped.

He ignored her, clicking her out of her restraints. "Do *not* run," he ordered her. "The chupacabra will chase you. Stay here, hide, and wait for me."

Elden was off, and she heard a barking dog, Hob definitely, and the soft "twang" of arrows being loosed.

The pinned creature let out the soft cry of the dying. Avalon popped open the glove compartment, rooting around in the mess a few times before her fingers found the cold metal of a knife.

The pinned chupacabra bit her when she approached it, crushing her hand and drawing blood. Her breath escaped in a hushed scream. She studied the chupacabra closely, identifying its throat before sliding the blade of her newfound knife across it. It wasn't as clean as she wanted, but Avalon lacked the skill to do any better. Wasn't that always the case?

The irony of her killing a creature solely due to its inconvenient bloodlust was not lost on Avalon.

"What are you doing here?!" Elden's pale face was grey and furrowed. His shoulders heaved with fatigue, trying to catch his own breath after dealing with the rest of the pack.

Ignoring him, Avalon reentered the off-road vehicle, putting herself in the passenger seat this time. She stuffed her borrowed knife back into the glove box, not wanting to be caught with a weapon, and Avalon waited while Elden dragged the chupacabra corpses underneath the dead tree.

Hob appeared and nosed her knee until Elden returned and made him jump into the bed. "You're in his seat," Elden explained bitterly, struggling to start up the now damaged engine. He smelt like the chupacabra and a tang of blood—a rather unpleasant mixture. He didn't sound particularly grateful to the person who had just saved his ass.

After a successful turnover of the engine, he reversed the vehicle to head back towards the inn, and her feylight floated lazily after them before burrowing back inside her chest. Elden's eyes burned when he witnessed that exchange, and she knew they would be having another late-night conference.

CHAPTER 12
ELDEN

Elden pressed his fingers against his eyelids before moving upward to massage his temples. "I don't even know where to start." He had led her to the outdoor wedding venue at the lake, of all places, and he sank into one of the pews. Avalon sat across the aisle from him, kicking her feet back and forth. Clean wooden benches lined either side of a white stone aisle that led up to a wooden arch with the lake as its backdrop. The arch was alive, made from woven branches that twisted into a large, vine covered circle.

Elden waited for her to take control of the conversation, as his irritation was causing him to hesitate. His temper was up, and everything he tried to say sounded like a line that belonged in a witch trial. As confounding, confusing, and secretive as the woman was, Avalon did not deserve such heavy-handedness.

Avalon said, without preamble, "I'm a Seer."

Elden laughed loudly, hysterically. He threw his dark, wild head back as he leaned against the pew, both arms sprawled across the back. The bow he used earlier was cast to the ground—a long, wooden recurve style. "Of course, you are."

His reaction was clearly not what she'd expected. Avalon gave a little more detail, her eyes wide at his outburst. "Listen, I didn't think that it was relevant. I'm a *very* weak Seer. Otherwise, would I have stumbled through that mound like that?" When he buried his face in his hands, distorting his amusement poorly, Avalon snapped. "I didn't want any of this! Most of the time, I don't see far enough ahead to even do anything about it!"

"You're a changeling and a Seer, and you somehow have a *will-o'-the-wisp* doing your bidding." Elden straightened and cut her a humorless smirk. "If I wasn't so pissed, I'd be impressed."

"Will-o'-the-wisp?" she echoed, and he groaned again.

"Unbelievable. At least understand *what* you're bargaining with, Avalon."

"That light is a will-o'-the-wisp? Following it blindly into the darkness now seems terribly idiotic." At least she had the sense to sound embarrassed.

He wanted to laugh again, but held it in to avoid startling her a second time. Feasibly, the wisp had happily led her to him, hoping the chupacabra would take care of both of them.

Elden didn't give her a second to regain control of the interrogation. He continued, "Why this information wasn't included when you were begging me to trust you, I have no idea. Seems foolish. As foolish as making a deal with a will-o'-wisp of all things." He looked at the center of her chest, as if he could see the pulsing, blue light within. "Admittedly, it does help your stance that you didn't know what you were doing in the feylands."

The night air and Elden offered no comfort. Avalon hugged herself, shivering.

"What did you offer it, changeling?"

"Stop calling me that." She had taken on a new tone—it was very nearly threatening.

Elden refused to let her avoid the truth. "Living in denial won't change what you are."

"Fine. Keep spitting it in my face," she fumed, a shiver stuttering her words. "Keep reminding me that I don't belong anywhere. That I stole someone's life. That I'm the hated, terrible thing that every new parent fears."

If she wasn't so exhausted, Elden doubted Avalon would have slipped and revealed all that to him. She looked quite small as she trembled in the pew. "Avalon."

"What, Elden!"

"I apologize."

Her eyes darted over to his. He kept going, something rare and talkative coming out in him. The nearby lake lapped at the shore, the repetitive sound settling his temper. "I can understand what it's like to feel as if you don't belong. Look at me— what I am. And where I am."

She blinked. "You'd rather be in the feylands?"

"Arawn, no! But," he clarified, "I don't truly fit in here, do I? I can't run this inn, can't form relationships with the guests—fey or otherwise. And it's not any better back with my father and my half-siblings." He moved pews, now sitting at the end of hers. "Avalon, I won't call you that again."

She leaned forward, placing her folded arms on the back of the pew ahead of her. Avalon rested her head on her arms, studying him from her new angle. "Fine. And about the wisp? I tried to offer something that wouldn't bite me in the ass later on. So,

I asked if it wanted my favorite song."

He clicked his tongue, revealing, "You might have given away more than you think."

"I can find a new favorite—"

"You won't." Sympathy didn't suit him, twisting his face into something unfamiliar. Elden softly said, "My family, my mother and I excluded, are all orators. I know how these deals usually go, how to see the true cost. What you gave, Avalon...you didn't give away a single song. You'll *never* have another favorite song. *That* is what you gave away. It would explain why that murderous lantern is helping you, instead of leading you over a cliff."

She looked away, hiding her forlorn expression from him. "Can you ask what you really want to know?"

What remained of the moonlight was fading quickly, leaving Elden's features in shadow. He shifted, stretching out his weakened and sore limbs. "Now, what did you see, and how did that lead to you charging through the woods to find me?"

She was taking too long to answer. Was she trying to lie? Elden scowled as Avalon's answer came out slow and steady. "I was *told* that the chupacabra might be more than you could handle. Tahoma and Kenan weren't onsite, and I was afraid we were running out of time. I don't see very far ahead." Kicking up the grass at the bottom of her shoe, Avalon added defensively, "I was worried about Hob."

"Hob takes care of himself. And he can take care of me." Elden couldn't help feeling insulted. "It would take a lot more blood-suckers than that to pose an actual threat."

"The vision wasn't exactly crystal clear. Like I said, I'm—"

"A weak Seer and nothing at all for me to worry about?" Elden guessed, almost managing to sound sarcastic. "Perhaps that's why you were brought to the mortal realm as an infant."

"What?"

The timid way she spoke stabbed a tiny shard of shame into his heart. He had never heard of a changeling making it so long in the human realm. After a few years, most parents would have caught on and the switch back would be made. And the fey family responsible severely punished.

It was a child's wish to know why one had been abandoned. Elden couldn't fault her for it. Life as the governor's daughter seemed ideal, but there was nothing about her that was well-adjusted. Time in that household had done something to her.

"Seers are always taken to work directly for one of the feyrie rulers. A life of delivering bad news to royalty is rarely a happy one." He darkened, pausing. "I have seen how my father treats his own."

"Well, don't leave me in suspense." Avalon couldn't keep her shivers from leaking into her voice. "Should I expect the Commission in the morning or..."

His surprised cough turned into a laugh. "You think I should send you away for this? For trying to rescue me? Whether it was needed is a moot point. But you thought it was. And still you came."

"For the *dog*," she muttered.

That nearly made him smile. Yes, couldn't have him getting confused, could she?

"Sure." Now when he watched her, it wasn't with the cold calculation of a warden, deciding if she was guilty or innocent. He was looking for something else in her, and, if she knew, she would hate that even more. "You're cold. And we need to keep that bite from getting infected."

Avalon didn't appear to appreciate either of his

observations.

CHAPTER 13
AVALON

Her wrist burned from the alcohol Elden had poured over her wound. The inn's office had a first aid kit that was alarmingly well-stocked. Elden's long fingers had curled tight around her wrist to keep her from jerking away from the antiseptic. Which, as pathetic as it made her look, Avalon had tried once she realized how much the disinfecting would hurt.

Now alone in her room, after promising Elden that she'd keep her wound clean and notify him the moment it looked off, Avalon had plenty of time to mull over their last discussion. She couldn't get it out of her mind, what Elden had revealed about the lives of Seers in the feylands. Had her parents, her birth parents, been doing her a kindness by giving her to the Golightly family?

No, there was no use reading into that. There were a hundred reasons she might have been swapped with the Golightly's eldest daughter. It did not matter if it had been an altruistic act—what mattered was the consequences of that act. The abuse she, and Odele, had been subjected to. The situation she was in now, one wrong move from being sent to the Commission.

Not to mention what must have happened to the newborn you replaced.

"Shut up," she muttered out loud, scolding her own insecurities.

She had hoped that Elden had kept her, possibly superfluous, rescue to himself. Judging from the ridiculous stack of extra bacon Lyra had presented her at breakfast (and the over-the-top smooch on the cheek that left Odele scowling at her sister), Avalon knew she could kiss that dream goodbye.

Avalon didn't want Odele to discover she had taken matters into her own hands last night. Odele was already sensitive regarding her inability to physically prevent her own premonitions. If she learned that her sister had risked her own life for it...

Odele would track her down later, she knew, but for now Avalon tried to act as though it was normal for a single person to be given twelve pieces of bacon.

Odele's caulking gun poked her in the chest. Avalon's back hit the wall of the hallway Odele had cornered her in after breakfast.

"What the hell happened last night? All I got was a single text at dawn that read 'it's done'."

Avalon blinked, her face trying to feign dumb innocence until she deemed it impossible. "And that was completely correct."

"And I'm not even going to *ask* about Lyra this morning."

"Then don't." This was becoming tedious. What she could tell Odele and what she couldn't. It was impossible to toe the line without the ability to fib. Not that she particularly wanted to lie to her sister. "Last night was handled. I *think* there were coyotes out last night, and *maybe* that was what you saw. Though the inn appreciated your warning. I just couldn't communicate to Lyra that *you* deserved the smooch and not me."

"That." Odele's tongue clicked in annoyance, her cheeks turning pink. "That isn't what this is about. I'm worried about you and I'm afraid I've been...well, I haven't been handling this well. I'm not used to you being the one to fall apart, and it scared me because I cannot, for the life of me, understand where it's stemming from."

Having to be the "big sister" was frustrating. Avalon more than appreciated that. And she knew what had caused Odele's earlier reaction to Avalon pleading with her to leave. Odele was afraid to lose what she had only gotten a glimpse of—a safe place with friends.

Forgiveness came too easily when Odele was involved. "Perhaps you won't ever understand it, Odd. It just *is* that way, for now. But this isn't permanent. We'll be okay."

"I know that, but I needed to apologize. I love it here, even though we've only been here a week, and I thought, for a second, you were jeopardizing that out of jealousy." Odele banished the silence that hung between them. "What *is* hard to believe, though, is that you ate all that bacon, and when Kenan tried to take one, you tried to stab him with your fork."

"In my defense, I said I would do exactly that, and he chose to take that chance. What jury would convict me?"

Avalon struggled through her hotel management presentation, having commandeered one of the inn's few meeting rooms for guests staying while on business.

There wasn't a way around it. Thompson required the same training to be given to all new managers, with no allowed deviations. He was uncharacteristically strict about his management slideshows, and Avalon wasn't going to argue with the man who actually let them use their vacation days when they asked.

It seemed Elden had escaped death by chupacabra to experience, instead, death by slideshows.

Tahoma stayed awake throughout the day-long presentation by constantly fidgeting. And dropping her water bottle four times as a result. Her brother was a nodder, waking when his forehead drooped low enough that he slammed it against the conference table.

Elden perfectly avoided either of those routes by falling asleep the second she turned on the projector. Knowing he had spent the night fighting pests with four-inch fangs, and subsequently having to dispose of those carcasses, Avalon allowed the slight.

Her final slide said "Questions?" in Comic Sans, another upsetting choice made by her employer. Kenan's hand shot up; the most alert Avalon had seen him all day.

Hesitantly, she prompted, "Yes?"

"Were you really trying to hit that chupacabra, or did you just miss Elden?" Kenan tapped his fingers on the table, the rhythm reaching a crescendo after he discovered another possibility. "Or is it that you can't drive?"

This was headed in a brilliant direction. "Nothing management related, then."

"She wasn't trying to kill me."

Elden, choosing now to pay attention, began helping himself to the donuts she had provided this morning, a desperate apology for the slideshow she had begged Odele to retrieve for her.

In between large, half-starved bites, Elden declared, "Though she made it quite clear that her rescue was intended for the dog. And not at all for me."

"Well, Hob's adorable," Tahoma laughed. "You? Not so much."

"You try being adorable when you're this size."

Avalon was on the outskirts here, watching friends' banter while she tried to listen without seeming too interested. College quickly came to mind, and Avalon shoved those friendless years she was without Odele aside.

When Avalon returned foggily to the rest of the world, she discovered that the twins had departed, and Elden was throwing away paper cups and napkins.

Hob was eating a strawberry jelly-filled doughnut. The sight was upsetting. If that doughnut troubled Hob's stomach, neither of them would sleep tonight.

The inn's meeting room was by far the most modern looking room in the inn. It was also the least personable. The screen for the projector barely seemed out of place, though it was rarely used, if Avalon had to judge from its aversion to being rolled and unrolled. She watched helplessly as the screen made it halfway up and stopped, the handle now comically out of her reach.

A shoulder lightly bumped against hers as Elden easily

guided the screen back into its home.

Too close. Avalon sidestepped out of his way. She defended herself before he could even speak. "I am not short. I've seen the statistics."

"That's not something secure people say." Elden stood by as Avalon gathered her laptop and an extra-large thermos that was covered in the most ridiculous stickers Odele could find. "And that presentation was really..."

"Let's not discuss the presentation." As cathartic as it might have been, bad-mouthing Thompson's over-complex slideshow wouldn't do her career any good. "Anyway, the best way to learn this is through practice. I'll shadow you and your co-managers for the rest of the time and lend a hand as needed."

"That doesn't seem like enough work for you. Since you've been here, you've been tearing up my office—"

"Organizing your office," she interjected.

"—and we rarely even see you for lunch. Lyra's beginning to feel insulted."

Was he questioning her whereabouts? Protecting her innocence, Avalon fumed, "Hob is with me the entire time."

Elden tugged at his hair before catching himself. "That wasn't what I was implying. No one, no one," he echoed, "believes you can outmaneuver Hob." Elden folded his arms, the grey leather armor creasing at his shoulders. It was still startling to see him strutting around, fully armed and dressed like an evil Prince Charming. "I meant we should make better use of this time. You need to master changing your form back to human. I don't expect you'd like to stay here forever."

"I've tried. My body won't listen! It's like I'm trying to flex my leg and instead my hand punches me in the face."

His mouth quirked up, for a second, before Elden was, once

again, all business. "You need a coach. Someone who has experience changing forms." He handed her one of the inn's business cards, his personal number scrawled on the back. "We can start tonight, after dinner. Text me if you're up for it."

She was more surprised that his ancient phone could even receive texts than at his offer to help her.

It wasn't her proudest moment, but Avalon gave him a small, accepting nod. "Who did you have in mind?"

"*Him?*" Avalon bristled, regretting instantly (as she had known she would) that she had ever trusted Elden to help her. While the wind gusting off the Pacific chilled her, she eyed Kenan and his shit-eating grin distastefully. "What am I going to learn from him? How to offend everyone I meet?"

"I think we can agree that you have that covered all by yourself." Kenan had taken a wide stance on the beach, his heels digging into the stony surface. He and his sister both had gym bags lying at their feet. Though the sea air was chilling, neither of them appeared the least bit bothered.

"How is this going to help me?" she demanded. She had done a little research on the selkies after Odele had made that scarily accurate joke. "I don't have a skin I can take on and off."

"There's more to it than that," Tahoma insisted. She unzipped her bag, pulling out her sealskin carefully, lovingly. Though Avalon failed to see how this performance would help her, she knew a selkie's sealskin was a precious thing and even seeing it was a privilege. Elden must have worked very hard to convince the twins she was a worthy enough cause.

Or maybe he had informed the twins of the consequences

of Avalon's failure to revert to her human form—that she wouldn't be free to leave until she was successful. Meaning that they could be stuck with her for the unforeseeable future.

Even Avalon could admit that would be one hell of a motivator.

She tried to remain hopeful as Tahoma described, in visceral detail, her transformation.

"Wanting it isn't enough. You have to *need* the change." Tahoma waded into the ocean until she was knee deep. Avalon danced along the shoreline, dodging the ice-cold waves as best as she could. "Changelings make the initial metamorphosis in order to survive. You need that same level of fear, of desperation."

That would explain why the feylands forced her to revert back into fey. Avalon had believed, had *known*, that her life was in danger and her body reacted accordingly. But how was she to convince herself now she would be safer human? It was completely counter-intuitive. As she was now, she was stronger, faster, and even needed less sleep.

"You'd think having to stick around this guy would be enough to scare anyone."

Elden returned Kenan's joke with a scathing glare. But was he wrong?

Tahoma's sealskin settled across her shoulders. A wave crested, blocking Avalon's view and when it waned, Tahoma was gone. Avalon glanced wildly at the ocean, straining to find Tahoma again until Elden appeared at her side. He gently touched her shoulders, turning her body and pointing out Tahoma's seal form in the distance.

Elden and Avalon were both acutely aware that no matter how many times Tahoma and Kenan demonstrated their shifting powers, Avalon was no closer to finding her old self again. Elden caught her staring longingly at an old picture on her phone, her fingers tracing the softer, rounded curves of her facial features from a year ago.

"I've asked around, trying to find another changeling that could help you." He grimaced, and Avalon guessed at his failure before he could speak it. "It's not a straightforward task. Most changelings that are returned to the feylands—"

"Die some horrible death?"

"Or become extremely good at hiding." He paused. "You could learn to glamour. But some witches can see through it. And, depending on your skill level, most feyries might, too."

The man was brutally honest. She could appreciate that.

"As much as it pains me," Avalon confessed, "I'll have to refer to your judgement on this. Seeing as you've had, what, like a thousand years to encounter shapeshifters, you'll be my best bet to find a decent teacher."

"A thousand *what*?"

Lyra had a snack prepared for Elden and Avalon at her house, a cute tiny home set on the inn's expansive property. The walk from the beach to Lyra's had been silent and disappointing.

Avalon had previously noticed the two houses that sat north of the inn; a cottage, garden included, and a larger main house. The buildings were mostly hidden as the trees had grown in a way that neatly shielded them. Perhaps that was not a coincidence. Lyra seemed to have a natural way with plants. Manipulating a few trees didn't seem out of her power.

Lyra had claimed the cottage all to herself, her own personal touches visible everywhere. Huge pumpkins and squash took over every available patch of earth. A small fire pit was set off her porch, wooden Adirondack chairs gathered around it.

"S'mores!" Lyra advertised, waving a melting marshmallow sandwich around. The sight both made Avalon's mouth water and filled her to the brim with envy. It wasn't fair for someone to have that much energy for this late hour.

"She thinks I'm a thousand years old."

Elden was apparently not going to let that one go. "Every-one—" Avalon maintained her position. "—knows that fey can live for hundreds of years."

Lyra's astonished laugh caught in her throat. Taking pity on Avalon, Lyra clarified, "While that may be true for some, Elden's not even thirty, and younger than I am. Only by a few years, before you jump to conclusions about *my* age."

Avalon bit her lip and considered the situation. Should she apologize for that? Elden seemed to be waiting for something, by the way he was irritably and openly glowering at her. No. No! That was ridiculous. He was nearly, no, actually holding her hostage. There wasn't a chance in anyone's hell that she'd atone for over-estimating his age.

Avalon solemnly held up a s'more, her eyes wide and falsely naïve. "Can you even eat this with dentures?"

Her joke must have hit a sore spot. "*Dentures,*" Elden loudly repeated as Lyra left to wash her hands of sticky, marsh-mallow residue. Avalon couldn't keep a smirk from forming— he was clearly livid about her overestimating his age, and it was such a silly thing to be enraged about.

Her satisfaction dimmed, sizzling out as a not entirely un-welcome shadow fell over her. Elden stood directly behind her, leaning in so close that it sent shivers racing down her back.

Disturbingly close to her neck, he threatened, "Maybe I should bite you and prove your words false."

Her heartbeat stuttered, replaying every low, dangerous word. Was this him flirting? Or was it a warning? Unsure what she feared more, Avalon made herself become as calm and unbothered as an eye of a storm. She continued forging her s'more, keeping her movements precise. "Well?" she demanded. "I'm waiting."

What the hell was taking Lyra so long? Only years of tapping down and hiding her emotions kept Avalon from jumping. Was she imagining it or was the phantom chill on her collarbone not just her imagination? Whatever it was, or wasn't, the touch vanished when Lyra's cottage door swung back open.

"Just what I thought." Her voice was a little shaky, but it was small enough that she doubted Elden would notice. She faced him, finding that Elden had taken several steps back from her, his gaze narrowed and dark. "All bark and no bite. Just like your dog."

"Dammit," Lyra suddenly groaned, running back inside her cottage a second time. Avalon whirled around to beg her to stay, but was too late. Lyra's voice trailed off. "I forgot—"

His cousin out of sight once more, Elden darted behind Avalon and nipped her earlobe once. Her hand smacked her ear, too slow by a mile and completely missing him. She felt a few indents and swore. "What are you trying to do? Pierce my ear?!"

Elden showed no remorse. In fact, the fey looked extremely pleased with himself and with her over-the-top reaction. He had won, Avalon admitted inwardly. Now Elden knew he had some sort of strange, and irritating, effect on her. "*That's* what you get for insulting my dog."

Hob took that moment to snatch the marshmallow bag and

shake it back and forth, sending large, sugary pillows flying. Elden cursed and surged forward, racing Hob to see who would get to each marshmallow treat first.

Avalon rubbed her neck, her soft laughter hiding her uncertainty.

CHAPTER 14
AVALON

It took many, *far too many*, additional unproductive lessons with Tahoma and Kenan before Elden would finally call it. Avalon was grateful and disappointed at the same time. Grateful she wouldn't be freezing her ass off every night, exposed to the heavy ocean winds. And disappointed she hadn't so much as transformed a pinky finger.

Elden swore to her he would find an alternative, and she believed him. Not just because he could not lie. His life would be infinitely less complicated the less that Avalon was in it.

But he left her with a stern warning. "The next teacher I find may be rather cruel. Is returning to your mostly human state *truly* what you want?"

"Cruelty doesn't frighten me." Trapped and relying on Elden, or another feyrie, to keep her glamoured and hidden—now, that was bone-chilling horror.

"Are you *certain*? We may have different ideas of what's cruel."

"I can take a little tough love," she argued and wished she

had chosen her words more carefully.

"Rumors are going to be flying around this place if we don't find a better way to do this. We spend so much time together that I think some of your staff is getting the wrong idea. "

While she and Elden were sneaking out of the inn in the bare light of day, sparrow-sized fey she learned were *pixies,* were flitting behind them, chittering to each other and giggling. The blue-skinned creatures were too quiet, too high pitched for Avalon to catch on to what they were whispering, but she doubted they were complimenting her last-minute outfit.

Her socks, chosen while Elden barked at her to hurry, didn't even match.

As she followed Elden away from the inn and through the surrounding woods, she noticed they were suspiciously close to where they'd fought the chupacabra—if Avalon was to judge by the smell alone. It was high-noon, though the sun did little to warm her when she was in Elden's company. The man radiated winter from his very being.

Elden walked with purpose while Avalon lingered a few feet behind, rubbing her still slightly sore ear. He had left markings on her lobe, something that renewed her annoyance with him every time she looked in a mirror.

If that truly had been the feyrie's attempt at flirting, she wanted nothing more to do with it.

Her earlier concerns about the smell were confirmed. That rotting stench belonged to the corpses of the slain chupacabra.

"Can the inn's glamour hide this smell?" she whined, pinching her nose and cringing. "If you think I'm going to help move those carcasses—"

A length of iron chain appeared in Elden's armored hands.

She saw the plan formulating in his mind before he had a chance to enact it.

Avalon began her sprint, her unruly hair flying with the abrupt movement, before flying chains of iron wound themselves around her legs and chest. She tripped, eating a face full of dirt. While the iron was still working its way around her, coiling around her like a python and diminishing her willpower, she managed to pop an arm out.

Something flipped her onto her back. Elden straddled her hips, trying to tighten the iron chain around her. She reached out and clawed at his face, swiping wherever she could reach.

Despite her scratching and twisting and snarling, Elden overpowered her, looping the iron around her skin, singeing her, before he started dragging her in the direction of that barren tree from the other night. Setting her against the trunk, Elden secured her in place. There were no locks in place, only multiple lengths of chain wound around her to keep her there. It would be a simple escape, if she could heave off the chain, but the irons properties weakened her to the point she could barely wriggle.

Her rage tore its way out of her throat.

Elden let her scream. "These corpses have drawn something here. I felt it slip through the mound last night."

Flies buzzed, hovering around the deceased chupacabra. The dead tree she was strapped to was in the middle of a large clearing and above her was nothing but clear, blue sky...that was dotted with a large, blank winged shape.

"Ellén Trechend," Elden observed, indicating the shadow in the sky.

"What did you say?" His accent had seemed thicker just then, and his words were nonsense to her. She couldn't take her eyes off the shadow, trembling as it circled. Each turn it grew closer.

"It's a vulture."

That was as close to a lie as he had come. The bird swooped down suddenly, blocking the sun for just a moment. That wretched thing had three damned heads.

She swallowed her need to scream, her fury burning in her lungs.

"The Ellén Trechend feasts on our dead. But a trapped, living fey is not a treat it can resist."

Elden stepped away from her, his face an unmoving marble statue crafted in times of war. She searched for something, anything, for an ounce of sympathy and came up empty. He possessed that unnatural stillness she'd seen in other magical creatures, that moment when their mask fell, and it was revealed how far from human they were.

His departure gave the creature the opening it was waiting for. It landed, the tremors that accompanied it shaking loose from her another fearful shriek. Gods, that thing stunk. It was ostrich-sized, with three naked heads that wove and studied her like snakes.

Elden didn't intervene as the bird stomped around Avalon, trying to find which part of her it wanted to taste first. The corpses had drawn it in, but this vulture seemed more eager to try fresh, feyrie flesh.

Looking at Elden was a waste of time—he would watch her eaten alive, those beaks tearing her apart bit by bit, and wear that same void expression.

The next teacher I find may be rather cruel.

She wanted to laugh—the lunatic had been talking about himself.

What was the simplest solution to a changeling that couldn't change back? Chain her to a tree and let a three-headed feyrie vulture have at her was evidently the answer. She thought birds went for the soft parts first. She shut her eyes in fear.

"Fuck you, Elden!" was all Avalon managed to curse with the iron burning into her skin. It was infuriating. The iron, if she were human, would be a simple thing to slip out of.

Only one thing could give her a miniscule chance of survival.

Change.

That single thought infuriated her. If she couldn't do this meditating on an empty beach, how was she going to do this while death stared her in the face?

Had Elden done this on purpose? That desperate to get rid of her, she could return to her human form and escape this haunting bird...or she could be torn apart and left to rot alongside the chupacabra.

Avalon stretched her limbs as much as the chains would allow, doing her best to ignore the searing pain the iron's touch was unleashing upon her.

It was counter-intuitive, trying to become human while something with inhuman strength assaulted her. Could she ever let herself become that vulnerable?

A thought slipped into her mind. *Don't let Odele watch you die.*

What better motivator than that could there be?

That ache, the one she had experienced in the feylands, returned at the tips of her fingers and toes. She leaned into the feeling, letting it pull her in.

The iron hurt a little less, and its python-like grip slackened enough to give her some wiggle room. If there was anything that a changeling could understand at a molecular level, it was survival. They would do anything for it.

The bird's sour breath fanned her face. Fighting the urge to vomit, Avalon caught the edge of that transformation, desperately held on to it, tugging with all her might until—

The temperature dropped.

Her eyelids flickered open to witness a wall of ice growing before her. That feyrie vulture was attacking the shield, its three beaks stabbing against the ice.

Whatever Avalon had been on the precipice of left her, leaving a void that had always been there, but now the echoing emptiness of it was unbearable.

The iron vanished as if it had never been.

The loss of what she'd been so close to achieving was more terrifying than the monster. Elden and his axe cut at the molting bird. When it tried to take flight to flee, Elden encased its talons in ice to weigh it down. It fell, and he took the opportunity to decapitate all three of its heads.

Elden knelt next to her, catching her as she tipped forward. "Avalon?" He pressed his fingers against her wrist, searching for the weak pulse of life within. His hair was darker now and drenched in red that left tiny droplets of blood against his sharp cheekbones. Three harsh, bleeding lines were etched down his face, starting just beneath his eye. It seemed she'd done some damage to him, after all.

Avalon vomited. Now that she wasn't in danger, the smell of the bird's breath could no longer be ignored. She was shaking so badly that Elden had to grip the back of her shirt to prevent her from falling into her own sick.

"Asshole."

"I know." And one glance told Avalon that Elden did, in fact, know. Gone was the statuesque blankness. Now he looked terrified and cold, raw power rolled off of him in waves, unwavering and uncontrolled.

"No, you *don't* know." She scrambled to a seated position. Gods, she was trembling. "*I almost had it.*"

"Truly?" His eagerness died instantly. "No, that was a mistake. You nearly died."

"It nearly worked!" She slammed her fist against the unforgiving ground, the pain vibrating up her arm in a way she oddly liked.

It was comical how obvious the answer to her problems had been. *I need to let myself be weak.* That might have been possible for literally anyone else. Avalon had never allowed herself to lower her defenses before she was surrounded by murderous fey.

Elden's response was sharp, unsympathetic. "We are *not* trying that again."

"It won't work, anyway." Her frustration boiled inside her. She had been so close! Elden couldn't have been psychotically brutal for one more damned minute? "Now that my body trusts you to save me, I won't be able to find that fear, that motivation." *What a waste. Of all times to form a conscience.*

"Trusts?"

She had meant a different word, honestly, but it was too late to amend it. With the bird gone, there was nothing to distract her from her own panic.

"You're shaking." Elden stood, lifting her to her feet by her elbow. "Avalon, you're going into shock because of the iron." Where he gripped her, frost crawled across her skin, turning everywhere it danced an icy blue. He quickly released her arm. "We need to get you back. Somewhere warm, too."

"My room is plenty warm enough." But the words came out slurred and she couldn't be sure that Elden had understood her. Her vision was growing spotty—the panic attack unpreventable at this point.

"I'm not one you can bullshit about this."

Movement, too fast for her to follow, prevented a witty retort or simple swear from spilling from her mouth. Her world turned upside down and her forehead met with Elden's back.

Absolutely. Not. This would *not* be withstood.

Her fists rained down on whatever she could reach. "Put me down!"

"Why?" Elden tightened his grip, keeping her waist pinned against his shoulder. "Afraid of heights?"

She thrashed, searching for an angle where she could put her still sharp teeth to use when the combination of the cold, her fatigue, and her former iron prison took over.

Dog breath fanned Avalon's face. Hob nosed her temple until she opened her eyes. Then he pawed her chest until he got the attention he deserved.

Her aching hands buried into his coat. Avalon didn't know how long she had spent wrapped in that iron, but she had been left nearly crippled. Every muscle or joint she could feel *hurt.*

An argument floated within her hearing, taking place somewhere she couldn't see from her prone position on...gods, she was on the *floor* of someone's extravagantly decorated home. What kind of hospitality was this?

"Idiot!" A shrill, womanly voice came from her left. "Idiot, idiot, idiot!"

"Your point was made the first twenty times." That was Elden; his rumble was unmistakable.

"You're lucky that woman is insane." Ah, that was clearly Lyra. And she was pissed. Good. Elden deserved her worst. Wait. *Insane?*

"Lucky wouldn't be the first thing that comes to mind."

"I know you were raised to believe that only *results* matter, not the path taken to get there, but Avalon could have been hurt. She *was* hurt. She's just not dead. That's not a win, Elden."

Rolling onto her hands and knees, Avalon surveyed the room she was occupying. Hob rested, panting, in front of a fireplace taller than Avalon was. The walls were a light grey in most places, patterns of winter themed wallpaper hidden in smaller sections of the walls. Multiple intimate couches were arranged around her, all black leather and not designed for comfort.

Lyra and Elden entered, Lyra rushing to Avalon's side in an angry fit. "You left her on the floor?"

He had never looked less princely, and he averted his tiny cousin's gaze. "I thought the rug would be warmer."

He did have a small point there. The rug mimicked a fur coat and would certainly be warmer than the leather settees. Blankets were piled around her, and Avalon dragged them closer to her.

"You're still in your dirty clothes!" Lyra helped Avalon to stand and started leading her out of the main room. Avalon leaned heavily against Lyra, and she paused to shoot Elden a last, scathing glare. The iron had completely zapped Avalon of energy.

Elden had one last defense. "Wouldn't it be worse if she was in different clothes?"

Lyra led her to a bathroom and after weeks of using that tiny, cramped shower in Whimsy, Avalon almost told Lyra to leave immediately. Swallowing that command, Avalon listened while Lyra pointed out where the good towels were and promised to bring her a change of clothes.

For thirty glorious minutes, Avalon enjoyed a shower without feeling cramped or fearing that she'd touch the shower curtain. Hell, she could have even held her arms out and twirled around had she wanted to. An obvious slip hazard, so she refrained.

While Avalon dressed in the clothes Lyra had left for her, she checked her phone for any messages from Odele. Considering her near-death experience with the feyrie vulture, Avalon had expected a hundred missed calls from her banshee sister. But there was nothing. Which meant Elden never considered, not even for a moment, letting anything happen to her.

Lyra's old clothes were a little snug, but fit otherwise. An oddly recognizable aroma drifted from the kitchen, enticing Avalon to follow its delectable trail.

"Chicken nuggets?"

Her question was met with further exasperation on Lyra's part. "I was busy yelling at Elden. Sorry, it's not filet mignon."

"No, this is perfectly fine. Keep yelling at Elden." Lyra's meals were all delicious, but secretly the Golightly sisters had a stash of cheap, frozen pizzas and chips in Odele's cabin.

Elden looked tired. He always looked tired. And now he watched her eat store brand nuggets like she was sampling rat poison.

"Now, what did we rehearse?" Lyra asked in a singsong

voice. Elden and Avalon both sighed at her melodic tone.

Elden had the posture of a man who had been read his last rites. He monotoned, "I shouldn't have let you believe I was going to let you die. And I shouldn't have chained you to that tree. And I shouldn't do anything ever again unless I run it by Lyra first."

"You shouldn't have rescued me!" Avalon countered. "You could have waited another minute." Her response caused Lyra to sink her head slowly onto the kitchen counter, refusing to make eye contact with such foolishness. "I mean," Avalon clarified, "if you're going to go through all that trouble, why wouldn't you follow it through? What a waste."

Elden motioned between the two women in his house, frustrated. "I'm too harsh, I'm too weak. Which one is it?"

Avalon and Lyra answered differently at the same time.

The fey healed quickly, though, in Elden's case, not quickly enough. He claimed the more difficult cosmetic glamours were beyond him, which left his wounds, courtesy of Avalon, completely visible. The morning after their failed attempt to force Avalon to transform, Odele had spotted Elden's trio of scratches and asked if it was from a cat.

Elden said carefully, "That would be the easiest explanation."

"The inn has a CAT?"

Avalon shot him a look that clearly said, Odele-thinks-there-is-a-cat-so-there-had-better-BE-a-cat.

Later that night, Elden returned with an orange tabby that fought hard against his grip and practically leapt into Odele's

waiting arms. Where he had gotten a kitten on such short notice, she could hardly guess. A barn cat from Abernathy, perhaps?

Even though this act had been the direct result of Avalon's
silent threat, it still made her feel strange.

The cat's eyes were mischievous enough that Avalon dug
out the feyrie book in her room, flipping through the illustra-
tions until she came upon the *cait sidhe* entry. That Cheshire
grin on the pages made her feel slightly less pleased with Elden's
rare act of kindness.

The fool had gifted her sister a feyrie cat.

The hotel's front desk was no longer the same ghostly, cob-
webbed, deserted island it had been on her first day exploring
the inn. For the past few weeks, Avalon had been manning the
counter while the twins were stalking elk in the Olympic Forest.

The guests must have sensed fresh blood, and she was
quickly overrun with complaint after complaint. Most of them
were technology related, as the fey seemed to have a special
knack for breaking anything that ran on electricity.

When Odele's contractor and his crew weren't busy with
her demands of repainting and replacing worn out materials,
Avalon had to borrow them to make repairs as they were
brought to her attention. There was no sign of a maintenance
log, another thing to implement.

The requests were an endless stream, threatening to drown
her, and seemed to increase in ridiculousness the more she tried
to appease them. Avalon almost missed being oblivious to the
inn's many, *many* fey guests. Though, and it irked to admit it,

the challenges that accompanied a fey hotel were mostly annoying, but also a little fun.

When the fey weren't pushing it with the complaints.

"They're messing with you."

And don't I know it! Avalon's internal, not customer friendly voice begged to be released. Ignoring the career-killing urge, Avalon instead turned to smile at the fresh voice. "Can I help you?"

Now who the hell was this? Avalon half-expected a tumbleweed to bounce along in the background, going along perfectly with the women's sepia toned western wear. The woman's beaver fur hat was an odd shade of grey, possibly matching her morals, and her high-waisted black jeans covered a pair of scuffed boots, a vermilion stain blooming on one toe. Her hair, black as the void, and tightly wound in a single, long braid, didn't have a hair out of place. But barely any of that registered to Avalon as the woman roughly placed a rifle on her counter.

Avalon stared at the weapon, blinking slowly. "Now you don't want to touch that," the woman warned, sporting a grin more friendly than anything else about her. The sleeves of her shirt were loose, beige, and cuffed at the sleeve, revealing strong, tanned arms. "It's cursed."

"Why are you armed with a cursed gun, Darling?"

That endearment was not meant for Elden's mouth. Was this his girlfriend? Avalon couldn't decide if the two made sense together or if this woman was far too good, and witty, to be with a grumpy stick-in-the-mud like Elden.

The woman paid no mind to what he called her. "I *just* got that rifle sighted in. You want me to throw that away because some witch said it would abandon me when I need it most? Sounds like it'll work fine most of the time." She leaned against the counter, giving Avalon a conspiratorial wink. Or a flirty wink. Avalon couldn't determine which, but blushed anyway. "Men. No sense of loyalty. By the way, I'm Jesse Darling." She extended a hand, which Avalon accepted. Jesse made a shooing gesture at Elden. "I won't bother with you. I remember how you feel about handshakes, as un-American as it is."

Avalon decided she liked Jesse. And not solely because she had revealed that Elden's resistance to handshakes wasn't an isolated incident.

But her surname was Darling? That had to get irritating.

"It's nice to meet you," Avalon slowly began, trying to find the right words on the fly. If anything could sound rude, it absolutely did when it left her mouth. "But why are you here?"

"Oh. I work for the Commission. Return and Rescue division. And sometimes *execute* but they tend to leave that part off the pamphlets."

The oddly pleasant exchange continued on without her. Avalon's world suddenly became minuscule, her vision narrowing down into a pinpoint.

Return. Rescue. Execute.

What was an agent of the Commission doing here? Did Elden call them? Without any sort of warning? Knowing he was essentially giving her a death sentence?

Of course, he called them. What are you to him if not a liability? If her insecurities could smile, they would have done so with bloody teeth.

What had made her slip up like this? Avalon was always so careful, so observant. She had fooled herself into believing that the past week was anything but a test. The humdrum and routine of her job had served as the perfect distraction, allowing Elden the opportunity to betray her.

She should have let him die. Let the chupacabra tear him apart and drag his entrails away from his corpse to store in their den. She should have helped them, or, at the very least, watched as—

The letter opener was cold, her fist squeezing the metal hard into her palm. Elden's hand rested on the front desk, the back scarred and bruised. When she spiked the letter ripper through his hand, squeezing it between two of his knuckles, she wasn't sure which one of them was more shocked.

Avalon left the rifle behind, as its curse ensured that it would be useless to her. Jesse tried to grab Avalon around the waist, letting go when Avalon slammed her head backwards against Jesse's face.

Avalon ran out the door, sprinting for the relative safety of the trees.

A shot rang out, and she fell forward, the world spinning.

Running away appeared to be out of the question. And if stabbing was out of the question, there was little left in her wheelhouse. She couldn't overpower either of them. Could she make a deal with Elden? Not that she had anything to offer that he would ever want. Anyway, Elden did not seem the type to bargain. He even seemed to abhor them, judging from his reaction to her deal with the wisp and his aversion to harmless handshakes.

Avalon whispered, "Don't let Odele see."

Jesse's smile had yet to fade, though at Avalon's beseeching tone it had quivered uncertainly. "What is she on about?"

Elden had no answers for his friend. Puzzled, his eyes searched Avalon for clues.

Despite her vision, the letter opener had found its way into her hand. Avalon let it clatter loudly onto the counter. "I don't understand what I did wrong, but don't let Odele see her take me away. She'll try to come with me."

"Take you away..." Elden's voice was a distant echo. The letter opener caught his attention while he analyzed her plea. "Avalon." The raw apology in his tone was too intense for her comfort. "Avalon, she isn't here for you." He reached for her hand, but retracted his unexpected touch quickly. "Jesse is here to take tissue samples of the chupacabra. Those things are usually in her territory. The Commission wants to know if some disease is behind their northern journey."

"I don't think rabies can affect the behavior of those mutts, as insane as they already are, or cause them to migrate, but, hey, I'm not an overpaid scientist who has to justify their ludicrous budget." Jesse never asked what Avalon thought she'd be taken in for. Was her trust in Elden's judgment that unwavering? Not that Avalon wanted to push it. Still, it was bizarre.

Jesse pushed off from the counter, silver glinting at her throat. "Hob can show me where those bodies are? You seem to have your hands full." After Elden gave her a nod, Jesse inspected Avalon for an impolite amount of time.

There was no avoiding that questioning stare. Desperate for any distraction, Avalon pathetically offered in return, "I like your locket."

Jesse seemed far too pleased by such a half-assed compliment. The trinket must have meant a great deal to her. "Thanks. It's haunted."

That seemed in character.

As soon as Jesse left, Hob proudly leading the way, Elden was quiet. Not unusual for him, but to Avalon, right now, it was incredibly aggravating.

"You could have let me know that an agent of the

Commission was expected."

"She arrived early." When that failed to rescue the situation, Elden deepened his frown. "In my defense, I don't think there's much I can do to get you to trust me," he argued.

She had little sympathy left, and none at all for him. "Be less threatening?"

"Were you going to jab me with this?" The letter opener in hand, Elden raised a single, incredulous brow her way.

Avalon had never understood asking questions one already knew the answer to. "You'll remember to add me to the email chain next time," Avalon retorted. She wouldn't ask forgiveness for almost stabbing someone. Who had the time? "And I won't accept your extremely advanced age as an excuse."

He graciously let that quip go. It was all too obvious that what had just happened unnerved her. She was shaking too much to even hope that Elden, who already spent far too much of his time studying her, would miss it.

CHAPTER 15
ELDEN

It was supposed to be a quick project. Avalon had been complaining about the loose handrail on the staircase that went directly to her room, and Elden had moved it to the top of his list before he could question why he was doing so.

He sighed at the carpets that spanned the hallway in front of the stairs. Once they were brilliant crimson—now they were faded and worn. Avalon had promised Odele would find the right company to restore them, but Elden had his doubts. If damage was done, and he had to replace another thing that had been carefully curated by his mother...

Avalon's sister was quiet on approach, and then much less so. "Hi!" Odele sang from behind his left shoulder.

Elden twitched. He wasn't used to someone speaking directly into his ear. Odele was very tall—something he somehow knew Avalon must be jealous of. "Hello, Odele," he answered, hoping he could turn back to his work.

Odele circled to stand in front of him. Elden quickly

shooed away the brownie that tried climbing the stairs up to them while balancing a mug of coffee. The brownie took his dismissal poorly and dumped the drink meant for Elden into the nearest potted plant.

"Grand."

"What are you doing?" Odele asked, ignoring his exasperated sigh and remaining oblivious to the tiny feyrie cursing down below.

"Trying to fix the banister."

"I see." Her voice was critical, and Elden crossed his arms to wait for her to leave before starting again.

"I have it *handled.*"

"Oh, I didn't mean..." Odele's voice trailed off as she eyed his tool bag and frowned. "Anyway, that isn't why I found you."

So, this conversation had a purpose. "Am I about to spend more money on crown molding or something?"

Odele looked up the stairs and saw Avalon's hotel room door was closed. "No, and sorry if this is awkward, but it's about my sister. Did she...well, did Avalon upset you?"

"Upset me?" Elden blinked. Avalon had complicated his life, something he didn't need help with, and she continued to win the upper hand in all of their arguments. But Odele shouldn't have noticed that.

Unless Avalon has found some way to tell her the truth about the inn. The truth about you.

No, that made little sense. Odele wouldn't be casually chatting with him if that was the case.

Picking at a string on the hem of her shirt, Odele replied, "Yes. She can have that effect on people. Avalon is..."

"Feral." The word escaped before he could think better of

it.

"So, she *did* say something to you! I knew she wouldn't let that stupid handshake go!"

"Handshake?" he echoed, his earlier task completely forgotten. "I never shook her hand."

Odele nodded. "That's the problem! She thinks you avoided it to slight her." She tested out the handrailing as she continued. "And now she's taken her revenge. I've noticed you staring at her night and day. She really must have done it this time. Please, don't fire us!"

This was a problem. Odele's head was not as far in the clouds as he had believed. She knew he was watching Avalon—that wasn't something he could explain away. *Not without lying.*

Their conversation didn't need to be a back-and-forth, it seemed. Odele was happy enough to do all the talking. "What did Avalon say to you? Wait, let me guess—"

"Do not guess."

"But I need to know what to apologize for!"

How codependent were these women?! "There's nothing to worry about, Odele." Elden was shocked he could even string those words together. "Avalon...she has not hurt our professional relationship whatsoever. Your jobs are safe."

She only relaxed for a moment. "If she didn't insult the very core of your being...why do you stare at her in a dingo-watching-a-baby kind of way?"

Now you've done it. What are you going to tell her? That you know her sister is a changeling, and you have to watch her in case her "accidental" journey into the feylands wasn't so random?

Elden pinched his brow, the right words forever escaping

him. He wished he could call his trickster of a sister and ask her for the right combination of half-truths to give this girl.

"Oh no." Odele coiled a lock of hair around her finger and pulled it. "*Oh no.*"

"Oh no?"

"Exactly. This is even worse." Odele made a few uncomfortable faces before picking up his tools and beginning to work on the banister. It was as if she suddenly and desperately needed a distraction. "Elden, Mr. Cavanaugh, it brings me no pleasure to say this, but...you should reconsider."

Was that a *threat*? From a woman wearing tie-dye? "Reconsider *what*?"

"Reconsider Avalon. Not that you aren't her type!" she hurried. "As an uninterested party, even I can see that you are a nice-looking man, but you are also technically employing us. Avalon would never date an employer, and if she notices the way you intensely stare at her, she'll let you down robotically *and* awkwardly." Odele moved her arms in a way that he assumed was supposed to be mimicking a robot dancing.

He'd had worse conversations, Elden was certain of it, but in his current nightmarish situation, nothing came to mind.

Once again, his input was not needed in order to keep this conversation thriving.

"It's better you hear this from me," Odele assured him. "Avalon isn't so gentle. I know she looks cute and harmless, but she's a real psycho sometimes. I say this with love."

He stumbled over an explanation. "Odele, I—I'm not—"

"I won't say a word to her!" she vowed.

Elden refused to let this miscommunication stand. "I don't have a—what is the word your kind uses? I'm not harboring some *little crush*."

Her brow knitted together. "*My* kind? I think we're in the same generation, if that's what you mean."

"Oh. Sure."

"You don't need to feel embarrassed." Odele checked her repair, and, satisfied, she placed his tools carefully back into place. "You just have to cut out the staring, man."

While Odele may have thought she had done Elden a great service, warning him about Avalon's aversion to dating employers, all it had done was make him hyperaware of the way he watched Avalon.

Was he staring too much? Were his eyes wandering impolitely? Suddenly, he questioned everything.

Maybe this was some plot to throw him off. Odele and Avalon were working together against him, trying to get away with...something.

No, that was silly. When would Avalon even have time to plot against him? The woman worked herself to death. He grew tired simply observing her.

Not to mention she was routinely skipping meals. He was currently on his way to Avalon, bearing leftovers from Lyra. It was an overstuffed container of chicken Alfredo that Nora Lee had insisted he be the one to deliver.

Avalon was in the tiny kitchenette the inn had for the guests. It was seldom utilized as few dared to miss out on Lyra's meals. Stirring a pot on the stove, Avalon stifled a yawn as she cooked. Elden planned out his approach until he saw Avalon wipe her eyes hurriedly.

He froze, quickly backing away until he hit a body.

Odele was not pleased to see him standing there, clearly staring at Avalon as she fought back tears. "I can see that our earlier conversation was a waste of time, lover boy."

Lover boy?! Elden would not address such nonsense. "No, this time I wasn't—"

She gently took the container of food from him. "Let me give her that. She's just overtired from working herself too hard. She always does this." Odele waved him away. "If she knows you saw her cry, she'll really hate you."

He winced, lingering for a moment before heading out of the inn and to home.

Even at home and in bed, there was no refuge from his trailing worries. If Avalon *was* innocent and had found herself in the feylands on accident, then her hatred for Elden was completely warranted. He had her under guard, and even if the guard was furry and adorable, she was technically his prisoner.

But for how long?

Avalon would need to change back to human, eventually. So far, he had failed to be any help with that. There were a dozen reasons she could be crying for, and they all led back to him.

Elden groaned, tossing and turning so much in his bed that even Hob had jumped down from the mattress with a huff. The dog flopped in front of the fireplace instead. Elden could hardly blame him—there would be less interruption down there, and it would be considerably warmer.

This icy magic...would it ever feel normal? Would he ever feel at ease with it?

Sleep fought him, but when Elden finally relaxed his mind enough to rest, his dreams were no comfort. He should have listened to Odele and ceased stalking Avalon around the inn. He had spent so long in her presence that she took center stage in his nightmare.

Avalon straddled his waist, her legs bare, and Elden skimmed his hands up her thighs to settle on her hips, resting underneath the t-shirt she wore. Her appearance had interested him from the moment they met, and now he wondered if some part of him had guessed at her true form.

Elden wished to see that soft, bright hair undone, but even in his own dream he knew better than to try.

Her nails raked his chest, slowly tracing out a circle around his heart. The knife she plunged into the pattern she drew woke him instantly.

Hob raised his head, watching his master as he struggled to catch his breath.

Elden inhaled, forcing his pulse to slow. *Well, that was grimly realistic.*

Innocent or not, he needed to decide Avalon's fate soon. He doubted that too much sorting through the inn's tax records was the real reason for Avalon's tears.

CHAPTER 16
AVALON

Could feyrie magic multiply filing boxes? Avalon had sworn she had counted them *twice*, and now there appeared to be three more boxes to be organized.

I've done so much work in this damn office. And it's only getting worse.

Was she cursed somehow? Or was Kenan pranking her? It had better *not* be the latter. He didn't want to learn what a motivated Avalon could accomplish when it came to revenge.

Her phone, for lack of a real speaker, played through a metal playlist that enticed the will-o'-wisp attached to her out and about, bobbing along in what she could only assume was its version of headbanging.

The door opened a crack before Elden gave the frame a quick knock in warning. "This looks..." He squeezed through the small path Avalon had carved through the junk. His unsettling eyes focused on the wisp, rose a brow, before glancing back at her. "This looks..."

"Listen, I already know you can't lie. Stop trying to work around it." She stopped a pile of papers from falling over with her foot, sighing when she over-corrected and sent them scattering the other way. "I know it's impossible to say anything nice about any of this."

He folded and unfolded his arms, a nervous habit she had never witnessed before. "This looks like...it was a lot of work. Was that anything?"

What a weirdo, Avalon thought with a small half-smile. She offered, "It was certainly something. Anyway, I should get back to it."

And that should have been the end of that. Now Elden would mutter a farewell, intimidate her into behaving, and then vanish for the night. Avalon cheerfully prepared herself mentally for a night of alphabetizing and having some priceless time to herself.

"Jesse is leaving in the morning."

What the hell was he doing? Avalon had provided him with the perfect opportunity to leave! "Oh." Normally she was quite happy to let chit-chat dwindle and die, was elated to stomp out its ashes. However, she needed to remain on Elden's good side, and her attempted, needless rescue had already done wonders for her reputation. She couldn't risk undoing her hard work now. "It was nice to meet Jesse. You know, after you finally let me know she wasn't here to arrest me."

"Yes." Elden readily agreed, and, to Avalon's horror, he took a seat at one of the desks.

No, no, no! This was not heading in a direction that Avalon could easily evade. Searching for something harmless to add to move things along, she asked, "Does the Commission send agents often?"

"Not really. Before you came along, I've been able to handle everything thrown at me."

"Excuse me if I don't apologize for that." The situation was becoming too surreal. Was she honestly having a heart to heart with her captor? The Stockholm Syndrome was strong tonight.

"I didn't come here to discuss that."

Finally. "Is it about my working late? I can adjust my work schedule to start later and avoid charging you—"

"I'm not worried about that. The Commission pays me to maintain the mound's border. It'll more than cover your costs." Elden straightened a few of the papers stacked on his desk and then speedily retracted his hands to his lap. "Sorry. I shouldn't mess with whatever system you have going on. Anyway, with some of the other feyrie mounds losing the power to even stay open, we've been receiving more funds from the Commission. The Summerland's Arizona mound vanished this year."

It was hard to imagine a fey entrance in that desert climate. Avoiding obsessing over the terrifying news that feyrie mounds could and did lose their power, Avalon inquired, "Then *why* did you come here tonight?"

"I saw the way you panicked when you realized what Jesse is. And," Elden soberly said, pushing his chair away from the desk and stretching his legs, "I wanted to tell you I'm done observing you. For suspicious activity. You can roam without Hob at your heels. But!" He looked at her sternly, as if he was about to scold his dog for even contemplating the idea to chase Abernathy's roaming chickens. "As your sister is human, you *must* not tell her about the mound. The Commission has witches skilled in mentalism, and they are *not* picky about what memories they destroy."

The Commission became a scarier foe by the minute.

Leave it alone, Avalon. "What the hell made you change your mind?"

"The fact that you've been doing such a *horrible* job of proving your innocence."

She must have made a face. No, she *knew* she did, because Elden's eyes had brightened so much she could see flecks of blue within them.

He explained before she could pry it out of him. "*If* you were some sleeper agent, you wouldn't have risked me finding out more of your secrets by trying to save me. Or made a deal with a wisp. Or contemplated stabbing me with a letter ripper."

"I suppose I can see how those wouldn't exactly give off an international man of mystery impression," Avalon muttered bitterly.

Elden argued, strangely sincere, "You're not without your talents, Avalon. Bane won't stop complaining about his arm. That certainly makes you more likable. To me, at least." Her questioning look in return must have been too much for him because Elden prattled onward. "And you're a Seer."

"Barely," she countered.

"Sure, you're no Nostradamus, but there's no harm in practicing. Back in my father's kingdom, he threw an extravagant party whenever his Seer attempted a prediction."

"Are you saying you'll throw me a party if I try? I'm not exactly what you would call a people person," Avalon said. His sudden change in attitude was strange. Was he being playful? Elden gave the appearance of it, the lax position, the lazy, *almost* grin. It gave her chills. "I can't look for winning lotto numbers, if that's what you want."

"I wouldn't ask you to try. When you have a vision, are you seeing through your own eyes or—"

"Sometimes, but more often it's like I'm floating above the scene and looking down at what's happening."

"Let's try something simple. Tell me, is there a method to this madness?" He indicated her various and precarious piles of files. "Is this office ever restored to its former glory? My mother, despite what it may look like now, planned for everything. Her backup plans had backups."

Tell him goodnight. You don't even have to mean it.

"As you wish." What was she saying? Avalon immediately felt foolish. No one, other than Odele, had ever watched her try, purposefully, to predict the future. Normally, her visions smacked her in the face mere minutes before they were about to occur.

Nothing happened. For minutes Avalon sweated it out, her eyes shut tight to avoid seeing Elden's expected disappointment. Or worse, perhaps this would serve as further evidence that she was *nothing*, nothing at all to worry about. A hapless, unlucky stooge that—

It came to her in a mist. The office appeared blurry initially before the cleaned, surprisingly bare room came fully into view. The never-ending loose papers were gone, stacked in boxes that were labeled and sorted by year. Even the coffee bar was neat, clean, and restocked with new and various coffees and teas, all too fancy to have been chosen by Avalon. Odele, or even Lyra, must have lent a hand.

"It looks like a different place," she murmured, searching for anything in her vision that would give her a date. Gods, she hoped that this wouldn't take her weeks to accomplish. "It's even alphabetized."

The image cleared, taking on that rare 3-D appearance that her Sight was rarely strong enough to achieve. Avalon's current surroundings faded, the Sight taking her fully into the future.

Elden entered the scene, his back to her. Avalon got the feeling she was at the tail end of a discussion, something menial and mundane and comfortable. She was handed a steaming mug of coffee—it was terrible and she told him so.

The bird's-eye view that normally accompanied her visions wasn't present—instead, she was looking through her own eyes.

He laughed and tossed sugar packets at her until she threatened to throw her coffee back. "You're the one that made this coffee, Avalon."

Allowing the mug to warm her hands, Avalon found herself openly staring at the man. She noted the awkward way he took up his chair, like he rarely found himself lounging at all. This office was too small for him. His voice bounced off the walls, loud enough that her poor hearing caught every word. His words were clear and overly enunciated.

The sugar did nothing for her coffee. When she mentioned it briefly, Elden swooped in to retrieve her mug, so close that a few wild strands of midnight hair tickled her face.

She did not move away. Not even when one of his scarred hands rested over her own, squeezing her fingers before he left to dump her coffee down the drain.

"For alternatives, we have tea, which no one actually drinks. Or I can show you how to actually make a good cup of coffee. Which I would have thought an American would already have mastered." He paused, smiling down at her. "Or there's Tahoma's secret stash of whiskey."

"No feyrie wine?"

Jokes, they were joking with each other as easily as if they had been doing this for years.

What was the *date*? When was this going to happen?

Disturbed, Avalon tried to shove herself out of the vision, aware of Elden, the *real* here and now Elden, calling for her.

She must have missed something, for Elden was now much, much too close. He hovered over her, spinning her chair until they were face to face, and she did not flinch or shove him away. She—she wanted this. She'd been waiting for this since he entered, had contemplated jumping him the second he had walked through that door and they found themselves alone.

He actually grinned at her, and she couldn't stop imagining those sharp teeth nipping at her skin, at her throat.

A hand in her hair, gentle. Fingers deftly lifting her chin. A brush of their noses. And their lips—

She returned too quickly, the real world vaguely dream-like after her hasty escape. Something had her by the elbow. Elden, looking concerned of all things, was the one thing keeping her standing upright.

"Your eyes..." Elden released her once she steadied herself. "You weren't yourself. Avalon, you're frightened."

She was terrified. Never had she been unable to remove herself from a vision. Was her proximity to a feyrie entrance causing this? Or, now that she was physically fey, would her visions be this strong for good?

All she knew was she was *never* cleaning this damned mess. The office could drown in an ocean of paperwork for all she cared.

"I need to go to bed."

"Avalon, what did you see? Is something bad about to happen? I need to know." Elden, the warden, was back. She was almost thankful for it. Whatever he had been playing at earlier did not suit him.

"I said, I need to go!"

His scowl settled back into place, and with it, all the light-heartedness of the evening vanished. "I'm not keeping you prisoner."

"Yeah, as of ten minutes ago. What a hero. I'll ask my dad about getting you a key to the city."

Avalon didn't care how nasty she sounded. It got her what she wanted. Elden didn't say another word as she walked out of that office and sprinted to her room, her heart only slowing when she had a locked door between them.

CHAPTER 17
AVALON

Her secret clawed at her insides, searching for the quickest path out. The Catholics' lax way of running confessionals appealed to her. Confess your darkest, bloodiest sin, dirty your knees, say a few prayers, and then never think on it again. Wash yourself clean until you did it all over again.

Lacking a dude in a white collar, Avalon turned to the next best thing.

Odele. Odele, who did not appreciate Avalon lurking outside her cabin door in the wee hours of the dawn, frantically, pathetically tapping on the door frame until, sleepy eyed, Odele finally answered.

"I'll kill you," Odele yawned, ushering her inside to escape the chilled air. Winter was approaching far too early, thanks to Elden, and a sheet of frost was already visible. Avalon inhaled, taking in the crisp, biting scent of snow on the horizon. A scent that was becoming far too familiar. "Just give me a weapon."

Odele then face-planted back into her bed, the rest of her instructions muffled. The orange tabby, who already had a purple collar with a name tag that read "Clancy", nestled in his own corner of the bedding. He looked quite pleased with his throne of blankets and she was certain that fey cat would be running Odele's life soon enough.

Avalon was also certain that she'd never be able to separate the two.

"I had a dream I made out with…" It was nearly impossible to put into words. As if she spoke it, it gave the vision more power. "*Elden.*"

An unclear *"what"* could be heard from the mattress. Odele sprang up, propping herself on her elbows. "You have to be kidding me. Not you, too." Before Avalon could ask what Odele meant by that, her sister rushed onwards. "Avalon, you say it was a dream, but from the way you're losing it, you're leading me to believe that it was really a vision."

Avalon didn't know what gave her away, but suddenly Odele leapt from her bed and was shaking her by the shoulders. "He. Is. Our. CLIENT. Don't you like our jobs? You're not going to find a bigger pushover than Thompson. We cannot lose that!"

"I know! Why do you think I'm panicking?"

"When does this allegedly happen?" Odele didn't bother asking for the why. How does one explain the impossible?

"I can't be sure," Avalon started, collapsing into Odele's nest of blankets. "But it happens after I organize the office. So. There's one thing I can do. I'm not stepping foot into that dump of an office ever again."

"Or don't smoosh faces with our client?" Odele proposed. "Don't you hate him? Wait, is *that* why you did it? If that's the case, please spare me the details."

Avalon didn't want the details, either. "Can changelings get possessed? A possession would certainly make more sense than legitimate attraction."

Odele cringed. It was an unspoken rule that they never said the word "changeling" out loud. Never admitted that they, while not directly responsible, had replaced two humans, two real, living people, *children*, and had stolen their lives. It was a step too close to thinking about where those children were now. Dead certainly, but how?

Sometimes Avalon had nightmares about it.

Cryptic was not appreciated.

Avalon stared at the message slipped underneath her bedroom door, a few sentences scrawled in Elden's unruly handwriting. It didn't matter how many times she reread it—nothing became any clearer.

Get dressed for dinner out. I don't care what you wear, but if you want to avoid standing out, dress for the occasion. We have work to discuss.

Dinner out? Where the hell were they going to go? The only "restaurant" Fair Harbor possessed, besides the inn, was a solitary coffee stand that served dry muffins.

There was a joke there that Avalon was too stressed to address.

After their spat in the office, she was not looking forward to spending more one-on-one time with the man. She'd spent the past days avoiding him to the best of her ability. Was this invitation related to that?

Avalon rifled through her clothing, not happy with her selection of hoodies and jeans or, at the complete opposite end of the spectrum, business casual clothing. Borrowing from Odele was out of the question—unless she wanted to look like a child trying on adult clothes.

Oh, gods. Avalon knew what she had to do.

Odele's front porch was covered in a fine layer of sawdust. A pile of cut wall trim was stacked next to the rocking chair Odele was resting in, a ceramic mug with the inn's logo in her hand. She was completely at ease—there was even a small bit of cinnamon in her drink as a garnish. A plate of pumpkin-shaped cakes, Lyra's work obviously, sat next to her.

Avalon interrupted her picturesque break. "Where is it?"

"Where is what?" Odele sighed, her face fighting to remain serene while her brow threatened to furrow.

"I know you packed some kind of cute, outrageous outfit for me so you could try to wrangle me into a picnic or something equally sickeningly adorable later. Well, I need it."

Odele blew on her steaming drink, idly sipping from the mug and leaving Avalon in dreaded suspense. "A rather *suspicious* request for someone who recently saw themselves smooching our employer."

"Don't call it *smooching*. I'm sure it was strictly sexual, no emotion involved."

"Spare. Me. The. Details." Odele watched her with a shrewd, disbelieving eye. "What does it matter what you wear? I know you have *plenty* of work outfits. We're both terrible over-packers."

Oh, gods. Did they need to get into this? Avalon started half a dozen sentences before finding one and sticking with it. "I want to feel *confident.* I don't know where we're going, but I'm sure we'll get stared at. It's hard not to ogle at a dinner date between the Prince of Darkness and Little Orphan Annie."

"I have a few issues. One, you called him *Satan,* and two, please never refer to yourself like that again. It pisses me off, and I will use violence against you. Or put all your skincare on a tall shelf and make you grovel for it."

"That's what ladders are for."

"Nope, in this scenario, I have destroyed every ladder in the world." Giving a sigh of defeat, Odele retreated into her cabin and, upon her return, tossed an article of clothing at Avalon's face. "Try to keep it in your pants. Or skirt, I suppose."

"And the shoes?"

She shouldn't have asked. Odele wound up like a pitcher and beamed those at Avalon's face as well.

Avalon had expected the worst, something floral, something neon, but Odele had contained herself and picked an outfit that had a chance of Avalon wearing it.

The outfit ended up being a grey dress, which was an appropriate color for a work dinner. It was properly cinched at the waist to show off her hips. There were laces in the back that would have allowed for an even tighter fit, but Avalon left those alone. The skirt had black lace appliques in a few random places, and stopped mid-thigh. Black tights helped her fight off the frigid weather.

Covering up against the cold, Avalon threw on her long

work coat and did up every button. She was slightly embarrassed at being so dressed up and was fine with waiting until they got to the restaurant before she let Elden see.

Gods, this *was* western Washington. He could very well be taking her to some rustic lodge where she'd be terribly out of place. But her fears quieted when she met him at the inn's garage and saw black slacks underneath his own winter coat.

There was one thing that they needed to discuss before she would set foot in a vehicle with him again.

"Is this a dinner to fire us? Or just me? Because if it is, I will make a scene."

Elden nearly dropped the garage door he'd been lifting. "By Arawn, can't you ever lead into these things? No, I am not firing you. Or Odele." He pushed up the door again and vanished, rolling out with an old truck, the white paint in many places worn until shiny silver was revealed. Elden hopped out, closed the garage, and, worst of all, opened the passenger door for her.

"Do not lift me into this truck," she warned, scrambling up on her own and nearly slipping twice.

"Why would I need to? You *are* above the national average height for women."

What the hell was he doing, remembering things she had previously said to him? "My gods, this thing has a cassette tape player."

"That's how the seventies worked."

"Well, you would know."

"I would not." Elden already looked like he was regretting this evening together. Good. "This was my mother's truck. I'll drive this thing into the ground, so get used to it."

Thankfully, their painfully silent journey was a short one. They pulled into a gravel drive and Elden, waved on by a child in green overalls, parked next to a large barn. If one had to describe Old McDonald's farm, this would be the blueprint.

Though, the old, white tree—bare of leaves or life—distracted from the cozy scene. The width of the tree rivaled that of a redwood. It didn't seem natural.

Elden leaned over to her. His whisper was far too intense for the current setting. "I have to ask you a favor. Do *not* tell Lyra we were here."

Being asked to keep secrets was not her preferred start to a work event. "I don't even know where we are, Elden."

He said it like it was something unspeakable. "We're at Abernathy's farm."

"Let's speed up the exposition, please and thank you."

Speaking low as though they were planning a mutiny, Elden clarified, "Every year Abernathy hosts a farm-to-table dinner for the end of the harvest. If Lyra finds out we're being fed by her once a year competition, she's going to do something awful. To *both* of us," he added, souring Avalon's sadistic smile at the thought of Lyra torturing her cousin.

Realizing this night would never end otherwise, Avalon silenced her protestations and went along with it. She promised, "Fine. I won't mention it. But our inability to lie may be our downfall." The truck cab felt claustrophobic. "Can we head inside now?"

"Right. I'll get your door—"

Avalon threw open her door and jumped down, her flats squishing into the grass. The child in overalls ran over to their vehicle, holding two neon glow sticks she wielded like she was directing air traffic. The girl guided them to a white and grey barn which had its main door propped open enough to let people walk inside without also letting in too much of the evening air.

The Abernathy family had transformed the barn into a makeshift restaurant. Once Elden and Avalon were led to their table, a small, candlelit, hodgepodge of kitchen furniture, Avalon removed her coat and allowed the child to take it. "Wait," she called after the disappearing child to no avail. "I didn't get a ticket for my coat."

By this time Elden's jacket had been whisked away as well, revealing his outfit. Simple black slacks, black tie and waistcoat, and a long-sleeved shirt that was the color of her dress exactly.

"We match," he observed calmly.

"We look like we're going to prom," Avalon observed less calmly.

He wasn't nearly as upset as he ought to be. Elden shrugged, as if this wasn't the most embarrassing thing in the world. "This event is filled with hedge witches and nymphs. It wouldn't be a problem to get a corsage made for you."

"Now is not the time to develop a sense of humor." She took her seat, settling her dress before looking up to glare at him.

Whatever cutting remark she'd been prepared to give died on her lips. Elden's brow knitted as he undid the buttons on his cuffs. He rolled his sleeves carefully, displaying impressive forearms that were ordinarily hidden by armor. The candlelight flickered as she watched him, throwing gold into his eyes. As dangerous as Elden may be, he was just as enticing.

He met her stare and explained, "I'm not used to actually wearing human dress clothes. They are...restrictive."

"Well, I don't think there's normally a frost giant section in clothing stores."

"That's not at all what I am and you know that."

As a blonde woman in a jean jacket poured them wine, Avalon remarked casually, "This is a strange place for a business meeting." The other tables were occupied by pairs, couples, unlike themselves. Strands of dimly lit orbs that weaved throughout the beams of the ceiling gave the venue a very dreamy, romantic vibe. "It might be too dark in here to take notes."

"I don't think notes will be necessary." Elden poked the small plate placed before him. "What is this?"

"A palate cleanser." Life with the Golightly family had involved many forced, fancy dinners. "Leave it alone." A thought struck her. "Aren't you a prince? Shouldn't you be familiar with all this?"

"They're making this event fancier every year. I was raised differently than my elder siblings. My mother always intended for me to be the next warden." He pushed the plate to the center of the table.

Don't ask about his family. It's nothing you need to know.

Avalon told herself she needed every bit of information that she could gather about the fey. Her survival might depend on it. But none of this was helpful. It was Elden's personal life. Still, the question escaped from her traitorous tongue. "Your mother was the warden before you? Isn't that strange, if she was the queen?"

"She had little interest in royal life. She was married to my father in order to seal a weapon's deal, not for love, and my father had little interest in having another person to answer to. Her life among the humans suited both of them."

"Do you miss the feylands?"

He nearly choked on his whiskey. Elden cleared his throat twice. "You've been there yourself. What do you think?"

"I wish I'd never stepped foot in that place." Just thinking about her mistake soured her mood enough that the food, though delicious, could not save it.

"Now, that is interesting. I would have assumed a changeling would harbor some wish to see where they came from."

"Bruce said it would be suspicious if I developed an interest in such things. He wouldn't even let Odele take part in *A Midsummer's Night Dream* her senior year of high school, in case someone might connect it to me."

In the end, Avalon had ignored her father and read every book their local library possessed on the fey. But the legends contradicted each other or were too vague. The fey did not care to be known, and the literature reflected that.

"I can tell you what I've guessed from observing you these past few weeks." Elden hesitated, giving her ample time to protest. "Well, you're obviously Unseelie."

She rolled her eyes. "Obviously."

Now that he had opened the gate, Avalon couldn't help but try to get as much information as she could steal. "Do redcaps normally have, ah, wintery powers?"

Shut up, shut up! Listening to her common sense, *finally*, Avalon apologized, "I shouldn't be prying. I've already asked you too much."

Elden swirled his drink before taking a taste. "I don't mind. I don't have anyone else to tell who doesn't already know."

What? Why would he confess that to her, of all people? It guilted her into giving him a single nod.

And so began a private feyrie history lesson.

He began with the redcaps, explaining that they were violent, cunning creatures that loved instigating wars in their spare time. His mother's family were blacksmiths and enchanters. They could control fire and heat the way Elden's father could command wind and ice. Rarer was the ability to enchant the metal the redcaps forged—his mother had been gifted as such, and it had driven a wedge between her and her brother.

"When my mother died, her power was supposed to return to the rest of her family."

"What do you mean supposed to?" She silently cursed herself—she was listening too intently, getting too involved.

Elden was silent for several minutes, a sign he didn't want to speak the truth. "It's...complicated." The slip of family drama made him look away before he dove into a broader, less personal feyrie explanation.

Seelie and Unseelie were easy enough to keep straight, as they were polar opposites. Nymphs like Lyra and other happy, more nature-inclined fey were Seelie. And redcaps, orators, and banshees, beings more associated with darkness, were part of the Unseelie.

It gave her a small amount of comfort that she and Odele were at least both Unseelie. Whether they were actually related to one another was anyone's guess.

There were two kingdoms, something Avalon already knew, and two rulers. The Seelie Queen ruled over what was called the Summerlands while the Unseelie King ruled the Winterlands. Elden's father, King Taliesin, could call the north wind and, less impressive she thought, could convince anyone of anything.

"He can cure addicts or turn puritans to the bottle with a single sonnet. But he doesn't speak a word that doesn't benefit him."

The appetizer had been a vegetable medley soup and so fragrant that it cleared their sinuses before they had a single taste. The main dish was composed of roasted sweet corn and squash, grilled steak, and mashed potatoes so creamy that Avalon let out an audible hum when she took that first bite. Quickly turning pink, she covered her mouth with a hand as if she could stuff that sound back down her throat.

Elden gave her an amused glance. "It's as good as I remember. We absolutely can't let Lyra know we were here."

He must have gone to these dinners with his mother. But that was much too personal to bring up. She directed them back to their earlier conversation, eager to cover up her unnaturally long pause. "What determined how your powers manifested? I've seen you control winter, but do you also share your mother's gifts?"

"That's not normally how the fey families work. Every fey has a specific gift. Two feyries with different or opposing gifts will bear a child that will usually lean toward one. Some of us," he said and poked at his food, deciding on his next bite, "could lean either way and must choose. *Sometimes* we choose without realizing it." This he directed at her, and she leaned forward, more interested than she cared for him to know. "You are a Seer, short-sighted as you are, but that might have been what you needed most as a child. Blind and unaware as you were, you still made a choice."

Her Sight had shown up some time after Odele's premonitions of death had started. Avalon had needed that five-minute heads up to run to Odele's room to quiet her wails before—

"My mother was married off to my father after the first Unseelie Queen died. She was part of a weapons trade that my eldest brother arranged. I think Jin wanted to take Ashling away from her family because of her abilities to forge magic weapons. She was less of a threat away from their forges."

Avalon was becoming lost with all this talk of magic and

bargains. Elden sensed her fading ability to keep up, and he spoke faster. "Ashling, my mother, hoped she could keep my birth a secret from her family. I was raised with my father's knights, pretending I was his, ah, illegitimate child. But after my mother...well, my father ensured that the court now knows all about me."

Avalon winced. No child deserved to be treated as a dangerous inconvenience.

Elden had continued through her quiet pity. "If I had accepted my mother's gifts, her family would've noticed my presence, and one of my redcap uncles likely would have abducted me."

Her attention snapped back to him. "Your uncle would have taken a child?"

He actually laughed at that. "Avalon, did you forget what you are?" She flushed, so used to hiding her changeling secret that she'd said something foolish. "My uncles and grandmother would have done everything in their power to put me on the throne to be their puppet. That's what my mother was meant to do—why her mother allowed her to marry my father in the first place. The Unseelie Throne rejects anyone without the royal bloodline. It froze a man to death when I was eight." Elden sounded tired. "But that's all been avoided. I was properly hidden, and I have done a somewhat decent job of convincing my siblings that the Winterlands are theirs to squabble over."

It surprised her that he had no ambition regarding the throne. Did he enjoy the human realm that much? "I hope Bane isn't the eldest."

"I have a sister and brother ahead of him, thankfully."

She thoughtfully clicked her tongue. "Your mother's

family couldn't be satisfied with a prince for a nephew?"

"Redcaps are rarely ever satisfied. They would consider a prince to be a waste of talent. They'd want a king or nothing. If I had kept my mother's powers, that would have taken away from their own. Only having a king in the family would justify the power loss." He paused to drain his whiskey. "Or so my mother explained it to me. I've never met them in person—only viewed them from afar."

Elden's family drama made her homesick. She joked, searching for a new topic. "You don't learn any of this in Unnatural History class."

"Yes, I'm sure that course mostly covers ways to avoid us, or, better yet, kill us."

He wasn't wrong, but it prickled her anyway. "Fey aren't exactly innocent, Elden. Not even our children are safe." She spoke as though she still believed she was human. Elden was kind enough to not remark upon her mistake.

"You misunderstand me," he said, straightening. He took on that noble, still posture that separated him from humankind. "I've spent half my life in the feylands and the other half here. I can tell you with certainty that in many cases, the only good a feyrie will do is to rid the rest of us of its presence."

What a morbid position to hold, she thought. *The only good feyrie is a dead feyrie.* Did he count himself amongst those numbers?

Dessert was a huckleberry tart. It was delicious, making Avalon feel like she was betraying Lyra somehow. She ate slowly, savoring the tart filling while Elden spoke briefly with Abernathy.

The witch had dressed in his best jeans and collared shirt, topped off with a white cowboy hat, the edges a faded red. With that ridiculous dark mustache, Avalon imagined Abernathy had been quite popular in the seventies.

Even immersed in his own conversation as he was, Elden saw her rub her arms, a lame attempt to ease the chill racing through her. Wordlessly, Elden passed his whiskey glass toward her, continuing to argue with Abernathy about the proper way to deal with a kelpie.

Though she knew the liquor would only give her a false sense of warmth, Avalon took a few sips. She was careful to avoid placing her mouth where Elden's had been, cringing at the faint burgundy print her lipstick left on the glass. When she pushed the glass back in front of him, Elden didn't take such care and took a large swallow immediately.

It left a strange, flushed feeling across her skin. To avoid thinking about it, Avalon dove back into her dessert.

With her tart gone, she thought the dinner would now turn to things work related, but Elden did not appear to be in a hurry to begin, despite the late hour. He decided, instead, "It's your turn to give me something. I've been talking far too long. Tell me a secret."

"A secret?"

"It's only fair, after I bared my heart to you." He grinned then, the first she'd seen from him, and it perfectly displayed that stunning great white shark smile.

It was so close to the vision she'd had of him in that office that her face turned bright red at the memory. And worse, Elden *noticed.* He blinked a few times before averting his gaze.

There had been no denying he was handsome when they initially met, but once she could see past his glamour...could see the unruly, dark hair, the too sharp, almost alien angles of his face, and even the teeth, each slightly pointed... It all came together to stir some wild thing inside her.

Dammit. Avalon hurried. "My name isn't really Avalon. Don't you ever use it, but I'll give it to you. Ava Golightly is my real name. Odd—I mean, Odele—gave Avalon to me. I think we watched too many King Arthur cartoons that year."

Elden transfixed her with a deep, angry stare. "Why the *fuck* would you tell me that?"

"Don't talk to me that way." Just when she thought he was changing, that she was too judgmental of his actions in the fey-lands, Elden did something like this.

He let out a breath, his hand forming a fist on the table. "I apologize. But that wasn't a secret. I'm a *feyrie*. I already knew Avalon wasn't your true name."

Was that all that was? Her secret wasn't good enough? "Elden, you already know my biggest secret in the world." She wasn't pouting, but she was getting close. "What more do you want from me?" If he started calling her Ava, he could bare his heart to her all he wanted—it would just make ripping it out even easier.

"I want a lot more," he said flatly, but there was something almost wistful in his tone. "Forget it. Turn around and wave to Nora Lee." He pointed over her shoulder. Feeling like a character in a horror film, Avalon slowly turned to see the bloodcurdling scene behind her. Nora Lee, seated with a man—her husband Avalon assumed—at another table, waved at both of them, a witness to whatever the hell was going on tonight.

Nothing about this dinner looked like it was remotely work related. Avalon pinched the bridge of her nose. Surely, by morning, the rest of the inn would discover how the pair of them had spent their evening. If Nora Lee hadn't already sent a group text, prom picture included.

It had to be getting late. "I think I distracted us for long enough," Avalon sighed. In fact, the dinner was practically over. "What did you want to talk to me about? The work thing, I mean."

"Ah." He looked solemn, like he was about to send her to the gallows. Even more so than when he had threatened to do literally that. "There's a wedding coming up. Initially, I meant to only involve you a little, but now that I know you're fey..."

"So, it's a fey wedding?" Avalon asked, frowning. Was that all he had to tell her? This dinner was the worst example of "could have been an email" that she'd ever seen.

"The daughter of one of the Seelie Queen's wardens is getting married. Her Unseelie bride is arriving tomorrow to begin the preparations."

"Do we have anything to go off of, or are we starting from scratch?"

"That's one of the many negatives about this situation. My mother was our event planner. And I have no idea where her files are." That certainly wouldn't go over well with the brides. She could read from Elden's expression that there was more bad news. "The bride doing all the planning, Maetta, is an Unseelie bridezilla."

It was her turn to snicker at him, though the sound came out far too cute and high-pitched for her comfort. "I've helped plan a wedding for a bride that forced her father to take out a second mortgage to pay for it all. If there's one thing you don't need to worry about, it's my ability to deal with the most unlikeable personalities and have them be none the wiser."

What was that flinch? Did he think he was included in that list? And what did it matter if he did? Still, Avalon rode that fence, unsure which side she'd tumble off of until a decision was quietly made.

The more she said, the less likely she was to improve the dead air between them. But Avalon made a go of it, anyway. "Look, Elden, I'm sorry for how I overreacted the other night. I don't have any excuse that's acceptable. I saw something upsetting, but it wasn't world ending. Please, don't take it personally."

He became animal-like once more, taking on a predatory blankness that was impossible to decipher. When he relaxed, Elden merely said, "You're a redcap."

As if that explained or excused anything at all. "So?"

"Redcaps are naturally cruel. I expect you to be mean. *I'm* mean. Honestly, a few nights after I threatened to call the Commission on you, I dreamt that I woke up to find you in my bed, carving my heart out of my chest."

Her brain had short-circuited when he said, in that gruff voice of his, "find you in my bed". Avalon laughed, startled. "Carve your heart out, Elden? I considered the idea."

"I wouldn't expect anything less, you feral woman."

He'd called her "feral" before, but now it was almost said with an endearing softness. The night was becoming too surreal. She blurted, "Why did you bring me here?"

"It's an apology." Elden glanced at the dying candlelight, eyeing it until it returned to life, even brighter than before. "And I wanted to."

For some reason, one she refused to analyze, those words made her unseasonably warm.

Elden, unfortunately, had more to say.

"Since you apologized, Avalon, I need to explain myself as well. I spoke harshly to you tonight, but I will not say it wasn't warranted." His tone had become quite grim. Suddenly, the fey leaned over the table to whisper to her, the winter breezing off his body and chilling her flesh. With only inches between them, it was impossible to ignore the ridiculous size difference. She shuddered as he growled, "Do *not* tell any fey besides me your true name."

True name? The fey course of Unnatural History came flooding back to her. She had just doomed herself. Did she really just give *Elden,* of all people, her true name? She met his eyes, but that only cut the distance between them even more.

She knew all fey had a "true name" which could be used by another fey to have some power over them. It still was hard to consider herself anything other than human.

Her heartbeat was too faint. Avalon asked, nearly whimpering, "So, any fey that knows my name can control me?"

"Any fey you *give* your true name. Simple introductions won't cut it. It must be offered. The power is in the offering. If you'd been less dramatic, Avalon, this could have been avoided." Elden waved a hand. "There's no use antagonizing over it. It can't be undone. Just ensure that I am the only man who holds you."

He said man, not fey, but surely that was unintentional.

Avalon lifted herself from the table, swaying on her feet. How could she have let this happen? All that pride she had in her paranoia, in her attention to detail...

She was such a fool.

Elden called to her softly. "Avalon, are you okay?"

She felt him lightly touch her elbow, but her vision had begun to dim as her mind raged at her mistake. "I need some air."

Did he even hear her? Her own voice was lost amongst the roaring in her head. Avalon wiped her sweaty palms on her skirt, taking slow steps toward where she guessed the exit was.

With her true name, Elden could make her slice her own throat if he wanted.

"Avalon, I'm going to touch you for a moment. Don't bite me."

Elden's words held no meaning until her feet left the ground and suddenly he was carrying her. *Bridal-style.*

"My gods, Elden, put me down!"

He ignored her, taking her all the way back to the truck and neglecting to stop for their coats. Elden dropped the tailgate and sat her down on the cold metal. His hands caught her shoulders, steadying her. "I assume you know what to do here, Avalon, but I'll say it, anyway. Count down from ten."

Count from ten. Name five things you can see. She knew the spiel. Avalon tried to push him away, but Elden's chest didn't budge an inch.

"Avalon, I won't let you go until you play along. The cold doesn't bother me, so I'm happy to stand here all night."

"I see a stubborn jackass in front of me. I see a barely functioning truck. I see—"

His hands moved to her face, feeling her flushed skin. "You're too warm. Let me help." Elden held his palm against her forehead, his winter magic working to lower her feverish temperature. The cool touch of his hand allowed her some time to even out her breathing.

Avalon must have finally visibly relaxed because Elden muttered, "Good girl," and released her. His praise made her want to kick him. She tried, but he easily dodged her attempt.

"I see you're feeling better." He almost smiled before Elden helped her to the front seat. After he started the truck and drove them back to the inn, he asked, "When I found you in the feylands, fighting with my brother, you weren't nearly so panicked."

Avalon answered the unasked question. "Because that situation wasn't my fault."

She let him walk with her back to the lobby. Not that Elden gave her any choice. Avalon headed for the staircase, turning to tell him goodnight.

"Come here, Avalon." Elden was unlocking the office behind the front desk. "I have something to show you."

Don't go. Pretend you didn't hear him. It's believable with your piss-poor hearing.

She knew what he was going to show her. And still she followed, each step a slow-motion dream.

He showed her an office that was not only tidy, but also organized for future success. This was how she had avoided him so easily the past few days. Elden was holed up in here, shredding papers and filing and scrubbing dust off the walls. The coffee bar was even restocked, like she had seen in her vision.

"You know, this inn was built by my mother to be something great. We were the first feyrie mound to offer such a place. It's time I helped rebuild it."

CHAPTER 18
AVALON

The arrival of Maetta Bradigan was given the same dread that normally accompanied a funeral procession. All the inn's staff was crowded around the feyrie entrance, waiting for Elden to open the gate to allow Maetta through.

It seemed silly to Avalon, even though Elden had made it vividly clear she would be the one to inform Maetta that all her previous wedding planning had been misplaced. Sure, the plans had been lost due to a tragic death (possibly tragic, Ashling was a sensitive and confusing subject around the inn), but rarely did a bride care *why* they were being inconvenienced. They just wanted it fixed.

Now Avalon eyed Elden critically. Was the man *sweating*? She'd witnessed him battle far nastier beings than a pissed-off bride.

"Flowers for Maetta?" She skeptically indicated the bouquet in his hand.

"I panicked."

Elden had panicked earlier as well.

Avalon had texted him, already a *mistake*, to ask what was for dinner. Elden, who clearly didn't know how humans texted, sent the eggplant icon. Avalon, after staring at her phone for ten minutes, dumbstruck, had marched into his office and threatened to whip her cellphone at his head.

While Kenan exploded into laughter, Tahoma had explained, fighting back her own giggles, that Lyra was making moussaka.

Gods, Avalon couldn't have a normal moment with the man.

Elden fidgeted. "There's a bouquet for you, as well. In Whimsy. An apology for the...unfortunate text."

"One of the twins told you to do it, didn't they?"

"Tahoma was *very* convincing that it was a known symbol for moussaka."

This grudge was silly, and while the thought was also silly, Avalon wondered what sort of flowers waited for her.

The inn had never looked better. Without the glamour obscuring her vision any longer, the inn's grey stone sparkled in the sunlight. Avalon had hired a cleaning and landscaping crew for the main entrance of the inn, and, boy, did it pay off. Avalon didn't bother fighting the pang of pride in her chest as she took in the Refuge on the Moor.

"Beautiful," Elden whispered. Avalon nearly jumped at his interruption. He motioned toward the inn's front entrance. "The, uh, landscaping is well done."

Avalon merely nodded, turning back to check in on everyone else. She knew Lyra was doing her part and slaving away in the kitchens. Standing next to her and Elden, waiting for the feyrie entrance to be opened, Kenan and Tahoma were even dressed as they were supposed to be every day. With sleeves.

It was time to prove her worth. There had been a lot of doubtful glances between the rest of the staff when Avalon had ensured Elden she could deliver the news to Maetta without losing her business. She let them underestimate her—it wasn't so hard to imagine *why* they questioned her peace-making abilities. She hadn't much opportunity to deploy these skills, what with her life being threatened every other minute.

Another reason for Elden's worry—this wedding was *full* of feyrie politics. The Seelie Queen and Unseelie King were sworn enemies, though Elden explained that they no longer fought each other as the seasons shifted. Now the transfer of power between the feyrie royals that accompanied the changing seasons was symbolic, rather than gory.

Despite this "friendly" exchange of power, the families had been, initially, less than pleased with the match. "They'd be fine with bedding an Unseelie," Elden had said of the Seelie court, "but Arawn forbid they *marry* them."

Since Maetta was arriving through the feyrie mound, Elden was dressed in his heavy silver armor. With that bouquet in hand, he looked like he belonged on the cover of a half-priced medieval romance.

Elden was present each and every time the mound was opened. Without his ability to move the iron gate magically, it wasn't as if the fey could come and go as they pleased. After the gate creaked open under his command, Elden greeted Maetta awkwardly, nearly shoving the flowers into her, and verified some papers. Once the admin work was completed, Avalon was brought over to meet the Unseelie bride.

Maetta was a redcap herself, those enhanced angles and slightly sharpened teeth present. Her hair was dark brown and shaved in the back, the rest left to hang around her ears and eyes. Gold earrings glittered from every available space on her ears, the largest earring of all matching with the ruby engagement ring on her finger.

Her face was void of any makeup, heavily pierced, and pissed. "Who's going to be the one to tell me how much you've botched this wedding?"

Ah. Showtime already? Elden mouthed something to Avalon from behind Maetta's shoulder. It looked suspiciously like he was sounding out, "*no biting*".

Avalon smiled.

"I still don't understand what happened!" Kenan was louder than usual, the beer in his hand surely getting warm with all this talking he was doing. The bartender at the rustic tavern they were visiting paid Kenan's volume zero attention. "I mean, Avalon, you were poised, *charming*, and by the end of it you had Maetta *happy* to be starting her wedding planning over."

"I was honest with her," Avalon shrugged, sipping her own drink and trying to convince Odele that cotton candy beer would not be as good as it sounded on the menu. "I'm the spawn of a career politician. The truth can be presented in many ways. You'd be surprised by the talents my tongue possesses."

The table erupted into laughter, proof of how drunk they all were. Kenan leaned forward. "Oh, would I?"

Avalon flushed. Rarely did she *mean* to sound flirtatious. Kenan seemed to read this and laughed, smiling as if to say, "don't worry about it", before turning and starting a conversation with Lyra.

Grateful, Avalon decided to slow down on her drinks, setting her beer aside and looking up to find Elden staring at her with the determined, haunting gaze of a serial killer.

She hadn't been explicitly warned about it, but she had felt the compulsion to keep the inn's secrets leave her as they drove further and further from the Refuge. If she was able to sneak Odele away, she could tell her sister *everything* and get Odele out of there. Convincing Odele to leave without her might be difficult, but Avalon had to try.

Of course, Elden was watching her, hawk-like and intense, to ensure that didn't happen. It didn't bother her in the slightest that he didn't trust her. Her first thought, when Lyra announced she wanted to celebrate away from work, *had* been, *how do I get Odele alone?*

They lingered at the bar for hours—Avalon felt her social meter deteriorating. It wasn't that she wasn't having a good time, more that she was unused to company that wasn't her sister. She had to gauge her facial reactions and her responses, which was never easy for her. It had been her and Odele against the world for so long that she was unsure how to include other people in it.

Her replies became shorter, the uncertainty detectable. Odele was, at least Avalon hoped, the only one that noticed and she offered a distraction from the discordant chatter.

After flipping through the many photographs Odele had taken of the inn's current renovations, an obnoxiously tall shadow fell over the sisters. They removed their attention from Odele's phone, waiting for Elden to cease his lurking and finally speak.

"I'm heading back, Avalon. Would you like to ride with

me?"

Kenan jerked away from the conversation. They had taken two cars to get here, the girls had all piled into Tahoma's Jeep, blasting girly bops at a volume even partially deaf Avalon protested. Her glamour hadn't wavered during the drive, thanks to Elden, in that old, white truck, riding their bumper like his life depended on it.

Unhappy to lose his place, as Kenan had ridden alone with Elden, he whined, "You're *ditching* me?"

Elden didn't even spare him a glance. "I'm paying the bill."

"Then ditch away."

It was clear what this was. Elden was tired of pushing his luck and wanted to take away Avalon's one chance to tell Odele everything. This wasn't an option.

Avalon was tired of losing battles before she even had a chance to fight. "Alright." She promised Odele she would text when she made it back to her room. Odele kissed Avalon's cheek as she headed for the bar's bathroom.

With her sister out of sight, Kenan teased Avalon, his laughter drawing far too much attention. "If you two go somewhere to park and make out, we'll *know*."

Elden's eyebrows shot up to the top of his head. He showed Kenan his middle finger before turning it upside down and sticking it into his beer. As the Winter prince removed his finger, Kenan's dark beer froze.

Kenan pushed his drink away. "You know, you didn't need to *freeze* it, Elden. The finger was enough."

Avalon pointed at Tahoma's glass. "Tahoma laughed too, Elden."

Quickly covering her drink, Tahoma barked at them to leave already.

The drive back to the inn was around half an hour, just long enough to make things feel awkward.

Avalon's buzz from the evening was fading—she hoped it would last long enough to help her fall asleep. "I didn't tell Odele about the feyrie mound. Though, you know humans all learn about the fey in high school. I still can't see the point in keeping this so secret."

Elden's grip relaxed on the steering wheel. "As I said before, that's the Commission's call. They want to avoid a panic. Or avoid more humans trying to cross to the feylands to make deals that will never end in their favor."

The fey that lived on the human side of things were all carefully monitored. Bargaining with the fey was strictly outlawed, and for good reason.

"Well, it's not like you have the entrance properly locked up, from this side at least. Seems like *anyone* can waltz right in."

His mouth became a grim, tight line. She'd hit a nerve there. "That's the nature of the mound. It wants victims. Humans, I mean." It always amazed her how much he was willing to reveal to her. Was he this upfront with *all* his fellow fey? "The iron door stops most feyries. But if I were to cover it in chains and padlocks to keep any nosy humans out..." He glanced away from the road to glare at her. "Then the mound would quickly find somewhere else to be."

What a frustrating conundrum. Contain something enough to avoid incidents like the one Avalon fell into, but not enough to destroy the magic and overall nature of the mound.

"If you keep it unlocked, at least unlocked for humans, you must have protection spells or cameras or..." What needed to be contained was her curiosity. Questions like these were suspicious. There was no need for her to know the scope of the inn's defenses.

"There are *multiple* forms of barricades and methods of detection—that's how I was able to locate you so quickly." If her inquisition bothered him, Elden hid it well. "There's little to worry about."

Little, but not *nothing*. Elden's inability to lie was sometimes a comfort, though not always.

The inn crept into view, an impressive prison emerging from the dark. "Well, thanks for the ride," Avalon said with a touch of sarcasm.

"Yes, you..." He turned off the vehicle, sitting for a moment quietly in the dark of the garage. "You had looked like you were running out of the right things to say. I've experienced that same aloofness. It feels like you're pretending while everyone else is honestly having a good time. It makes me feel—"

"Disingenuous?"

"Yes."

Was that why he offered to drive her back? Not because he was afraid that she'd spill his secrets to Odele?

His concern was...well, concerning.

Neither Maetta nor Avalon were ready for another round of wedding planning. The inn had, of course, a tearoom and Avalon decided all wedding planning would take place in there. Soft oranges, browns, and yellows filled the tearoom, matching perfectly with the porcelain tea sets. It surprised Avalon that Ashling had such delicate taste as she had assumed Elden took after his mother personality-wise.

Maetta and Avalon had stared at so many napkin swatches that Avalon could no longer tell the difference between sandy beach and blanched almond. Avalon saw Maetta's fingers grip the edge of the table, and she quickly pushed down on the surface to prevent Maetta from flipping another table.

"What did I say before we started this?" Avalon reminded her. "No one remembers what shade their napkin was at a wedding. And if they do, they should be executed."

"*You* haven't met the Seelie," Maetta argued. "They bullied me into choosing this wedding venue, no offense. When we finally announced the date? Oh, the angry messages they left! All of them were so pissed that we didn't want a spring wedding."

Avalon waved that away. "Does Sabella care about finding the right shade of napkin?"

"Sabella wanted to elope. In Greece. I'm a fool to have suggested otherwise."

Avalon felt for Maetta. The fey wasn't planning this wedding so facetiously because she wanted to compete with another wedding or had to have the "greatest wedding of all time". Maetta was just frightened of disappointing her future in-laws.

"So, you don't get along with the in-laws," Avalon summarized. "Is a napkin going to change that?"

Maetta wasn't the heartless fey Avalon had expected, only grumpy and stressed. Some of Ashling's plans were salvaged, thanks to Maetta's stellar memory, but there was still a lot of tedious rework to be done.

Finally, the bride-to-be pointed to a napkin in the middle of the pile. "Screw it. Go with that one."

The inn had two weeks before the Seelie were to arrive for the wedding. Elden was seldom seen; he had brought a few of the Unseelie King's guards to the inn for extra surveillance. So many fey arriving through the mound at one time was rare—and dangerous. Though the Seelie were generally considered to be rather harmless (by fey standards, at least), Elden had been on edge since Maetta had arrived.

The guest list had been limited, and the number of attendees from each land had to be equal. With so much work to be done, the days flew by, a flipbook racing before Avalon's eyes. As their contract continued, Avalon wasn't sure that she'd be returning to Seattle at the end of the ten weeks. Despite that fleeting feeling of change she had in the face of that three-headed vulture, she hadn't been able to replicate it since. Still, Elden persisted with their "changeling lessons", which he was running out of ideas for.

The latest had involved Lyra jumping out at her from behind doors or corners, as if she could scare the fey out of her.

Avalon was doomed.

"I can extend the contract. For as long as you need," Elden swore, a promise that put Avalon's stomach in knots. If her situation was so desperate that even Elden felt the need to be kind to her, she was lost. "Though, I'm afraid of what changes Odele might make if she finishes all the repairs and starts to get bored."

What if I'm stuck like this forever?

Either those words had actually escaped her mouth, or she was easier to read than she knew.

"There will always be something else to try."

Yeah, until there wasn't.

CHAPTER 19
AVALON

Shrill and searching, a wailing started around midnight and frenzied an inn that was already on edge. Every feyrie knew that, in the morning, members of opposing courts would arrive in numbers that even an axe-wielding Elden may not be able to control. So, hearing the warning cry of a banshee in the wee hours of the night was not at all welcome.

Avalon nearly threw herself down the stairs from her room, almost falling out of her sneakers. The inn quickly developed into a madhouse. The human guests peeked outside their doors, glancing down dark hallways for any sign of the inhuman, sorrowful keening, while the fey knew the source instinctively and kept their doors firmly shut and locked, with perhaps a knife clutched in their claws, guarding and waiting.

If Elden and the others heard Odele's wail, and how could they *not*, would they believe the sound to be merely the result of night terrors? Would Elden fall for something so common, so *human,* when he already suspected her?

Avalon raced to the front lobby, shouting down the halls, "Stay inside your rooms! It's a mountain lion!" She hoped there wasn't a good old country boy, dragged to the inn by his wife, who could call her on her bullshit.

Avalon burst out of the inn, the fresh, November air cutting through her clothing. The moonlight was bright, a full orb suspended amongst all that inky black. It wasn't bright enough to account for how well she was seeing through the darkness. No, she had her fey side to thank for that.

As the eldest daughter, a good portion of her time, when a more relaxed person might have been idle, was spent preparing for impossible scenarios. This constant anticipation ensured she already knew the quickest path from the inn to Odele's cabin, where, to her instant horror, she found the door to be wide open and swinging in the late-night wind.

Avalon stormed into the cabin, scouring every cranny of the tiny home. She upended the bed, not knowing her own strength, and threw the wooden frame against the wall. Underneath was bare, disappointing, useless.

Her hands twisted into her hair, and she swallowed her own scream.

Gods, let me fucking see!

Her head snapped backwards, her arms flailing, wheeling, from the force of her vision.

Odele, barefoot, dried leaves crunching beneath her cold heels. She wore that long, ankle-length black nightgown, the one Avalon had purchased online for her after Odele had stared at it in wonder, whispering, "Now that's an outfit for a real banshee."

Dried branches caught at the lacy, vintage fabric. The moon was obscured by clouds.

The woods! Maybe Odele was on part of a trail? It had been hard to tell. Avalon's head was pounding from the effort it took for her to see something so specific.

She should have borrowed a coat from Odele's cabin—the hoodie she was wearing did little to keep her warm. Desperate, Avalon looked to the sky, noting the wisps of vapor beginning to veil the edges of the moon. She had to move fast. If only Hob was with her. The downside to Elden beginning to trust her a tiny bit more was that he had removed her canine overseer. Right now, she did not appreciate it.

She had to find Odele before anyone else did. Before Elden did. Before he found out she was omitting even more important truths from him.

She followed the first trail she stumbled upon, a thin hunter's path that Elden must have carved during his routine patrols.

Trying to find Odele through her cries was a dead-end. Odele's song of future death seemed to come from every direction. And when a siren went off, Avalon clutched her ears and ground her teeth together.

"What the hell is *that* for?" Avalon had reviewed the inn's emergency procedures—for a missing person there was never a mention of a siren. She glanced backwards, her own sweat covering her in salt, and saw the gardens, the mound, was lit up with sterile, white light that rotated in a repeating sequence. What did that mean? Was something else going on? Something that Odele was predicting?

A distraction. That's all it was, all it could be for now.

"Odd!" she half-shouted, afraid to risk anyone hearing who exactly she was searching for. Again, her voice cracking, "Odd!"

If Odele was sleep-walking, this premonition was *bad.*

Why, *why* had she let them get separate rooms? She should have, Odele's feelings be damned, thrown a tantrum and demanded they get those adjoining rooms she had asked for. Boundaries were for those who could safely afford them.

She cupped her hands around her mouth, ready to shout, when she caught a glimpse of flowing, dark cloth in the distance.

Odd!

Avalon's muscles tensed, preparing to run further into the woods when a voice she wished she didn't recognize spoke from behind her.

"This night keeps getting better and better. How convenient to find you here and without another witness in sight."

That velvety voice...

The hair on her arms prickled, though it wasn't the night air that was chilling her. Avalon knew she couldn't outrun him, the third Prince of the Winterlands. Did Bane's sudden appearance have something to do with that siren? Was there some sort of security breach at the mound?

As on and off as her relationship with Elden was, she doubted he would neglect to tell her if Bane had submitted the proper paperwork to enter the human realm.

She could not win in a fight against him, but that wasn't what was important. What mattered was she distracted Bane long enough to give Odele time to get away.

Odele, wake up and run!

Avalon felt lightheaded as she faced him. Bane dressed in simple black robes—nothing as extravagant as he'd been wearing the last time. What could she say to get him to leave? Revenge glimmered in his cold eyes, his dark intent clear and promising. She would not leave these woods tonight, and if she did, she wasn't sure if it would be in a state much better than death.

Bane's head cocked to one side, considering. "No," he muttered to himself, "I should still have time." He brightened. "I'm sure its keeping the warden busy. *Let's play.*"

Desperate, Avalon said, "Your brother isn't far." Her throat begged for water. But it wasn't exactly a lie—she wasn't *too* removed from the inn. Clearing her throat, Avalon continued, her bravery waning, "I'm not too proud to scream."

His laughter was too high-pitched, too prolonged. If sanity was a thing the fey could possess, Bane had missed that gene entirely. "My dear brother is a little preoccupied with his own battle, and who's going to hear you over that lunatic banshee? He isn't coming." Bane pushed a strand of hair out of his face that had escaped his braid. Tonight he was armored in quiet, dark leathers, which seemed excessive considering Avalon was not known to be carrying anything armor-piercing. Well, she had her teeth, as he must remember from their first meeting, but that wasn't enough to warrant full armor.

Bane shortened the space between them, and Avalon froze. Another step and she again forced her body to remain still, to at least not show him the horror that was churning her stomach. "I couldn't ask for a more perfect setting. The moonlight tonight—" Bane grinned, his voice taking on a dream-like quality. "—will reflect beautifully off your blood."

Gods, Avalon suddenly knew whose death was invading Odele's dreams. It made sense now that Odele was sleep-walking and unable to control her keening.

Odele was seeing the gory, visceral murder of her sibling.

CHAPTER 20
AVALON

Hot tears swam in Avalon's vision. It didn't matter that she had her newfound fey strength. Bane was just as strong, if not more so. And the redcap ferociousness she had been leaning into, rather than shoving down, wouldn't matter, either. Bane was a prince of the Winterlands; he must have had some sort of combat training. Years of it. Maybe centuries. Even if it had been a fraction of what Elden had experienced while training to be the warden, it would be more than enough to overpower her. A handful of women's self-defense classes would mean nothing here.

I have to buy Odele time.

What if—acid burbled up from her stomach and touched the back of her throat—*what if Odele was awake and consciously searching for her?* If Bane so much as *looked* at Odele, Avalon would lose it.

Avalon could thank Bane for one thing—he kept her from spiraling further.

He tackled her, the move rough and not what Avalon had expected from him. She had thought him more precise than that. Her feet went out from under her, and all she could do was grab hold of Bane's clothing as they tumbled to the ground. His knees pressed into her chest; the air forced out of her lungs while she flailed uselessly at his face. Her thumbnails dragged underneath his eyes, her reach too short, and twin bloodstained tears were carved on either side of his face.

Desperate, Avalon grabbed his long hair and yanked, over and over, until his knee found her windpipe.

She gaped like a fish and something metal clacked against her teeth. The cold implement seemed to open, forcing her mouth wider. For a split second, Avalon thought of the dentist and her stark reality hit her.

He was going to remove her teeth first. Just as he promised.

She squirmed, clawing and shoving at Bane's tremendous weight. Her head thrashed until one of his knees pinned her throat, the choking weight too much for her.

Another tool found one of her back molars—pliers—and jerked upward. The pain was throbbing and unbearable—she clawed into the dirt, crying with abandon.

A fey prince wouldn't keep such common tools on his person, especially not one as vain and soft-handed as Bane. If Bane had pliers at his disposable, that meant that this, all of this pain, had been carefully planned.

The pliers slipped, digging around until Bane caught another tooth. This time his grip was sure, the metal biting into gum and bone. When he pulled, her tooth came out, a bloody, stringy thing he tossed to the ground.

The edges of a blackout hammered into her sight. She tried to shake her head, and his knee pressed harder into her throat until she stilled. Bane switched sides and gripped another tooth, but this one didn't come out as cleanly. He wiggled and yanked before freeing it.

Her own blood flooded her mouth, threatening to drown her. She spit, desperate to save herself. Bane gave her enough leeway to turn her head and rid her mouth of the liquid.

"How many teeth do you have left? I might need some help counting down." Bane adjusted his tool, the sound of metal against her teeth unbearable. "Maybe we go for one of the front ones this time? Sure, yanking the back ones brings more pain, but the front—" He smiled, his teeth normal and unbloodied. "We could end this if you'd like. If you gave me something of value, little changeling."

She didn't respond. Bane had reduced her to a crying, snotty mute. The pain he had inflicted on her made speaking impossible.

Her silence didn't dissuade him. "Give me your true name, and I promise I'll stop. You can keep the rest of those razors in your mouth. Unless..." Bane squeezed her jaw, and she yelped. "Unless someone already owns you. My *brother*, perhaps? Elden's acts practically half-human himself, which makes him just as tainted as you."

A vision, a teasing glimpse of fur and fangs, filled Avalon's heart with hope.

There was a primal fear attached to certain nighttime sounds—the quick, racing footsteps of an unknown quadruped was one of them. Even Bane stilled, his onslaught paused while he peered dumbly into the darkness. She could pinpoint the instant that Bane knew he was fucked.

A black shadow attacked, partially tearing Bane off her chest. She squirmed from underneath Bane, sinking into the mud, taking her first and maybe only opportunity to escape.

The involuntary sounds Bane was making made it impossible to separate the beast from the fey. The angry jaw of a canine caught Bane's arm and shook him like a doll.

That's my cue, she thought and attempted her getaway.

Something caught her ankle while she tried to run. Avalon's chin connected with the ground as she was jerked off her feet. She didn't want to look back, but her ankle refused to move. Ice had formed, was *still* forming, around her ankle and was creeping up, up, up to her knee. Kicking against the ice block with her free foot, Avalon now had a front row seat to Bane's mauling.

Hob didn't look like himself. His hackles raised, an angry mohawk running down his back. *His size.* The canine had grown three times his usual height, a shimmering magic glazed over his fur. Hob circled the fey, watching warily as Bane summoned a thin sword formed of ice and fey magic. As Bane was now distracted, and his magic focused into that icy blue blade, the ice around her ankle melted.

When she pulled herself to her knees, Avalon heard the sharp, shrill cry of a wounded animal.

Avalon crouched, frozen in a runner's position. It hadn't occurred to her, not that there had been much time for deep reflecting, that Bane would be able to overtake Hob. She could run and...

There was no use even finishing that thought. There was no way she could leave that dumb, slobbery dog behind.

Red dripped from Bane's sword and from a gash in his shoulder. Hob limped, refusing to put any weight on one of his back legs. Bane kept his attention on Hob, even as wounded as the dog seemingly was.

I need a weapon. It seemed ludicrous that Avalon was waltzing around a fey-infested inn without so much as a pocket knife. Not that she had any idea what to do with one if she *had* a weapon. And yet, when Hob lunged, so did she.

The wet shredding of flesh was audible even with her poor hearing. She had been a step too late. Bane had summoned spears of ice that sprung from the ground and caught Hob mid-lunge, dark, angry wounds appearing all over his abdomen. Hob landed, off to the side, twisted and on his back. His howl competed with Odele's banshee wails in terms of volume.

It was heartbreaking, but the sound disguised Avalon's footsteps and she was able to catch Bane unaware. Not knowing what else to do, she took a page out of *Dracula*, and sank her redcap teeth into Bane's neck.

He yelped, turning and trying to make a grab for her, but she persisted. She tore what flesh wasn't covered by armor until he somehow caught her and threw her over his shoulder. Landing awkwardly, she rolled away from his kicks and positioned herself in front of Hob's shaking form.

She was a useless shield, one of mere flesh and bone. One hand she held out in front of her and the other she had to use to keep Hob down, preventing him from trying to protect her in his bloodied state.

A hand pressed against his neck, Bane looked at them both with disgust. "What that *mongrel* is doing all the way out here when there's much more pressing problems than me..." He trailed off, but Avalon gleaned enough information from that slip than he probably intended.

Something else was attacking the inn. And the gods only knew how long Elden would be preoccupied with that before he even thought to look for his contracted hotel manager or his dog.

Hob's body was warm and wet against her back. She leaned into him, waiting for the killing blow. This, at least, would be less painful than having her teeth removed one by one.

It began to rain, a fitting background to her soon-to-be death. Avalon hoped those quickening droplets would soak Bane's robes thoroughly. The least the universe could do for her before she was murdered, was make her killer slightly uncomfortable.

Bane ignored the rainstorm, approaching them with a fiendish delight until those raindrops turned to snowfall. Avalon pressed closer against Hob, that ice blade in Bane's hand filling her vision with terrifying focus.

Snowflakes collected on her lashes, melting and partially obscuring her vision. Blinking them away, Avalon saw past Bane and caught that fantastic silver armor, now marked with swirls and splatters of a black, metallic liquid, emerging from the woods.

Elden was rage incarnate—frost and wind danced around him as he took large, silent steps toward his brother. That double-bladed axe was in his hand, and his next steps were fast— the movements of a trained killer.

A glint of silver caught the fading moonlight. A wet, upsetting sound as something splashed upon the ground, upon her face. It took some time for her brain to admit what it had witnessed, a half-hearted attempt to protect her. To give her time to look away. But she did not.

Elden swung that axe down on his brother's shoulder, the leather armor Bane wore the only thing preventing his torso from being split in two.

CHAPTER 21
ELDEN

One swing and Elden was, once again, the villain in her story. Captor, kidnapper, executioner. A list Avalon could add to at length, he supposed, and far less polite in her description.

Elden would have *liked*, for his own moral code, to say that hacking through his brother had been difficult. But with a clean blade and such a practiced swing, it had been the easiest thing in the world.

And it had shut that bloody banshee up.

Bane, however, now shrieked instead. The force of Elden's swing had caused Bane to fall to his knees. He pushed at the axe embedded in his shoulder, wincing as he yanked his gloved hands away from the steaming metal. "It's hot! Why does it *burn*?" The brothers shared the same eyes, but Elden doubted his own had ever looked so cold, so dead. Bane sneered, "You would kill me for a half-human monster? With one of your mother's twisted experiments?"

"I'm going to kill you for a dog," Elden answered.

The axe was white hot, and Bane studied it with fear, but also interest. "*That's* where Ashling's been this whole time?" Bane asked, brow furrowed. "Of course. All those gifts your mother possessed, all that power, and she stuffed it all in a blade for her baby boy. As if you weren't spoiled enough."

How did Bane even *know* that his mother's power was missing? That it had never returned to her family? For now, Elden would ignore it. It was just another reason he needed to kill his brother.

Morally, Elden knew he was in the wrong. There were other options. He could report Bane to their father and let Taliesin sentence him. A century in the dungeon would be more than long enough to keep Avalon safe. Once she returned to her human shape, she'd be dead long before Bane was released. A prison of ice was not an easy one to escape.

Logically, though? Elden wanted to keep his promise to her, after failing once again to keep Avalon safe, and there was only one way to absolutely guarantee it.

He pushed down on the weapon, sinking it further into his brother's flesh. A headshot would have been cleaner. Not *cleaner*, but more efficient. But the thought of Avalon witnessing him do what came so naturally to him...

His mother had wanted him to be different. To be kinder than she had been, and to avoid the merciless warmongering that ran in their redcap blood.

It was hard to find that goodness now. All Elden could think was that hesitation was not a sign of moral superiority— it was a sign of weakness.

The war axe had been a gift from his late mother, forged with the last of her waning strength. A task he had begged her not to undertake while her body was failing.

You need something from me, she had said, that misplaced smile shining. *I let your father have too much of you when you were meant to be like me.*

His mother's anger and frustration at her weakened muscles, muscles that strained and struggled to hold her hammer, had been beaten into the metal. Elden scarcely cared to wield the wicked thing, though situations like this seemed to cause it to fall perfectly into his hands.

The blade appeared to absorb his brother's blood, the silver sheen turning a shade of rust. Bane grunted, lifting the axe blade up and out so he could escape. That idiot had made it so easy to find him, using their family magic like that. Elden had been able to home in on Bane's location instantly. Desperate, Elden had even abandoned the twins, leaving them to clean up the remains of that confusing battle at the feyrie mound.

He had to kill Bane. Bane would have tortured Avalon until he grew bored and then killed her. This thought alone stirred the embers of his fury.

Again! Again! The smoking axe screamed for more, and Elden was happy to oblige.

There was more to Bane than a lust for torture, though. Large shards of ice shot from the snowy ground, forming a triangular defense around Bane. Elden cursed, hacking at the ice until a snowstorm whipped around the barrier and blinded him. When the snow and wind cleared, Bane was gone.

He had forgotten Bane's magic, so like their sister's, allowed for such trickery. What else would he fail at? Elden did not want to turn around to face Avalon. But Hob's panting was growing faint, and they had little time. Little hope.

In the distance, against the blanket of white upon the ground, Elden spotted a few droplets of red. Hob scented the blood and struggled forward on his belly, ready to resume the hunt. Elden raised a hand. "*No, no, no.* Stay down."

Elden finally forced himself to observe Avalon. Watched as her attention was slowly pulled from Bane's sudden disappearance and up to him.

Her face, mostly her jaw, was mottled with purple and brown bruises. And she was *shivering*, freezing in only a hoodie. She hadn't been prepared to be out here—that was one point in her favor.

"Here." Elden unpinned the navy cloak from around his shoulders. His voice came out a little muffled as he fumbled with the clasp. "Will you take this?"

Her head twitched to one side, confused, as she watched him undo the cloak. She didn't respond, watching him and waiting.

Hmm. He'd expected something like this. Though she failed to mention it, Elden had suspected there was something off with her hearing. Sometimes she answered his questions as though she had guessed at some of the words. Elden paused until she looked at him, repeating louder, "I want you to take this. I don't need it."

"Okay..." Speaking was a visible effort for her. Adjusting the cloak around her shoulders, she grimaced, and said, "Is there an after-hours large animal doctor in town?"

"What." Asking for a doctor had been a possibility he considered, but one for *Avalon's* trauma.

"Hob needs a *vet*," she said, her tone quickly losing patience. Her chattering teeth beat out a desperate tempo. "He tried to save me from Bane. I'm sorry—I shouldn't have been out here."

Why *was* she out here? A question he honestly didn't care

to have answered, but he added it to the never-ending list, anyway.

Why was Avalon in the middle of the forest?

What had attacked the mound?

Where had that banshee come from? There wasn't one listed in the guest book.

And, embarrassingly, *what would Avalon think of him now that she'd witnessed him try to commit fratricide?*

Elden knelt down, rubbing Hob's ears as the dog whined. He tugged off his scarf, the cold barely a discomfort, and placed it against Hob's wound.

She gave them a moment alone, before, "What do we do?"

"Not *we*," he corrected. "You're in no shape to help anybody." If he didn't need to keep applying pressure to Hob's wound, he would have taken her into his arms and carried her back home to personally care for her injuries. Whether she hated his touch or not, he would help her.

"Fuck you." Now *that* had been expected. Avalon stomped a foot into the icy ground in her fury. "I can help. I doubt Bane is going to be much of a threat with a wound like that."

Avalon was the Seer, not him, and yet Elden knew the outcome of this argument before it began.

But he had to at least try to dissuade her. "Something tried to attack the mound tonight, something other than Bane. Some...creature. The twins and I fought it off, but—"

"What kind of creature?" Her voice was shaking, and she turned away to spit out more free-flowing blood. "Do you mean the *banshee*?"

Interesting. She recognized that sound as well, despite her human upbringing. "No, I haven't found the banshee. But she gave us warning, whether she meant to or not. I'm grateful for that."

Avalon relaxed. "What am I looking out for?"

"They looked like snakes…" he trailed off. Those writhing arms had seemed like snakes, but that answer was too simple. A black mass of arms had attacked the mound's entrance, its origin unknown, and Elden, with the help of Tahoma and Kenan, had beaten it back until the tentacles retreated into the inn's lake. "I don't think it could make it this far." He couldn't think of what it could be. He hadn't encountered anything like it in his travels in the Unseelie lands.

"Then let me help."

The tools Bane had used on her teeth glinted in the moonlight. They were familiar, items Bane might have grabbed from Ashling's forge. The thought of Bane digging through his mother's things made his jaw clench.

Avalon waited on his answer. Was she in shock? She must be in so much pain, and yet, he knew she would not rest until Hob was safe.

As he studied her, Elden felt a vulnerability in his heart that heightened his wariness. It took him far too long to understand what it was.

No, he could not be feeling *that* for the one person who would never reciprocate. As small as the emotional flame was, the longing still bothered him. He was quite careful with his affections. It was illogical that Avalon, a half-feral woman he'd just met, could cause such want.

Was it because a changeling might understand how he lived? With one foot in the fey realm and one in the mortal one?

Elden relented, defeated, and worn out from searching with his magic for any more intruders. "Do you remember the way to Abernathy's farm?"

"Point me in the right direction," Avalon begged. "Bane made me get turned around but—" Elden raised a finger and she took off, her orange and pink halo of hair bobbing in the distance. That damned wisp appeared, emerging from her chest, and becoming a guiding light that Elden's gaze followed until they vanished.

Hob's magic sheen wavered, and his size returned to what they considered normal. Reaching Abernathy's farmhouse was no easy sprint. Elden's heartbeat quickened—the witches may not take kindly to a wild fey tearing into their territory, a will-o'-the-wisp alongside her. The siren would have put them on high alert, as well.

Avalon was too far from him for Elden to maintain her glamour. Not that glamours ever worked on the old man to begin with. She'd have to convince them to risk crossing their protective boundary, based all on a feyrie's word, to rescue an injured fey creature. She had performed a miracle on Maetta, sure, but this was a fool's errand. And she was no orator.

Futile. All of it. As futile as trying to stop the winter storm that continued to rage around him. Sure, Elden and Abernathy's goals may have aligned from time to time. And the old man loved to tease him, had always picked at him, even when he was a boy and spent half the year in the human realm with his mother. But Abernathy had his own family to protect. Fey neighbors were something the witches lived with because they had no other option.

The soft cries his dog emitted tore at Elden. Snow, wind, and ice seemed like such useless magic when his best friend was dying. If Hob didn't make it through this, Elden didn't know what he was going to do.

Elden sat next to Hob for a long time, hollow and

incompetent, until twin beams of light temporarily blinded him, befuddling his Unseelie night-vision. Human technologies, like the damned high beams on Abernathy's farm quad, screwed with his heightened feyrie senses.

Abernathy hadn't ridden over alone. Abernathy's granddaughter, Maddox, was with him, the least annoying one in Elden's opinion, and was riding her own quad. Avalon had tagged along with Maddox and hopped off, running to check on Hob.

The dog's breath was faint and uneven, but Hob forced each lungful of air down and out despite the pain.

The farmer wasted no time. "I'm going to need you to ease up on your protections, elf. I'm about to use some serious magic."

Too exhausted to ask for clarification, Elden shut his eyes, straining to alleviate the wards around the inn. Earlier in the evening he had strengthened them, and it went against his instinct to oppose them now.

Thrusting both of his hands into the earth, Abernathy muttered some chants while his granddaughter placed a hand on his shoulder for support. The ground groaned underneath them: thick, dark roots emerged from the dirt to wrap around the fading dog. Elden tensed, letting Hob go when Avalon softly touched his back and guided him away. Hob kicked and whined as the roots covered him until he was no longer visible.

That tricky old man, Elden thought. Abernathy had sworn that the roots of his family's witch tree did not extend to his property. Clearly, with the speed that the roots had arrived, that had been a lie.

To his granddaughter, Abernathy barked, "Maddox, he'll arrive at the greenhouse. Go prepare the rest of your sisters. I'm going to need everyone to be available for this."

Abernathy's family shared their power, the majority of it resting in their patriarch (or matriarch as it had been the case with the previous generation). If he needed every single witch in the family to aid him, things were certainly looking dire for Hob.

"Meet us at the greenhouse when you can." Abernathy glared up at the sky and the snow falling in large, fast clumps. "This weather better not affect *our* land, elf." Abernathy got back on his quad and rode away, sparing Elden a sympathetic glance that was unexpected.

After Abernathy's exit, Avalon's eyes danced between Elden and out between the trees. Was she searching for something or simply on the lookout? She settled on him long enough to ask, "What the hell happened tonight?"

By now, Elden's powers had run rampant long enough to leave an inch of snow upon the ground. He hated to admit this. "The mound was almost opened. Something was trying to force its way inside."

"Bane said you were too busy to come for me. He made it seem like this was planned, and he was taking advantage of the chaos," Avalon said. Elden knew why she mentioned that bit, even though he had heard it as well. Avalon wanted to make it very, very clear that this breach was something that had been planned on the *other* side of the mound.

It was cute that she still thought Elden considered her a threat.

The situation was bizarre. While Avalon waited, Elden reviewed the little security camera footage available through an app on his phone. Bane seemed to have been the only visible figure around the fey entrance. And once those snakes, or whatever they were, had attacked the mound's doorway, nearly tearing it open, they had curled around the nearest security cameras and crushed them.

What had been Bane's goal here? As far as Elden was aware, while Bane did not like to use the PNW entrance, the other feyrie mounds let him in and out without issue. Why would he need to try opening this particular entrance?

And were Bane and those snakes somehow connected? It was not magic Elden thought Bane possessed.

Elden asked, "What *are* you doing out here?"

Avalon's answer came quickly, something she must have prepared in advance. "Odele gets night terrors. When I went to check on her, she was missing from her cabin."

The snow continued to fall, a beautiful, sparkling death sentence. "We need to find her." As much as he wanted to be with his dog, Odele wouldn't last long in this weather. He had invoked the spirit of Winter, and this was not something that could be undone.

He looked at her, about to start talking strategy, *you go this way, I'll go that way*, and this time he truly saw her.

She had run over a mile in the frozen night. The wisp hovered over her shoulder, but that small heat would have done little against the impending storm he had wrought upon the inn. There was no trivializing her wounds—Bane had hit and bruised and scratched wherever he could.

Avalon needed rest. Warmth. Not to go winding through the wood on a manhunt.

Elden was not looking forward to telling her so. "Tahoma and Kenan are out, looking for any possible intruders that we may not have picked up on the security footage. I'll tell them to adjust and start searching for Odele."

"Good. The more, the merrier."

"But," and here was the danger, "we need to get you out of the snow. You can wait at my home until we locate Odele."

"Go—"

"Screw myself?"

"That's the PG-13 version, yes." Avalon adopted a fierce, wide stance that Elden was already far too familiar with. The *I'm-about-to-get-my-way-or-do-great-and-terrible-harm-upon-you* stance. "How do *you* think this is going to go?"

"Everything with you goes poorly, Avalon. That's no surprise." This wasn't something he could compromise on. "You're going to freeze. There's an office back at my house where you can flip through our live security feed. If Odele *is* still wandering about, that's the only way I'll let you search for her."

There was a long, *long* silence. One where Avalon was clearly cursing him, silently, and gauging her ability to outrun him.

"Fine." She wasn't pleased. But perhaps she had finally calculated the height difference between her legs and his own. Avalon wouldn't be beating him in a sprint or a marathon, with or without his armor weighing him down.

Once they made it out of the woods and inside his house, Elden ushered Avalon into a tiny room where a few monitors had been set up. "I can't believe," she said, using the mouse to flip through different black and white camera views, "that you didn't even have a computer for the inn, but *this* was sitting here the entire time."

"Tahoma had it installed." The security feed was on a local network and no one else, not even the Commission, had access to it.

Avalon had made it through each camera feed and started

her loop again. Without glancing away from the screen for a second, she said to him, "Go check on Hob. I'll be fine in here. But if you lock me in, I'll burn this place to the ground."

She didn't seem to mind Elden's silences; the spaces left empty after her joking and prodding. Avalon spun around, meeting his eyes for a second before she returned to tracking down her sister.

"Hob will be okay," she promised.

And she couldn't lie.

Before Elden exited the house, he turned up the heat and called Tahoma to update her about the situation. The twins quickly changed directions, one searching for Odele and the other verifying that Bane had fully left the grounds.

His brother had been a monster, even for feyrie standards, but there was a right way to handle these things. If he wanted to keep the moral high ground against his sociopathic family, he needed to tell the rest of his family that Bane was wounded and on the run.

Bane could die out there tonight.

It was unnerving to think of a feyrie in the past tense, considering their lifespans. It brought back memories best laid to rest, memories of his mother. Her dark hair thinning and pale, her voice hushing itself until she could scarcely be heard.

Abernathy's farm was lit up, every light in the house bright and yellow. Even the string lights the witches hung early in preparation for Yule were on, twinkling, a bright background for a grim situation.

Elden found the farm's greenhouse with the aid of one of

the younger grandchildren, a small boy in footie pajamas. The boy ignored Elden's thanks and stumbled to his grandfather, climbing onto a lounge chair that must have been dragged into the greenhouse for Abernathy. The old witch was sunk in the armchair, snoring lightly. Hob rested at his feet, his breathing a slow but steady rhythm. That one-eyed raven stared at Elden from its perch on the old man's shoulder.

Every single plant in the glass greenhouse was dead. Drained. A dust bowl level of famine.

Abernathy stirred, awakened by the young child's babbling. Those cunning eyes narrowed at Elden's presence before they relaxed into a tired, shit-eating grin. "He's going to be okay. The family was just able to pull this off."

Elden cut a glance at the decaying potted life around them. "This must have cost you a great deal," he frowned. Abernathy had gone to far greater lengths to save Hob's life than he had expected.

"A good dog is worth all this many times over."

The old man said this easily, as if that was that and there would be no strings attached. Elden even got the feeling that if he offered monetary repayment, Abernathy would only get pissed.

Generations of Abernathys shared this land, something Elden had always been jealous of. He had spent the summers and falls here, as a child, staring over at the bustling farm over the boundary. Everything was shared, everything given without cost. Elden had watched the Abernathys and understood, for a second, why his mother risked everything to live with the humans full-time.

"Let the dog rest here," Abernathy cautioned. "That amount of magic, and unfamiliar magic at that, would take a toll on anyone."

It was hard for Elden to speak, the silence forming a pit in his chest. He wanted to respond, to show the proper gratitude, but years of watching his words, guarding his intentions, left him mute. It was so easy, being the only redcap in a family of orators, to fall prey to a bargain through a simple *"thank you"*.

"It's okay, son. Go get some rest."

The endearment unsettled Elden's stomach. He would have preferred that the old man called him "elf".

CHAPTER 22
AVALON

Elden was going to discover the truth. And there was not a single thing Avalon could do about it.

Odele was found wandering the moor by Tahoma, while a *banshee* was on the loose. It would be all too easy to connect the dots. Maybe the warden already had.

If that was the case, then Odele would be trapped here for observation, too.

Avalon watched Tahoma bring her sister to Lyra's cabin while she hid in Elden's front window. She kept the lights off to avoid being seen. Lyra would take care of Odele, though the nymph had admitted earlier that her healing skills were relatively unpracticed.

Elden stood by as Avalon peered outside. "She shouldn't see you like this, Avalon."

Being unable to care for her younger sister made her grind her teeth. And then fight back tears from the resulting pain. To distract herself, Avalon demanded, "Why can't she see me? Do

I not look pretty?"

Elden made a rather strange sound in answer and then walked away.

Announcing that Odele was asleep, Lyra stopped by to check on Avalon (and cook more food than anyone could possibly eat) when there was an outraged *thumping* against the main door.

Elden answered the knocking, motioning for Avalon to remain out of sight.

Odele's voice was cracking, damaged from a night full of warnings. "Get out of my way! I *know* Avalon is in there, and I *am* going to see her!"

This. Would. End. Poorly. But Odele's voice was a comfort she craved and so Avalon stayed out of sight, retreating further into the house. She leaned against a wall for support near enough to hear her sister call Elden an overgrown twit.

Odele's recovered quickly, despite the night's violence. Avalon relaxed into her relief.

Lyra's thumb hovered around her mouth, the struggle she was having to keep herself from biting her nails evident. "We need to get Nora Lee."

It wasn't hard to guess why Lyra wanted to get a human involved. Avalon asked bitterly, "So she can *lie* to my *sister?*"

The chef's eyes flashed, hurt. "I couldn't tell the truth to Odele even if I *wanted* to. Not with the inn's magic preventing me from doing so. The warden has to make that call." Lyra tapped hurriedly onto her phone, texting Nora Lee no doubt. Another futile attempt to rescue a doomed situation.

"Why can't Elden *glamour* my bruises away?" That solution had a much higher success rate in her mind. Convincing Odele to *wait* to see her *sister*, who Elden explained had gotten hurt while searching the woods for Odele, was an awful plan.

"Have you looked outside?" Lyra remained zoned in on her phone. Avalon glanced through the window the nymph had pointed to and found there was a foot of snow on the ground. "Elden's powers are drained. He can't even maintain your *usual* glamour right now. And, honestly, casting a glamour on another fey is difficult and not something he's particularly skilled at." The nymph chewed her lower lip. "Glamours on another are beyond me. It's more an Unseelie skill."

Back in the foyer, Elden's control of the conversation—not that he ever really possessed it at all—was slipping. "Odele, your sister needs to *rest*. She should be asleep. It's better if you see her later." The man couldn't even convince himself. The half-truths in his words were all too apparent.

There came a pause, the emptiness swelling throughout the entire house. Avalon shook her head, fearful that her tinnitus and hearing loss had caused her to miss something. Finally, Odele, in a monotone, said, "Okay."

Oh, shit. Avalon knew what *that* meant.

"Okay?" Elden's repetition was mistakenly hopeful.

"Yes, I'll come back in the morning." Avalon recognized that tone, that false surrender. Odele normally reserved it for their parents.

When he returned, Elden was foolishly optimistic. Perhaps it was the sleep deprivation. How else could he miss something so obvious? "She's going to return in the morning. That gives us a *little* time to at least heal the surface damage."

Avalon didn't need to use her powers to predict what would happen next. "You might want to step away from that window."

The rock that came crashing through the glass had

"welcome home" painted on it. In purple. With rhinestones.

Odele came climbing through after it, broken glass slicing a wicked gash down her forearm.

Ever the gentlemen, Elden helped Odele manage the window. Once through, Odele shoved him aside, shouting hoarsely, "Avalon!"

Elden's magic tingled weakly over Avalon's body, another poor attempt at a glamour. A glance at a wall full of artfully arranged, ornamental mirrors let her know he had managed to round out her ears...and nothing else. She could keep her mouth shut to hide her teeth, but the rest of it...

At her sister's beckoning, Avalon abandoned her perch against the wall, stepping into the light of the foyer Odele had bullied her way into. Odele's rage was a tangible thing, if Avalon would have opened her mouth she would have been able to swallow it and let the fury settle uneasily in her stomach.

Avalon's face was still visibly swollen, her missing teeth the culprit. If there was any further bruising or lacerations, Avalon was blissfully unaware of them, full of painkillers as she was. Odele's gaze flickered over her wounds, eyes almost bulging, though this must have been exactly what she had expected.

"*We are leaving.*" Odele stomped to her, slipping Avalon's arm over her shoulder despite her sister's weak protests. "And *you* had your chance to speak. Get out of my way."

Elden stood his ground, blocking the doorway and exchanging glances with Lyra. Was he trying to buy time until Nora Lee arrived? To let her spin some lie Odele would never believe?

Because Odele already knew.

Odele must have dreamt of Avalon's near-death experience. It would explain why she was out sleepwalking, searching for

Avalon even in her unconscious, foggy state.

Tahoma and Kenan appeared, entering from some side door Avalon had been unaware of. Had they found Bane? Or was he still out there, waiting for her?

Odele saw the twins for what they were—*a threat.* "I'll ask nicely *once*, Elden. Get away from the door and let us pass."

He was a braver man than Avalon. Elden gritted his teeth, planting himself firmly in their way. "Not with Avalon. She has to stay."

His words were not well received.

Odele had always been the stronger one, as much as Avalon tried to live in self-denial. The banshee's fey side was too close to the surface, too wild, unpredictable. It was surprising that Avalon had been the one to revert to their roots and not the other way around.

"You're going to wish you had that axe now," Odele seethed. Elden took a step back, confusion flooding his expression as he tried to make sense of her words and failed.

Pressed together as they were, she felt Odele's power build, a fire that had been given way too much fuel. There was no time to warn the others, Avalon could barely slap her hands over her own ears before Odele happened.

For twenty-four years Odele had never once let her powers reach their full potential. It had gotten close, *far too close*, when they had accidentally accepted a contract in the territory of a serial killer. But even then Odele had fought against her own powers as hard as she could, the effort damaging her vocal cords nearly beyond repair.

The sound now forced Avalon to her knees, and she had anticipated it. This was not *wailing*, not a drawn-out warning, or a pathetic cry for help. *This was an attack.*

Odele alone remained on her feet. The fey around her had met the floor quite quickly, covering their ears against the onslaught. From experience, Avalon knew their damage control came too late. She was glad that Hob had been left with the Abernathy's. She hated to think what Odele's sound waves could do to an animal with more delicate hearing.

The banshee inhaled, taking a brief pause to survey her work. Lyra was curled up on the floor while the twins were struggling to stand, the discombobulation fighting them every step of the way. But it wasn't until Elden halfway rose, his fingers grasping at Avalon's pant leg, that Odele assailed him once more.

This time, every nearby piece of glass in the house shattered.

A vengeful wraith, Odele's vintage gown whipped around her legs, her pale hair lifting from static. She held that striking note until her voice grew hoarse and everyone else in the house was curled up on the floor, hands pressed against their ears.

With Avalon in tow, Odele kicked Elden's outstretched hand away from her sister. Odele stepped over his body and supported Avalon while they left Elden's home and marched back to the inn's parking lot.

"Odele," Avalon whispered while she stumbled to keep pace. "I can't leave."

"*Shut up.* I understand now. Well, I understand enough." Odele's head swung back and forth, inspecting the forest. "You tried to warn me. I don't know why you couldn't *tell* me what the danger was, but it doesn't matter. We're getting out of here."

Even getting into their tiny car was an effort. Avalon let Odele buckle her in. She had so little strength left, unable to put into words why leaving was a bad idea. The hike back to the car had drained what defiance remained. Now all she could do was slump into the passenger seat, her eyelids fluttering.

As Odele reversed, barely checking her mirrors, Avalon thought she spotted Elden's unmistakable form racing down the path they had taken.

They passed Nora Lee's bright bicycle on their way out, the early morning light illuminating the woman waving them down while Odele raised her middle finger in answer.

They drove down the inn's driveway in silence, Odele's grip on the steering wheel sure and unrelenting. The radio stayed off, and Avalon could only be thankful. Her head was still ringing from Odele's brutal shriek.

She hated to imagine how the others were faring.

"Who *was* that man? The one Elden tried to chop to pieces." Odele swallowed. "The one that attacked you and the wolf."

Odele had seen *everything*, then. There was no use trying to answer her questions now. Avalon still felt the compulsion to keep the inn's secrets. "Keep driving."

"Avalon—"

"*You have to keep—*" The car lurched forward, and Avalon's head sunk further back into her seat. Odele pressed down on the gas pedal until their aging car protested with a few sounds Avalon was not looking forward to mimicking for a mechanic.

The frantic pull of Elden's magic was fading. She prepared herself to tell the truth, to reveal secrets she had unwillingly promised to keep, but there was no need.

"What is happening to your *ears*?" Odele drove a few more yards before she whipped the car off to the roadside. "Avalon!"

The glamour must have reached its limit. Wordlessly, Avalon reclined her seat back, sighing, and revealing to Odele a shortened version of the past few weeks. When Avalon finished, she had hoped she would have felt some sort of relief, a lightening. All she could find was exhaustion.

Brimming with tears, Odele rasped, her voice barely usable after her display of power, "You couldn't tell me *any* of this?"

"No. There's some sort of spell that prevents talking about the feyries here while on the grounds. And I couldn't sneak us away to tell you because I was being watched. And," she motioned to her face, all angles and sharp ears, "partly because of this. Elden cast a glamour over me to hide it, to appear human. I have to rely on him to hide me until I can change back." Her own attempts at glamours were pitiful. Elden had her practice making an apple appear as an orange and somehow she ended up with a lemon.

"I guess you haven't mastered that skill yet, have you?" Odele groaned and softly beat her head down on the steering wheel. "What are we going to do? If you get caught out like that, Dad—*Bruce* will lose his mind."

"I don't know, Odele." It wasn't often she could admit that to herself, let alone to her little sister. "But we cannot ask *them* for help." The thought of seeing their "parents" like this, like the fey she was, made Avalon want to throw up.

The rumbling startled them, another presence entering the empty gravel road they had parked on. There was no mistaking that great white truck. Elden had found them.

Frantic, Odele tried to get the car out of park and peel off. Avalon stopped her with a hand on her knee. "Wait."

"Wait?" Odele swatted her away, but Avalon had stepped out before Odele could make their escape.

Elden's truck slowed, parking behind them. He waited inside the truck, watching, until Odele stepped out to join her sister.

Had he actually taken the time to discard his armor? Was it to make him appear less threatening? Elden walked over, each step carefully precise, like he didn't want to spook them. He wore a green canvas jacket and dark pants. Normal clothing, safe clothing.

"Make this quick," Odele commanded. "You're the one dressed for the weather."

They all stared at each other for a few awkward minutes. The least impressive showdown in western history. Two half-dressed changelings versus one giant fey prince.

His voice was too loud, the timber of someone who had returned from a concert where they had neglected to remember hearing protection. "I want you both to come back."

Avalon quirked her head at him. That hadn't been a demand, his preferred form of communication with her. Elden sounded...hurt? No, that wasn't exactly right. Concerned? Afraid? Desperate? She decided to leave it at that. It was tiring enough understanding her own warring emotional depths.

"Burn in hell," Odele scoffed, making Avalon flinch. She didn't like what this had brought out in her sister. Not that she meant Odele's newfound strength...it was this *callousness*. Avalon had never wanted that for her.

"Avalon must have told you what she's been going through." Elden paused until Avalon gave a short nod. He didn't look upset that she had spilled the inn's secrets. He wanted to correctly assess the new circumstances.

Odele stalked up to him, her chin raised and back tall. There was little height difference between them. "You threatened her with *what* evidence? You silenced her. Isolated her from me. Through your negligence, your own family attacked her not once, but twice. I had to crawl through earth and mud, panicking every time I touched something cold and wet because it might have been my sister's battered body."

Elden took it all, unblinking. He replied, "She was meant to be safe."

"She wasn't. She was never safe with you."

"Odd," Avalon whispered. "I can't go back to Bruce and Valerie like this. I-I don't think I could take it. Throwing it in their face, what we are...what we have done to them."

"You two didn't do anything."

Odele snapped at Elden, "Shut up. She knows that." She searched Avalon's eyes, frowning. "You *know* that wasn't our fault."

Logically, yes, of course she knew that. She had told Odele the same thing over and over, huddled together at night when the guilt began to eat away at them. But...

"You damned fey couldn't have let me have my children?"

Valerie, as terrible of a mother as she was...was still a mother. And in one night she had lost her children, *both of them*, for good.

Odele presented another solution. "Okay, so we don't go directly to our parents. We can still figure this out. *Without him.*"

The discussion went downhill from there. Odele was open to any option—even going to their estranged parents—that would take them far, *far* away from the Refuge on the Moor and all of its inhabitants. Avalon didn't know if Elden was remaining silent because he was being polite...or if he was afraid of Odele attacking him again.

The holes in Odele's plans were large and plentiful. Avalon argued, "We'll lose our jobs."

"I'm sure we can bully Thompson into hiring us again, after we figure out how to change you back," Odele promised. "You could learn to glamour."

"The glamours don't work on everybody. And I've been trying that, too, and failing." Avalon wiped at her eyes, her deficiencies too much to take. Avalon was no closer to transforming back than she had been the first time she tried it. "We can't take that much time off work, either." They couldn't afford to skip that many paychecks. They owed a debt, and a pause in repayment wasn't something they could risk.

Gods, if they couldn't pay, Bruce might make them work on his reelection campaign. It was insane that Washington state had no term limits for the governor.

"We cannot miss paying those medical bills, Odd." It was a harsh truth, one that made Odele flush. But Odele's guilt over a few bills was wrong and unwarranted. Avalon never blamed Odele for their financial situation. Vocal cord repair was something that Avalon had been acutely aware of, had even started a fund for. Odele, in her human state, hurt herself badly every time her banshee powers flared.

Tonight might have done more damage, damage a surgeon might not be able to undo. Avalon listened for any rasp to Odele's voice, a breathy attribute that would signal injury.

"I can't let you go back with him." Odele remained firm, though the mention of their bills had thrown her. "Not after all that's happened. Not after what I watched that *feyrie* do to you."

"And I can't go back to Bruce."

"You were begging me to leave weeks ago! What the hell

changed?" Odele hugged herself, shivering. She scowled at Elden when he offered her his jacket.

"Just take the damn jacket," Avalon returned, her temper rising alongside her sister's.

"Just get in the damn car!"

"No."

"No?" Odele's voice broke. "That isn't logical, and that isn't you!"

The cracking in Odele's raised voice broke her. Avalon cried, "Dad told me if there was ever a chance we'd be found out to be changelings, he'd send us back." Tears slid down her face, hot in contrast to the winter winds. Crying wasn't as embarrassing as calling Bruce "Dad". "He swore he'd make sure we were taken to *separate* feyrie mounds with *nothing*. I can't let that happen, Odele. I won't survive it."

And, for the first time, their two-man team had split. Avalon stormed over to Elden's truck, climbing up into the passenger seat. Her side of the argument was over. She'd rather face Bane a thousand times over than show up on the Golightly doorstep looking like the changeling she was.

I ruined everything. I can't repeat that. Can't endure it.

She should have said those things to Odele, but was too cowardly. It was one thing to inwardly know she had torn up their dysfunctional family beyond repair. It was another to hear it confirmed from the only person she loved.

Odele pulled at her hair before she threw herself back into the car. After Elden peeled out in his truck and headed back to the inn, the small car stayed motionless for a few too long minutes before Odele followed them.

True to his character, Elden didn't utter a word during the drive back. Avalon had half-expected him to interrogate her, not give her the proper space she needed.

How infuriating.

Avalon wasn't a chatty person. But there were exceptions. Sure, Odele was following them back—that didn't mean anything. It could have gone either way back there. And that thought was surely going to eat at her the next time she tried to sleep.

Twice she almost spilled her guts to him. It felt easier than it should have.

Elden parked right in front of the inn and shut off the engine. He cut off Avalon's third attempt to speak before it could begin. "I'll tell everyone to leave you two alone for a while." Elden stayed behind in the truck as Avalon dropped herself to the ground. "There's plenty for us to do, anyway. With the security breach and Bane and—"

She asked loudly, aware of the damage his eardrums had suffered earlier, "Did Hob make it?"

His irritation at being interrupted was over in an instant. Elden nodded quickly. "Abernathy ruined an entire greenhouse to do it, but Hob is going to be fine. I'm going to pick him up tomorrow." He fiddled with his rearview mirror; a motion that had to be useless as Avalon sincerely doubted he let anyone else sit in the driver seat of his precious, hand-me-down truck. "You could come with," Elden offered. "To see him."

"Okay," she accepted the offer, seeing it for the olive branch it was. It was pointless, though. Even if he and Avalon became besties, now there was Odele to deal with. And while Avalon's temper flared white hot and faded quickly, usually because she had discovered a new thing to be furious about, Odele was quite the opposite. The banshee was generally quite a happy person, so when her anger finally manifested, it was there to stay.

She was afraid to ask. Bile crawled up her throat as Avalon inquired, "Did you find Bane?"

"No, we did not. He bled quite heavily, though. We can hope—"

"I don't think I can 'hope' right now."

Odele slowly drove past them in her car, glaring at Elden through the driver's side window on her way to the gravel parking lot. Elden told Avalon, "The glamours won't work on her now. You might want to catch up with her to avoid any scares."

Yeah, she was certain Odele wouldn't appreciate running into any of the fey guests on her own. Especially the boggart in room thirteen. "You know why I couldn't tell you what she is, don't you?"

"Of course." He replied as if it was insane that it had to be answered aloud. "I behaved boorishly toward you when I pulled you out of the feylands. So, I know *precisely* why you kept Odele's nature a secret after I threatened you. My ears don't appreciate the secrecy, but the rest of me understands it."

Somehow, she had suspected that Elden, whose logic was as cold and twisted as her own, would understand.

"Can I ask..." He paused until she told him to go on. "You are *both* changelings? *And* you were born on different dates?"

"It's hard to believe that one family could be stolen from twice, right?" She shared that disbelief. "As to why they chose the Golightly's both times...your guess is as good as mine."

"Desperation rarely can be explained."

That would have to be good enough. She had no desire to continue a pointless conversation that would have no happy ending. Avalon waved goodbye after hopping down from the truck, the gesture awkward and feeling even more so when the Winterland prince, just as uncomfortable, waved back.

Odele refused to look at her when Avalon caught up to her. She let Avalon trail behind her as she pushed her way into the inn's hospitality closet and grabbed herself some toiletries. She then led them up to Whimsy, locking them inside.

"We have a lot to talk about," Odele scowled. "But I crawled through snow and mud and stinking, fey blood looking for you. I get the shower first."

Avalon presented no argument, undressing and waiting for Odele while making use of the fluffy inn robes. Her sister reluctantly allowed her to clean up as well. Avalon rushed into the bathroom, climbing, once clean, into the bed that was not at all large enough to hold both of them.

"We shouldn't be here." Odele yanked the covers further over to her side of the bed. "It isn't safe."

"I'd rather die here than live and get thrown at separate ends of the feylands."

"Avalon, you'd kill anything in your way until you found me."

Odele sounded so sure. After finding herself underneath Bane, helpless and in such pain, Avalon knew otherwise. *She believes in me like a child believes in St. Nick.* The hateful thought formed, and Avalon squelched it back down, ashamed.

Odele remained oblivious to her sister's poisoned inner workings, and the blankets moved westward once again. She vowed, "If we get murdered by feyries, we get murdered together."

Avalon poked Odele to make sure she was listening. "Despite what happened tonight, I don't want you to lose your new friends. Lyra, Tahoma, and Kenan...all seem relatively harmless." The twins could be deadly, but they had been born in the human realm. That meant something.

"I see you left someone out."

Even if Elden had rescued her from his brother, Avalon doubted she could convince Odele that the man meant well. At least not now. "He's a thousand feet tall. Of course, he's capable of doing harm."

"Didn't stop you from jumping into his truck, did it?" One last tug and Odele was completely cocooned in the quilt. Her voice turned low with exhaustion. "That man could have selfish reasons for keeping you here, Avalon. If I have to take over being the paranoid one and break you out of whatever feyrie spell he has you under, so be it."

Avalon wasn't even annoyed that her feet were now uncovered. In fact, she didn't feel much of anything.

Some far away portion of her brain was screaming how illogical staying at the Refuge was. But the numbness that was swelling throughout the rest of her body washed those worries away. She tensed and untensed her muscles, trying to restore feeling to her body. Nothing helped. That pain, that *taking*, had caused something in her body to switch off. In a desperate act of survival, her own mind had destroyed itself to prevent feeling that pain.

And even now, when she was as safe as she could be, that deadening of her psyche had lingered.

Avalon had not chosen the safest option—which was unlike her. Instead, she was giving Elden another chance.

It didn't bother her that she had watched Elden try to kill his own brother. It bothered her that he did not succeed.

Now if only she could undo this unwanted serenity and return fully to herself. In more ways than one.

CHAPTER 23
AVALON

Avalon slept until late afternoon, while Odele had awoken earlier and grabbed them a shitty breakfast from the coffee shop in town. Avalon crumbled her muffin and threw it away. There was no way she'd be able to eat anything solid after what Bane had done to her.

Maetta accepted, through a phone call, that they would hold off on wedding planning for today. The breach in security hadn't been something that could be kept quiet. Avalon could see on her phone, as she was logged into the Refuge's new reservation system she had installed, that a few couples had checked out early. It was hard to blame them. Sirens in the middle of the night were not included in the brochure.

The fey wedding guests were due to arrive that morning, but Elden pushed it off until tomorrow night, using the promise of an all-inclusive cocktail party to appease any frustration.

Avalon preferred not knowing how much it cost to provide alcohol for that many fey.

With a room as small as Whimsy, Avalon easily convinced Odele that they needed to stretch their legs. She led Odele to the wedding arch at the lake, wanting to check on the landscaping before the judgmental Seelie laid their eyes on it.

Their walk was accompanied by Hob, who attached himself to Avalon's leg as her own personal guard. She avoided the mound as best as she could, glimpsing its vague shape through the impeccably trimmed hedges and huge rhododendron bushes. Landscaping was not really something the inn needed help with. But, with the Seelie's expertise in the nature department, she was sure they would find something to complain about.

Past the gardens, the lighted stone path continued and took a short-lived jaunt through the woods before Avalon came upon the lake. Approaching it in awe, the sisters admired the Monet-esque lily pads and lilies until the abrupt sight of something black and wriggling entering the water shook them out of their wondering. Hob rushed to the shore, his sharp barks ringing Avalon's ears.

Odele jumped back. "Was that a *snake?*"

"It could be some weird sort of feyrie," Avalon guessed, readjusting their hiking path.

Taking a wide berth around the water, the trio explored the shores from afar, tripping over three dark roots Avalon swore hadn't been there before she put her foot down, until she found what she had been looking for—where the weddings were held. Elden had brought Avalon there the night the chupacabra attacked, but it was difficult to find it again on her own.

The lake made for an elegant backdrop, so dazzling that even Avalon, who gave little thought to her own future wedding, had a split-second where she envisioned herself in a lacy, white gown.

She shook that horrific image away, finding herself whistling to Hob to call him off the frog he was hunting, and followed the path back toward the inn.

In the middle of convincing Odele to order room service for dinner, there was a rapping on the door. Avalon rose to answer before Odele shoved her backwards onto the bed. Avalon fought with the tangled mess Odele had reduced their blankets to while her sister answered the door.

"What the hell do you want?"

Well, clearly she was speaking to Elden. Odele would be cross with her if she intervened, so Avalon remained where she sat. Finally, after a few more veiled insults, and even more, less veiled ones, Odele returned.

"He's booked you a dentist appointment."

"Oh." Avalon dug around for her purse and shoes. Odele turned any room she was in into a disaster area. "I haven't said anything, but my mouth is *killing* me. Am I allowed to go?" It wasn't an exaggeration. Simply speaking almost brought her to tears.

Odele worried her lip, staring at Avalon's mottled face. "I would go with you, but he said his dumb, stupid truck seats two."

"That's *exactly* what he said?"

"Exactly."

"I don't know what Dr. Lim will be able to do for you," Elden admitted during the drive over to the dentist. "But we can get some painkillers and make sure it's not going to become infected."

"I'm sure whatever it is, it won't be covered by insurance."

"Send me the bill," Elden demanded, quite serious. He spoke over any protest. "Or I'll wire you an amount of my choosing that will be grossly inaccurate."

She tapped on her front teeth and paled. "Wait...glamours can only hide so much. He's going to notice it's like *Jaws* in here once he starts poking around."

He wasn't worried. "Dr. Lim's fey."

What an awful occupation for him to choose. "That leaves him open for a lot of tooth feyrie jokes."

"I'd refrain until he's finished the exam, at least."

Dr. Lim was a dryad, a Seelie who had been born in the human realm. He required that Elden remove the glamour from her, so his human assistants would be able to see what was going on.

It wasn't pretty. One of the dental assistants handed her a card with information on the nearest women's shelter.

The dentist gave her a normal pain prescription, along with a small, glowing vial of lime-green liquid. "I don't give this to the humans," Dr. Lim explained. "But it will speed up the healing process for you tenfold."

Avalon drank the potion greedily, already feeling the ache in her gums subsiding. Dr. Lim gave her a few more vials to take home and told her to schedule a follow-up appointment so he could replace the teeth she had lost. When Avalon returned to the waiting room, Elden let her know he was going to warm up the truck and wait for her outside.

Once he had departed, the woman manning the front desk leaned forward while Avalon finished up some paperwork. "We were," the receptionist began, whispering conspiratorially, "trying to figure out if he was your husband or your stalker. It's an even split."

What horrifying options they presented. "He's my employer," Avalon corrected.

"And he scheduled a *dental appointment* for you?"

Avalon's pen scribbled faster. It was time to end this conversation before it delved into deeper, less easily explained territory. She had been saved from having to describe to the dental assistants how two of teeth had been ripped out by some quick spell from Dr. Lim. But Elden hadn't replaced her magical disguise yet, and she felt exposed. Why didn't she bring a hat? It was winter, after all.

The waiting room was empty, save for one unassuming, thin man. He slunk in his seat, playing a game on his phone at full volume. Avalon hurriedly passed the clipboard across the counter. "That should be everything."

"Golightly?" The receptionist repeated the name thoughtfully, her pen tapping unhygienically at her mouth. "Golightly...where have I seen that name before?"

"Your voting ballot."

Avalon turned in time for the man, no longer slinking, to snap a picture of her with his phone. She startled, recovering quickly enough to make a grab for him while he ran past her for the exit. Catching the corner of his coat, she pulled hard enough to make him stumble before he slipped out of his coat entirely. It was an unexpected move, considering the weather, and it cost her the upper hand.

Flying outside after him, Avalon nearly slid on a patch of

ice, losing her ground. The man fumbled on his phone while he ran, which gave her time to catch up with him.

Her tackle wasn't pretty. She wrapped her arms around his waist and twisted, sending them both flying into the asphalt. They crash-landed in the middle of an empty street. The man scrambled with his phone until Avalon caught it with her foot, punting it into one of the brick buildings lining the street. As it sailed, she heard the horrifying sound of a message being successfully sent.

She sprinted over and retrieved the phone, swearing when she confirmed the worst. He had sent someone that bloody photo of her, bruised and disheveled—and very clearly fey.

Avalon spiked the phone on the ground and stomped on it until she could see its insides.

Useless, maybe, but therapeutic for sure.

Her attention wandered, ire and fury shadowing her features. Now she focused her anger on the correct target—the piece of shit who thought it was perfectly acceptable to take unwanted pictures of women.

Her feet left the ground. Elden's arms had snaked around her from behind, hooking under her arms and lifting her. She kicked like a toddler about to be put down for a nap.

"Avalon, stop." Elden spun around, still carrying her in that awkward way. "You'll kill that idiot."

"So? There aren't any witnesses." She squirmed, trying to escape his hold.

Elden sighed, "Murder is not the answer."

She slackened in his grip, her limbs numbing with dread. "He took my picture, Elden. Everyone is going to know what I am." Panic kept her from saying more. Coherent sentences were outside of her current abilities.

Now Elden paused, his grip tightening and pressing her back closer into his chest. He gently set her down before searching for the photographer.

The creep had made another run for it after picking up his broken phone. Elden conjured iron shackles around his ankles, with a chain attached that led straight to the warden. Elden heaved the man back to them like he was a fish on a line.

The man shouted, "Get this shit off me—"

Elden vanished the chains and, grabbing the man's shirt collar, lifted him to his feet. "*Tell me your name.*"

Avalon's blood turned cold. Elden didn't sound like himself—honestly, his normal voice was deep and a little too void of inflection. *Now*, there was a dangerous friendliness that didn't belong there.

"Lucas Stockton." Lucas frowned at his own admission, blinking.

"Lucas Stockton," Elden repeated. His countenance changed, the glamour slipping away to reveal the sharp cut ears, the unnatural angles, the *teeth*... Teeth that shone bright in his shark-like smile. "*I would like to make a deal with you.*" Silver threads spidered out from Elden's chest and crawled toward Lucas until they coiled around his throat. Avalon wasn't certain if the human could even see the magic noose choking him.

Even a sniveling exploiter like Lucas knew better than to accept a fey's bargain. "I don't want—"

"I didn't ask what *you* want. Like *you* didn't ask this woman if you could take her picture." Elden drew in closer, his voice melodic. "You are not a bad person, Lucas."

"I—"

"You weren't thinking about who you were hurting back there. You weren't thinking at all. But *now* you *think* you should do something to fix the hurt you caused. The choices you took from someone else."

"I—I..." He couldn't hold Avalon's gaze. "It was just a picture. I wasn't *hurting* anyone—"

Elden *tsked.* "The perpetrator doesn't get to decide if the victim was hurt, Lucas. *You know that.*" Avalon had witnessed this man try to kill his own brother, and yet, she'd never been more afraid of him until this exact moment. Elden sounded so much like a *feyrie.* Like the orator side of his gene code wasn't as useless as he claimed. Or as he wanted to believe. "Lucas Stockton, you will do *everything* in your mediocre power to ensure that photo does not make it to the public eye."

"I will." Lucas shook his head, the ensnarement fading. Had Elden lost him? A full, terrifying minute passed before Lucas, smacking his chapped lips, asked nervously, "What will you give me?"

It was a split-second flash, but Elden's eyes, the brutal victory she caught in them, terrified her.

"I'll give you a winter's breeze whenever you start to sweat."

Lucas's eyes narrowed. Such a gift was lost on someone like him. To Avalon, that sounded like having a permanent "cool side" of a pillow. In summer, in an over-crowded apartment building with no air conditioning, that was invaluable.

The man's taste was more material than ethereal. Elden presented a clenched fist to the man, opening it as a sapphire the size of an orange slowly appeared in his palm.

Elden pulled the stone away before Lucas could snatch it. "Ah, but you have to *promise* me, Lucas. *Swear that you will do as I ask. Swear on your life.*" Sickly sweet, Elden held out his other hand; open, steady, and waiting.

And after a moment's hesitation, Lucas took it.

The silver noose snapped fully into place, and the bargain was struck.

After Lucas left them, Elden said, disgust clear in his voice, "I did not want to do that."

Avalon swallowed, glancing down at her shoes. "I'm sorry..." The words trailed off as she was not sure what she wanted to apologize for first. "You shouldn't have *had* to do that."

He remained emotionless, unblinking. As if the bargain was decades in the past. A regrettable mess, but nothing more. "I said I did not *want* to do it. Not that I would take it back. It's my fault—I should have been with you in there."

She wanted to hold her curiosity back and failed. "What will happen if he can't hold up his end of the bargain?"

Elden's face was grim. "Something bad."

"Is that why..." It seemed silly to bring it up, after all that had happened between them. "Does this have something to do with you refusing to shake my hand when we first met in Seattle?"

He sighed, as if he'd been waiting for an opportunity to clear this up. "We were talking business. I could not risk taking your hand and accidentally striking a bargain." He helped her climb into his too-tall truck before she could remember to protest. "I've been involved in a life-or-death deal before, and not through my own choice. I would not subject anyone to that."

Yet Elden had crossed that moral—and legal—line for *her*. The thought, the implications that it held, was dizzying.

There was nothing to be done about the photograph. Perhaps the man had sent it to a friend, trying to share a bit of gossip about the governor's daughter. Elden's bargain with the man may help, but it could also have meant nothing. That picture could already be circulating before Lucas could do anything about it.

It didn't matter that *she* was numb to this disastrous situation...

Odele was going to lose it.

It was only a cocktail party. Granted, it was a last-minute one. Avalon found herself running all over the inn, setting up chairs and throwing on tablecloths where she could.

The party was being contained to the garden around the feyrie mound. Which, with the fall weather, had confused Avalon until Lyra explained that once the Seelie arrived, it would be more than warm enough.

Avalon moved from station to station around the circular garden; advising the bartending staff to limit drinks to a few signature cocktails to streamline the process, helping Lyra prep the hors d'oeuvres, and replacing a few of the strings of twinkling lights that had burnt out. She had barely noticed she was beginning to feel dizzy until Elden caught her arm, halting her spin-cycle.

"You need to slow down." He guided her to one of the ready tables and urged her to take a seat. "You're fighting through some strong painkillers, and you don't need to overexert yourself."

"You and Lyra are the ones that decided to throw a party with no preparation," Avalon scoffed, but did as he requested. Her head was foggy and now that she was resting, it was even harder to ignore.

"I apologize for that. I admit that I am grossly unaware of

the effort that goes into event planning. Or running an inn."
His eyes kept drifting to the mound—now that Avalon was fey,
she could see what the mound really was. Before she had seen a
small utility closet door. Now the feyrie entrance revealed a
large, iron circular gate that was set in the hillside. Black vines
twisted throughout the bars, so thick it was impossible to see
through them. On the vines grew dark blue flowers that were
beginning to open as night crept closer. Elden returned his attention to her. "I wish *you* could manage all of this. I'd gladly
give you the reins and stick to being the feyrie mound's warden
and nothing else."

She rolled her eyes. "Yeah, give me that mansion of yours,
and it's a deal."

Elden leaned forward; his brow drawn together. "Truly?
You can have it. Just know there is a dog door in the kitchen,
and Hob *will* enter as he pleases—Oh." He sat back, posture
tightening. "You were kidding."

"I thought you were kidding! And Elden, that's a *terrible*
bargain. What's gotten into you?" Avalon protested. "Do you
really want *me* hanging around here for the foreseeable future?
I can try to look ahead, but I'm sure we'll be at each other's
throats before Christmas." *Not that the holiday would mean a
thing to a fey.*

Her concerns didn't faze him at all. "I'm sure I'll deserve
whatever you throw at me. Still," Elden continued, momentarily squeezing the hand she had rested on the table. "Think on
it."

The man was certifiable. "I'll never convince Odele." It had
to be said. She needed to set him straight and forget this nonsense. "This morning she called you a *pile of shit even a dung
beetle would pass on.*"

"Yes. It's hard to forget something like that." A smile threatened to lift one corner of his mouth. "It seemed *very* unlike her. Are you sure those were Odele's words? They seemed...rehearsed."

Avalon backtracked. "She may have heard me say something sort of similar once, but—"

His laugh was so loud it startled her. It was cut short by one of the extra guards Elden had borrowed from his father. The Unseelie royal guard whispered something and led Elden back to the mound.

Odele was a ghost—pale, silent, and foreboding. She appeared out of seemingly nowhere and spun Avalon's chair away from the table to glare down at her. "Why was he laughing, Avalon? You shouldn't be entertaining the enemy!"

What would surely be a tedious discussion was able to be completely avoided.

The Winterland's entrance to the feylands was opening.

CHAPTER 24
AVALON

Elden stood before that circular gate with his hands raised before him. The feyrie mound remained unmoved, as if it didn't want to open, until sweat formed on the warden's brow. The iron gates slowly creaked open, the sound setting off the ringing in her ears. Avalon wished her unreliable light would make an appearance—it was eerie being exposed to the feylands through a dark tunnel. What was left of her humanity warned her that anything, *anything*, could come rushing out of that darkness.

She heard them first. The steady, discordant marching of two opposing sets of people. As her anxiety blossomed, the will-o'-the-wisp warmed her chest, a comforting heat against her ribcage.

Elden loomed large, weapon ready and wearing that full silver armor she'd almost grown accustomed to seeing him in. The axe he had used against Bane was nowhere to be seen. Instead, he had a short, single-blade axe. There shouldn't be anything to worry about, he had reminded the inn. These fey were arriving for a *wedding*, after all. For the joining of two of their most in-fluential families.

Ideally, Hob would be present. The dog could be heard all the way in the gardens, his howling echoing from Elden's home where he was currently contained for his own health. Avalon didn't envy Elden's throw pillows. Hob might be tempted to take out his fury at being locked in on the décor.

The Unseelie emerged first, a motley crew of redheads and other, darker colors. A few pale blonds dotted the crowd. The group favored clothes with rich burgundies, browns, and cop-pers. And all of them were armed with wicked looking weapons that gleamed with enchantment.

The forefront of the ensemble was led by a man who was as giant as Elden was, wearing a silver helm that came to a point between his eyes. The metal took on a suspicious red sheen. He alone was armored—the rest wore clothes better suited for a party. If the party was held during the Black Plague.

He approached Elden, removing the helm and shaking out a head of dark auburn hair. "Nephew," he smiled, those sharp teeth marking him as a redcap. "It's so good to *finally* meet you, now that your mother can't hide you away. You certainly take after her looks. Any other similarities you'd like to share?" There was accusation in his words.

Elden was normally stiff, but it was still apparent how tense he had become at his uncle's greeting. "Warden Evander of the Highland mound. Your presence was not announced."

"How formal, and you forget I control the main entrance to the Winterlands, kiddo." The modern nickname sounded wrong coming from a man wearing chain mail. "I have all the proper paperwork."

That condescending jab did nothing to shatter Elden's calm

demeanor. Elden checked and double, triple checked the man's work. He took so long that Evander's brows began to lower dangerously.

"Welcome to Refuge on the Moor," Elden said, his tone unreadable. "Maetta and Sabella thank you for celebrating with them."

"Thanks, I'm eager to see what Ashling built here." Evander's grin held promises—none of them good. "And what else she's been hiding besides her *heir*."

Avalon nearly jumped as Odele pinched her in the side. Avalon's eavesdropping on Elden's family drama was over with—Odele stole her attention as she dragged her as far from the feyrie entrance as possible.

"I didn't want to be here in the first place," Odele said, leading them toward the outdoor bar. "But I understand why we need to continue doing our jobs until we can get you back to yourself. I will, however, protest standing right in front of the portal to feyrie hell."

"Fine." No part of her could argue against that. In fact, Avalon was embarrassed that she hadn't considered the dangers first. She had been too concerned with watching Elden—to see how he handled such an onslaught of unfamiliar fey—to see the threat right in front of her.

With her inward chastising over with, Avalon foolishly went right back to watching her warden for any sign he needed someone to come to his rescue. Elden had been apprehensive about this wedding, dreading how exposed it would make the inn. But it was what, she had been told, his mother loved to do. Bring fey of all kinds together to celebrate and overlook their politics.

As the Seelie entered, bearing giant bouquets of flowers

and pitchers of wine, it became more and more apparent that whatever hosting skill Ashling may have possessed did not go to her son.

"I need to go do my job," Avalon told her sister sternly. She gently moved out from Odele's grasp, though she hated to abandon her sister when all manner of fey were wandering about.

Odele let her go, though she watched Avalon intently as they parted. Avalon passed by Nora Lee, a seasoned veteran of all this fey nonsense, and asked the human woman to stick close to Odele. Nora Lee agreed, floating off to join Odele and lead her to one of the many piles of teacakes Lyra had spent all morning baking.

As Avalon approached him, Elden offered her his left arm. The right one was currently occupied by his axe, which had yet to return to his belt. With everyone watching them, Avalon didn't hesitate to take his offer. Even if it seemed rather strange. But Elden was a fey who spent a lot of time among humans, living with one foot in the fey realm and one in the human one. He was prone to his oddities.

Wasting no time, the Seelie had formed a circle around the party, their arms raised to the cloudy sky. Slowly, the clouds parted, and the sun shone with a terrible, supernatural heat. The snow around the inn started to melt, and Elden's jaw twitched.

The grand display of magic made her shiver. Avalon felt exposed a tiny bit, and she couldn't help tightening her hold on Elden's arm.

Elden had explained earlier he was terrible at glamours (*your hair*, he had mentioned, *I think I've been making it a touch too pink)* and had to leave her without one. There were too many feyries arriving that would be able to see straight through it. This was something Odele was not happy about, though there was little currently going on that pleased her sister.

When Avalon thought no more would arrive—here came the bride.

Sabella led the small group, lifting the skirts of her off-white gown, the tulle overstuffed with flowers. The nymph was as awe-inspiring as Maetta had insisted. Sabella's hair was in a short afro, spotted with daisies. Her brown and freckled skin glimmered with the essence of life—she was the ideal Summer-lands feyrie.

Behind Sabella, who had gleefully thrown herself into Maetta's waiting arms, stood her parents.

Sabella took after her mother, mostly. But instead of flow-ers in her mother's short hair, the fey had different types of mushrooms forming at the edges of her hairline. They were mesmerizing, and beautiful in their own, eerie way. Sabella's dryad father, one of the Summerland's few remaining wardens (a fact Elden had mentioned in passing), had black hair so shiny it appeared wet. His olive skin shone with that same shimmer of golden spring that Sabella's bore. Running up and down his arms were dark, always moving vines. They even dove under-neath his clothing.

"Good to meet you, Warden Dimitrios of the Seelie Court."

Thankful Elden addressed him, as the proper term for the man before her had evaded her, Avalon took over the rest of the introductions. Khaira, when Avalon met the Seelie Warden's wife, eyed her suspiciously and allowed her gaze to wander down to Avalon's stomach.

Avalon tried not to let it bother her. Could Khaira some-how tell she was an oddity? That she was a *changeling*?

There was no time to dwell on it. The Seelie Warden, after asking Elden a dozen complex questions about how the inn was faring, introduced them to two more of the Summerlands' citizens.

"I've brought along our Seer." The man in question hobbled forward, his thin limbs barely holding him aloft. The Seer was dressed in fine clothes, in the golden tunics that the Summerlands fey wore. But his physical state...

"Seer Ilias," Dimitrios continued, oblivious to Avalon's discomfort, "already had his yearly foretelling. He'll be spending this trip recovering. Now, we want to see this lake our daughter will be having her ceremony at!"

Ilias turned his head to Avalon, his chapped lips in a firm line. His eyes were covered in a red bandage, and he did not speak when she kindly asked if he wanted to be escorted to his room. He twitched every so often, seeming to hear things that were not there. Avalon had the sinking feeling that he was drugged.

Avalon saw Odele staring at the disturbing scene, and taking long, graceful steps toward her.

Odele had waited until she had dragged Avalon inside her cabin and locked the door before she started ranting about the fey. "They are savages." Odele paced a small circle with Clancy, the cat, at her heels. "There was something wrong with that Seer. That could have been you!"

"I know." Avalon picked at her cuticles. "I *know*." After seeing Ilias, Avalon had begged Elden for a moment to compose herself. He had released her, but he had also stared after her as she and Odele had fled to the cabin.

Now Avalon worried she had caused a scene—at someone else's bridal celebration. The shame might kill her if Maetta didn't get the chance first.

Odele complained, "That was messed up."

Avalon took the opening. "Odele, you can still leave. You should visit Valerie—I'm sure she'll be so zoned out in her own little world that she'll barely notice that you're even there. *You* can work remotely with the contractor, and *I* can stay behind and help supervise."

"I'll stop you there." Odele flicked Avalon in the forehead. "Quit being an idiot."

"How eloquently said," Avalon quipped. "But I need to swallow my pride and to get back to the party. I'm sure they'll do something as amateurish as run out of ice."

"Elden's an *ice prince*. And, yes, I am aware of how ridiculous that sounds." Odele blocked the cabin door with her body. "Let him wiggle his fingers and summon magic ice sculptures or whatever. You don't need to go back out there."

"Oh, but I am. We both know that I'm stronger than you."

Odele's laughter was not encouraging—it bordered on insulting.

Avalon did, in fact, escape. But it had taken more tickling than it had brute strength.

The garden party was unrecognizable. The spirits definitely hadn't been neglected. The Seelie were dancing, the reel encircling the mound and dragging in the Unseelie, who looked happy to be left on the sidelines. Avalon didn't see Lyra among the dancers. The twins stood close to the mound, which Elden, the only one who—besides Evander and Dimitrios who stood nearby and observed—could manipulate the iron gate, had started to close for the evening.

The atmosphere, which had a pleasant breeze before—courtesy of the Seelie and an early wedding gift from their queen—now took on a chilling bite. The iron gates swung back open, pushed outward from a wind whistling from within the tunnel.

Tahoma and Kenan jumped to the entrance, waiting for further orders from Elden. The warden was not as disturbed as his subordinates.

"I recognize that magic," Elden mused aloud.

I should run, Avalon rationalized. On any other day, this idea would have completely taken over. All other thought processes would halt until she finished that vital task. But another whisper crept into her mind.

I want to see what happens to him.

This wasn't morbid curiosity. Somehow, concern had entered her heart. For someone other than her sister. For a man she *barely* knew.

What a useless emotion to feel for a man who can saw someone in half.

Elden entered the tunnel, disappearing for a minute, and Avalon cursed how her stomach had dropped the second he fell out of sight.

It's because you're surrounded by unknown entities and Elden is at least somewhat understood, she told herself.

His return came with a petite woman on his arm, her face obscured by a light blue and silver fan. Something metallic caught the light as she fanned her face discreetly, adjusting her long silver, glittering robes as she walked with Elden.

Was that a blade on her fan?

Avalon had a funny feeling she recognized this woman she had never met. There was a similarity that flooded icy panic through her veins.

Since the night with Bane, her previously frantic mind had quieted. *Numbed.* She felt static underneath every thought, buzzing and dulling her senses. It wasn't until she saw the woman with the fan that the static went away and alarm bells rang in her mind.

The woman acted as if she was unaware of Avalon's open stare, though it was apparent she was slowly leading Elden through the crowd in Avalon's direction. Snapping back to the present, Avalon spun to return to Odele's cabin and bounced off the back of Evander.

Evander half-turned, barely glancing down at her while she muttered some half-assed apology. She could address senators and governors and the like—the feyrie hierarchy was an entirely different problem.

Her apology irked Evander enough that he *really* looked at her. The Highland warden laughed, sipping scotch straight from the bottle. "Miss, if you want my attention, there are other, more pleasant ways to get it."

"Evander." The single word was more warning than greeting.

A week ago, Avalon would have sworn she would *never* be glad to hear Elden's voice butting into her conversations.

Evander seemed eager to escalate the situation, but luckily, or unluckily—time would tell—the mystery woman pushed herself in front of the Highland warden and inspected Avalon with a jeweler's judging eye. "Introduce me, dear brother," the woman demanded prettily. She ignored Evander's attempts to rejoin the conversation.

"Avalon, meet Crown Princess Hia. Hia," Elden gestured to her briefly before trying to lead Hia away. "That's Avalon."

The Winter royal was not to be moved. "*Avalon*," she sang, snapping her fan shut with a deft flick of her wrist. "We've heard so much about you. Bane is quite...*obsessed*."

Avalon snapped her mouth shut to give her time to find something that wouldn't make an enemy of yet another member of Elden's disturbed family.

Avalon settled on, perhaps incorrectly, "It's exciting to be a topic of dinner conversation around the Winterlands' royal table. I imagine, in a world of eternal winter, talking about the weather becomes rather tedious."

Hia laughed, any offense she may have taken hidden in those grey eyes. Her black hair was long, part of it placed in a braided bun while the rest trailed down her back all the way past her waist. A silver tiara was pinned in her hair, small teardrop diamonds catching the torchlight. "Yes," Hia continued. "And you've caught the interest of our father. Especially after what happened the other night."

Elden quickly looked down at his half-sibling. He nearly snarled, "What does that mean, Hia?"

His aggression widened Hia's smile. Neither Bane nor Hia shared Elden's sharp teeth. "It means," she explained happily, "that he wishes to meet her. Now. We're hosting our own soiree back home; in case you lost the invitation."

"He can request *my* attendance," Elden allowed before his tone darkened. "Avalon must stay here."

"What an odd show of disobedience, nephew." Evander found a way to weasel in and had gladly taken it. "I'd *hate*," he drawled, "for one of his own citizens to piss off Taliesin. Such a lack of respect should have deadly consequences."

Fix this, Avalon silently demanded. How Elden would decline this command, she had no idea. *But he had better do it.*

The dilemma—Elden could not lie. And he could not reveal her as a changeling. There was a hefty reward for exposing changelings to the Commission and she didn't trust any of these fey to keep her secret.

And even if she was a fey that had citizenship in the United States, whatever feyrie kingdom she originated from could still legally lay claim to her. Feyries had to have dual citizenship. If the fey criminally misbehaved, the government needed somewhere to send them back to.

Elden was an orator's son—surely he would come up with some solution.

"What does father want with her?"

Oh no. That sounded like he was conceding.

"To *talk*, dear brother." Hia removed her arm from Elden and snaked it instead through Avalon's. "You sound so paranoid."

Avalon did not care to "talk" with an orator. She had barely avoided succumbing to Bane's ensnaring words the first night they met. There was little hope she would fare any better against an orator king.

She could see a flash of that redcap brutality—Elden was contemplating whether they'd be better off starting a fight here and now...or taking their chances in the Winter King's palace.

Avalon knew what *she* preferred.

She so rarely got what she wanted.

CHAPTER 25
AVALON

When Avalon entered the feyrie mound this time, it was with her eyes wide open and unglamoured. The march through the lightless tunnel was still awful (was it too much to invest in some solar lights?), and approaching the Winterlands was like walking into a deep freezer.

She pulled Elden's borrowed coat, one he wore for doing chores and outside work, tighter around herself. It smelled of pine and earth—and something that was entirely Elden. Her cheeks grew warm trying to nail the pleasant scent down.

The feyrie garden was a perfect mirror to the inn's landscaping, but here in the Winterlands there was now a few feet of snow blanketing the ground. Unlike that first night, the gardens were completely empty, with no footprints marring the virgin snow drifts. The king's party was being held somewhere else. Somewhere *indoors*, Avalon hoped.

Hia had come fully prepared. Four horses were tied off outside the gardens; two belonging to Unseelie soldiers that had accompanied the princess. Avalon watched Hia being helped onto her own horse, a pure white mare with a mane that shone iridescent like a pearl, and asked a question she already knew the answer to.

"Why are we short a horse?"

Elden gave no reply, opting instead to grab her by the waist and lift her up until she was able to scramble and seat herself on top of the horse. He, even weighed down with armor as he was, annoyingly pulled himself effortlessly behind her.

Their ride was dapple gray and *massive*. It didn't even seem to notice their added weight until Elden gave a few light kicks with his heels.

She had been on horseback before, but never through such deep snow. Often it was like riding an avalanche—at every bump she expected to end up buried in a drift, never to be seen again.

"I'm sorry for this." Elden's breath brushed the back of her neck. "Hia is the crown princess: she has more sway than I when it comes to our father." He contemplated the situation. "Though I don't think she orchestrated this. My father does wish to speak with you."

Those words were spoken with the grim finality of a death sentence.

"He's going to ask me about Bane," Avalon realized.

"That's the most likely outcome, yes."

She wished Elden would elaborate more, but, true to his character, he neglected to add any superfluous fluff to make her feel better.

Their ride took them to a mountain pass, and then to a small, winding trail that went around a black, snow-covered peak. An aurora weaved across the mountains, rippling colors that seemed to dance along with the wind. The right side of the path sheared off into a cliff. The drop was so vast that Avalon shut her eyes, unconsciously leaning back into Elden until it was over.

His arm had snaked around her waist, and a quick pinch let her know when that part of the trail was finished. But, even after the danger was gone, the weight of Elden's arm remained looped around her. Avalon looked ahead, eyes adjusting to the dim light reflecting harshly off the snow, and saw the Winter King's castle.

A towering pagoda was built into the side of the mountain: three halls branched off from the building, and one hall even went inside the mountain itself. As they grew closer, Avalon was able to take in greater details of the architecture. Demon masks had been carved in white stone, with sapphire eyes that seemed to glow with magic. These masks were littered throughout the buildings, hiding and staring at Avalon as they passed. She wouldn't be surprised if those masks were helping someone watch their arrival.

They dismounted, and Hia regarded Avalon's clothing as the guards took care of the horses. "I'm afraid I can't bring you before my father wearing *that*."

Avalon pressed her mouth shut. *There's no point in arguing,* she told herself. *This is a woman used to getting her way. You need to save your energy for surviving the king.* "What would you have me wear? I'm not hiding a second outfit under here."

"Oh, I'll find something, Avalon of the Unseelie court." Hia's hand on her back guided her inside the palace. To Elden, Hia called back, "You need to change as well, brother. You look as if you're dressed to cause trouble. Like you expect there to be violence at a party."

Avalon had to imagine the sour expression sliding over Elden's face: Hia had quickened her pace and was pushing Avalon along a little faster than was polite.

The castle was made of several long halls, each one leading in a different cardinal direction. The center of the castle, the largest building and the only one with multiple floors, was glowing with warmth and light. Hia led her to the easternmost hall, pushing her into a dressing room with paper dividers with swirling patterns of snow-covered mountains painted on.

Avalon became aware of two things.

One, there was a beautiful gown placed on display. It was full of sparkling silver designs that reminded her of snowflakes, set on top of the deepest black she'd ever seen, and she had no idea how one would be able to get anywhere with that voluminous skirt.

And, secondly, more importantly, there was a cow-sized spider perched in one far corner of the ceiling.

Avalon made for the door, slamming into it as Hia closed it behind her. Trapped, Avalon instead flattened herself against the wall and let out a series of expletives any sailor would be proud of.

"The dress isn't that hideous," Hia began, laughing prettily at Avalon's expression. "Oh, are you talking about *Weaver?* He's a snow spider, and mind how you talk about him—he's quite shy."

She didn't want the spider's *tragic backstory*—she wanted it far away from her. Weaver scuttled down from the ceiling, stopping at the dress. The sound those eight giant legs made was the stuff of nightmares. *Too many legs,* Avalon groaned. *I don't want to hear all of them.*

Those front mandibles clicked a few times, and Avalon was starting to think she'd rather be back in those woods with Bane than be locked in this room with Weaver.

"I do hope you can dress yourself. As the crown princess, I certainly can't act as your handmaiden." Hia placed a hand on the door, glancing back haughtily. "You can ask Weaver for assistance, should you struggle. Be quick about it. My father is a patient man, but let's not test that, shall we?" Hia vanished before Avalon could protest.

Avalon slid the dress on, though it took a lot of jumping and twisting—during all of which Weaver was a silent, judging witness. The neckline was sweetheart shape, and the dress came with long, tight lace sleeves. The corset was not as tight as it should have been, but there was nothing to be done about that. As long as her breasts didn't fall out when she addressed the king, she'd be fine.

Always wearing her hair up made her look professional and made her feel prepared for anything, but tonight Avalon tugged her hair loose, letting it fall to her shoulders. A nearby vanity provided a comb for her to wrangle her hair into behaving.

Avalon stared at her previous outfit, accepting that she was never going to see those clothes again. Finding her way back to the party wasn't difficult. The rest of the wooden halls were quiet and empty. The only sound she could hear was a mass of string instruments playing a haunting song that chilled her bones. Fey music always seemed to have a purpose—this wasn't for art or entertainment...it was a *trap*.

Despite the sinister violins, it was a much classier affair than the first Unseelie garden party she had stumbled into. Blue paper lanterns hung from every available hook, each one filled with bouncing lights that almost looked like her will-o'-the-wisp. The crowd wasn't dancing, despite the music offered. Instead, they were forming a large circle, and she had to fight to get herself a place inside it.

In the center of the circle sat a man in white robes. As his audience stared and chittered, he carefully measured out oils and poured them into an incense burner. The circle parted at one end, leaving room for an ominous white throne. Magic pulsed from the seat, and the arms of the throne were made from pale tree branches that dripped icicles. The throne stood on a raised platform and seated upon it was a man she knew instantly had to be the Winter King.

Taliesin lounged comfortably, one leg kicked up and resting on a small table that had papers scattered on its surface. Occasionally, he leaned forward and snatched a paper, scribbling ink across it and throwing it back to the pile with the others. He and Hia shared many features; the small stature, grey eyes, and long, straight hair among them. Taliesin's age was shown in his locks, streaks of silver marring the deep blackness of it.

Hia had a smaller throne next to her father's where she sat more primly, her posture straight, and with a well-armored man standing slightly behind her.

It thankfully didn't take long for Elden to find her, and he attempted to pull her out of the circle. "You don't want to see this."

"I don't want to be here at all, but—" Her heels skidded them to a stop, her weight becoming an anchor. Turning to Elden to argue, instead she stuttered, "You—you look like a *prince.*"

He had never looked more insulted, and she had actually insulted him many times. Elden's dark hair curled wildly around the blood red crown jammed on his head. His eyes were unnaturally bright against the dark fabric of his clothes, lined in intricate silver designs. And he had never worn clothes so tight, outlining muscles she had assumed he had due to his lifestyle but hadn't personally seen.

Elden yanked at his collar dramatically. "These clothes are five years old—I'll tear a seam if I breathe too deeply."

Avalon laughed. Leave it to Elden to unknowingly ruin his princely image on his own. "As a woman whose mother jammed her into overly-complicated outfits quite often, I find it difficult to feel sorry for you."

"I doubt you're trying at all." He coughed once, looking pointedly away from her. "That dress suits you, though it makes me wonder how long they have been planning our arrival. And your hair..." Elden became very interested in adjusting his crown's position. "I've wondered what would convince you to take it down."

She longed to ask what Elden had thought would loosen her hair, but changed topics to avoid embarrassing both of them. "Everyone in here is staring at you," she remarked, shuddering under the eyes of so many fey.

Elden nodded, looking as displeased as she felt. "My father, as soon as my mother passed, introduced me to the court officially. I'm sure they're still gossiping about the *secret prince.*"

Their conversation accomplished what Avalon had wanted—whatever was meant to happen inside that circle was now happening. She leaned in closer to see, despite Elden's warnings. The man in the white hanbok had a large, smoking chalice in his hands, his long, grey fingers shaking as he brought the cup to his face. He inhaled deeply several times until he suddenly threw the thing aside and thrust his arms skyward.

"Avalon," Elden said, trying once more to lead her away.

Something inside her told her to stay, to watch. Avalon shook off Elden's touch. This was important.

The man fell into a bow, landing harshly on his knees and sliding his arms slowly forward. It was then that Avalon noticed the rest of the party, previously chatting and clinking glasses, were dead silent. Even Taliesin, who had seemed so relaxed, so uncaring at his own celebration, now leaned forward, nearly rising out of his own throne.

As if he had finally accepted he could not persuade her, Elden moved in close and left a hand on her elbow with a reassuring squeeze.

She was in the midst of a land that held magic in its very bones, and yet she was still startled when the man began to rise from his prone state, lifting up, up, up until he floated a few feet off the floor. His words were deep, monotone, and it was as if someone else was speaking along with him, but a tad off-beat.

"A flower opens only to close another's eyes forever."

Avalon inwardly laughed; the words, the setting was too surreal. *Why was he speaking like a horoscope? Vague and could apply to anything.* Elden had mentioned that when a Seer worked it was a huge event. This felt like a wind-up.

There was more. The hovering man gained another foot of air as he intoned, *"Forge an unwanted bargain with one who can travel leagues in a single step."*

Was *this* how a Seer was supposed to work their craft? Gods, how many times did she complain about her last-minute visions? She'd prefer her five-minute warnings over this cryptic nonsense any day.

And the levitating? What a show-off.

Her light-hearted jabs soon became shameful. The Seer

crumpled to the ground with a loud *smack*. And not a soul moved to help him. The party turned away in unison, bored with such a vague premonition that wasn't about any of them. The king leaned over the arm of his throne to speak with his daughter. Hia and the king began exchanging heated words back and forth.

It was only for a second, but Taliesin's eyes flickered back to the center of the hall and something triumphant flashed in his stare. Avalon turned to discover the reason for the sudden change in the king's mood and found Elden was helping the Seer to his feet. Avalon hadn't felt Elden leave her side, but now a phantom presence was lingering on her arm where his touch had previously been.

When Elden returned, he stared down at her until she spoke. "Now I understand why you told me not to be so hard on my own abilities. That was utter nonsense."

Mentioning that night in the office warmed her face.

It could have ended differently, had you let it.

Her inner voice, for tonight, was a suggestive and perverted moron.

"Utter nonsense for us," Elden agreed, looking to the throne where his father and sister were still in discussion. "But I imagine *someone* benefitted from that nonsense."

"Who's that man standing behind your sister?"

"Why?" Elden's words were too sharp for such an innocent question.

Avalon wanted to pinch him for his attitude. Considering she had been dragged here against her will by *his* family, he could at least be kind. Or get her a snack. "Because he's coming this way."

"That's Jin," he whispered quickly. Elden stood his ground,

but pressed Avalon tightly against his side. She couldn't find a reason to protest—no, that was an unspoken lie, the last deception she was still capable of. There were *plenty* of reasons to not lean into his body, and Avalon found herself ignoring them all. Elden continued, oblivious to her moral dilemma, "He's second in line and commander of our armies." There was a hint of jealousy for that latter part. "And Hia's unofficial guardian. He wants the throne even less than I do—and I have no desire at all."

"It benefits him to keep Hia alive and well," Avalon summarized.

"There's been few assassination attempts. Jin sends them back piece by piece. It discourages further attempts quite effectively." Jin had nearly arrived. Elden muttered, "He is Bane's greatest obstacle. They hate each other."

"Elden, and you're not alone, I see. How unusual." Jin was allowed to wear armor to the party, sporting white, clean plates over his dark blue robes. Avalon was certain that irked Elden. She knew Elden wore his small axe on one side—and she felt a sheathed sword on the side she was leaning against. Jin wore a grey bow and quiver, and a short sword on his hip, with the bright orange hilt facing behind him.

The brothers looked like polar opposites—Jin was the light to Elden's darkness. Their swords were even different styles. Elden's blades appeared more European-inspired, while Jin's short, single-edged blade, inexpertly judging from the palace's architecture, might have been similar to the mortal realm's Korean blades.

"What does Father want with us, Jin?" Elden scowled; his patience was already worn through. "If it's about Bane, Avalon was a victim, nothing more. We don't know where he is now, or if he even survived." That sentence involving her didn't sit well with Avalon, but now was not the time for semantics.

If anyone was watching the brothers converse, one would have thought they were discussing the weather. Elden's lack of outward emotion must be from his father's side. "Bane is a fool. Father recognizes this." Jin wore his silver hair as short as Elden did—more warrior than royal. "You've done me a favor. Bane needed to be knocked down a peg. Perhaps he has finally learned his lesson, but I doubt it."

The temperature dropped, raising the hair on Avalon's arms. Elden snapped, "Then why bring us here at all? I can't imagine you've all missed me."

"But you're so pleasant to be around, Elden. And your conversation skills—*perfection*." Jin mocked him before revealing, "There's been talk about your lady since the garden party you two ruined." *Oh, how terrible*, Avalon thought. *For a people who hosted an event every other week, you'd think that they'd hardly notice if one of them was cut a little short.* "Rumors have been surrounding you two for weeks now. Bane hardly helped put out those little fires."

What exactly did those party guests think was going on when Elden practically threw her back through the mound? Some sort of Persephone situation?

Jin offered some explanation, though nothing to appease Elden. "Father is curious. You've sworn you have no machinations for choosing, or making, an heir, but here you are. Arm in arm with the woman you almost killed your brother for."

Jin spoke about her as if she was something meant for breeding and nothing more. *What would Jin's blood taste like?*

"I have no heir and no plans for making one. I'll *choose* a successor when things at the inn settle down, and they can be properly trained. And I can find someone that wants the job and isn't a megalomaniac," Elden said, his grip on her tightening. "Apologize to Avalon," he snapped, his voice rising along with his temper.

"You're right. That was boorish of me." Jin bowed low. "If you wanted to go about it the old-fashioned way, I imagine you'd first need a lady that doesn't hate your guts."

That's not true, Avalon almost argued. But the words didn't fit quite right, and she would have hated to fumble them in front of Elden. *You did hate him. He threatened your way of life and so threatened Odele.*

What a useless reminder when she was currently depending on Elden for her safety. But what she felt for him now was unexplainable. Was it purely physical? Did she still hate him? Did she want to even *know*?

Elden's hand found hers, lacing their fingers together for reasons she couldn't fathom.

Jin eyed their entangled hands with disdain. "I can't believe you let Evander into your territory."

She didn't think anyone had the balls to condescend down to Elden, but Jin apparently was packing. Jin continued, "This damned wedding gives him the perfect opportunity to spy as much as he pleases. Do you think Evander gives a shit about the wedding of his architect's daughter? The Highland warden barely recalls my name."

Elden's grip on her hand tightened. "You think I want him there? Evander has the proper forms, legally I can't—"

"Don't speak to me of legalities with our brother's blood on your hands." Jin was not finished with Elden yet. "Evander was here at this court, mere days after your mother passed, offering his services to be the Refuge's next warden. Imagine his surprise to learn that you, his unknown nephew, would be taking over instead. Ashling left a mess for the rest of us to deal with by hiding you away all your life," Jin scoffed. "And for what? As if her family would have a real chance of seating you on the throne. You can barely manage your little inn."

Avalon felt a kinship toward Elden—his birth and her own were both riddled with decisions they had no control over.

At the mention of his mother, Elden had frozen. Wanting to cover for him and sick of being a silent bystander, Avalon said, "A party is not the time for such discussions. And family matters should be handled in front of family. Not shouted in the middle of a ballroom."

Her complaint drifted into the open air, raising one of Jin's eyebrows. Jin asked her outright, "What is my brother to you?"

She scrambled to answer. "For your information, Elden and I are in business together." How convincing would that be when Elden was holding her hand?

Elden groaned. "That's worse, you realize."

"What business?" Jin demanded.

How could she be any clearer? "We have business with the inn." Was that sufficient?

"With the mound?" Jin guessed, his face darkening.

"No," Elden answered, and this appeased Jin. Despite the feys' inability to lie, they were quite known for twisting the truth. Elden, however, seemed incapable of such double-talk, and his word was accepted at face value.

But he is capable of ensnaring humans, she reminded herself. *Look what he did to that creepy photographer. Not that it wasn't deserved...*

"You've found yourself quite the little viper—she even has the fangs to match. She doesn't seem to care how she addresses her prince. How dangerous."

Jin was referring to himself when he said, "her prince". He thought Avalon was part of his court. "I didn't vote for you."

"Avalon," Elden warned her.

Now Jin stared her down, and a malicious smile spread slowly across his face. "Your lady needs help with her corset, Elden. How neglectful of you. Can't have your guest walking around here half-dressed. Imagine what people will *think*."

She pulled back on her corset, trying to hold it taut and act as dignified as she could manage. Elden startled, his eyes flickering over to her back and seeing the mess she'd made of her laces. It might have been her paranoia, but she thought, for a second, that he had glanced at her chest before correcting his gaze.

"Come with me," Elden ordered, pulling her away from Jin's stupid grin. They left the main hall and wandered until they found a secluded hallway. Unknowingly, or so she assumed, Elden backed her into a corner. "Turn around."

A dark thrill ran through her as she did what he asked. His fingers were cold as he undid and redid the laces, occasionally pulling them taut enough to jolt her. "No one helped you dress?"

"Hia left me with that damn spider. I apologize if I wasn't able to properly dress myself with a giant arachnid staring at me."

"Weaver." Elden sounded amused at her plight. Avalon wished he could see her irritated expression. "Hia loves that thing."

"Really?" Hia came in pretty wrapping, but she was clearly as insane as the rest of her family.

"After tonight, I think you'll know more about my family

than anyone." The words were hesitant, almost regretful.

"Even more than Lyra?" The idea seemed laughable.

"She has her own family issues—I'd hate to add on to that with my own."

I think Lyra would argue against that. However, standing in his former home was not the time or place to correct such self-destructive thinking.

Elden was taking his time with her laces, much longer than Avalon suspected was necessary. "Why are you so good at tying up corsets? Were you a bit of a rogue back in your day?"

"Back in my day? We're the same age. And did you say good?" Elden laughed. "You should see the back of your dress. I'll have to cut you out later tonight." His fingers faltered. "Ah, I meant..." Elden's words trailed off while he raced to finish the lacing.

One final tug and it was done, interrupting the upsetting silence he had caused.

"Thank the gods," Avalon sighed in relief, though now it was more difficult to take full breaths. "Let's get out of here before people think we slipped away to have a secret tryst." She turned away from the wall, startled to find Elden still standing so close.

"When did Avalon Golightly start caring what the fey think of her?" Elden had yet to move, staring down at her with half an amused smile. He had recovered from his earlier embarrassment rather quickly.

Claustrophobia, and something less certain, sank in her stomach. She prodded his chest with one finger, holding it there as she said, "Get out of my way, Elden. Unless you plan on taking me against the wall, there's no reason for us to linger."

She meant to shock him or disgust him. Either way would

clear her path and get them back to the crowd. Before, her teasing would instantly end any conversation with the warden. Tonight, Elden rakishly warned her, "Be careful what you ask for." He took a step forward, the action sending her heart into overdrive. Gently, he pressed a hand on her neck, his thumb finding her pulse point. "You're flustered."

"I'm—" Her throat dried up, unable to form the lie.

"Your heartbeat says otherwise, Avalon." He moved closer still, taking up all of her vision, all of her attention. "You shouldn't tempt me like that unless you're certain you're ready for the consequences." When her eyes darted away, his hand moved from her neck to thread into her hair, tugging until her gaze returned to him. "Keep looking at me, Avalon. I want you to understand what I'm saying."

Avalon heard every word he said, his voice loud and clear despite the noise from the nearby party. Even if she hadn't been able to hear him, she would have understood. Her heart, which was already racing, doubled its speed. She realized why Elden always stared at her so intensely. He was making sure she was watching his mouth, making sure she could read his lips. He had noticed, though she'd never told him, that she was hard of hearing. And he was making certain she would have no difficulties communicating with him.

Her parents never offered her such accommodations.

Odele even forgot sometimes.

She nervously raised a hand, placing it against his chest to maintain some distance between their bodies. Elden took that hand and tugged it toward him, pressing them together in one quick, strong movement.

He leaned down, speaking clearly into her ear, somehow guessing—*or knowing*—which was the least damaged side.

"Avalon, if I believed for a *second* that you wanted me to press you against this wall and have my way with you...we wouldn't be having this conversation."

In that instant, if Elden moved to kiss her, she would have met him halfway. Instead, he dropped her hand, backing away, and her intense disappointment was alarming.

He must have seen the slight crash of her features, because Elden's face looked wickedly triumphant for a moment. "It isn't fun being *teased*, is it?"

Avalon couldn't help the slight pout of her lips—the taste of her own medicine embarrassingly bitter. "Rogue *and* a tease," she goaded him.

Elden retrieved something from his belt and placed it in her palm. "Enough of this game between us, my feral lady. I wanted to give you something." Her fingers curled around a leather sheath, and she revealed a small, intricate dagger inside. "I hope you don't ever need it. But I had hoped that before and look where we've ended up. *Look at what's happened to you.*"

She swallowed, banishing the memories he brought forth. Avalon wanted to appreciate the gift, but she blurted, "This isn't a weapon in *my* hands. I don't have the skill to use this—it will be turned against me."

"Here." Elden adjusted her grip on the dagger, forcing her to thrust the open blade against his chest, piercing his heart. She wanted to scream, the sound catching in her throat as she tried to pull back and away from him.

"Avalon, stop. I'm okay. I wanted you to get a feel for your target." Elden slowly removed the dagger, letting her see that the blade had completely vanished, leaving a black and ruby hilt. Once the dagger was completely free, the golden blade returned. "My mother had this made for my tenth birthday. A dagger that can never be used against me. Well," he amended his statement. "Fey magic is rarely so straightforward. It can't be a weapon against where my heart lies. Even my mother was prone to such mystical nonsense."

If it was that precious, why would he give it to her?

Weren't you listening? It can't be used against him. He can't trust you with anything else.

No, she knew that was wrong, just a weak shot from her own psyche. Elden sheathed the dagger and handed it back to her, saying, "You may not have the skills to use this in a fair fight. *Don't fight fair.* No one should know you have this until it's sticking between their ribs."

She took it, nodding numbly. His logic was sound, but she still wasn't convinced she wouldn't end up on the wrong end of it.

While he turned to lead her back to the party, Avalon, for lack of a better space, slid the dagger down the front of her corset and hoped the outline wasn't obvious.

After all that, it was impossible to pay any attention to the festivities. Every time Elden accidentally brushed her skin or touched her to point something out, she fought to keep herself from reacting.

How much longer is the king going to make us wait?

Meeting Elden's father had previously filled her with dread, but after hours of wallflowering, she wanted it over with.

Her third prolonged, impatient sigh caught Elden's attention. He seemed to mull over something before he took one of her hands, stepping back from her before bringing her hand up and almost to his lips.

She knew exactly what he was about to do. "What the hell are you about to do?"

"Asking you to dance." He brushed her knuckles with a polite kiss that made her think of rather impolite things. "I can tell you're bored. Unless you wish to return to our dark, secluded alcove instead, this is the only activity open to us."

She wanted to do both. And neither. "Elden," Avalon squeaked. "I can't dance. In this world or the one we left." It had driven Valerie to madness, Avalon's graceless stomping around on the dance floor at various fundraisers. She, even at that young age, had been more occupied with purposely stepping on the feet of her usually unpleasant dance partners than with actual dancing.

They were moving, Avalon tugged lightly along by their entwined hands. Elden spared her the center of the dance floor, opting for a less busy area instead. "Good. Because this portion of my training was vastly overlooked. I'm pleased that *I* won't be the one embarrassing *you*."

He touched her waist without hesitation, helping her into the proper position. He still was cold to the touch, though this did nothing to cool the heat moving through her veins at his proximity.

Avalon didn't know where or how to move, but he worked around that, cleverly guiding her with two large hands on her waist, rather than trying to whisper instructions over the music.

"It seems you remember your lessons better than you thought," she remarked. This dance was close to a waltz, the dance she recalled best. Her ability to keep up with him, with his world, was oddly thrilling.

His hands moving swiftly over her body, leading her and pressing on her lower back, were an entirely different, terrifying sort of thrill.

"You think that because you have no idea what to look for."

He offered another option. "Or you secretly like being twirled around like a princess." He brought them tightly together, and when he let her go to spin her, he seemed almost reluctant.

"I'll step on your toes and won't bother making it look like an accident." She shouldn't be so distracted. She was in danger here. So why was it so easy to relax into his grip and pretend she was perfectly safe and content?

Her threat made him laugh softly, the sound overwhelmingly intimate. When the song ended, she had been so distracted by Elden's light touches that she'd nearly forgotten what came next. Meeting the Unseelie king.

After most of the guests had said their farewells and respects to their liege, and suspiciously after more guards had entered the hall, Taliesin bid them forward.

All that waiting...what would come next? Avalon suddenly wished she and Elden were back on the dance floor, circling each other and avoiding the inevitable.

"I didn't agree when your mother appointed you as her heir," the king began. *That's a great way to start.* Taliesin's ink-stained fingers tapped on the arm of his throne. "I told her you belonged in my court. Not wasting your life among the mortals." Avalon averted her gaze from the king's open stare—she didn't want him to see how furious he'd made her. She still considered herself more human than fey, despite what she may look like. "I don't know what your brother was up to—"

Elden cut in. "Bane waited for an opening and stalked a woman who had insulted him. He showed no remorse—"

Taliesin laughed dryly. "Your brother *never* shows remorse."

"I made a decision. I have a duty to the *humans* as well, to keep them safe."

Taliesin scoffed. "That human government is paying you so much that you value money over family?"

It was like arguing with Bruce—with his political skills, it was impossible to win against someone who had no desire for truth.

Elden didn't wish to speak or didn't know what to say.

Taliesin scoffed, crossing one leg over the other, his foot bouncing distractedly. "Do you honestly believe Bane risked punishment solely for revenge? Though I doubt he thought you'd try to split him in half."

"No, I don't believe that."

Avalon swung her line-of-sight back to Elden, worried. It would have been better if Bane *had* been simply waiting for a chance to enter the human realm to hurt her. If there was something else he'd been doing, and she'd been just a happy opportunity...

Well, that would be horribly concerning.

The feylands were full of terrible, harmful things, but even in Elden's world it was rare for such an obvious attack on a feyrie mound to take place. What had been the point of those mysterious snake-like things Elden had fought? It seemed like...a test.

Elden cut to the chase. "If you brought me here to find out why Bane acted as he did, you'll be sorely disappointed. Or where he is now. That I don't know, either."

"I'm already disappointed. No," the king said, shaking his head. "As you are aware, I know of all bargains made by my subjects. Let's discuss the bargain you formed with the human, Lucas Stockton."

Elden's face greyed. "Are you going to miss one precious stone?"

Jin cut in. "You know that's not what we're getting at. All these years, you've acted so superior to the rest of us...all because you refused to strike another deal. Something," Jin emphasized, "that should make you ashamed."

Elden tried to make light of the blow. "The humans don't have anything I need," he scoffed. "Or want."

"But is that true, dear brother?" Hia hid half of her smirk with her fan. "Something prompted you to break your streak. To do what you so despise and strike a bargain."

The guards, who had been acting as merely ceremonial statues, now closed in on them. One of them grabbed Avalon by the arm, her blasted skirts getting in the way of her ability to dodge. Elden whirled toward her, his eyes frantic.

The Unseelie King rose from his throne. "Third son, Elden, I would like to make a bargain with you."

CHAPTER 26
ELDEN

The weapons in Elden's hands were a calming force, the sword in his left and the axe in his right. The trained warrior in him told him to survey the room, the approaching guards, his brother, and look for weaknesses. The redcap in him told him to make them all *bleed*. His eyes kept glancing back at Avalon, who looked more annoyed than afraid, as if she had spent so much time at the mercy of fey psychopaths that it was now merely an inconvenience.

"Perhaps you'd like to hear the terms of our bargain before blood is spilled?" Taliesin sounded amused. "I'm sure the lady will appreciate it."

Hia sat tall on her throne. Jin and another skilled guard were standing beside her and armed. "Elden," Hia softly spoke, "your reaction betrays you. Accept the bargain and you and your lady can leave."

He could spend a year deciphering the terms and loopholes in Taliesin's deal and still never find all his tricks. "This is why you invited us here?" Elden spat, turning back to his father. "To see if she was someone you could use against me?"

How long had his father been waiting for such an opportunity? Lyra was Seelie, and her Summer Queen would never allow Taliesin to demand her presence. Tahoma and Kenan had no allegiance to either court. Avalon was the first part of Elden's entourage that Taliesin could sink his talons into without consequence.

Again, Elden's attention wandered until he found Avalon, and he saw her glassy-eyed stare, the stare of a Seer. Avalon blinked, large golden eyes releasing a single shining tear.

His mind came to the correct conclusion too late—Avalon stepped forward, pulling free of her captor.

"I will bargain with you." She repeated, her voice breaking the second time, "I will bargain with the Unseelie King."

"Why would I bargain with *you*?" Taliesin asked. "The task I have in mind is for Elden alone."

"No!" Elden's weapons returned to their sheaths, a brief flash of sanity keeping him from dropping them on the ground. His hands clasped Avalon's arms, making her face him. "Don't you *dare*, Avalon." Her eyes gave her away. Avalon must have had a vision, and whatever she saw was horrible enough that she would accept any terms Taliesin came up with.

But even as Elden tried to stop it, silver threads of magic were already beginning to bind her to the Unseelie King.

Avalon wiped at her eyes. "What would you have me do?" Her nose scrunched up like an angry rabbit. She whispered, keeping her voice low enough that only the two of them could hear as pressed together as they were, "I *saw*, Elden. I saw what happens to you if I don't step in." She stepped out of his grasp, and, defeated and shocked, Elden let her.

Avalon faced his father once more. "Whatever task you give

me, Elden will ensure it is done."

And if she didn't believe it, the words would not have formed so easily. How could she trust him when he brought her before devilry such as this? He had damned them both in his hesitation.

"Do you want to hear the cost?"

Avalon spat in the face of Taliesin's false generosity. "What good would it do me? We're at your mercy. Tell me the task and let us leave."

Those silver strings of magic were tugging at her heart, leading her up to the throne. Things were moving too fast, and in his panic, Elden nearly let her do it.

The threads of the bargain forced her to kneel in front of his father and Elden became undone.

The redcap bloodlust flooded his vision. Elden's hands flew to his weapons. A second later, Jin threw himself in front of Hia, his bow already in his grip.

Jin's first fired arrow met with a shield of ice that Elden barely had time to finish forming. The arrowhead slid off and Elden, with a single thought, sent the shield to rotate around Avalon. She remained in place, shock-still, obscured every other second by the circling, reflective ice shield.

"Elden!" Hia leaned out of her throne, no longer the prim and perfect princess. "Accept the bargain! There's no need for this!"

Three blades of dark ice hovered behind Jin, each controlled mentally while he still pulled back on his bow—a difficult piece of magic only Jin was able to fully master.

Fine. Perhaps Elden's own magic was not as flashy or as pretty, but Ashling hadn't trained to impress. He'd been trained to get results.

Elden threw out his sword arm and an iron chain flew like a spear, materializing from nothing, and wrapped around Jin's neck. Another wave of his hand and the chain yanked Jin backwards and out of Elden's path to the king.

Hia leapt from the dais and her mouth opened, the first lyrics of one of her haunting songs released. An over-the-mouth gag of iron took care of that attempted ensnarement.

Taliesin stood, an arm stretched towards his youngest son. Elden attacked as his father did the same. It was a near thing—Elden threw his single-bladed axe like a hatchet, just as the Unseelie King's shard of ice hit him in his opposite shoulder. The force was enough to hurt Elden's aim and send the axe harmlessly thudding into the wall behind his father.

The flying icicle pinned Elden to the wall behind him like an entomologist's butterfly display. Elden's hands grabbed at the ice and melted the shard, dropping down to the floor.

Two of the royal guards grabbed Elden's arms from behind, wrenching his wounded shoulder. Elden ground his teeth as he fought the bleeding pain and tried to fight off their grip. He would pull out of one's grasp and two more would take their place—the feylands' second most annoying hydra.

Avalon turned to look back at him from her kneeling position, and Arawn, he would have killed everyone in the castle for her. But her eyes were angry, silently commanding him to let her handle this. What she had seen in their future, he could only guess.

"What," Avalon asked Taliesin, "would you have us do?"

"I need you to retrieve something for me. Something my position prevents me from obtaining myself."

Elden paled. That could only mean one thing. His father was sending them into the Summerlands—into Seelie territory.

Taliesin stood, clutching in his fist a handful of the silver threads that were attached to Avalon. "On the Island of Gorgons lives a flower that blooms at night, violet in color and rare in number. Fetch it for me and you'll be released."

The royal scribes usually scrawled Taliesin's contracts on scrolls that, when unraveled, would span a few dozen feet. Tonight, however, the king had given his word and nothing else.

A flower. Such an odd and seemingly insignificant request that set all of Elden's senses on edge. What could Taliesin need a flower so desperately for?

The flower's location did give some insight—it was located on the Island of the Gorgons in the Seelie Queen's territory. Not exactly vacation material. But Elden was the only one of Taliesin's inner circle that might be able to risk entering the Summerlands and not enrage the Queen. He was a warden and wardens could control where in the feylands their mound opened. Elden could slip into the Summerlands, and no one would be the wiser.

To ensure he remained undetected, he would have to convince Lyra, who *hated* the Summerlands, to guide him.

There were a million ways this could go wrong, and now Avalon would have to come, too. The bargain was in her name and her name alone. It was his honor that bound him to her. Elden needed to convince her he would never abandon her to such a fate.

Hia had been considerate enough to lend them a carriage, saving Elden the pain of being wounded on horseback. Now he and Avalon sat opposite each other, avoiding catching the other's eye. While he fought and failed to find a way to thank her, Elden applied pressure to his new wound, cooling it with his family's magic.

His reluctant savior, chin in hand, stared listlessly out into the night of the Winterlands. Keeping her eyes outside the carriage window, trailing the line of the dark, feylight filled forest, Avalon asked, "Does it hurt?"

Her eyes cut to his shoulder, studying him. Elden covered what he could. "It's fine," he assured her.

That angry bunny face was back. "That much blood is *fine?* Huh." She shut the curtain to her window with more force than a tiny scrap of cloth needed. "Make sure you at least get some on the upholstery."

"Already done."

Her eyes kept darting to his wound.

Was that...concern?

Yes, she's concerned. She's indebted to your father. If you die, she's doomed. How's one little changeling going to make it on or off the Island of Gorgons?

Elden shook off all thoughts that weren't productive and focused on one—Avalon was concerned.

He feigned a wince. "I'll need to treat it to avoid infection," he said. Something he had plenty of practice doing on his own.

Ah, there it was. Avalon hesitated before she hopped from her side of the carriage to his. "Let me see," she commanded while Elden tried not to laugh and peeled back his shirt for her.

As far as Elden was aware, Avalon had no medical training. So, what she planned to do with the wound was anyone's guess.

"Don't poke it," he cautioned her, worried about her wandering fingers. Fingers that skimmed his chest, circling the wound. It was fun, though ridiculous, to imagine she was happily using his wound as an excuse to touch him. "Nothing can be done with it now. You can help me stitch it up when we get back."

She frowned with an unusual sincerity and said, "Okay."

The carriage had left them at the mound's entrance, and Avalon had followed Elden through the night to his residence, needling him about his wound. He let her worry about him. Her attention was surprisingly pleasant.

Once they made it home, Elden sat at the kitchen island while Avalon, standing beside him, pressed his wound closed and watched him apply small, even stitches. Her lips were pursed, keeping any "helpful" criticisms to herself.

Taliesin's ice shard had, luckily, been quite thin. Though, perhaps that had been on purpose, so Elden wouldn't be too damaged to complete the bargain.

The repetitive and extremely painful act of stitching himself up gave him time to think. To remember that Hia was onto him.

At the pre-wedding party, Hia had linked her arm through his, the imperious smile plastered on her face an obvious mask. To everyone else, it must have looked like two siblings innocently catching up.

"I've wanted to check in with you, dear brother, since Ashling's funeral rites. But," she had continued, "I feel her all around us. It's like she's still here, at the inn."

Elden had tried to ignore the obvious hidden meaning. "Ashling knew how to leave an impression."

She had smiled at his curt answer. "I think you understood

what I meant, so please answer me plainly. I prefer your normal straightforwardness—I've come to count on it."

"If that's the case, hear this. Leave."

That made her laugh, the sound like the clatter of knives onto a marble floor. "I'm trying to help you. You've let a snake into your territory. There are things Evander may find that would be better off in the royal vaults. Think on it, and act soon."

The worst feeling was the knowledge that his sister was right. There was no way Hia knew about the cursed axe—the princess must have been concerned about any of the other deadly weapons in Ashling's arsenal. If the royals ever found out what Ashling had done, what she had left him...

Elden didn't possess the manpower, or the stone vaults, to properly deal with the war axe. If only Ashling had kept some of her power, her being, from the blade. But, as with everything his mother did, it was all or nothing.

Trying to get rid of me so soon, my wayward son?

He cringed, returning to the present and glancing at Avalon, though there was no way she would have heard the axe's words. He needed to give up the enchanted weapon, and he could have easily, if it did not grant him the opportunity to hear his mother's voice.

"That was *gross*," Avalon said when they finished with his wound, grabbing him out of his thoughts. It was unavoidable, but his blood had stained her fingertips while they worked. She stomped to the kitchen sink, presumably looking for the soap when he swooped over.

He clasped her hands in his equally bloody ones. "I promise you, Avalon, you won't be in this bargain for long. I'll do whatever it takes—"

"Elden," she huffed. "I know that."

But how could she? "I can bind myself to you."

She made a face and leaned back from him. "What."

"I'll give you my name, my *true* name. That way, you'll be absolutely certain that I can't abandon you."

Avalon tightly set her jaw. "I don't want your true name, Elden."

"But—"

"*Elden.*" One of her hands gently rested against his cheek, freezing him. "I don't need it. So, drop it, and cut out the weird feyrie shit."

The rejection of an unbeneficial oath didn't bring him relief. She moved away from him to clean her hands, glancing at the oven and scoffing at the hour.

Avalon wouldn't know this, but time in the feylands and time in the human realm did not proceed at the same speed. It was past the witching hour in the human realm—no one had been in the gardens to see them enter back through the mound or to see Elden pathetically leaning against Avalon, as if he was too wounded to walk himself back to his door. He had kept her up even longer, and the slumped position of her shoulders told him how worn she was.

He really should stop playing the invalid.

But instead, he asked her, "Help me up the stairs."

"Was something other than your shoulder wounded?" she questioned. Though she still remained at his side, hoisting one of his arms over her shoulder. Their height difference was so vast that this did nothing at all to help, something Avalon was purposely ignoring or was oblivious to.

She led him upstairs and into the bedroom he showed her, glancing around at his décor and furnishings with a mild curiosity. Avalon let him go and wandered over to the stone fireplace across from his bed frame. Hob was at the foot of the bed, snoring and lightly kicking in his sleep. "I draw the line at tucking you in," she announced, tracing the mantle. Her eyes settled on the mirror above the mantle, and she laughed. "You enjoy admiring yourself, Narcissus?"

Elden simply stared back at her, waiting.

Avalon looked from the mirror, to Elden, and back to his bed a few times before her face turned red. Elden laughed at her expression. "I'm *teasing* you. I didn't hang that mirror before you go on thinking I'm some sort of pervert."

Avalon sniffed. "It's no business of mine if you're a pervert." She nearly clipped his side as she hurried out.

"*Avalon.*"

She didn't turn, merely paused.

Again, he wished to ask her what she had *seen*, what had caused a single tear to roll down her cheek. Forgoing his own wants, Elden swore, "You won't be alone in this. I won't abandon this task. Or you."

"You won't," she agreed. "Because Odele will kill you if you do. And, unlike me, she has the strength and the stomach to do it."

CHAPTER 27
AVALON

What a ridiculous dress. What a ridiculous *man*. Pretending he was mortally wounded. It only worked because Avalon had never stabbed anyone, or been stabbed, and there was a tiny percent of her logic that was not quite convinced he was perfectly fine.

If Elden died, she'd never find that stupid flower.

She had returned sneakily to her room, hoping Odele had stayed in her cabin and wouldn't see her in her ridiculously ornate outfit. Or if Odele was in Whimsy, Avalon hoped her sister was still asleep.

Her hopes were dashed. Odele sat up in Avalon's bed, rubbing the sleep out of her eyes. "Of course, you're dressed like that."

"It wasn't by choice."

Odele gave a humorless laugh. "How horrifying. Did you get attacked by a 16th century version of our mother?"

What a terrifying prospect. "Help me out of this before I

lose my mind."

"I ought to let you suffer in that forever. I can tell you've been doing something stupid." Odele threw off her covers, the twisted knot she had turned those blankets into, and started working on the laced mess that was Avalon's dress.

"You can't assume I was—"

"Being stupid? Yes, I can." Odele gave up on the knots and Avalon heard the snip of scissors. "You ran back to that party to find *him*."

"I went back to do my *job*."

"Since when is *event planning* your job? You always said it was just something to give you more versatility."

Avalon let Odele complain all she wanted. "The website is done. This is all I have left to focus on."

"You should try focusing on *it* then," Odele grumped. "Instead of pretending to be *Mrs.* Refuge on the Moor." Her barbs didn't end there. "It's like you've been possessed by our mother, running around and trying to make a man's event perfect."

"That isn't *fucking fair*." Avalon rarely took on a harsh tone toward her sister, but her inner bitch came out fighting. And then quickly died when she turned and saw Odele's wide, wet eyes. "Alright, alright," Avalon consoled her, giving Odele a one-armed squeeze. How long had Odele stayed up tonight, worrying over her? "Things have gone to shit. And will continue to do so until we leave. But." She made Odele look her in the eye. "You made friends here. You were *happy*. Hell, you even had a few weeks of perfect sleep. I would say that's an improvement, wouldn't you?"

"That was *before* we learned what we're sleeping next to."

Avalon swiped Odele's phone off the table, winced at the 3% charge, and handed it over. "Odele, call Lyra and Tahoma.

Go have a girl's day. Or night. Or both. I'm sure they would jump at the chance to reconcile with you."

Odele had clear instructions, and her paranoid sister's blessing, and still she remained where she was. "When did *you* get so optimistic? It's bad timing."

"It's not optimism—it's certainty." Avalon paused, unsure about this next part. Clancy, the cat, seemed to glare at her, threatening her not to ruin his new, spoiled lifestyle. "About your cat..."

Odele grumbled, " *What* about my cat, Avalon?"

"It's a feyrie cat. Elden gave you a feyrie cat."

"Of course he did." Odele bundled Clancy into her arms and peppered his head with tiny kisses. "If you betray me, you'll be introduced to Hob," she warned the cat.

Neither Clancy nor Avalon believed her.

With Sabella at her side, Maetta's unreasonable wedding requests were easily talked down. Working together, Avalon and the Seelie bride convinced Maetta that there was no need to redo all the flowers because some nymph had called the arrangements "basic".

Sabella was exactly as Maetta had described her; bright, charming, and she possessed an unhealthy obsession with nineties romcoms.

The brides were most excited for the around-the-world cruise they had booked for their honeymoon, despite Maetta's penchant for seasickness.

"The mound my father oversees is in Georgia," Sabella frowned. "I'm trying to see as much as I can of the human world before I'm trapped in one place forever."

"It won't be so bad," Avalon offered, though in reality she had no idea what being a feyrie warden was like. It didn't seem like Elden was having a good time at the moment, but she was led to believe that this was unusual. "Look at how beautiful Refuge on the Moor is. I assume that the other mounds locate themselves in similarly picturesque landscapes."

She got a bewildered look from both brides, one that said, *Shouldn't you know better?*

"The Summerlands' Georgia mound is located—" Sabella laughed without humor. "—in a *swamp*. It's beautiful, sure, but I hope you like unusually large alligators and mosquitos that seem capable of revenge." Avalon could see that being a tough sell. Sabella continued, "We *also* have a hotel on the property, added a few decades after Refuge on the Moor. Having so many humans and feyries nearby gives the mound life—gives it power. But our guests are rare, and when they come, they're usually entomologists that are more interested in the *bugs* than the spa."

"*Anyway*," Maetta blurted, "we have a gift for you."

"It's a regift," Sabella said honestly. "My nymph cousins have been *very* particular about what they wear as bridesmaids." A pile of gauzy and tulle gowns was dumped out on the coffee table. Maetta scrambled to cover the coffee and biscuits. "*These* are the rejects."

Picking one at random, Avalon held the dress aloft and noticed the immense lack of fabric. "Need I remind everyone that it is *winter?*"

"Not while we're here." Sabella rolled her eyes. "Spring has come prematurely this year."

The Seelie *had* done a thorough job of clearing out the

snow and ice around the inn when they had first arrived. Apparently, they would be keeping that up. "Well, thank you." Avalon repacked the clothing neatly. "I'll wear one to the wedding."

"We've outfitted your sister similarly." Maetta rubbed her eyes. "We're up to our elbows in pastel tulle."

"But we *do* want to express our thanks," Sabella stressed, "and not just pawn off our excess things. When we heard all the rumors and drama surrounding our previous event planner—"

"Rumors and drama?" Avalon blinked. "What happened to Ashling?"

Sabella initially shook her head, but answered anyway. "Ashling declined rather rapidly. Sometimes feyries don't do well in the human realm. But this seemed like more than that. It was faster."

"Like it was foul play?"

"We *should* stop gossiping," Sabella announced curtly. "If we speak bad thoughts aloud, we'll only give them power."

Unsure how to ask anything more without pushing the subject, Avalon nodded and sipped her tea.

CHAPTER 28
ELDEN

Lyra served Elden spaghetti without pasta sauce—the surest sign she was upset with him. It also earned him strange looks from the Golightly sisters, who now must have thought he was some sort of man-child— or sociopath—that ate naked pasta. He wasn't certain which would be worse.

It was hard to hold his sauceless plate against Lyra—he had delivered her the worst news this morning. Not that he had allowed Avalon to get roped into making a bargain with his father, the Unseelie King. Or that he would have to trespass upon the Island of Gorgons, a deadly place full of snakes and cursed women who, while they could turn men to stone with a single glance, honestly deserved to be left in peace.

It was more the fact that Elden had asked, had begged, Lyra to...*speak to her family.*

Arawn, his garlic bread was garlic-less. That was over the line.

"Something wrong with your plate, cousin?" Lyra held her

butter knife like it was a lethal weapon. In her hands, perhaps it was. Elden glared in return.

"Looks fine to me," Kenan laughed.

"Isn't that always how he eats spaghetti?" Tahoma asked, her face stone straight.

The twin's ability to stretch the truth farther than the rest of them, thanks to their *very* distant fey blood, was, at times, more irritating than useful. At least Odele was amused by their antics. It was better than her new dinner routine, which mostly entailed sitting between him and Avalon and trying to stare daggers at him.

Things *had* been looking up for him—after dinner, Avalon had escaped Odele's clutches and asked to speak with him privately. Though he knew it would likely concern the bargain she'd made, it was enough to unknit his furrowed brow.

He should have known better.

Avalon led him to one of the conference rooms, avoiding the office like the plague. Once the door clicked shut, the inquisition began.

"I want to ask you something, and you're free to tell me to fuck off—"

He sulked. "I'm not going to tell you that, Avalon."

"That's presumptuous. You seem rather sensitive to the discussion of fey bargains. Not that I'm for them!" she clarified hurriedly. "But considering your family, it seems odd."

There was no reason for her to know this. No reason for her to care enough to even ask him.

"Is this something you really need greater detail on? Isn't it enough to understand that I despise feyrie bargains and those that make them?"

Avalon seemed to soften, sitting down at the room's oak

conference table. Elden followed, grinding his teeth at the thought that this discussion would last long enough to necessitate sitting.

"I do want to know," she answered. "You've made a bargain because of *me* and..." Avalon rested a hand on the table, her fingers drawing into a tight, shaking fist.

He knew he could distract her and leave this conversation to die, but, strangely, some part of him did want her to know.

"I made a bargain with a prisoner. It was part of a test—one I had no choice but to pass. I was twelve, a child, and the man I bargained with failed to uphold his end of the deal. So, his life was forfeited. The bargain killed him, and it made me stronger. I don't like knowing what that feels like."

Those golden eyes widened in fear. Elden tensed, waiting for what was sure to come next. *You're too dangerous, too damaged, too cursed. Because of you, I'm constantly in danger.*

"You must hate me."

"*No,*" Elden reassured her, his tone sharper than he intended, and then he commanded her, "Explain."

"I accepted that bargain with your father, even though you begged me not to. I knew you wouldn't abandon me if I took the deal. I'm just like—"

"Do not," he seethed, "finish that sentence. I *know* you made that deal because you saw no other alternative. Do not waste another moment thinking that way." He set his hand, palm up, next to her closed fist. "Here."

"What's that for?" She looked eagerly for a distraction, for a segue into lighter topics.

"Your nails are cutting into yourself. Take this." He nudged her with a knuckle. "You can squeeze your anger out all you care to."

She was hesitant to take his hand. "I don't want to hurt you—"

"With those baby hands, you couldn't hurt me if you—"

Snatching up his hand, Avalon gave it a fierce squeeze, her nose scrunching from the effort. She felt like fire in his hand, and Elden wondered who he had really done this for. When she grew tired, she left their hands on the table, still entwined together.

"Would you feel better if I pretended that hurt?"

Those golden eyes narrowed at him, and she slipped her hand out from his. "Unless you want my pity, don't give me yours." Her fingers tapped on the tabletop, barely grazing his as they moved. "Elden, you don't have to answer, but what was your mother like?"

He didn't *have* to answer, but he sorely wanted to. Elden had loved Ashling, even in the end when she had become half-mad with rage, and he felt an ache knowing that Avalon would never have the chance to meet her.

"Ashling was mischievous. She used to torment Abernathy to no end. You might have already guessed this, but she was messy—or as she liked to say, she had an 'artist's soul'. She loved photography, and took pictures of everything, especially her creations." It was easier to speak of her than Elden had thought. He coughed once, buying himself time to think of things that didn't hurt to say out loud. "She made so many things—weapons, mostly, but not always. I have a storage room filled with enchanted things I'm afraid to touch because my mother didn't write down what they did." Avalon said nothing, only listening, her face tight with concentration. Elden shrugged. "And she was tall."

Avalon's laugh was a comforting sort of quiet. "I could have guessed *that*, Elden."

There wasn't anything more in that particular topic that Elden felt capable of saying. He quickly jumped tracks. "We're going to need to discuss our...road trip."

"Road trip?" Avalon echoed. "I suppose we could call it that. I haven't told Odele about the bargain yet, so finding a code word for it might be a good idea. Although," she held a knuckle against her chin thoughtfully, "It might frighten her more to think we're planning a road trip together, rather than taking on a dangerous task in the feylands."

That reminded him. "I'm going to need you to save me at breakfast. Odele keeps sitting next to me and *accidentally* stepping on my toes."

"We'll see. It's hard to oppose her when she's this determined."

"I'll save you a seat."

Avalon considered his offer. "*Perhaps* I could wake up a little early tomorrow. But I'd wear steel toes just in case."

Dealing with Avalon always left him with excess energy. Elden decided to perform his rounds a second time that day, Hob bounding in front of him.

The forge lay on the outskirts of the property, the overgrown weeds stabbing at his guilty conscience. He was about to speed past it, not wanting to relive any memories of his mother teaching him to hone a blade, before he noticed movement inside.

Wanting to scout out the situation first, Elden angled himself so he could peer through one of the forge's windows without being seen. Evander lurked inside, lifting his sister's hammer and tongs with something that *almost*, through the dusty glass, looked like grief.

Elden shoved open the door, startling his uncle who, despite being caught unaware, managed to gently lay the tools back down. "Find what you're looking for?" Elden sneered.

Evander glared at him before replacing it with a smug grin. "Just looking for a bit of warmth from the elements. A cold forge should be a crime. Though, I suppose *cold* is all you can supposedly do, isn't it?"

Elden showed his teeth. "Care for a demonstration?"

"If you feel like embarrassing yourself."

Letting the insult slide, Elden began putting the tools his uncle had moved back into their proper places. While his mother had kept the inn's office a mess, her forge had always been immaculate.

Evander leaned against the workbench. "I heard you attacked your brother. Why?"

Who had even told Evander that? "If you've ever met Bane, you know why."

"You should have killed him. One less of those silver-tongued devils in your way." Evander leaned far too close. "Was *that* why you assaulted that bastard? Or was there another reason?"

That was enough. Elden sent a winter wind at his uncle, effectively throwing him out of the forge. Another gust slammed the door shut, cutting his uncle's swearing off.

Evander was a problem. A serious problem. And while Elden doubted the man knew exactly what he was looking for, there was still the danger Evander might stumble upon his mother's legacy.

There *was* an upside—Evander was here alone.

CHAPTER 29
AVALON

So much work still to be done and while Avalon's heart was firmly in it, her head was off in the clouds, replaying Elden's dark confession. She was working in the kitchen today, knowing there was always a tedious, mind-numbing task available. Avalon set up a station for herself, folding napkins for dinner on one of the clean dining tables. The repetitive movements allowed her plenty of time to think about Elden. Who would force a child to make such a hopeless bargain? She shuddered to think what her own father, more politician than man, might have asked her to bargain for if he had thought to use her for her fey powers, rather than hate her for them.

Avalon kept focusing on *stupid* things she couldn't forget. The feel of Elden's rough hand in hers, cold as always, but a comfort all the same.

Lyra butted into her workstation, nudging Avalon out of place with her hip. "As much as I admire your work ethic, the outcome leaves a lot to be desired."

Avalon had folded twenty napkins incorrectly. "Sorry." Avalon quickly began her rework until Lyra gently took the napkins away.

"I think you can rest today." Lyra left the task to the kitchen pixies and returned to Avalon, that shrewd gaze cutting through her. "You have more important things to think about and prepare for."

"You're right, the wedding—"

"The wedding? What are you...I mean the stupid bargain you made with Elden's father! *That's* what is most important right now."

"Lyra," Avalon pleaded. "I have no idea how to prepare for that, and if I start thinking about it at all, I'm going to have a meltdown. So, please, drop it."

"Fine." That battle was surprisingly short-lived. Lyra lingered, toying with her hair a touch too long. "Elden told me he offered you a job."

Gods, Avalon had completely forgotten about that. "It's hard to believe he was serious."

"Why? I heard Tahoma end a business call with, '*sounds like a personal problem*'. That's what we're working with."

That phone call would certainly come back to bite Avalon in the ass. "I have too many things to think about. Elden trying to snipe me from my current job cannot be one of them."

Lyra straightened out the corners of a tablecloth with a few tugs. "You know how bad Elden is at glamours, right?"

Avalon thought of Elden's admission she had been running around with pink hair. "I've become aware."

Lyra's dark eyes twinkled. "Nora Lee told me when they went to your office in Seattle, Elden saw you before you came into the meeting room."

"So?" *Where was this heading?*

"It's easier for him to glamour an outfit he has physically worn before. Hence, the wannabe lumberjack look he usually dons."

Avalon didn't know if that 'wannabe' part was accurate—she'd seen the man use an axe, and neither wood nor bone stood a chance.

"Anyway," Lyra grinned, moving on. "When he saw you before the meeting, Elden switched up his glamour."

Avalon could easily, and in great detail, recall the pristine navy suit he'd been wearing—glamour though it was, he had still managed to look uncomfortable in the imaginary stiff collar and tie. "Why the hell would he do that?"

"It's the current topic of discourse in our group chat, to Elden's despair," Lyra laughed, leaving Avalon to contemplate the unsettling answer on her own.

Avalon took a walk around the lake, verifying that there was no landscaping that needed to be tended before the ceremony. With nymphs and dryads present and awaiting the wedding, it was a complete waste of time. In fact, the Summerlands warden and his wife had personally taken to tending the inn's gardens, particularly the areas where the wedding events would be taking place—namely around the lake and the mound. The inn's greenery had never looked better.

Avalon was postponing her inevitable revelation to her sister. But breaking the news that she'd be taking a short, but deadly, trip into the feylands was not something she looked forward to. Odele was already climbing the walls. The way the banshee watched the feyrie entrance, stalking back and forth with her tabby on her heels, one would think Odele was gunning for Elden's job.

Avalon also suspected that Odele was scrounging the inn for anything incriminating enough, or dangerous enough, that could convince Avalon to leave.

When Avalon finally found her courage and started her search for Odele, Odele found her first.

"Why haven't you been answering your phone?" Odele's thin hair was standing on end, a halo of static hovering around her head. "I called you fifty times."

Avalon shrugged, prepping herself to deliver the bad news. "I needed to disconnect."

"This." Odele waved a hand wildly around them. "*This* is not the place to be disconnecting. I need you focused, and I need you to answer your damn phone when our parents decide to visit!"

Bile threatened to crawl up Avalon's throat. "Bruce and Valerie are *here?*"

"They're currently threatening Kenan for a room. We're booked up from the wedding."

They, under no circumstances, could be allowed to stay here. "Odele, they can't see me like this." Avalon drew her hair around her ears self-consciously.

"Then we better find your stalker." Odele frowned, taking Avalon's arm and dragging her back to the inn.

They crept around, searching his usual haunts for Elden. The garage proved fruitful, finding Elden underneath his truck on one of those wheeled creepers. Avalon gripped his ankles and tugged, sliding him out into the open. His scowl vanished when his gaze landed on Avalon standing above him. "You're a much better sight than I was expecting."

"Expecting Kenan, were you?"

"Yes."

Avalon ignored the warmth his words brought. She gestured to the truck. "How's it looking?" Odele glared at her for the unnecessary chitchat.

Elden sighed. "Seems to be electrical. You know how feyrie magic acts around that sort of thing. Or maybe you don't. Anyway, I'll have to ask Abernathy for help, and he'll make me hold the flashlight for him, which is emasculating."

The silly image of the farmer and the warden working together—and ultimately badgering each other to death—made her smile. Avalon hid a yelp as her sister poked her hard in the side. She got to the point. "I need a glamour. Now."

"You *could* use this as an opportunity to practice your own glamours," Elden said, sitting up.

He frowned when both of the sisters snapped, "NO!"

"Elden, we don't have time! Our..." Avalon hesitated. "Our parents are here."

That was enough to get him moving. Elden quickly packed up his tools and scrubbed his hands in a paint splattered sink. "What are they doing here? I'm assuming they don't know either of the brides." One of his hands lifted her chin, and Elden studied her as the familiar touch of his glamour ghosted her skin. "Is this about Lucas?"

Avalon winced. Recalling the deal Elden made with Lucas to protect her changeling identity filled her with guilt.

"Lucas?" Odele's tone was almost shrill. "Who's Lucas? And I thought glamours were a hands-off kind of magic."

Elden quickly dropped his touch. "I see you two have something to discuss on the way. Let's go meet the parents, shall we?"

Bruce mentioned he was the governor four times while Avalon, Odele, and Elden entered the inn's foyer. Both of the sisters cringed at his volume, which had started to draw a crowd.

"You've spoken to all the managers," Tahoma was insisting. "None of us are capable of making a room appear from thin air."

"That is precisely *why* I requested the *owner*, not another manager."

"He's no magician, either," Kenan grumbled. He ignored Valerie, who continued to try to hand him her bag.

"*I'm* the owner," Elden announced, stepping forward.

Avalon took a place beside him. "Hey, everyone! Did any-one mention that we're having a completely complimentary cocktail hour in the dining room?"

Her offer quickly cleared the room. The crowd dispersing, Bruce turned away from the desk, at which point the twins both slipped into the office and shut the door. "What seems to be the problem?" Avalon hated to even ask.

"The lack of rooms seems to be the problem." Now that Bruce had seen her, he only had eyes for Avalon and ignored Elden, which was quite the feat considering the man's size. She read it in Bruce's eyes. *This is your fault.* "We came to visit our daughters, and it was quite the drive. One that I'm not making again in the dark. Find. Us. A. Room."

Elden looked like he wanted to rip the man's state flag pin off his chest and stab him with it.

Avalon felt herself mentally finding solutions, which she hated herself for. Where was their usual entourage of security and personal assistants? Avalon glanced at Elden, who wordlessly gave her the lead. *Your parents, your call.*

Avalon pulled out her phone and called Nora Lee. "I'm so sorry about this, Nora Lee, but can you help Odele pack her cabin and get the room ready for two guests?" Odele, who had been hiding behind Avalon and Elden both, bristled, but said nothing. She turned on her heel, vanishing in the direction of her cabin.

"I didn't say we wanted a cabin—"

"And, yet, that's what you're getting, *Dad.*" The word stuck like peanut butter on her tongue, nearly impossible to get out. Bruce and Valerie insisted on maintaining the normal familial endearments in public. Though it was strictly business, it didn't make it any easier. "Your car is the other option."

"Fine," her father said. *Not that he had any choice.* "Arrange a private dinner for the four of us. There's much to discuss."

"Of course." She'd better eat now. Once she sat before her parents, her appetite would vanish and her stomach would sour. "How's six o'clock?" she asked, knowing whatever she said would be wrong.

"Make it seven."

"Brilliant."

Kenan reappeared, begrudgingly piling the Golightly's luggage onto a cart. "Would you like me to show you to our cocktail hour? Our head of housekeeping will let me know when your room is ready."

Once they left—Valerie whispering something to Avalon she had no hope of hearing on their exit—Elden offered her his hand. Avalon took it without question, squeezing out her frustrations until *her* hand hurt from the effort.

"Better?"

"Not even close."

Elden squinted down at her. "Who do you think makes more backroom bargains? Your father or mine?"

Her dry laugh was her answer.

Avalon's parents had her brain so occupied, so frantic, that she completely forgot that the Refuge was filled to the brim with feyries—not all of them as friendly as Maetta and Sabella.

"Dammit." The boutonniere she'd been fixing pricked her finger, drawing blood. Avalon brought the cut to her lips as a large hand clamped around her wrist.

Her throat dried as she panicked, hating that she'd been caught unaware. Avalon glanced up, noting auburn hair and a height that rivaled Elden's.

Evander. "Let go of me."

Her demand was ignored. Instead, Evander fished a handkerchief from his belt and wrapped it around her finger. He squeezed the minor wound until the throbbing pain made her wince.

It was shameful, a Seer being caught with her pants down—figuratively. Just where was her head at? Avalon scowled up at him. Gods, he looked so much like Elden, aside from the hair. And the eyes.

Looks like Elden will age gracefully, the bastard.

"I have a few questions for you."

"And I don't have the time for them."

Evander kept speaking as if she never had. "I've noticed you spend a lot of time with my nephew. And he pays quite a bit of attention to you."

What answer would satisfy him? Why did he even care? "I work for him. Do you think he has any idea how to run an inn?"

"And that's it?"

What else did he want? "If Elden doesn't want to spend quality time with you, it's not my fault. I imagine your issues can't be solved with a few fishing lessons."

"What do you know of our issues?" There was triumph in his tone, like he'd won some dark secret from her.

Shit. "When you corner a lady like this, hurting her, one would assume you have issues with everybody."

"How cruel of me. Here." Evander removed the handkerchief, sucking the blood off her finger before she could—if she even had the strength for it—jerk her hand away.

Evander had the same predatory smile as his nephew, but she never feared that Elden would bite her hand off.

"It was nice getting to speak to you without interruption. Let's chat again—after the wedding."

When he let her go, Avalon sank to the ground, her knees giving up entirely. That did it. She was buying bear spray on the next trip into town. See if Evander kept smirking with capsaicin sprayed directly into his eyes.

Bruce ordered their meals for them, from the appetizer down to the dessert. A bold move, an aggravating move, and totally normal for him. Valerie hadn't ordered for herself in years. Both sisters picked at their salad. Odele had been caught up to speed on the Lucas and Elden bargain situation and was, as she should be, terrified.

At least there wasn't an audience for their family drama—

Bruce had requested a private dining area, and with so much going on at the inn, Lyra's staff had been forced to convert one of the inn's break rooms into one. The couches had been pushed against the photograph covered walls to make room for a small dining table.

It was unnerving how quickly Bruce could revert them to their teenage selves. Pushing their fancy food around on their plate, counting down the seconds until they could be excused and return to their safe haven—their shared room. They each had been given their own room, each decorated in accordance with Valerie's vision, but they stuck to one at night. Avalon and Odele would be sharing Avalon's room tonight. *Just like old times.*

"How did you find us, Dad?" Odele stared down at her plate. "I don't remember mentioning it during our monthly call—"

"You didn't. And that chittering employer of yours wasn't any help."

Valerie took over, her small voice forcing Avalon to read her lips. "We know you two value your privacy, but we were worried, dear."

Avalon doubted that. "Can we skip the pleasantries and get to the real reason you're here?" Avalon tore up a piece of bread, if only to have something to concentrate on.

"Funny that *you* have to ask." Bruce pulled out his phone, displaying that blurry photo Lucas had taken of her. "This nearly got into the wrong hands. Luckily, the idiot tried blackmailing us first, which gave us time for her friend to contact us with her information."

Lucas had upheld his end of the bargain in a way. By selling out his friend. It was difficult to feel sorry for either of them.

Bruce zoomed in on the photo, focusing not on the bruises mottling her face, but on the almost invisible tip of a pointed ear. "What the hell is this?"

"A very shitty photo edit." Avalon pushed her hair behind her ears, hoping Elden had worked his glamour on her well. "What do you want me to say? Some creep recognized my name and took a picture of me at the dentist. Should I start wearing a bag over my head in public?"

Bruce put the phone away, scowling. "In this, you look...you look like one of those *creatures*."

I am one of those creatures. Avalon nearly wished she could show Bruce her new teeth. "Is *this* why you came all the way out here? What a waste of time. We may as well take the yearly Christmas photo now and save us all the headache."

"You're already expected at the Christmas party," Valerie sniped, downing her wine and rummaging in her bag, searching for her various and ever-changing medications, no doubt. "Let's keep the plans as is."

Valerie. She was the most confusing of the pair. When Avalon had revealed them, accidentally, as changelings, she had taken it the hardest. Avalon had been called her "miracle" baby, as the attempts before had been unsuccessful. They had tried for another child after the horrific, changeling reveal, Avalon knew, and could not carry to term. She wished that they had— she even internally swore she would watch over her almost sibling and ensure a fey swap did not happen again.

Odele shrugged as Avalon met her eyes. *Thanks for trying,* she communicated.

Whatever. The Christmas party wasn't all bad—the apple tarts came immediately to mind and nothing else, but...

Avalon spared a glance for her mother, whose gaze had

settled on a particular picture frame adorning the inn's wall and refused to move away. Her mother must be adjusting to a new prescription.

Done with Avalon for now, Bruce settled his attention upon Odele. "I hope that color you painted our cabinets isn't the one you're staying with."

Avalon let Odele have the bed to herself, cocooned as her sister was. She was tired of fighting for a scrap of blanket.

Avalon left Whimsy and wandered the inn's grounds, telling herself she was only taking a walk to clear her head. When she ended up before Elden's house, she couldn't help but search for some sign of life within.

She told herself she was there because Elden was the only person she knew, besides her sister, who could relate to having a father whose words could never be trusted.

There are other reasons you're seeking him out. Her heart laughed at her mind's rationalizing.

It did no good to dwell on it. Once they stepped foot on that island, there was no guarantee that they would make it off. Better she buried such thoughts deep, *deep* down. She'd at best make a fool out of herself—at worst, she'd distract Elden and cost them their lives.

A light was on in one of the windows. Elden was still awake and this bit of information both frightened and thrilled her.

CHAPTER 30
ELDEN

Elden wasn't shocked at Avalon's late-night appearance at his door. He had been spending so much time with the woman that Avalon, sitting ravenously at his kitchen island at one in the morning, seemed natural.

Avalon was still in her pajamas, a coat thrown over the purple striped set. She finished eating the omelet he prepared her after she complained that she'd been physically unable to eat during her family dinner. "That was delicious. I'm impressed."

"Lyra is an excellent, and unrelenting, teacher."

"What else can you make?"

"Let's discuss why you're here." To avoid embarrassment, he'd have to learn to cook something else soon. He'd been spoiled growing up in a hotel with a full kitchen. Elden blinked. He had never considered himself spoiled before. That wasn't a word normally reserved for a child that had drawn blood at age eight.

"It's *not* to relive the last supper from hell," Avalon

frowned. "I think we need to discuss the bargain and how I'm going to keep it from Odele."

"Time moves slower in the feylands. I doubt she'll miss you." *Unless we die. That will not go unnoticed.*

"Convenient. But, if gorgons can turn us to stone if we look at them, how the hell are we supposed to find this flower? I'm not even going to ask why your father wants this stupid plant."

"I had an idea." He paused, as his best and only idea involved Avalon's direct participation. "I had hoped, once Lyra leads us to the island, that you could stay behind with her. That you could stay safe."

"Not liking where this is going, Elden, but I made the bargain. I'm not going to try to weasel my way out of it." She hopped down from the island, her elbow bumping into him as she began drying the dishes he cleaned. Working together with her on something so simple, so domestic, put thoughts into Elden's head that were better left unsaid. "As terrifying as an island full of snake-headed ladies is, I won't leave you to perform the task yourself. Though," she frowned, flexing her biceps and showing a definite lack of muscle. "I can't imagine how much help I will be. I don't have magical ice powers like you, Jack Frost."

"Who's Jack Frost? An ex of yours?" Elden worked on easing out this strange jealousy from his tone. Avalon giggled at his response.

Elden rushed onwards. "I'm not asking for that sort of assistance. I think we can both agree that I have that covered. No," he cringed, wishing that his plan didn't entirely depend on her. "I need you to be my eyes."

She nearly dropped the glass she was drying. "Sounds like a good way to end up as a gorgon's garden gnome."

"I need you to *see*. To look ahead a few seconds, mere minutes, and lead me to where we need to go."

"The future is uncertain," she replied uneasily. "I can't guarantee—"

"Nothing in the feylands can be guaranteed," he countered. "I'll take a mirrored shield with us, but I'm afraid they may know that little trick."

"I suppose I must try," Avalon relented, sighing with her whole body. "It's hard to imagine we'll be around real gorgons. Sometimes the things you say make me feel like I'm living in a dream."

"Dreams are better than nightmares." Could he push his luck once more? "What did you see that made you take my father's bargain? I know that you detest our feyrie deals as much as I."

Elden did not expect her to tell him, but Avalon took it one step further—she showed him.

He did not care for the shadows that danced in her golden eyes. It reminded him too much of his father's Seers. They used hallucinogens before they attempted to call forth a vision.

Avalon stepped toward him, eyes shining, and carefully she placed her hands on either side of his face. Elden startled, that warrior's instinct yelling at him for allowing anyone to get so close, before he leaned into the touch, eyes closing languidly.

Avalon's vision was blurred. Elden blinked a few times, calling up a tiny measure of his own magic until he could see the scene clearly.

Armored guards closed in on them, and Elden fought his siblings on his way to Avalon. Much of the battle at the palace was the same—Elden used his iron against Jin, and was preparing to defeat every single one of the court's guards for their hopeless escape attempt when Avalon dug her nails into his shoulder, spun him in the opposite direction, and ducked.

Elden caught the guard's sword with his own, disarming him easily. Before he could decide where to turn next, Avalon shrieked, "Left!"

He caught on to this new dance of theirs swiftly. Avalon crouched, clinging to his back, shouting directions and numbers at him. It worked well—for a time.

"She has the Sight," Taliesin seethed and raised both of his arms to the ceiling.

A winter's gale blew from the king's direction, low to the ground, and knocked Avalon off her feet. An icicle, like a murderous stalagmite, burst from the floor and pierced her leg, immobilizing her. She screamed, distracting Elden enough to allow the guards to band together and drive him to his knees.

It was as if he'd gone mad. He strained against his captors, trying to crawl toward her—all logic and tactics forgotten.

"Father, don't—" Elden would offer anything to prevent Avalon from becoming trapped in Taliesin's possession. "She can't stay here. She has a mortal life. Please."

"A changeling that escaped her duties to the Crown?" Taliesin left his dais, stepping slowly, deliberately, over to Avalon. He vanished the ice embedded into her leg, and she shrieked.

"Let her go." Elden was still fighting to stand. "I'll do anything. I'll go anywhere you need. I'll kill anyone you ask me to. I'll—"

"You will," his father agreed. "You will do all that and more if you wish her to have a pleasant life here."

She became his father's new favorite toy, sitting oceans away from him across the royal dining table, silent and sightless—a blindfold covered Avalon's eyes, a mask that couldn't be removed without Taliesin's magic.

Elden watched himself in the vision as he left his warden duties to stay with Avalon, speaking more often than he liked, and loudly, so she'd be aware of his presence.

The vision's location changed abruptly. When Elden saw himself next, he had burst into Avalon's room in the palace after knocking out her guards.

She rushed to him, clinging to his arms as he spoke.

"I'm going to be away for a long time. I can't say anymore. Don't look for me, Ava Golightly. Not physically or with your Sight."

Her nails dug into him, infuriated that he had used her true name to command her. "Take me away from here, Elden."

"Not just yet. Wait for me."

He jumped scenes again, Avalon's weak Sight unable to give him the entire picture. Now he was dripping with blood, and his axe, Ember, was hot in his grip and steaming.

Taliesin lay on his own dais, dead. His siblings, Hia and Jin, were wrapped in Evander's iron, spread-eagled, and chained to the floor.

Elden stalked to the back of his father's, now his, throne. Avalon sat behind it, still blindfolded and hugging her knees to her chest. When she heard his steps, she blurted, "Don't kill me! I have the Sight!" If she didn't know who he was, she must have overused her powers to support Taliesin's defenses.

"My feral heart," Elden muttered, kneeling down next to her. "I can see the knife you are hiding."

The blade clattered to the floor as Avalon lunged for him. "How long?" she cried, burying herself against him. "How long has it been?"

"Three years," he answered, and she sobbed at the information.

"Take the throne, nephew. The Matriarch is waiting." Evander kicked at Jin's body, sneering at the restrained royals. "I still think we should kill them."

Elden said nothing. He would not discuss with Evander the bargain he had forged with his maternal grandmother. He made Avalon stand, leading her to the front of the throne.

Elden sat, the throne steaming but allowing the new ruler to stay. His grandmother, the Matriarch, took Hia's former seat and smiled at him, her pointed teeth stained red.

"It took far longer than I liked to get you there, but Ashling was always contrary." Despite the battle to overtake the Winterlands palace, not a single white hair was misplaced on the Matriarch's head. "That Seer certainly didn't make things any easier."

One of his father's former servants rushed forward, gaze downcast, and presented Elden with a blood-red crown. Once the crown was on his head, Elden jerked Avalon towards him until she sat on his lap. He tore off her blindfold as Taliesin's magic could no longer keep it in place. She slowly blinked, adjusting to the dim light of the throne room after years of darkness. His bloody appearance seemed to frighten her.

"Oh, Elden. What have you done?"

"*Enough.* Please." Elden couldn't stand seeing anymore. The misery he had experienced in Avalon's dark future made him ill. "You witnessed *all* of that?"

"I can't be sure. It's hard for me to remember. It comes to me in a blink." Avalon rubbed her forehead, swearing. Her feet swayed and she would have fallen backwards if Elden hadn't caught her. "I'm sorry—I've never done that before. I couldn't stop it."

"It's alright," he said, though nothing was alright.

She slackened in his grip. "Evander scares me," Avalon muttered, so low Elden barely caught it. "They, your mother's family, want you on that throne more than anything."

"I know." He helped her sit on a couch, though he loathed to let her go. "You really need to stop risking your neck for me."

Avalon ignored that. "I don't think I can make it back to Whimsy."

"Spend the night here, then." It came out as a command, which wasn't something Avalon responded well to. He needed to smooth that over, turn his demand into a caring offer, and still he ignored all those smart, sympathetic notions. "I'll get a room ready."

She slid off the couch, stretching out on the plush rug that lay between the furniture. "I can just sleep on the floor. Just throw down some pillows and blankets."

Their first sleepover and she wanted to spend it on the floor? "Do you always have to be so contrary?"

"Who the hell are *you* to call *me* contrary?"

That he overlooked. Elden stomped upstairs to return with armfuls of blankets. He would not let Avalon sleep in an unruly pile and made her move so he could lay out each blanket neatly, creating a lame princess and the pea stack of quilts. "This," he growled, "is more work than using one of the guest rooms."

She didn't respond as she crawled under the blankets and slid the enchanted dagger he gifted her underneath her pillow. "Good night, Elden."

An idea formed, and a bad one at that. Whistling once, Elden sat down among the blankets. Avalon peeked out from under the covers at him, squinting suspiciously. Hob made his slow, sleepy way down the stairs and situated himself between them with an uncaring flop. "Yes," Elden agreed, laying down on the other side of the mountain of a hound. "Good night."

"Oh, absolutely not," Avalon hissed, fighting to be heard over Hob's impressive snoring. "Get out of here."

"You needn't worry—I will remain on my side. Hob isn't going anywhere."

"I won't be able to sleep knowing you're there," she whined, but with the tired tone of defeat.

Amused, he inquired, "Why not?"

This she would not answer.

Elden waited for Avalon's breathing to slow, a sure sign she was asleep, before attempting to get any rest of his own. He had nearly drifted off himself when Avalon's rhythmic inhales became full of gasps, and he sat up to glance over at her. Both of her hands covered her mouth, and while she trembled, tears ran from her eyes and into her hair.

What she was dreaming about, Elden had exactly one guess. If he ever saw his youngest brother again, he would kill him.

Should he wake her? Comfort her? The latter thought left him lost and unsure. Luckily for Elden, Hob shifted and placed his head on Avalon's stomach. The weight was enough to quiet her nightmares, leaving Elden off the hook.

In the morning, Avalon tried to sneak out without him hearing. Ridiculous, but Elden kept his eyes closed and feigned sleep to save her the embarrassment. Mid-morning Lyra stopped by, ready to help fulfill Avalon's bargain.

Lyra listened to his recap, frowning when he revealed the

foundation of the plan relied on Avalon's weak Sight.

"I'm surprised you're even letting her step foot on that island, cousin." Lyra had been quietly working on a rough map of the Summerlands' shoreline and scattered islands. What little Lyra recalled from her childhood, at least. "The older ones used to dare each other to grab a seashell from the gorgon's shore—no one ever accepted."

Just the kind of anecdote he did not want to hear. "I will bring along something reflective, but I am hoping to avoid the gorgons entirely. They are traumatized women—and cursed—and I have no wish to harm them."

"I doubt you'll have a chance to open a dialogue and reveal your good intentions."

"Still, we must try to avoid a conflict. I have no desire to drag us into battle—if I am forced to use my powers, the Summerlands will become aware of my presence. Something my father must wish to avoid if he has gone to such lengths to send *me* and not Jin." With ownership over a feyrie mound, Elden could control where the entrance sent him—in Unseelie *or* Seelie lands. The border between the two kingdoms was heavily guarded by both sides. Only a warden would be able to travel betwixt the two without being detected.

What did his father *want* with this flower? And why did it have to be done in secret? Trade was common between the lands, so why could he not simply request it from a Seelie merchant?

It was best not to be too involved in the Unseelie King's workings, but something about this bargain continued to eat at him. Like there was some puzzle he was too close to solve.

"Not to add *more* stress to the situation," Lyra began cautiously, "but I remembered something from my days living in the feylands. The Summer Queen sent the gorgons a rather malicious gift. A mirror that could change one's appearance once they looked upon it."

"A mirror a gorgon would covet, but could never use." He shook his head, wondering once again how the Seelie were seen as the least cruel of the fey.

"You understand why I would mention this?" Lyra probed, finishing her map with a flourish.

Did she think he wasn't listening? "Of course. This could solve all of Avalon's problems."

"*So,*" Lyra drew out the word. "Are you going to tell her about it?"

"What? Why would I not?"

"Really?" She rolled her eyes and repeated, "*Really?*" in an exasperated tone. "Elden, you've never played dumb before. Why start now?"

"Please," he sneered. "Enlighten me on the situation."

"Don't take that haughty tone with *me*—you sound like the rest of your family."

Chastised properly, Elden asked without his previous poison, "Lyra, why wouldn't I tell her about something that could make her life better?"

"Because then she will leave."

She let him sit with that for a minute. Elden protested. "I have been doing everything in my power to make that happen." He moved his thoughts away from the recent memory of running to his truck, discombobulated from Odele's attack, and chasing Avalon to bring her back.

"Elden, you idiot, I heard you offered her a job."

"That was strictly a business decision—"

"Oh, cousin! You're acting silly enough as it is. A *business* decision? Like that dinner at Abernathy's farm? Don't think I didn't find out about that. No one in their right mind would have thought anything work-related was going on there. A business, candlelit dinner. Insanity." Lyra softly sighed, shaking her head at his antics. "I can see that you have been trying to help her—nothing else could explain that situation with the Ellén Trechend. That doesn't mean that you want it to happen. We can all see how lovesick you are. Perhaps except, as it usually goes, the object of said foolish affection."

Elden began several counter-arguments—all of which Lyra shot down. She shook her head, pushing her dark curls somewhat back into place. "I knew you were doomed the day I first saw the glamour you placed over her."

Now that was ludicrous. "I barely knew the woman then."

"Yes, which only proves my point. She looked *beautiful*, Elden."

He didn't argue with that. Instead, he snapped, "And how am I responsible for that?"

"She'd just been attacked in the feylands, hadn't slept, and still she looked beautiful because your glamour made her look that way. Because that's how you see her."

An uneasiness settled upon his senses, dizzying him. "Oh, fuck."

"Exactly right," Lyra said, and left him there to stew.

CHAPTER 31
AVALON

Avalon needed a clear mind before they descended into the feylands. Though she had learned in school that the Summerlands were considered less hostile than the Winterlands, this did nothing for her anxiety. At least Elden knew how to navigate the Winterlands. They were relying on Lyra to guide them to her family home, where she would remain while they explored the island.

Her cowardice begged to join Lyra in secluded safety, and Avalon had to quiet such pleas by reminding herself *she* was the one to make the bargain, not Elden.

Never mind, she had little choice in the matter. *Damn you, Taliesin.*

A clear, calm mind was hard to achieve—Lyra was tearing apart her wardrobe with overwhelming efficiency.

"Why don't you possess anything that a nymph would wear?"

Avalon laughed at her question. "Have you *met* me?"

"That is a fair point." Lyra left Avalon's wardrobe a mess, leaning back to stretch when she caught sight of the bag of dresses the brides had gifted Avalon. "Ah, finally."

"It's winter," Avalon blanched, trying to wrestle the bag of weather inappropriate clothing from Lyra's clutches.

"It's never winter in the Summerlands." Lyra examined each dress carefully, pressing the fabric against Avalon's skin. Lyra was dressed in sage green, with gold bracelets twinkling on her wrists and ankles. A chain of real daisies hung from her earlobes, and a collar of gold adorned her neck. Avalon was spared from such heavy jewelry—she needed to be as silent as possible once they reached the gorgons.

"Lyra, I wanted to ask about the gorgons. Can they really turn people to stone? How did they come to be?"

The nymph's eyes softened. "They are women cursed, unfairly I think, by the Summer Queen. They used to be nymphs, dryads, and the like."

"That's why Elden is bringing me along," Avalon realized. "He doesn't want to hurt them, and I can use my Sight to avoid them."

"Exactly. He's a good man." Lyra decided on a pale lilac for Avalon, turning around to give her some privacy. "Have you been able to look ahead at all? Do we all die or what?"

Her mouth a thin line, Avalon focused on pulling out any wrinkles in her silk dress. "It's difficult for me to look further than an hour ahead. It's rare when I'm successful and leaves me drained, whether it works or not. I didn't want to risk not having the strength later on." This outfit was ridiculous—identical slits were cut up her thigh, nearly high enough to reveal her underwear. The chest was equally embarrassing, diving toward her navel. "Why bother wearing clothes at all?" she complained.

Elden waited for them at the feyrie mound, looking as unhappy with her attire as she was. He scolded Lyra, instantly pinning her as the one responsible. "What have you forced her into?"

"We can't go prancing around—"

"No one's going to be *prancing*, first of all—"

"—the Summerlands in jeans. We need to blend in," Lyra finished loudly. "Not that you make that easy."

He shook his head, indicating his own outfit. "It's green. What else do you want from me? It's bad enough that I can't wear my regular armor." Instead of his princely silver plate, he was dressed in simple brown leathers over a dark green shirt. The short, one-handed axe was at his side and a round shield, polished until it was reflective, hung on his back.

"It takes more than wearing green to blend in with the Seelie," Lyra groused.

"Fine. If anyone seems suspicious of me, I'll start talking about orgies. That should make me fit right in." Elden checked his weapons, turning to Avalon and getting another red-faced eyeful of her skimpy outfit. "Avalon, I don't see your dagger. Do you have it? And did you tell Odele—"

"Yes, to the first thing," she interrupted, opening the leather satchel she'd been given to carry human food, water, and a second pair of warm clothes to wear to the Winterlands. She showed him the dagger nestled within the clothing. Elden gave her a belt and sheath to carry her blade with instead. "No, to the second. You said we'd be back before she notices."

"We can *hope*," he clarified. "I noticed that your parents are still here."

That was due to some scheme of Valerie's, most likely. She'd try to guilt her daughters into attending another sponsor dinner or something equally dull. "I didn't tell them where I was going, if that's what you're asking. Though, I'm sure if I disappeared into the feylands, never to be seen again, Bruce would find some way to spin it into more votes."

"Still," Elden grimaced, rubbing his neck, "I can't help but feel that you've been continuously coerced into entering my world without your consent."

"It feels like that because that's—" Avalon considered her words, considered how he might take them. "It *is* like that, Elden. I can't deny that. But, were we going anywhere else, I wouldn't hate being strung along with you."

"You don't hate being at my side?" His chuckle became a nervous cough. "For *you*, that's nearly a proposal."

"Shut up." She cringed. "Odele must be right—I'm suffering from Stockholm Syndrome."

As she had hoped, Elden searched for a distraction. He spoke, but she had looked away from him momentarily and missed some keywords.

"My wet dreams are none of your business!" Avalon snapped, her pulse racing.

Elden actually jumped back with his hands raised in surrender. "I said 'bad dreams', Avalon! *Bad!* I asked if nightmares were the reason that you looked tired. You were tossing and turning all night."

"Wait." Lyra busted into their conversation. "Elden, how do you even know that?"

Avalon wanted to melt into the ground. Initially, her dreams had been unpleasant. Filling first with memories of Bane, and then making the deal with the Unseelie king, before it gave way to images of Elden, his sword swinging to catch another's, straining with all that effort just to hopelessly try and save her.

And after, her dreams had changed.

Elden tugged loose the laces of her corset, rather than secure them. They occupied that same quiet alcove she remembered from the Winterlands' ball. Only now he had her pressed firmly against the wall, his large, rough hand wrapped around her throat from behind.

"You're flustered, Avalon." She tried to protest, but the hand around her tightened just slightly. "You can remain quiet, but your heartbeat can't."

His other hand started climbing underneath her dress. "Say it, Avalon. Say what you want."

She could not speak a lie. "You."

From there, the dream had spiraled into territory she couldn't admit just yet, not even to herself. It was no vision, just her mad imaginings based on her sexual frustrations toward her captor and employer.

Avalon demanded of him, "Can we hurry this up? It's cold enough already and you standing so close to me isn't exactly helping."

Elden stiffened and headed to the mound, doing his dramatic hand-waving until the gate swung open and a warm breeze drifted through. "I got us as close as I safely could. We don't want our entrance to be noticed."

As much as Avalon wanted to sprint inside, into the warmth, she contained herself and slowly followed at Elden and Lyra's heels.

The Summerlands was splattered with color, a regular Jackson Pollock of yellows, greens, and endless blue sky. The trees, taller and wider than anything Earth possessed, were filled with life. Large spiders, Weaver's size, were thankfully keeping to the upper branches. Small homes, reminiscent of birdhouses, hung from the thickest branches and had butterfly-winged feyries flitting in and out. The scent of the ocean reached her, but Avalon could not see or hear the source.

"My family isn't going to be happy that I brought you, Elden. But they will be *very* happy to provide a boat for you to reach the Island of Gorgons." Lyra led them down a narrow path, avoiding the larger main road Elden had dropped them on. "Their joy will fade upon your return."

"It's to be expected. It's not a fair thing to ask of them, to help an Unseelie prince trespass upon their lands."

"I don't know what this flower means to your father, and I honestly don't want to. At least he provided a description."

That would help marginally. Avalon doubted Elden was much of a botanist.

This was such an insignificant task—the sort of quest she'd expect from a feyrie king. Something stupid and most likely going to get them killed.

Lyra's family lived on the seaside, in one of many white washed, blue roofed homes that hugged the shoreline. The neighborhood they strolled through was cramped, each home threatening to encroach on its neighbor, and it was loud. Nymphs and water spirits flooded the streets, offering their wares to one another, and once their hopeful eyes saw Elden and Avalon, unrecognized customers, they thrust thin scarfs and various treats at them. The food looked *so* delicious—especially a pastry that was soaked in a berry sauce—that Avalon, though she had been warned against it, was sorely tempted.

Elden snatched her away from the vendor, turning his nose up at the dessert. "That sauce is cooked with Seelie wine. Unless you want to lose your mind and run around the Summerlands naked, I would stay away from that."

What a horrifying image. His scare tactic worked, and she allowed him to rush her through the market. "Try not to gape at anything. Or smile. If they see our teeth, the game is up." Elden kept close to his cousin, dragging Avalon along so she'd keep up with his long-legged pace.

Once they survived the Seelie market, Lyra led them to a house that stood on a cliff side. One building was on its way to sliding down said cliff. Lyra's family home was two stories, the same white and blue combination as the others in the area, and it was overrun with family. Kids ran around the home, playing some made-up game, until they saw Lyra approach. Most ran to her, hugging her legs, but one older child sprinted back to the house, vanishing inside to reemerge with an older woman. Lyra slunk forward to this newcomer, dragging her young siblings along, and had a tense, and loud, conversation.

"That's not boding well," Avalon remarked to Elden, who had a gaggle of children gathered around his feet, staring up at him with wide, brown eyes.

Hurrying back over, Lyra led them away from her home and down a stone staircase that was cut into the nearby cliff. Avalon glared down at each crumbling step, cursing each and every feyrie she knew, and especially cursing the carver for making the steps so steep.

They landed on a white sand beach, and the light glinting off the sand blinded their winter-adjusted eyes. A sun-bleached skeleton of some fey creature that resembled a whale but was *not*, sat on the beach so large that they did not walk around it, but through the rib cage. The skeleton had no eye sockets in its skull. A small dock became visible through the bones, a few small, but well-kept boats attached.

"Sorry you didn't get invited to dinner," Lyra apologized, scratching her curls and looking away. She held onto Avalon and Elden's spare clothing intended for their inevitable journey into the Winterlands. "My family is usually the type to grab people off the street and bring them to the table."

"We understand," Elden shrugged. "It's not up to you to solve our world's politics. It's enough that they are willing to lend us a vessel. And feyrie food has nothing on your cooking, Lyra."

Lyra's brightness returned, though weakly. Elden and Lyra then exchanged a meaningful look, and he said, "Avalon, there's something else on this island we need to retrieve. A mirror." Elden avoided meeting Avalon's questioning stare. "If we can find it, you'll be able to change your appearance permanently. You could return to your old life."

"How did you know about this?" Avalon thought she might be sick. All her problems could instantly be solved by a simple, enchanted trinket.

"It's something we don't like to talk about," Lyra explained. "But I think it's important to remember our people's cruelty. That mirror was given to the gorgons by the Summer Queen. A callous gift, and one the gorgons will never be able to use on themselves."

Elden had explained that the curve in his reflective shield would prevent him from looking directly in the gorgon's eyes, but if a gorgon looked directly into a hand mirror—they would turn themselves to stone.

If Avalon was the gorgon that had received such a "gift", she would have spiked it on the ground.

Lyra hugged them both, squeezing Avalon hard enough that her back cracked. At that physical sign of affection, it began to dawn on Avalon exactly what they were undertaking.

That numbness she'd encountered after Bane was nowhere to be found. Familiar and incapacitating, Avalon's anxiety crept back in, a rising whirlwind inside her. Any other time, with natural problems, no fey involved, she was a master at channeling this negative energy into angry motivation. But this was not a bit of code that was escaping her, or an unmanageable guest, and Avalon was losing herself in the spiral.

Why would he tell her about that damned mirror now? It added a layer of pressure she wasn't sure she could handle without preparation.

Watching Lyra walk away, reluctantly climbing the staircase (something Avalon dreaded as much as rowing to this island), made her breath come in short, rapid shots. She even let Elden do the lion's share of the work, loading and preparing the boat himself. She was never one to be idle while someone else was working, and yet, even this guilt was not enough to move her.

Readying the boat didn't take long, which meant they had a long wait ahead of them. As they were to be stumbling around blind on the island, Elden had made the decision to wait until twilight struck, when the island's inhabitants would have the worst vision. The Unseelie, like Elden, had night-sight—they hoped the gorgons didn't possess the same.

Through all this, Elden said nothing, taking Avalon's satchel to place it in the boat for her. He returned, each step careful and silent, until he presented her with her blindfold.

That scrap of black cloth, caught by the ocean wind, hit her with a terrifying finality she could not shake. Avalon turned away from him, spying the perfect seaside neighborhood and the storybook forest behind it. Elden's index finger slowly moved her chin until she would look at him again.

Elden gazed at her for a moment too long before he turned her around so he could test out the blindfold.

Once the blindfold slipped over her eyes, and Elden tightened the knot securely, the idyllic, dreamy haze of the feylands vanished. Panic flooded her senses—the ones that remained. How was he so certain that they could rely on her Sight? Avalon had never used her powers for such an extended period. It didn't matter that she was merely looking seconds into the future—she would fail them both.

"Elden," Avalon whispered, whirling around and grasping, reaching for his shirt in the dark. Her hands fisted into the fine material. "What if I can't use the Sight? We'll be blind out there. I'll kill you. I—"

Elden gripped her by the shoulders, lightly squeezing. His voice was loud enough to overpower the ocean. "Then I will look, Avalon. If it comes to that, keep your eyes shut, and I will see for the both of us."

And if he saw a gorgon? He'd turn to stone, prince or not, and she'd be trapped, sightless, and responsible for his undoing. "I don't want to lose you. I..." She exhaled, finishing the rest of her statement silently. *I can't lose you, Elden. I can't be responsible for it.*

"I'll hold your hand the entire way. You won't lose me."

Avalon let his mistake lie. "The entire time? You swear?"

"If I let you go, know that it is because I am dead."

For an innkeeper, comfort was not something he could provide easily. Elden added, when his words failed to ease her troubled quivering, "Avalon, I know you can do this. I need you to do this. I need you."

He needed her? Needed a weak, pathetic changeling?

Avalon, sure her face was flush with shame at her own fear, begged, "Show me, Elden."

"Show you?" he repeated, doubt shadowing his tone. More serious, a rumble across her skin, he muttered, "*Show you.*"

She waited and, blinded as she was, the seconds seemed to pass like eternities. Avalon gasped as Elden's hands left her shoulders, cupping her face gently. He didn't go any further until she pressed closer against him, stretching up on her toes.

Droplets from the sea hit her back, carried by the winds cresting off the waves. The ocean crashed in her ears as she strained for any sort of clue as to what he was thinking. She couldn't remove her blindfold and look at him—she was too cowardly for that.

His thumb swept across her lower lip. When she turned her face up to his, Elden kissed her.

His kiss was no more a comfort than his words—the man kissed her as if nuclear sirens were ringing and he wanted her to be the last thing he tasted before their bodies turned to ash.

He held her so fiercely, as if he wanted to squeeze out her fear, and Avalon could not deny that this was exactly what she needed. What she *wanted.* A new, stronger despair overwhelmed her.

She now knew how it felt to have his attention, to have his trust. How cold his magic felt as they pretended death was not on the horizon. And it was easy to imagine how empty she would become without it.

He broke it off first, silently gripping her arm and leading her into the small dingy Lyra's family had provided. She peeked underneath her blindfold until they were settled. The boat rocked with their weight, and Elden sat facing her, his back to the island. She kept her eyes downcast so she would not have to meet his gaze. *How unattractively spineless,* she shamed herself.

Though she could not see all of him, she watched as Elden placed the oars down and leaned forward, extending a gentle hand. It was becoming a ritual between them—Avalon met him halfway and clutched his hand, crushing it with her own.

This small thing brought more heat to her face than their earlier embrace.

He rowed them over the increasing waves, glancing back—as they had discussed—only when he absolutely had to.

Her lips were pleasantly swollen—she fought to keep her fingers from touching her lips to soothe the slight tingle that remained.

"We're close, Avalon." How dare he sound so calm! "I need you to start being my eyes."

She would not allow this kiss, or her own fear, to let her fail him. Holding her breath, summoning clarity despite the edges of worry eating at her concentration, Avalon looked.

CHAPTER 32
ELDEN

Impossible woman. *Show me.* What was that supposed to mean? Elden rowed onward, the exercise providing some distraction.

Avalon spoke clearly, powerfully. The steady and sure chant of a Seer. "The shore is empty for the next five minutes."

Not much time, but this had been the plan. Elden lifted his own blindfold, looking to the shore without hesitation. Once the water was shallow enough, he dragged the boat to shore, leaving it high enough that if the tides changed, they wouldn't end up stranded. As he helped lift her out of the boat and onto the sandy beach, Elden forced his blindfold back on so he would stop staring at her soft mouth.

He could not linger upon the kiss—he could only wait and see if he would receive a painful call from Thompson's Hotel Management's HR.

They moved further into the island slowly, their hands clasped together, fitting as naturally together as a lock and key. Avalon spoke quietly, though her voice was certain, and did her best to keep them safe, keep them moving, and keep them from tripping on exposed roots.

The ocean made it difficult for Elden to hear any creatures, humanoid or not, approaching. Avalon had yet to predict any obstacles in their distant future, which set his teeth on edge. Things were never easy for him—why would that change now?

"Wait." Avalon tugged back on his grip, halting them. "I see...clouds. Over a field of purple flowers."

"A storm?" he guessed, but her silence said that wasn't it.

"Poison." But Avalon did not move them or give a direction to run. "All around us. We're surrounded."

"When, Avalon? Where?"

She guided him off the sandy path they had taken. When the terrain underneath him switched, he started to pull back.

"Are you taking us *toward* the field?"

"I can't see a way around it," she said, refusing to let him slow them down. "All roads lead to the murder field or some mystic bullshit like that." Avalon halted them, her fingers digging into his skin. "Elden, someone is—"

They weren't alone—he didn't need Avalon to tell him that. He felt the phantom in their midst, heard the muffled shifting of their feet. Still, Avalon whispered, "A woman. Ghoulish and too thin, and a cloud of dust rises as she moves."

"What nasty words, Seer. Let me pluck out your eyes, as it does not seem that you need them."

Elden sighed. He felt Avalon move in front of him. That foolish woman was placing herself between whatever was now speaking and him.

"What," Avalon scoffed, "is it about feyries that they are always threatening to steal parts of my anatomy? She's not a gorgon, Elden. I'm not sure *what* she is. But we can look."

Elden slipped the blindfold up, pushing his hair wildly out of place. A small woman, who looked made more out of nimbus than flesh, crouched before them. As they watched her, she held a purple flower, picking at the petals with black, pointed nails. "So many visitors," she muttered. "Who are you here to kill?" She stood at the edge of the field, the background of purple mist hovering above the fauna less than inviting.

"We aren't here to kill anyone," Elden replied defensively.

Her laugh was dry, clouds of dust bursting from her mouth with each exhale. "No one sees *me*, boy, with good intentions."

Something prickled in the back of his mind, murmuring doubts and fear underneath his next question. "Have you seen this?" He presented a drawing he'd been given from one of his father's scribes, the flower drawn crudely as if the artist guessed at some portions. That fickle feylight floated out of Avalon's throat, lighting the paper and also giving away their position to anyone nearby.

The woman studied the paper, amusement flaring on the being's gaunt face. "You sure you don't want someone dead, boy? This won't do for a bridal bouquet, if that's your idea. Even your bitter mouthed lady doesn't deserve hellebore on her wedding day."

"What's your name?"

Elden held back a groan. Avalon was still inexperienced in feyrie ways. That was not a question one simply asked.

"Achlys, not that you could do anything with it."

Avalon didn't understand how much of an insult that was, but she'd been given an answer. If it was due to her plain incompetence in the feyrie realm, did that matter? Elden could have asked a half-dozen times and received a dozen refusals.

"I hope you have something to trade. Something shiny,"

Achlys grinned, all malicious, blackened teeth. It was hard to miss the hint.

There went the backup plan, but as Achlys eyed the shield, greedily drinking in the moonlit reflection, Elden saw little choice.

"The shield for three of your flowers. Nothing more, nothing less." Could it be this easy? He held his breath, scowling, and waited for the inevitable complication.

"Eager to leave, aren't you? Smart. The gorgons hate men." But Achlys would not make this transaction simple. "What about the dagger on her hip? I need a new peeler."

"No."

He was surprised Avalon replied with such force. Surely the dagger held no meaning for her? Was she drawing a line for his own comfort?

Achlys's smiling, triumphant mouth tightened. "I'll take the shield."

Something was off, and Avalon seemed to agree. She pinched his arm, finding an unarmored section, and whispered, "Give it to her. Quickly!"

Elden made the trade, letting Achlys wander off into her poison field and pick three perfectly dangerous blossoms. He instructed Achlys to slide the flowers in-between pages of a journal he'd stolen from his mother's office. He wrapped the journal up with leather, stowing the book inside his shirt for safekeeping.

As soon as the book was out of sight, Avalon took him by the arm and pulled them back toward the shore. "Cover your eyes! She's going to—"

Achlys, he guessed, was using his shield as a drum, banging some metal instrument against it and drawing attention to their location. If Achlys could not trade for the dagger, she would instead pluck it from their corpses.

"MAN!" the poisonous woman screeched. "MAN on the island!"

They needed to get off this cursed hellhole before whoever or whatever Achlys was calling found them. Avalon dragged them off the path, leaping over bushes that snagged at their clothing.

"The mirror!" Elden reminded her.

She shouted back, "*Damn* the mirror!"

They ran together, the shore still so far away. "Don't look!" Avalon repeated, a frantic mantra that kept them zigzagging through the island. "Too many variables," she cried, her voice breaking. He tried to fight against her, to slow her down, as he sensed they were no longer alone. But Avalon was never one to relinquish control. Still, she pulled, panting, "I can't see! Elden, I'm—"

"Blind."

Their retreat halted. Elden couldn't say how he caught the movement—but he snatched the air in front of Avalon and grabbed a thin wrist. A voice cried out—not Avalon, but an enemy.

Avalon's hand, still gripping his free one, was shaking. "She—the gorgon—removed my covering."

Using the captured arm to his advantage, Elden pushed out at the new body, shoving them back and away from Avalon. Instantly, his short axe was out, his ears straining for the gorgon's new location. Odele's banshee shrieks had left a slight ringing in his ears that wasn't there before. The shield was gone, but Elden was meticulous in a way that wore callouses into his hands and fingertips. The axe in his hands was polished to a perfectionist's shine—Elden hoped Avalon's will-o'-wisp was near as he lifted his blindfold enough to see the ground beneath him.

A soft blue glow illuminated his axe, and the wisp gave him enough light to observe two shadows lengthening before him.

"Don't look at my blade," he warned them. One glance at their own image, reflected in his blade, would have turned them to stone, solving the current problem for good. He saw two pairs of bare feet and that was all.

A faint hissing rose, then quieted, as the women shushed what he could only assume was their head of serpents. "What an odd tactic. Giving away your only trick."

"Oh, that's not my only trick."

Avalon had worked her way behind him, pressing her forehead against his back to further shield her vision. Elden could freeze these women—and hack their frozen heads from their bodies—but he had trespassed on their island. A scouting party was only logical.

"We came to speak with Achlys, and that is done. Now we wish to leave." The mirror would have to be forgone—they had been betrayed by Achlys and spending any more time hunting for the accessory would be suicide. "But," Elden said, recalling Avalon divulging that one of the gorgons had stolen her blindfold, "if you so much as touch her again, I'll bring winter early and not let this island feel warmth again until hypothermia takes you all."

"Don't play the victim, Unseelie," one of them laughed, a rattle accompanying her dry amusement. "Achlys doesn't deal with innocents. You should have offered her more—she's been getting spoiled as of late."

Who else was visiting that poisonous woman? Elden knew

now he could no longer bury such questions. "Will you let us pass?"

"We should at least try to kill him. If we keep letting trespassers escape with Achlys's petals, more will come."

"We're held to a bargain," Avalon piped up, her hands twisting tighter into his shirt. "We can't return without the petals. Otherwise, we'd never have come at all."

"Bargains," the one who spoke without that rattling scoffed. "Why should we care about your bargain? You've done this to yourself."

"But she didn't." Elden saw an opportunity and ran with it before his logic could keep up. "She was forced to accept this bargain—or die at the hands of the Unseelie King."

"That is not the nature of a feyrie bargain."

"*Men,*" the other added, with a spit of venom. "Always taking. Always hurting. And *you.*" She must have been indicating Elden somehow. "Are you here to make sure she doesn't fail?"

He was, but not in the way the gorgon meant it. She was accusing him of being there as insurance, as a guard on behalf of the Unseelie King. Elden replied, "I'm here because I need her to be safe—because I want her to be safe."

"That doesn't make us hate him any less, does it?" The gorgons had a conversation without him, their raspy whispers undetectable.

"Leave," they said in unison, and one continued with, "And do not return. Though you may find the waters at night more dangerous than our appearances."

"We came for one more thing."

Avalon moaned, tugging at his shirt. "Are you insane? Let's go!"

"I believe the Summer Queen bestowed a gift of a mirror."

"A gift?" The rattling one laughed. "And he was doing so well."

"A cruelty," he corrected. "It's nothing but a danger to you all. Let us take it off the island." If it could be destroyed, it likely already was. But such things took great magic to unmake, and he doubted the gorgons had the capability. They might have tried throwing it into the sea, but such an act would offend the queen—and risking the royal's unearned wrath again was not something he could envision these women doing.

"A feyrie would know better than to ask for something without offering anything in return."

"You said Achlys has been drawing visitors—something you don't want. She betrayed us after accepting our bargain. She brings men to your shores." His plan was sure to piss off the Summer Queen. He'd have to ensure Taliesin would be blamed. "I'll rid you of her presence. I'll lay down a sheet of frost over her field of poison. Nothing will grow there again."

"*Elden*," Avalon warned. "It's not worth it. Enough feyries are out to get us. Let's not add an entire kingdom to the list."

"You act as if I don't know this," he snapped, and quickly regretted the tone he used. The gorgons wouldn't appreciate it, either. But why couldn't Avalon let him act in her best interests—even if it led to his ruin? He knew the possible consequences and was man enough to make the decision himself.

"Kill her, and we'll bring it to the shore. Perhaps it will annoy the queen to know an Unseelie has that damned thing and can actually make use of it."

The other chimed in, "You have a deal with us, redcap. But I'd avoid meeting our sisters. They may not see the wisdom in such a bargain. Achlys killed as many as she lured here."

This trip would not be without bloodshed, as Elden had

naively hoped. "Find Achlys again," he told Avalon, though he knew there was a very good chance that she'd ignore that and take them to the boat instead. He slipped his blindfold over Avalon's eyes and kept his own shut.

"Damn you, Elden," she swore, leading them away from the sound of waves and back to the fields. "Can't you ever leave well enough alone?"

No, it was a very well-known fatal flaw of his.

"I'm getting a little tired," she told him quietly, the terrain under their feet becoming familiar.

If she was admitting that to him, Avalon must have been nearing exhaustion.

"She's ahead of us," Avalon whispered, and Elden risked it and opened his eyes completely.

Achlys's beady eyes widened to see them alive. Her thin body stilled. That poison cloud hovering over her field darkened and rolled toward them. It was simple to send a winter gust of wind to dissipate the cloud. *Simple,* but using Unseelie magic might draw more danger to them.

Achlys cursed them and dug around in her pack, withdrawing a small parcel from the inside. She threw it at their feet, and Elden tackled Avalon to get her underneath him. The explosive began fizzling and releasing gas. He covered Avalon's mouth and nose with his hand, fighting her squirming, and dragged her away.

Another burst of wind cleared the air. Pressing her into the sand, he ordered, "Stay down until I come back." He passed the journal into Avalon's possession. "If too much time has passed, leave and fulfill your bargain with my father."

Elden walked away, leaving behind Avalon's angry protests. He kept a tornado of frigid wind around him, keeping his air clear of Achlys's poisonous clouds.

Achlys was so quiet, so slight, that it was nearly impossible to track her to her tiny sea cave. But Elden managed, his night-sight just powerful enough to find his way. He searched for the small woman's footprints, catching her trail after a few tense minutes of searching.

The interior of the cave was unlit until Avalon's damned wisp floated in from behind him, illuminating crates and baskets that were overflowing with jewels and weapons. Avoiding kicking over a woven basket filled to the brim with rings, Elden tried to shoo the will-o'-wisp away. Avalon would need the thing far more than he would, but the orb ignored his motions (though Elden knew that wisp understood him perfectly) and flew further into the tunnel.

Dammit. Elden tightened his grip on his axe, quietly trailing behind the wisp. That light would give away his position, but that wasn't something he was too concerned with. This cave seemed to be one straight tunnel. Achlys would know he was coming, regardless.

The wealth was unending—how many times had she traded material goods for someone's life? Did only the Seelie know about her? If his father had to send him for such a task, one could argue that the Winterlands didn't frequent the island. And yet, hadn't some of those jewels seemed to have his homeland's touch? Had these precious stones come from his father's many mines?

Even if Elden hadn't forged that bargain with the gorgons, ridding the realm of this poisonous presence was justified.

Something fell from the ceiling, landing on his back and digging claws into his neck. The wisp was in Achlys's face immediately, blinding the nocturnal creature and allowing Elden time to grab her and throw her to the ground.

She rolled, dodging the first downswing of his axe. Achlys ran back into the darkness, to attempt a second sneak attack, before she lurched forward, a blade of ice embedded through her back.

While he lacked Jin's ability to magic three ice blades into existence at once, one blade was well within his skillset.

It was hardly the most sporting kill. But Achlys was fueling murderers with deadly flowers—hardly the most innocent of victims. He strained so far away from his redcap nature to avoid unnecessary killing. It was rarely appreciated by the fey.

The wisp led him out of the cave, illuminating that field of poison. Killing the field was not so simple. Elden was sorely out of practice calling up so much Winter, and in the Summerlands, no less. There were multiple factors working against him, but he was finally able to bring a winter storm down and level the poison field.

Perhaps, as remote as this island was, no one would notice. No, that was foolish. There was no way the Summer Queen would overlook this.

Avalon had waited exactly where Elden and the wisp had left her, her arms crossed and mouth tight. When Elden announced his return, she flew to him, pinching his arms as she held him.

"Don't leave me like that again, Elden!" She hiccupped, continuing her angry ranting with, "I won't allow it! I-I don't know what I'll do to you, but I know you won't like it!"

Still blind-folded, she was unaware of the stupid grin her onslaught had given him. "I understand, Avalon." Elden allowed her scolding. "It won't happen again."

Barely satisfied, Avalon returned the journal with the

flowers inside to him, and Elden carefully tucked it back into the pouch woven inside his shirt.

They retraced their path, Avalon hesitating with her directions more and more. Now they felt as blind as they actually were. It was an immense relief when they could once again feel the salty spray of the ocean.

"We can look now. I think."

Not exactly reassuring. "I trust you." It even surprised him how easily the words left his lips. "But let me look first."

The beach was empty, and the boat was still safely tucked away from the water. Inside, underneath one of the planks that served as a seat, was the mirror, wrapped carefully in silk.

Elden grunted as he shoved the boat back out to sea. He went back to Avalon and lifted her by her hips, forgetting in his haste to give her a warning, and placed her in the vessel. He apologized, and soon they were hitting the water.

He rowed them back across the water to where safety lay. Elden's position gave him a perfect view of his partner, still blindfolded but alert, face open and searching.

Avalon had done her best to contain her hair by knotting the top half of it into a bun. After all that running, it was now a soft, rose-gold mess. Strands lifted by the ocean winds, illuminated by the moonlight, stole his attention.

It didn't matter that Avalon could only see minutes into the future—his secret would be discovered soon enough. Perhaps he even loved her. And, without the ability to tell a lie, there was a sure way to tell. If he could say the words, they were the truth.

With the mirror in hand, he knew she'd be gone in the morning. It would be kinder to never say anything. Elden gently removed her covering, watching her blink at him as her eyes adjusted to the pale moonlight.

"Avalon, I—"

Wet, cutting hands gripped him from behind, tearing him from the boat and into the water. Oceanic naiads, eyes white and large, began their quick descent with Elden in tow.

CHAPTER 33
AVALON

Cursing, Avalon stood up, the boat rocking her and nearly tossing her into the ocean alongside Elden. "Light!" she screamed, her voice a broken, hollow thing. Throwing herself to her knees, she inched as carefully as she could to the boat's edge. The wisp obeyed her, dancing above the black water uselessly. She could not see him. She could not see—

Her powers were all but spent, but she had no choice. With that leather armor strapped to him, weighing him down, Elden would be helpless against those ocean feyries.

Avalon looked with her Sight, the dark ocean giving her nothing until, with more strength than she had to give, she found him. Elden, sinking, no, being pulled by his legs down toward the trenches, where he would stand no chance against the closing pressure of tons and tons of water. He was frantically trying to unhook his armor—sodden as it was, it would surely keep him from resurfacing.

Such an image would have been useless—there were no

markings or objects that could help her determine his underwater location. But she saw, in her prediction, her wisp acting as a spotlight, highlighting Elden's pale, beautiful features.

The effort was too much—Avalon heaved into the water, her sides aching as she barely kept her stomach's contents down.

"Find him!" she begged, and, to her panic, the wisp only hovered in place. "What! What more do you want? I'll give you anything!" Such a stupid thing to say to a creature of the feylands.

The wisp dimmed—considering her desperate promise, perhaps—before diving into the water. Dumping everything off her person, save for the belted dagger she wore, she jumped clumsily into the waves.

The saltwater stung her eyes, but her Unseelie night-sight—something that had unnerved her at first—saved her now. The saltwater naiads, those bitter, vengeful monsters she recognized from the storybook in her room, were swarming, an underwater tornado of nails and teeth. They were mostly humanoid, fitted with gills and fins that attached to their limbs. The skin ranged from blue to green to black.

But why were the naiads bothering with them? Even Avalon knew that they didn't live close to the surface. It didn't make sense.

The wisp went to each naiad, illuminating a vulnerable part of their body. Avalon swam, feeling sluggish compared to the naiads' swift, smooth movements. The will-o'-wisp was well-versed in death—wherever the wisp lit, Avalon struck, delivering an unskilled blow that would still leave lasting, bloody damage.

All she needed to do, she told her rising terror as air became scarce in her lungs, was free Elden.

The naiads slashed at her, only retreating when the wisp zipped into their face. The naiads must have been used to blacker, deeper waters, and the light was too intense for their dark-adjusted eyes.

With the wisp playing goalie against the ocean fey, one of them torpedoed up to the boat and capsized it. All the items stashed inside sank to the bottom. A glint of the golden mirror caught Avalon's attention before it vanished into the depths.

The wisp could find it. If she asked the wisp to lead her down to the mirror, it would. But that would mean abandoning Elden. The will-o'-wisp floated in front of her face, waiting for her to change her orders.

Ignoring the unspoken question, she continued diving until she found Elden, struggling to fight off three naiads by himself. She reached him and started cutting any straps in his armor that her fumbling fingers could find. She snipped three before Elden took her dagger, held it between his teeth, and roughly pushed her back up to the surface.

Avalon burst out of the water with a painful gasp. Logically, Elden could have only been a few seconds behind her, but Avalon felt each thudding of her heart in slow motion. Each inhale to reclaim her breath seemed to take ages. *Where was he? Where—*

"Dammit!" Elden broke the surface, immediately cursing. "The boat! Where is the—" His swearing repeated, though this time more colorful than before—and all of it very fey. He slapped the water in his frustration. "The damn mirror! Avalon, I am so sorry—"

She hadn't the patience for any more apologies. "Shut up and swim! Lyra's waiting for us and—" She had to finish that statement in her head. *Not going to wait for us forever.* No,

Lyra would wait until her lamp burned out completely and then head the search party at first light.

Taking a deep breath into her soggy lungs, Avalon tried to decide between the backstroke or the breaststroke when her head slipped back underneath the water.

Some leftover naiad had her by the ankle and was jerking her back down. Her curse forced more water inside her. Despite how much she kicked with her other leg, her escape attempts were futile. Avalon reached for her dagger, only to remember she had given it to Elden.

How deep was it taking her? She was chilled—if the pressure didn't crush her, hypothermia would take her.

Their downward spiral slowed, and, to her shock, she was able to finally kick free. She floated above the naiad, giving it one last glance.

Elden held the naiad in his grip, blue swirls of magic in a whirlpool around them. He was freezing the creature, and slowly. The naiad fought for a time, before the cold overcame it and its white, dead eyes crystalized with frost.

He'd already used the Unseelie king's magic once on the island. Risking bringing even more winter to the Summerlands was insane.

Out of air, Avalon kicked up to the light, Elden following a few moments later. Without asking, he headed for the shore after taking one of her arms and slipping her onto his back. It wasn't an easy swim—though Avalon admittedly wasn't expected to do much—and Elden ended up half-carrying her to shore once their feet could touch sand.

Once ashore, Avalon focused on ridding her lungs of leftover saltwater. "Do you have the book?" Avalon asked, coughing between words. She sat quietly, the white, flawless sand digging into her wet skin.

Elden violently tossed the wrapped journal down on the beach. He stood, fists clenched and shaking. White, sparkling crystals drifted down from the gathering grey clouds and stuck on her eyelashes.

It was snowing in the Summerlands. Not a light flurry, but a full-on winter storm.

"We lost the damned mirror." Elden began to pace, hands pulling at his wild, dark hair. He barked at her, "You should not have entered the water, Avalon. What were you *thinking*? I can't understand why you'd act so foolishly, so out of character—"

Avalon's face twisted, and she knew with a horrifying certainty she was about to cry. Her anger rarely took on such a form, but occasionally her fury became shameful, hot tears.

She pushed the heels of her palms into her eyes. "Damn you, Elden. Fuck you for thinking that I should—that I would leave you behind. Is that what you really think of me? That I'm so selfish?" Her forehead hit the sand, and her voice broke. "I'll always be a changeling first to you. A lying, selfish cockroach that will do anything to survive. I *hate* you for that, Elden."

It was too much—the loss of the mirror, her greatest chance at returning to her old life, and the fact Elden seemed furious that she had jumped into the water after him, rather than leave him for dead. Those two thoughts collided around in her skull, infuriating her. Avalon curled into herself. Elden was trying to speak to her, but her ears were still waterlogged. She'd have to look up at him to guess what he was trying to say, and that was the last thing she wanted to do.

She felt him land on his knees next to her, lifting and burying her face in his chest. He was soaked to the bone, and painfully cold, and still she wanted to press into him, forgetting her bitter anger. And since that's what she wanted, she denied herself it.

Avalon shoved against his chest, trying to make space between them. He barely moved from her force, but he leaned away from her of his own volition. "Avalon, stop that." He didn't speak until she looked at him. "I'm sorry, Avalon. You...you frightened me. I don't think you are any of those things."

"And *I* wasn't scared for you? They almost had you, Elden! I don't want to hear it." Her rage was too familiar to her—she clung to it desperately. She didn't want Elden to say what she needed to hear. She wanted to resent him.

"You are the furthest thing from selfish. You made a fool's bargain for me."

Stop talking. "I made it because—"

"You can believe you're self-serving, Avalon. In my father's court, you told me you took that deal because you saw what would happen to *me*. And while you can feed yourself a lie, you cannot speak one."

With too many warring emotions inside her, she snapped. Avalon lunged forward, gripping the front of his shirt in both hands. "Stop fucking talking!"

She forgot that Elden's temper was also quick to rise. He pinned her to the ground by her shoulders, too quick for her to protest. "You feral, wild *thief*," he snapped, something strange and broken in his voice. "You merciless *raider*."

She maintained her hold on his clothing, her breath hitching as he towered over her, inches from her face. The memory of his mouth was too recent—it distracted her from the fury she wanted to sink into.

When he attempted to speak again, it was too much. Avalon jerked him further down, capturing his mouth and smothering whatever he'd been about to say.

How quickly they both came undone. His hands twisted into her hair, his kisses invaded, and one of his knees pressed between her legs, pooling the heat there. This was drastically different from the desperate, fear-filled kiss they shared before the island. There was only frustration and lust in this, and she writhed underneath him, her want flooding her veins and taking over her senses, pushing her anger out.

He flipped the wet fabric of her dress up, exposing her bare legs and soaked, to the point of being nearly opaque, underwear.

"You hate me?" Elden repeated, and it painfully dawned on her what she, unable to lie, had just said to him. *I hate you for that.* Elden bit down on her lower lip, though not hard enough to draw blood. "Fine. Hate me. As long as you want me, I can deal with the rest."

I didn't mean—

Avalon *had* meant she hated that he would think her so callous that she would leave him behind. His opinion mattered greatly to her, a terrifying realization, and one she was not ready for.

It was impossible to get a word in—Elden devoured her with a fury she wouldn't stop if she could. Avalon wanted him, the repercussions be damned. Wanted those rough hands on her body, those sharp teeth nipping at the most sensitive parts of her. She needed him to know how she felt. This terrible heat he forged in her—she couldn't stay silent and let him go another minute unaware of exactly what he did to her. Avalon halted his kisses by gripping his jaw in one hand and pushing him back.

His unnatural eyes weren't so terrifying anymore. They were open and afraid he had pushed her too far.

"I want *you*, Elden. Don't doubt that again."

They stared, consumed with each other, before Elden broke away to press harder into her and begin kissing her neck. Without Elden's armor, there was little fabric between them and still that was too much distance.

He hooked a finger under the band of her panties, beginning to gently tug them downwards as if performing an experiment. Avalon raised her hips in encouragement, waiting for him to free her. He slid her underwear down and off, running his hands down the sides of her thighs hard enough she was certain she'd return home with purple fingerprints against her skin.

When Elden suddenly stopped to glance over his shoulder, she wanted to kill him.

"Lyra's making her way back down."

The madness that had taken over momentarily vanished. Avalon slid backwards until she could sit up, fix her clothes, and work on slowing her breath. Elden quickly kicked a hole in the sand to bury her underwear in. She mourned the clothing, but she didn't really want the ocean-drenched thing, anyway.

Elden offered a hand and pulled her gently to her feet. Avalon brushed her clothes free of sand, or tried to, and blushed at the man's obvious staring.

"Did I...hurt you?" he asked, his fingertips grazing the new bruises on her thighs.

She was too embarrassed to admit how rough she would have let him be with her. "You didn't do anything I didn't want, Elden."

His words were soft, hoarse from the saltwater they had

both swallowed. "I can give you more than that, Avalon."

What? Why would he want to? Her hands shook as she adjusted her belt and her empty sheath—anything to avoid looking at him.

He slid the dagger back into her possession before Elden's attention left her and focused on Lyra's lantern bobbing down the cliff's stairway.

"Is everyone okay?" Lyra demanded upon arrival, setting the lantern down between them. "Elden, it's *snowing*. What did you do?"

"Naiads pulled me into the water." How did he sound so calm? "That was no random attack. Someone must have sent them after us once they realized we stepped foot on that island."

"Who would do that?" Lyra mumbled a quick prayer to some feyrie goddess. "We need to leave. Now."

"Agreed."

Why this couldn't be a simple handoff, Avalon had no idea. Hadn't they suffered enough defeat tonight? Being in the feylands was surreal enough—having breakfast with Elden's Unseelie family...that was a recipe for disaster.

They had quickly escaped the Seelie's territory, heading back through the feyrie mound and ending up at the inn. There was no time to clean up. They had thrown on winter coats and footwear before Avalon and Elden headed for the Winter King's palace.

Once they were before the king, Elden violently threw the journal to one of father's advisors. "The bargain is fulfilled. Release her. Now."

Upon receiving the flowers, Taliesin waved a lazy hand towards Avalon, the silver threads binding them together reappearing and snapping in two. Taliesin then announced they were to remain for the morning meal. Something Elden and Avalon both fought against to no avail.

Hia approached them, her nose crinkling. "You smell like the ocean. Clean yourselves up." This time, she did not lead Avalon herself and sent a servant instead. Apparently, now was not the time for one of the princess's pranks.

Elden went in another direction, after squeezing Avalon's hand briefly as if to say, *we're almost out.*

The servant brought Avalon to a large bathing chamber, the steaming tub filling the entire room. It was dark inside, but dozens of black candles were grouped along the sides to provide some light. A basket with towels and cedar scented soap sat on the edge of the bath.

Once she was alone, Avalon stripped down and quickly slipped into the pool. It was a shock to find how deep the tub went; her shoulders barely remained above the water. It was unclear when breakfast was served so Avalon washed quickly, scrubbing the saltwater out of her hair.

As she bathed, the flickering candlelight reminded her of the wisp, whom she had made a promise to—one she didn't fully understand. What would it take from her? As will-o'-wisps dealt so often in death, Avalon was not keen to find out.

The loud sound of a sliding door that desperately needed maintenance interrupted her dark musings. She stilled, lowering herself into the water until it reached her chin.

Elden entered the chamber, wearing a loose silver robe that really ought to have been tightened. When he finally noticed her, he stopped short. "They didn't tell me you were in here."

He scratched the back of his neck fretfully, his gaze turning up to the ceiling. But he did not leave.

"It's too dark to see anything, anyway." She was glad her face was already flushed from the heat. It hid how she was both excited to see him and feeling shy all at once. "I can turn around while you undress to protect your innocence."

"How gallant of you. I can see about having you knighted later."

It was annoying—she had never wished for her foresight more than in this moment, and she was too drained to even attempt to use it. Having run out of things to say, and the beach still fresh in her mind, Avalon faced the other direction and tried not to imagine what was happening behind her.

Some quiet splashing told her it was time to turn around just in time to witness Elden reemerging from underneath the water. It brought to mind a certain period film she may have rewatched far too many times.

His eyes, glowing with that silver Unseelie shine in the darkness, widened. "Can I wash up before you stare at me?"

He was rather self-conscious for a feyrie. But she quickly, and without judgement, did as he asked. This time, she waited until he gave her permission to face him.

"I see there are some perks to being royalty. This bath is larger than my apartment."

"There are minerals added to help with aches and torn muscles." When he stood, he was much more exposed than she. Elden waded over and grabbed her upper arm. His touch raised gooseflesh where he held her.

"Elden, I—" Her breathiness vanished as she realized what he was doing. Elden was examining the various scratches she'd received from the naiads.

"We need to get ointment on this. Let me." He dug through her basket and retrieved a small jar. He applied a thick green paste to the small cuts on her upper arm. "You were brave out there, Avalon. *Too* brave."

Sincere compliments set her teeth on edge, but she swallowed the need to minimize her actions. As focused as Elden was, it gave her ample opportunity to study him. Avalon drank in every small detail. The dark lashes, the semi-permanent down tilt of his lips...she could see him clear as day.

Wait.

"I can *see* you," Avalon whispered in horror. *The fucking Unseelie night-sight!*

"Yes?" Elden frowned.

"That means *you* can see *me*."

"Did you—did you just realize that?" He straightened and quickly let her go. "I mean, how do you forget that we can see in the dark? Your eyes are open."

"I thought, since I've been in here awhile, my eyes had adjusted to the dark. I forgot that—"

Flatly, Elden clarified, "So, you wanted to see me naked, but not have it go both ways?"

Horrifying, this was horrifying. "Get out."

"You're upset at me for this?" She could hear the scowl in his voice as she tried to turn away. "Avalon," he fumed, turning her chin back to face him. His voice softened. "While you have made your feelings toward me quite clear, perhaps I haven't offered you the same courtesy. I thought I had been quite obvious—not with my dialogue, as I admit that is not my strong suit, but with my actions toward you. If I have failed in that aspect, let me now be perfectly clear."

Elden had abandoned any attempt to sound at all human

with that confession. His eyes settled on her lips, and she was sure he'd kiss her again, but instead Elden used a thumb to place a small amount of ointment on a scratch along her cheek.

"Whatever you ask of me, Avalon, I'll grant you." A large hand enfolded one of her own, pressing it against his chest. "My heart belongs with you—even if you still want to carve it out of my chest. As long as you would accept it as yours."

The weight of his confession threatened to sink her. And she could not protest its sincerity. Elden had never lied to her. Even if he was capable of it, she knew he had no patience for dishonesty.

She hesitated too long.

Something new and cruel flashed in his expression. His large hands rested on her bare shoulders, thumbs pressing against her neck in slow, soft strokes. "Perhaps you still enjoy seeing me suffer." He began walking her backward until her back hit the edge of the bath, near where she had laid her towel out earlier. "Communication has never been our strength. Would you like a physical demonstration?"

"I'm not letting you have your way with me in public," she argued, pushing away the memory of what had nearly occurred back on the beach.

"Avalon, I don't want to fuck you. I want to *taste* you." He continued, his hands drifting underwater and dangerously close to her hips, "If my feelings haven't scared you away."

His words shocked her—and stirred a fire in her belly. Was he—did Elden really mean *that?* There was one surefire way to find out. Avalon nodded, any further debate dying instantly. "I'm not afraid of you or how you feel, Elden."

Elden grabbed her waist, lifting her out of the steaming bath and exposing her to the frigid air. He set her down on her towel, her legs still dangling in the water, and gave her a light shove to indicate she should lie down. She eagerly complied, gasping when he lifted her legs up to rest them against his shoulders.

His deadly teeth teased her inner thighs, sending waves of fear-addled lust throughout her core. When his mouth moved against her apex, it was all she could do to keep her hips from bucking against him.

She hoped there were no servants on the other side of those thin doors—the quiet sounds she was making couldn't be mistaken for anything innocent. She wanted to cease her babbling, but anytime she said Elden's name she was rewarded with more pressure, more pleasure, more *everything*.

"Elden, that feels so *good*."

She felt him laugh, sending a funny tingle to her center, but when she glanced down at him there was no humor in his stormy eyes. He brought her right to the very edge, teasing her mercilessly, pausing only to ask, "Do you want me to *stop*, Avalon?"

"What?" Anything, but that. "No, don't stop."

"Then beg."

She'd imagine him speaking to her this way, but to actually hear it? His voice, low and rasping, giving her orders? Her pride had no place here. Without missing a beat, Avalon pleaded, "Please, Elden, keep going. Keep...yes, Elden, *baby*, that's—"

His sudden absence from her made her eyes flutter open. Her hand shot out, reaching to grab hold of his hair and tug him back into place, but Elden ducked out of reach and then let her legs drop back into the water.

"There. Now we're both frustrated."

She reached for him again, and pleaded, "Elden, I was

almost—"

"I know." He darted forward to catch her hands, preventing her from finishing the job herself. Once her trembling stilled and she fell back onto her towel, groaning in resentment, the prince let her go. "I'm sending the servants in after me, so don't try to pick up where we left off." Without warning, Elden climbed out of the bath and grabbed his robe. "Keep putting ointment on your wounds. I'll see you in the dining room." His movements were so quick that Avalon didn't get the chance to avert her gaze.

She sat up, scowling at his retreat. "Ass!" she shouted, unable in her current state of mind to appreciate her own pun.

Elden paused, tying the robe around him as he glanced back at her. He snapped his fingers once before he left, and it only took Avalon a moment to realize what he'd done.

That magic *snap* had plummeted the temperature in the bath to nearly freezing, though there were earthly laws that deemed such a speedy change impossible. Avalon yelped at the frigid water, scrambling backwards to get her legs out of the bath.

Elden was trying to punish her with those antics. Avalon decided she deserved it. Grand speeches were not Elden's forte, and yet he had desperately tried for her...and received no answer at all in return.

His confession was proof of how fey he was. Such prose! Truly the son of a poet. And yet, it was so very far from the fey with open honesty in each word. How could he speak of love so easily! Especially after what she'd said, *shouted*, on the beach. Avalon hadn't said a word in response to his revelation, and here she was, feeling like a stone sat in her stomach.

Why can't I let myself take that chance? Why can't I allow myself to accept this weakness for him?

She answered herself quickly enough. *Because as much as he may wish it were otherwise, Elden is dangerous.*

Avalon groaned, cursing her inability to take what she wanted—damn the risks—and left the bath. It was confusing to be around him. She had been afraid to read into their kiss on the beach as she'd all but begged him to do it. And the second kiss she'd stolen from him. At any rate, this was neither the time nor the place to stew on it.

She wished again that they had saved the mirror. With that magic item, her decision would be simple. Despite how she may feel about the man, her desire for self-preservation would ultimately win. She would have returned to being mostly human, and left the inn, and Elden, without looking back. No matter how much it might hurt to do so.

There were servants waiting for her, waiting to push her into another cumbersome, uncomfortable dress. Avalon held her temper as her lungs felt crushed in the outfit—she liked to fight, to be obstinate, but after years of doing so, she had learned when it was a waste of her time. And Avalon actually *liked* dresses, but she did not care for being forced into them.

The dress they chose for her was white as snow, and the snowflakes sewn into the fabric sparkled in a way that seemed only possible through magic. Thankfully, this time she wasn't stuck in a ball-gown. The dress hugged her a little too tight for her comfort and had sheer, glittering bell sleeves.

She'd be dragging that material through her entrée, she was sure.

Elden was waiting for her outside what she assumed was the dining hall. She spied him first, allowing her to eye him from head to toe. Again, he dressed in all black, with small silver details woven throughout his fine outfit. The crown Elden wore nearly blended in with his dark hair—she only spotted it due to the rubies embedded around the black metal.

An overbearing shadow against the doorway, Elden appeared lost in thought. Oblivious to his watcher, Elden's expression was unguarded. At first glance, the redcap looked intimidating, vicious, but Avalon thought she knew the man underneath that scary presentation. How had Ashling raised a boy born capable of such violence, and with so much power, to be so good?

His mother must have known what her world would endure if her son had any interest at all in the Unseelie throne. Of the terror her family would inflict to put him there.

Avalon wondered if this strange man was as lonely as she was. Those achingly familiar eyes flicked up at her, brightening before some wariness dimmed their hope.

"I feel rather silly," she said, trying to banish her earlier misstep in the bath with self-deprecating humor. "From our conversation before and from being in this dress."

He ignored the former part of her statement. "You're speaking nonsense." Elden's words were short and clipped. As if her statement was too ridiculous to deserve a response. "You are as beautiful as you always are, and to say otherwise is foolish."

Only Elden could give such a lovely compliment so testily.

"Wait." *Stop being a coward.* "Elden, I wanted to be clear. I don't hate you." *Very romantic,* her inner voice mocked. Avalon reached out and lightly touched his arm. "I meant I hated that you thought I could—that I would leave you so heartlessly. I know how I am—suspicious and defensive—but I want to be more for you."

Immediately she felt light-headed, but if Elden could tell her he cared for her right after she said, "I hate you," then she could manage this.

Elden flashed her a quick, unsure smile. "About what just happened in the bath…I wanted to apologize." He exhaled, finishing with, "I may have gotten carried away."

"I wish you would have finished getting 'carried away'!"

That sweet grin turned wicked, and she knew Elden wasn't very sorry at all.

He led her into the dining room, her arm woven through his. The dining table took up the entirety of the long, narrow room. The table sat low to the floor, resting on a beautiful blue and white rug and had cushioned pillows gathered around it.

It was a trick trying to sit on the floor in such a tight dress, but Elden helped her manage. Elden's place was across from her, but because of the wide berth of the low table, he seemed so very far away.

Seeing the multiple spoons and forks next to her dishes made her grateful for her mother's constant needling about her table manners—something she'd never admit to the woman, ever. Every other setting had bronze chopsticks next to their plates. *Much less nonsense to memorize*, she thought glumly. She hesitantly reached for the correct fork.

Sitting near the head of the table, Hia didn't appear as cool and haughty as she had the first night they met. She snapped her fan open and shut several times—a nervous tick Avalon hadn't expected from the ice princess. Anytime a servant entered, she twitched. Her father, who had an elbow on the table, hand propping up his chin, was not so affected.

Jin wasn't anxious, either—only pissed off. "You made it *snow* in the Summerlands. If we wanted to be so obvious, I could have just marched the entire army over the border."

"No one bothered to explain to me that we were gathering ingredients to assassinate someone. Perhaps, if I'd known, I'd have taken more care."

"Brother, if you'd known the real reason, the entire Summerlands would be frozen over. Or in *ashes*, if you had one of your infamous little slip ups."

Avalon steadied her hand—she nearly dropped her fork at that. What did that mean, *in ashes*?

Hia's fan hit the table. "Jin, enough."

It was clear that this meal would end abruptly—or in a fight. Avalon began shoveling food into her mouth as quickly as she could—propriety be damned.

Jin and Elden's bickering lasted until a servant scurried in, knelt down next to Taliesin, and handed him a scroll. The king unfurled it with no dramatics, scanning the message a few times before he set it down on the table.

Hia and Jin stared at their father, waiting. Elden glared at Taliesin. "What is going on?"

"Our herbalists had ample time to study the hellebore you procured." Taliesin stood from the table, towering above them all. "They had determined that is what killed your mother. It must have been secretly administered to Ashling over a long period of time."

The oddly purple tea blend flashed in Avalon's mind, along with the vision of her heaving if she dared drink it. *Not expired after all*, she thought. What had nearly happened to her and what had happened to Elden's mother made her breath come too fast.

Nothing was said for the longest time. Hia, who was on Avalon's right, grabbed her arm hard enough to bruise. Jin's focus was on Elden, who had become statuesque in his stillness.

When the table caught fire, Hia tore Avalon out of danger. Jin leapt to his feet, leaving Elden alone, still sitting before the flames. Elden's breath dragged out in heavy, labored gasps. Whatever he'd done had nearly destroyed him.

Elden jumped to his feet, looking like the giant that Jack fought as he stalked over to his father. "What? Has she just been sitting on ice this entire time? You haven't even buried her?"

"The investigation hadn't been completed. We were missing the hellebore." Taliesin gave a lazy, shooing motion with his hand. "Cool him off."

Jin's magic, more silver than Elden's icy blue, wove throughout the room. The temperature dropped, and the magic continued to Elden, encircling him. Hia gave a single wave of her fan and the fire went out in a sudden snap—as if it had been nothing but candlelight. Her magic was a deep purple.

"Your mother was poisoned. Deliberately. The questions you need to think about, need to answer, son, are *who* and *why*." Taliesin was humorless now—a rarity that even Avalon recognized. "Don't get so caught up in discovering the former that you neglect the latter. Your mother may have made you an executioner's axe, but there's more at play here than you think."

CHAPTER 34
ELDEN

Elden couldn't stop shaking. His core was practically vibrating, the ever-present violence that soiled his heart would not abate. There was no outlet for his rage, the unknown culprit nowhere in his reach.

Start cutting, and by a process of elimination, one of the bleeders was responsible...

As much as he wanted to attribute that grim line to his own muddied stream of consciousness, the truth could only be ignored for so long.

Elden was barely aware of his surroundings as Avalon led him to one of his father's carriages. She bit her lower lip as she watched him. He should have said something to assuage her worries, but he lost himself to his memory instead.

His mother's axe, that double-bladed cursed thing, burned his hand the first time he had lifted it, as he had known it would. Ashling had hammered too much of herself into the metal. Too much of her power...and the rage, the bitterness that accompanied the frustration of a slow, incomprehensible death.

This was not how Elden liked to remember his mother. This was a version of Ashling that hadn't escaped the fires of her childhood. She had taken him there once, to the edge of her family's industry, to watch the black plumes of smoke rise up and blot out the sun. The fires never stopped, something Ashling had told him without a hint of pride. The hammers would fall all day and all night, and his grandmother listened to the pattern. There would be hell to pay if there was a missed beat.

Elden sat on that giant, decaying mushroom with his mother, listening and watching. Seeing what his mother had escaped.

"They can't know about you, Elden. They married me off to bear an heir, to make a *king*. How would you please them, my strong, brave child." She had that faraway stare that always came back whenever the feylands were mentioned. "A child in the family with a blood claim to the throne? Mother would never let a chance like that go. They'd unmake you—brainwash you into becoming the unfeeling, conquering warlord that they so desire. They can't have you. And they can't have my power."

That was when Elden received the dagger—not the first weapon he'd been given, but the first that hummed with his mother's complex enchantments.

"You will have a better life in the mortal realm. When I retire you're to be a *warden*, Elden. And you have things to guard in addition to the mound."

Avalon stirred Elden from his dream by lightly shaking him. Their carriage journey out of the king's territory was finished— it was annoying being unable to simply open a gateway back to the inn directly from the castle. But there were dozens of wards in place to prevent such a security risk.

"I hate to mention this now," Avalon softly began, jumping out of the carriage. "But when I first arrived at the Refuge, I discovered a tin of tea in the office. I had a vision that it would make me ill, but, with the state of everything in that room, I merely thought it had molded."

Elden's answer was automatic as he followed her out. "You couldn't have known."

"True, but it seems relevant now, don't you think?"

Honestly, he didn't want to think about this. What he wanted to do was collapse into Avalon's warmth, resting his head on her shoulder until she took pity on him and held him close. Even if she did not return the same level of feelings he had for her, she wouldn't deny him that. There was a kindness underneath her ruthlessness.

Elden stepped away from her, feeling the bite of winter more than he ever had before. "It was someone that knew her. Someone with access to another entrance. Or access to a human to do their dirty work for them. And," he continued, recalling the evidence presented by his father, "it was someone who could enter the Summerlands unnoticed. Or had help doing so."

What one person could fit all those requirements? No one he knew.

Once they were through the mound and back in the inn's gardens, Elden turned without a word to head home. Alone. He couldn't face another second of Avalon's pity.

She didn't let him go so easily. Avalon latched onto his back, squeezing his waist tightly from behind. Her embrace was brief, innocent, and she ran from it before he had a chance to respond.

Elden watched her vanish inside the inn before restarting his walk home.

Even after Elden built back up the fire in his living room, his teeth still chattered from Jin's overzealous spell. Now that he was at home and alone, and Avalon was safe in her own room, he had time to make one of his dreaded lists.

As Elden scribbled his list, he kept looking over at his mother's journal. It had been returned to him by a steward, void of those poisoned petals.

Who would have done that to his mother? *A coward.* It was not fitting of a master enchanter—a slow, shriveling death at the hands of some nameless villain. Worse, yet, had been that his father, who cared little what his mother did or whom she did it with, had been the one to unveil this murderous scheme. Leaving Elden to find the culprit.

That, at least, he'd understood. Taliesin believed his wife's killing to be a way to get to *him*. Elden didn't agree. Taliesin and Ashling saw little of each other once he'd granted her the wardenship of the Pacific Northwest mound. Ashling found the Unseelie king's court to be dull—its cruelty nothing compared to her own family—and was more interested in humans and their world. Killing the queen, if it had been done to send Taliesin a message, was a waste of time and effort. It was not clear what the message was, or who had sent it.

No, Elden's mother had been personally targeted. And the obvious culprit was Evander—yet, *poison*? Evander didn't have the stealth to commit such an underhanded task, if his pride would have even let him attempt such cowardice.

Whoever had poisoned Ashling had been after something, and Elden had a few ideas on what that might be.

He recalled his outburst in the dining hall. Setting the table aflame was nothing but a pathetic show of his temper. And worse, Avalon had witnessed his fiery tantrum. He was already so many red flags rolled into one that he could not afford to add *pyromaniac* to the list.

A little of his mother's fiery magic remained inside him, but it had been locked away so tightly that even using it so briefly exhausted him. Elden could only hope he had used so small a percentage of his mother's power that Evander would fail to notice. Elden had slipped up in his childhood and used it before without their knowledge. It was the only time that his mother had been truly angry at him.

His list stared up at him, as empty as he was trying to maintain his heart. *Avalon would be so much better at this*, he unwillingly thought. Her task lists were online *and* printed on stiff, professional paper. Her efficiency often bordered on psychotic.

Jotting a few items down and rereading them, Elden wanted to tear the paper to pieces.

Find Mom's killer. The "how" was not at all clear.

Consult the reservation book for suspects.

Speak with Evander.

Discover another way to return Avalon to her human form.

That, perhaps, Elden wanted to accomplish least of all.

Fine, he'd deal with the first. He'd search through his mother's things until he found anything remotely suspicious. As secretive as Ashling was, this might leave him with only more questions.

Ashling's disorganized security room proved unfruitful. The double-bladed axe, her final gift to him, loomed in its glass case—a case that was enchanted to hide the magic stored within. Her bedroom, a door he had not opened since she passed, was eerie, but uneventful as well. He'd all but given up until he recalled the journal.

He flipped through the pages—large sections were missing and her entries were sporadic at best. But a few pieces were written in a more legible handwriting, as if the information was something Ashling, unorganized as she was, did not want to risk forgetting.

No. *No.* Elden read the note, squeezing the journal so hard he nearly cracked the spine. He had briefly considered the possibility, but never did he think his mother might have known about it. Had *allowed* it.

There wasn't a chance Avalon would believe that he was ignorant regarding this exchange until now.

But he could not keep it from her.

It was difficult to breathe. He needed to take a walk as soon as it was light. To clear his head. To give him some illusion of peace before he tore his heart out.

CHAPTER 35
AVALON

It didn't feel right, leaving Elden while he processed the revelation of his mother's murder. But Avalon sensed that Elden wanted to be alone, and she couldn't refuse him that peace.

She'd witnessed more of Elden's family drama, and she—though it went against every fiber of her being—wanted nothing more than to talk to him about it. Avalon knew she was the furthest thing from a comfort one could get, but Elden was not one who needed to be coddled. She nearly believed she could be enough.

Elden watched her until she entered the inn, where she made her way to her room on her own. Her heart dropped into her stomach when she tried the knob and found her door unlocked.

Bruce swung the door open, appearing as tired as he should be considering the early hour, and hissed, "Get inside. Now."

Odele was sitting on the floor, using the bed as a backrest. "I tried to call you."

Valerie sat on the bed, uncomfortable and too formally dressed. A wine glass, half-empty, swirled in her hand. That wasn't terribly unusual, but Avalon would have hardly considered that breakfast.

This was not a simple family reunion—Bruce's two man security team were at opposite corners of the tiny room. Men in suits with walkies did not belong in a scene with pine tree patterned wallpaper and string lights.

"Oh." Avalon crossed her arms, slowly realizing how she was dressed. In that over-the-top dress and a coat Hia had gifted her and then threatened to take back when Avalon asked if the fur was ethically sourced. "So, the A-Team was here the entire time? You didn't care to mention that?"

"They were investigating," Bruce sneered. "There's always been rumors that there's something unnatural going on here. And my man inside the Commission confirmed it last night. This place is crawling with feyries."

"They know." Odele cut him off with a sigh. "With no help from me, I might add. Of course, walking in here dressed like that isn't helping."

At that, Valerie giggled and sipped her wine, earning her strange looks from everyone involved. *Was their mother hysterical?*

"What was your last election platform built on, Bruce?" Avalon demanded, refusing to cower. "Humans and magical beings cooperating. Well, that's what we're doing. Cooperating."

"I've been told that one of you," Bruce narrowed those lizard eyes on her, "is doing more than *cooperating.*"

Did those suits catch her outside the mound a few minutes ago? The thought of some creep in a tie watching her through a giant camera while she tried to comfort Elden as he dealt with his mother's death…how did people justify making their money like that?

"That wasn't—" The words died on her lips. Frantically she tried a few more sentences, all denying that there was anything at all to what they'd witnessed, but nothing would come.

"You will not disgrace our family *again*." Bruce turned from her. As if that one sentence would be enough to control her. At one time, it would have been. "We'll leave after breakfast. Once we're back in Seattle and out of the damn sticks, we can discuss finding new employment for both of you."

Valerie's laughter was an out of use bell—years of dust coating the inside and muffling the tinkling sound. "Oh, Bruce. Shut the hell up."

What was in that wine glass? Avalon exchanged stupefied glances with her sister.

"Valerie…" Bruce was just as mystified—only his skepticism came alongside a huge heap of asshole. "What did you just say to me?"

"Oh, shit." Valerie picked up her handbag from the floor, pilfering through its contents. "I think I took the wrong pill, or maybe I took the right one this time?"

"Obviously, the wrong one," Bruce seethed, making a motion toward one of the men in black. A pathetic move that said, *take care of her before I have to.*

"Bruce, Ava has never done what you wanted before. Give up. Stop ordering us all around. Let her go fuck the feyrie."

"Mom!" Odele was startled enough that the endearment slipped out.

"Mom, what?" Valerie scoffed, downing the rest of her glass in one go. "If—Bruce, let go of me. I'm perfectly fine. If

Ava wants to sleep with him, let her go ahead and do it. Why not? She's a feyrie, he's a feyrie. And he's so tall. *That's* reason enough as it stands."

Avalon never would have seen this coming. *Never.* She took the glass from Valerie's hand, worried it'd end up in a thousand pieces on the floor. "Valerie, I was comforting him. He's my friend." That was close enough to the truth.

Odele groaned. "I'd rather you said you just wanted to sleep with him. *Friends?*"

"Enough with the sex talk!" Bruce stamped a foot on the ground. His daughters ignored him. Valerie was being so much more interesting. And more *alive* than she had ever seemed.

Valerie pulled out a flask which Avalon quickly confiscated. Unperturbed, Valerie laughed, "Since you *refuse* to go to therapy with me, Bruce, I'm afraid I'm going to have to be the one that tells you...we were terrible parents. The only reason they still speak to us is that damn medical debt. Our own daughters...we're holding them *hostage*, Bruce."

"They have to learn—"

"I *told* you not to hire any feyries. And you wouldn't listen to me. *We have to show we believe in the campaign—we can't have an all human staff.* Which I never said I wanted. I just said no feyries."

Indignant, Bruce snapped, "You'd rather we not know what they are? That we'd still be pretending we're a big, happy family?" He waved a hand at his security and mouthed, *get the hell out.*

With the flunkies gone, Valerie really let her inhibitions go. "*I* always knew what they were. You—you never made it to any of my appointments. The doctors made it very clear how impossible bearing a child would be for me. Even so, you never rearranged your busy schedule to be there with me."

Bruce sniffed. "Why are you bringing all this up right now?!"

Odele and Avalon simultaneously sat on the bed next to Valerie. Odele patted her arm awkwardly. Valerie slumped into herself. "Blair...*she* made every single one of my appointments. She was there as I was poked and prodded and—" Valerie looked so very small as she said, "I couldn't stand any more doctors, and I couldn't disappoint everyone so I asked Blair if there was ever...if there was ever a case where a changeling was better off in the mortal realm."

"Are you saying..." Odele began and abandoned her thought.

Valerie's hand reached over and stroked Avalon's hair. Avalon did her best not to flinch. "I asked Blair to bring me one of those cases. She cast a glamour on me so I looked pregnant. When she brought you to me, Ava, your eyes were so open and judgmental even then. But I didn't care. You were mine."

Avalon froze as Odele released a half-cry. For years they had thought there was a human counterpart to them, trapped in the feylands. But Valerie had finally admitted her dark truth. Avalon and Odele hadn't been swapped with anyone, merely—and illegally—adopted.

She felt happy and sick at the same time. Her limbs felt so far away as she took it all in. No child was suffering in the feylands just because Avalon existed.

Valerie's hands were shaking. Avalon couldn't recall a time she'd heard her mother speak for so long. "When you got older, Blair wanted to tell you what you were. I fired her for it. I was awful. But I didn't want you to know, even with Odele's nightmares. Even if it might have helped. *Selfish.*"

Gods, this was too much to take in right now. What had caused Valerie to reveal so much? Was it seeing Avalon with another feyrie? Did Valerie feel guilty that she'd taken a part of her daughters' background from them?

Was this terrible timing on Valerie's part? Perhaps. But it was one less thing to weigh down Avalon's heart.

"It doesn't matter what happened in the past. These two are *lucky* their parents abandoned them with us. They lacked for nothing." Bruce continued, "You're seeing the doctor the instant we get back. Something's off with your medication. The rest of you...I'll need some time to figure out what to do with you."

"No. I'm staying here." Valerie shrugged, kicking her shoes off and watching them tumble across the room. "Check yourself out. Go back to Seattle alone, and I'll have a lawyer talk to you tomorrow."

Bruce gripped Avalon's wrist a little too tight. "Do something about your mother!"

Avalon stayed still—as long as Bruce focused his attention on her, Odele was safe. "I don't have to do anything you say."

"You don't?" He laughed, the edge of hysteria eating at his words. "Why don't we do what your mother wants? Let's have *everyone* know what you two liars are! You deceitful, fucking feyrie—"

Whimsy's door slammed open, and Bruce froze, his words cut off, with his fingernails still digging into his false daughter's flesh.

Elden took up the entirety of the doorway. He said, in a falsely polite tone, "You're going to want to let her go."

Avalon paled at the unexpected sight of him. *No!* Elden needed to be dealing with his own grief—not be a witness to her own family drama.

All semblance of propriety was lost. Bruce boomed a laugh at Elden. "Who the hell do you think you—"

"I'm one of those *fucking feyries*. And you've been making a racket." The large, arching window flew open. "Your options are the stairs or *not* the stairs. I wouldn't think about it too long. The winds here are unpredictable."

"I'm the *governor*—"

"And I'm a feyrie prince. Both mean jack shit here." Elden's fingers snapped, sending a speeding line of ice shooting across the floor and heading straight for Bruce. The governor jumped back, releasing Avalon, and pressed his back against the window frame.

Some of the floorboards lifted partially and acted like a slide, and Bruce nearly tipped out of the open window. The near fall was enough. "Fine!" Bruce fled to the doorway, awkwardly trying to fit around Elden as the floorboards snapped back into place. "Consider this my early checkout."

"It's been a pleasure," Elden smirked, watching the governor scuttle away. Instantly he was at Avalon's side, gently taking her arm and inspecting it for any potential bruises. He tilted her face up at him so she could see his mouth. His voice was low, and meant only for her ears, as he asked, "Are you okay? He looked too comfortable gripping you like that."

Valerie hiccupped at the accusation in Elden's tone.

With the visual aid Elden had provided, Avalon understood him perfectly. "Wouldn't be the first time."

His gaze darkened, and he glanced out the window as if he was contemplating running the governor down before he was out of his territory. When Elden turned back to find the other women staring at him, he nervously cleared his throat. "As long as you're all alright, I'll leave you alone. Goodbye."

She'd been privy to more than one of Elden's family fights, but it was still so embarrassing that he'd witnessed her dysfunctional clan.

Valerie spoke first. "That was the most attractive thing I've ever seen. Don't screw that up, dear."

After their father left the premises and Valerie returned to the cabin, the sisters were able to get dressed properly for the day. Avalon felt no relief from being free of her bargain with Taliesin. All she wanted was to find Elden and see how he was faring. Though he had handled Bruce just as he deserved, Elden hadn't lingered, grief still weighing down his shoulders. Elden's grieving process had restarted, stuck perhaps on anger for the foreseeable future.

Avalon would have to find him later. There was a lot of last-minute work still to be done for the upcoming nuptials. Maetta was second-guessing every wedding decision they'd made, and Avalon rearranged table settings until she wanted to smash the dishes on the floor. She wasn't free until dusk was threatening their daylight.

The kitchen was not where Avalon wanted to be. Lyra was remaking the wedding cake for the third time, and her sour mood could be detected throughout the inn. But if Avalon wanted to locate Elden, after failing to find him at home, the inn, or the garage, Lyra was her best chance.

"He's brooding in his brooding spot," Lyra shrugged, folding a huge bowl of purple icing.

"And if someone who has no idea where the hell that is

wanted to find it?"

"Ugh, no! That cake was meant to come out two minutes ago!" Lyra nudged one of the brownies away from the oven. "Avalon, I don't have time for...dammit, just find the creek and follow it."

Avalon vaguely remembered coming across a creek the day Elden accepted Abernathy's chupacabra hit. But she had followed Elden over every inch of the property that day...it was not clear in her memory where she'd stumbled into the creek.

One thrown wooden spoon later and Avalon realized Lyra would not be any more help.

Bundled in every winter accessory she owned, Avalon trudged through the woods, kicking the snow as she went. Alone, and slightly fearful she was heading in the wrong direction, she called out her wisp.

The blue light zipped out of her, probably excited to claim its prize.

"So?" Avalon prompted. She wished they had learned Morse code or something. "What am I to give you? We made a deal, and the terms weren't exactly clear."

The wisp just floated there, waiting. Avalon groaned. "I have to guess what you want? Lovely." What would a murderous flashlight even want from her? "Do you want me to take you back to the feylands?" she tried. The wisp buzzed almost in anger. "I'll take that as a 'no'? You don't want me to just set you free here, do you? I think I have some sort of moral responsibility to mankind to deny that."

Avalon had come to think of the wisp as her friend, a dangerous notion. She had asked a lot of it. It had helped her rescue Elden, and what could she offer that would be as precious as Elden's life?

"His words," she whispered, the quiet tears already streaming down her face. "When he offered me his heart, and I said nothing. Take them." Avalon didn't deserve them, anyway.

The wisp just hung there, waiting, as if it was giving her time to change her mind. Then it grew so bright she could not stand to look at it.

She silently repeated Elden's confession. How brave he had been to give it to her, and here she was, throwing it away.

My heart belongs with you—even if you still want to carve it out of my chest.

The taking was immediate, and the void inside her was more noticeable now. Avalon blinked slowly, wiping at her eyes and wondering why her face was wet.

What had she been doing? Oh. Elden!

"Can you help me find Elden?" she asked the light, which seemed more corporeal than before.

The wisp was happy enough to lead her to Elden and then promptly left, zooming through the woods where Avalon hoped it would not lead some unsuspecting hiker off a cliff.

Elden's spot was indeed perfectly set up for a brooding winter prince.

Tucked away in a towering, old grove of trees was a clear pool with frost snaking across the surface. A waterfall, maybe ten feet tall, poured into the pool, roaring happily in its seclusion. Elden sat on a large rock that pointed to the pool's middle. He did not look up as she approached, studying the water's ripples as a sheet of ice advanced upon the center.

He spoke, loud and annoyed. "I assume Lyra told you I was out here, *brooding*."

Avalon waited until his magic froze the entire pond and walked across the ice to him. "More or less."

"Well, I'm not." He stepped down from his perch, meeting her on the ice.

"It wouldn't matter if you were. In fact, it would make sense. You've been blindsided."

He wasn't wearing armor today—or a coat. Not that Elden ever needed a jacket, but he usually maintained the façade. He hadn't looked directly at her yet, and when he did, it was with a grim finality only morticians wore.

"What now?" she moaned, stepping closer to him.

"I have to tell you something, Avalon."

That didn't sound like it was going to be a proposal. "Is it about what happened to your mother?"

"No." Elden flinched.

The daylight was entirely gone now, but Avalon couldn't count on the darkness to hide her. A fact she wouldn't forget a second time. "Is it bad news?"

"Yes."

"If you *don't* tell me, will anyone get hurt?"

Elden grimaced. "I suppose not, but—"

"So, it can wait a few days." She stormed up to him, pressing a gloved finger to his lips when he tried to speak. "It *will* wait a few days. Let's just make it to the reception and get drunk on feyrie wine together. Maybe nothing made by a *nymph*, but you understand what I mean."

"Avalon." He gently pushed her hand away. "I *have* to tell you. It can't wait."

Avalon recalled feeling so certain when she had first started looking for him, but now she worried that those moments they shared together were purely physical. Perhaps he was only interested in her because they were the same type of fey? If she ever transformed back into her human state, and shed her redcap features, would Elden still hold a torch for her? *Dammit.* Avalon would have to do what she hated most—trust her own heart.

It was easy to grab a fistful of Elden's flannel—he was in no way expecting it. Avalon yanked him down to her level until their eyes met—his were shocked and hers were determined. "Listen, *my prince*, you'll have a better time with me if you do exactly as I say."

His face twisted into his signature scowl, bringing a smile to her lips. She preferred seeing that irritable frown rather than the melancholy he was stewing in earlier.

Any other day, the mere thought of unknown bad news would have driven her into a spiral. She would have thrust her powers out, searching the future for solutions or warnings.

But tonight, after everything...she was too tired of her own bullshit. Whatever he had to tell her, she knew Elden would help her deal with it.

"Damn you, Avalon. Now *you* listen to *me*—"

She lightly pressed her lips against his, not wanting to act too aggressively, too desperately, in case he was angry with her. Avalon didn't care what he had to tell her. It went against her very being to take this chance. All she knew was she needed him, and she had the strange feeling that they were somehow running out of time.

She melted the winter prince.

Avalon felt the tension, the stubbornness, leave Elden as he wrapped her into his arms. He still kissed like she was his life raft and he a drowning man, which was something he'd nearly been.

His fingers twisted into her hair, tilting her head back for a better angle. She was burning for him, but the man was ice-cold and pressed together as they were she was freezing. "Elden," she murmured, whenever the man gave her a break between ravaging her, "Elden, I'm too cold. I—"

Elden made a noise to signal his irritation at being interrupted and led her off the icy surface. Once they were on solid ground, he resumed kissing her and a staggering, supernatural warmth filled her. In their hazed embrace, it took her a few moments to realize that fire was coming from Elden.

How had he done that? While she knew Elden came from opposing families when it came to their magic, he had told her that he'd been sworn to his father's winter spells. Of course, she'd seen a flash of his mother's fire appear before, but that seemed to have taken everything out of him, burning through him until he was a husk of himself.

Here, though, on his mother's land, Elden did not seem to suffer that same weakness.

She didn't want to care about any of that. Not right now. Gods, she wished there was something that could stop the always suspicious, anxious gears in her head from turning.

Focus on him. Let it go. She suggested, "Can we head back? I would like things to continue somewhere with walls. And a bed." She could blame the pink in her cheeks on his heat.

There was no hint of humor in his tone as Elden said, "If I didn't think you'd end up with frostbite, I'd throw you down and take you right here in the snow."

"Need I remind you that I am a governor's daughter? I'm not used to such rustic manhandling." Her tone was completely playful.

"I'll manhandle you indoors, then." He stepped back and winter returned to her bones. "Hold my hand," he ordered. "I can keep you from freezing to death that way."

Avalon latched onto his hand the entire hike back, searching for that confusing fire of his. The wisp found them and disappeared beneath her skin. Elden watched the intrusion and said, "I should take that thing back, you know."

"We came to an agreement," she replied, somewhat defensively. "I'll let you know if it becomes too much for me to handle on my own."

"I'd hate to get involved once it reaches that point."

The snow silenced their walk. Avalon, warily, asked, "I'm not sure that I understand your ability to use your mother's power? In your father's court, it seemed like it exhausted you. But here...you seem at ease with it."

"I was under the impression you didn't wish to discuss anything serious."

"Once we get inside, I'll stop," she promised.

He didn't say a word until she squeezed his hand. "Fine, Avalon. I'll tell you all my secrets—"

"*Not* the bad news you tried to ruin the moment with earlier!"

"I think one of us, for this to work, needs to learn how to be less bossy."

"And I'm sure you'll be able to do it. Now, continue."

Elden let them trudge along for a few more silent minutes. "My mother knew she was dying. And I suspect now that she thought it was the result of foul play. She took some measures, some I'm not sure I agree with."

She pressed against his side as they walked. Elden sighed. "When she died, her powers were supposed to return to her familial line. And as my father's magicians had done their best to remove any ability to harness fire from me...her power would have skipped over me and gone to my uncles and grandmother.

Ashling feared what they may do with it."

Avalon guessed, "Her power is still here, on the property. Somewhere. And you've been borrowing it."

"While I'm here, on her land, I can feel it calling to me. But it's been twisted somehow. She was so angry, so frustrated. It has become this dark thing, not like my mother at all."

There was more, and she gave Elden the time to tell it. "I shouldn't have used it for something so trivial, but I hate to watch you shiver because of me. I would prefer to make you tremble for other reasons." Butterflies, something she'd never thought a man could give her, fluttered in her heart and stomach. "Evander must already believe that, despite my father's claims, Ashling hid her power within *me*. He'll make an attempt to retrieve it, eventually."

The way Elden said *retrieve* gave her shivers—the bad kind.

"Does that satisfy your curiosity?"

"Enough that I can move past it."

"Good."

They continued their hike, hand in hand, impatience clear in their hastened steps.

CHAPTER 36
ELDEN

Back at his home, Elden suggested Avalon shower while he made something to eat. While he wanted nothing more than to tear all those frustrating winter layers off of her and have her immediately, he also wanted her to keep up her strength.

He'd done his best to use his mother's gift to keep her warm, but a hot shower would still do her some good. He should have avoided tapping into that power altogether—it would only draw Evander's attention to that axe, *Ember*.

The blade wanted out of its cage. It haunted him, whispering lies and incantations to him when he let his attention wander freely. The worst part was that it used his mother's voice to call to him. Some days, he thought it would drive him mad.

Avalon tapped his chest, bringing his focus back to her. "A shower sounds good."

While she vanished into the bathroom, Elden worked on reheating some risotto he'd taken from the inn's kitchens.

Dinner settled, Elden returned to the bathroom to tell her

so through the door and strangely found it wide open. Unthinking, he stepped inside to address what he had assumed would be a fully dressed Avalon.

She liked to make a habit of proving him wrong.

It looked like she'd been working on getting dressed, judging by the robe and slippers she'd placed on the chair next to her, but had interrupted herself. Now Avalon stood in front of a floor-length mirror, having wiped away the fog, and examined her naked body.

Fuck. Knowing the longer he stood there without her knowledge, the worse the outcome would be, Elden cleared his throat.

She didn't startle, merely glanced over her shoulder. "I haven't really looked at myself. Looked at how my body changed. I just felt like a failure." Her brow furrowed. "If I return to my human shape, Elden, will you still want me?"

What a stupid—

Elden swallowed, interrupting whatever he'd been about to say, knowing it would only be the wrong thing. "Avalon, I didn't want you to know this, but...I may have adjusted my glamour when we first met. To impress you."

"Oh, Lyra mentioned something like that."

"Then why even ask—" That wasn't important. Whether she truly felt self-conscious about her human or fey form, or she was teasing him, did not matter. Not when he could so easily prove otherwise.

He had stopped calling up his borrowed fire the second they reached the house, so when he pressed against her back, he watched a shiver ripple down her spine. Nuzzling into her blonde hair, Elden said, "You will *never* ask if I want you, ever again."

He kissed her neck, one hand exploring downwards while the other knotted in her hair, holding her head in place to make her watch herself in the mirror. When he let his teeth just barely graze her vulnerable throat, she moaned in a pitch that made it extremely difficult to continue this slow teasing.

He was saved from having to maintain his composure. Avalon spun and demanded, "Take me to bed."

He should have known she'd be impatient. They had almost come together too many times before to waste a moment more. "I did say I would grant whatever you asked of me."

"Don't make yourself into a liar."

Once they reached his bedroom, they moved together with a frantic aggression his mind told him to curb. His want made that difficult, and when Avalon grabbed him, dragging his mouth down to hers with such violent pleasure, it became almost impossible to avoid mimicking her rough foreplay.

Avalon kissed just as he'd expected—harsh and biting. Elden attempted to slow her down, to return her ferocity with gentle nips and touches, and eventually Avalon adjusted her kisses to match his.

The fireplace in his bedroom roared, flickering shadows dancing across their bodies. His hands traced her curves, cupping her behind as he lifted her onto the bed. He swallowed hard as Avalon sat back on her elbows, opening up as though putting herself on display for him.

He ran a hand down her leg, smirking as he watched her shudder. There were markings on her thighs, markings from the way he'd grabbed her on the beach when he was nearly mad with his need for her. "You don't still hate me, do you?" He meant it as a joke, but realized his tone had slightly missed the mark. Elden covered his mistake by running his grip up each of her inner thighs, pausing at the apex and squeezing her legs. "You don't seem to hate my touch."

"No, I don't," she crooned, her hips rising from the bed as he toyed with her. "I love it."

You know what she meant. And what she did not mean.

Still, the words undid him. He slowly undressed, watching Avalon struggle to sit back and observe from afar. Finally stepping out of his pants, Elden covered the little distance between them instantly. He pushed her legs even further apart than she had placed them.

He wanted to bury himself in her, forgetting everything else. Avalon must have wanted the same. When they came to-gether—*Arawn, she took him so well*—, she hooked her legs around him, locking him in place.

Avalon turned her face, bunching a corner of the comforter against her mouth to muffle any sound. He tore the blanket away, chastising himself for his impatience internally, and made her meet his eyes.

"I want to see you. I want to hear you." Once she returned his gaze, he began shifting his movements, watching for—

Her back arched suddenly, and a keening sound escaped her swollen lips.

There it was. Elden repeated the angle, enjoying the sight of Avalon writhing underneath him in pleasure. He had always found her notoriously difficult to please—he was glad that did not extend to the bedroom.

"I've been thinking about this longer than you know." The words were muffled as he brought his mouth to her breast. "About being the man to break that shield you hold around yourself."

"How long?" There was genuine surprise coloring her tone.

"When I didn't shake your hand in Seattle and you looked like you wanted to skin me alive."

"What?" She tried to sit up, but Elden kept a hand at the base of her throat, pinning her. Avalon didn't seem to mind. "That *can't* be true."

"Unfortunately for me, it is. It's been very frustrating—at night especially. Having you so close, and yet knowing you'd never glance my way with anything other than animosity."

She pursed her perfect lips together, making him think about how badly he wanted to spread them apart. "I thought I was putting you in your place, and all it did was turn you on."

Her sense of humor, normally welcome, was now a distraction. Elden worked on drawing her attention back to him.

"For me—" Avalon's own sigh interrupted herself. "—it was when I realized you knew about my hearing. You made such an effort to speak with me clearly. That was when I realized how dangerous you could be for me."

Her words were sweeter than he had expected. It made him want to say all sorts of foolish things that would only scare her off. "I'll be worth what you've been through with me, Avalon. I swear."

"Oh!" Avalon quickly wiped at one of her eyes. "Elden, you don't need to—I mean, you already are."

They kissed again, and this time there was something both hopeful and desperate laced in it.

When it became apparent that Elden was happy to keep teasing her, edging her, Avalon shoved him off. While he sat back, she straddled his lap, reuniting them easily. Her teeth began exploring *his* throat, prompting him to warn her, "Easy. Those teeth are new to you, remember?"

"Oh?" She leaned back, that wild smirk surprising and

simultaneously driving him mad. "Do you need me to be gentle with you, warden?"

No. It shocked him to realize it, but Elden would let her do whatever she wished. Avalon could break him if she so desired, and he had nothing in his arsenal to combat it with. "I don't think you'd know where to begin."

She rolled her hips against him, smiling at each sound she drew forth until she emitted her own gasp of pleasure.

Wanting, needing, to hear that sound again, Elden clutched her close and moved with her until she tipped over the edge with him following after.

He kept the only thought he was able to string together to himself. *I love you, I love you, I love you.*

Avalon fell off him, exhaling a deep breath. She immediately tunneled underneath the covers, tucking them under her chin. He had stoked the fire, but during this part of the year, it was difficult to contain the winter that lived in his chest.

Around Avalon, he felt a warmth inside him, a steady heat that cradled his chilled heart. He felt whole, restored.

"I imagine this will be a godsend in the summer," Avalon murmured, her eyes fluttering.

"The *summer?*"

"Yes, I won't need air conditioning with you around."

Elden sat on the edge of the bed, staring at her. "You want to be here in the summer?"

She raised the blanket a touch higher, her voice now muffled. "I wasn't trying to invite myself. I mean—"

"Avalon, I *want* you here." He pushed the blanket, which had crawled up even further, off her face. "I can't make that much clearer."

"I'm not going anywhere for now." She grinned, appearing

uncharacteristically playful. "You'll have to drag me out from under here if you want me."

He reached underneath the covers, gripping her legs and yanking her to the side of the bed. From there, he flipped her onto her stomach, bringing her to his hips.

"Oh, I *do* want you."

Elden halted their exploration of each other after a time. The hour had grown late—Avalon's eyes repeatedly drifted closed despite her constant insistence that they were not.

Though it had been a very long time since he'd shared a bed, Elden could not remember ever being so excited for it. He dragged Avalon against his chest, paying no mind to her claims that he was too cold for this, and stroked her naked back until she fell asleep against him.

Their morning, meant to be a lazy start to a very busy day as Avalon had the wedding rehearsal to prepare for, was interrupted by a harsh rapping on Elden's front door.

"Don't shatter my window again," Elden shouted, opening the heavy door to let Odele inside. He wasn't happy to see Avalon's sister at the moment, and the feeling was clearly mutual.

"I want to say first that I already know she's here. So, no bullshit."

Elden let Odele push her way inside, eyebrows raising when he saw what she was carrying. A photo frame stolen from the inn was pressed against Odele's chest as she began shouting for Avalon.

He couldn't help but smile as Avalon stomped downstairs, dressed in his clothes, swimming in them, and barked, "Odele!

What the hell do you want?"

"Right now? A gallon of bleach for my eyes."

"How mature of you."

"I thought you'd be more concerned about our parents. But I can see that hasn't crossed your—"

Avalon threw up her hands. "If we're going to have a fight, I'm putting on real pants." She stormed back upstairs, out of sight, and left the pair of them uncomfortably alone.

"Sorry for spoiling breakfast in bed for you."

Odele was not a mean-spirited person—Elden had observed her quite closely, and this behavior was reserved only for him. He could empathize with her side of things, though this didn't keep him from adding, "Now, am I serving your sister breakfast in this scenario? Or is Avalon my breakfast?"

"You think this is *funny*?" Odele squeezed the frame in anger. "Yes, the idea my sister slept with her trafficker is hilarious."

She knew? Arawn, she *knew*. "I was a *child*," he protested. His mind raced to find a solution as he heard Avalon coming back downstairs. Elden stepped towards Odele, hoping to explain himself, and she flinched. Elden recalled how tightly Bruce Golightly had gripped Avalon's arm before he had stepped in. Had Odele also endured such abuse in her childhood?

Elden moved back, increasing the empty air between them and watching Odele visibly relax.

Odele's appreciation was short-lived. "Show me your birth certificate, feyrie, or save your tricks for someone else." Odele rushed to Avalon the second she stepped off the final stair and shoved the picture frame in her face.

Avalon leaned away from the picture. "Why am I looking

at this?"

"Valerie found this during that awful dinner. She said she recognized Nanny Blair instantly. Recognized *you*, Avalon." Odele tapped on the glass insistently.

"Me?" Avalon snatched the frame away, bringing it an inch from her face. "What kind of Overlook Hotel bullshit is this, Elden?" She showed Elden the picture frame, pointing to a feyrie in the background of a picture of the inn's dining room. The fey woman was dressed all in periwinkle and held a crying babe in her arms.

Elden fought his fey nature and spoke ungarnished truth. "It's what I was trying to tell you last night."

Odele rolled her eyes. "Likely story."

"Wait here." Elden went straight for his mother's home office, ignoring the buzzing from Ember, and returned with the journal. "I was searching through my mother's things for information on her...passing. Read this." He indicated the right page and passed it to Avalon.

Her hands shook as she studied it.

Elden had memorized the section with a horrifying efficiency. He had planned on revealing the truth *before* they...

He might have ruined everything.

It hurt to hear Avalon read Ashling's entry aloud for Odele.

"Last night, a feyrie named Blair visited me. She dressed in all blue, and, though still lovely in a kind, elderly way, her aging blonde hair was streaked in stressed silver and her face panicked. She bore with her a child, an angry, pathetic thing, that was pink and loud." Avalon paused her reading, glancing at Odele. "Odd, I don't want to—"

"Keep reading, Avalon," her sister demanded. "I want you to say it out loud."

Avalon continued, though quieter than before. "Blair asked me to let her through the mound and begged that I tell no one. She'd found a home for it and the babe was cursed with a gift that would keep her enslaved should she not escape."

Avalon roughly passed the journal off to Odele, who picked up the reading. "The babe is not much younger than my own. And though it did try to bite me when I tickled its chin, I feel some responsibility to it. After all, I am hiding my own child." Odele spared Elden a glance. "I do fear Blair may prevail upon my kindness again. Taliesin would not be pleased, but he does not pay enough attention to me, as absorbed in his writing as his is, to even notice."

Avalon sighed, hugging herself. "*This* is what you had to tell me?"

"Yes." The picture was a surprise—he was unaware Avalon was in one of the old photographs his mother placed around the inn. He kept his answers short, with no room for feyrie word-play. "This is what I wanted to tell you."

Avalon looked to the ceiling, tears catching the dim light. "I had considered that I—that *we*—may have been taken through this mound. But the idea that anyone here knew about it..."

"I *just* learned about it, Avalon. You've witnessed how the Seelie, the *Seelie*, treat one of their Seers. Perhaps Taliesin does not keep his Seers drugged, but they live a trapped life. An unhappy life spent trying to please royalty."

"Do you agree that we need to leave *now?*" Odele gripped Avalon's sleeve, begging for her focus. "I spoke with Mom. If Dad wants the divorce to go smoothly, he'll forget about our debt and keep his mouth shut about what we are. And Mom will help us fix you. We can stay with her until we find a solution."

"Odele—"

"Your work is mostly remote, anyway. And I can design for Mom's rich friends. Avalon, please. They trafficked *children* through here. I don't care what the reason was. It's unacceptable."

His mother's murder was too fresh on his mind for Elden to allow such slander. "My mother believed she was doing the right thing. She wouldn't have acted otherwise."

Odele's eyes burned in anger, her voice hoarse as she sniped, "We were given to a Kennedy wannabe. We're lucky they stopped lobotomizing difficult women. Bruce would have done that to us, just to keep us quiet."

Avalon's voice broke on her desperate words. "I don't want to leave!"

Her cry spun Odele up even more. Elden was afraid to speak as the sisters argued. "Avalon, just look! Look into your future with him and tell me you won't get hurt again."

"I don't need to do that."

"You don't?" Odele's laughter reached hysterics. "Avalon, how many times will you get dragged into the feylands? And don't think I didn't notice your last little trip. How many scars will you earn for him? How many *teeth* will be torn out of you? Will I be expected to bleed for this, too?"

"Don't say that."

"This isn't sisterly advice, Ava. This is an *ultimatum*."

Elden knew her answer perhaps before Avalon realized it. But what could he say? This was not something he could force himself into the middle of. Avalon would choose him, or she wouldn't. There would be no influencing her decision—not even the Unseelie King possessed words sweet enough to influence Avalon's shrewd mind.

Odele loomed over her sister, shoulders shaking with anger and fear. "All my life," she declared, "you've kept me from getting hurt with your damn visions. Don't eat *that*, Odd, you'll get sick. Don't leave now, you'll hit the train. You've kept me from getting hurt, from making poor choices, and you kept me in your control. Now, you need to listen to *me*. My dreams..." Odele hugged herself. "My dreams haven't been this bad since Chicago, Avalon. I haven't slept in *days*."

The banshee now pointed at Elden, seething. "You know what plagues me at night? When I look at him, all I see is *death*. Perhaps the when and where is uncertain, but I know the final outcome. And you would, too, if you would wake up and look yourself!"

Avalon avoided meeting Elden's watchful gaze. "I don't need to look. I trust him." Her words were sounding less certain by the second, wavering under Odele's cruel logic.

"I know you, Ava. This isn't like—"

"You don't know my feelings, Odele. Not in this." Avalon held one hand near her mouth, as though resisting the urge to bite her nails, and the other hand she slipped into his.

"Ava, *look*. You've kept me safe for years. Let me save you."

Odele gripped Avalon's face, towering over her. Elden nearly tore her off her sister, some last semblance of logic beating out the waves of rage flooding him.

Odele's eyes were shadowed, and Elden was reminded of the time Avalon had shared her vision with him. Was the banshee now doing the same? What was Avalon seeing?

"Do you understand now?" Odele almost seemed sad until Avalon failed to respond. She snapped, "Blood and fire, that's what I see. Your blood. His fire. Are you happy, Avalon?"

"Stop! *Stop.*" Avalon buried her face in her hands. "I'll go with you, Odele. Just stop. And let me talk to him for a moment. Please."

"Avalon—"

"I said I would go with you to Valerie's," Avalon relented, her tone sharp. "You're right. It's the safest option. I was being selfish. But," she added, quite unmovable, "I will be staying until after the wedding. I'm not disappearing on them the day of their rehearsal."

"Finally, you start to make some sense! I worried that he had you under some feyrie spell."

Elden had always suspected there was something inside him that didn't work quite right—and tonight had proven it. Avalon had broken his heart, and he felt it already trying to repair itself, covering the wounds with unfeeling scar tissue.

Avalon was leaving, but his own guilt admitted that might be for the best. It would give him time to settle the situation at the inn—to find whoever had poisoned his mother and bring them down. He was sure whoever had orchestrated Ashling's death was behind everything else going wrong at the inn. And while watching Avalon leave may pain him, he did want her safe.

Odele rubbed her forehead. "Make a clean break. It will be easier..." She hesitated. "For both of you. I'll tell Valerie you'll be coming with us."

After Odele slammed the front door, Elden began his case. "Avalon, please believe that I wanted to tell you—"

"I *believe* you, Elden. Honestly, I don't even care what mound we were brought through. I cared about the *children* we replaced, but my mother, I mean Valerie..." She placed both hands behind her head, trying to deepen her breaths.

"You should sit down." She let him lightly touch her arm, guiding her to one of the couches. "Hold your head between your knees and breathe."

After a few deep inhales, Avalon raised her head, her eyes red and watery. She held back her tears until Elden offered his hand out to her, just as before, and she crushed it with her own. "Valerie said there were never any children for us to replace. So, I'm off the hook. I'm not a monster anymore."

"You never were," he chided, squeezing her hand so tightly she would have to tear them apart. "Tell me what happened."

She hiccupped, shaking her head. "Elden, I shouldn't—"

"Lean on me? You shouldn't confide in me because you're leaving me? Is that it?" Elden ignored that and pulled her onto his lap, noting how easily she sank against him. "Be selfish with me one last time."

Her face buried into his shoulder, and he knew it was so she could hide her expression from him.

"Valerie lost it. She wants a divorce, understandably. Valerie also admitted that she asked our fey nanny to, ah, procure Odele and I." Her nails dug into him, but the pain was lost in a sea of it. "When I was sixteen, I did something...bad. Because of what I did, we found out that we were changelings. And I've *hated* myself ever since. All this information does is let me hate myself a little less."

"I wish I had the time to convince you to feel otherwise," Elden said, stroking Avalon's hair as they sat together. "It kills me to hear you hate yourself when I—"

"Don't, Elden." Avalon twisted her hands together. She sighed. "When we learned we were changelings, everything we did was blamed on that. I was too temperamental, I was too silent, too introverted...all of it blamed on being fey. But it shouldn't have *mattered*. I could have been completely human and still be how I am. Why wasn't I enough? What about me was so wrong that something needed to be blamed for it?"

She would not let him console her any longer. Avalon jumped up and dug through her clothes from yesterday, choosing now to return his enchanted dagger to him. She had kept it tucked inside her winter coat. "Please, take this back before I go. I'm out of excuses to stay. If Valerie can really keep Bruce controlled, I shouldn't risk being here."

It was unfortunate, but Elden had realized this about Avalon rather quickly. She was a changeling, and they were meant to survive under any conditions. It was in her nature—it was a defining point of her personality—to keep her, and Odele, safe at all costs. The fact she had risked so much to be with him—though it was only one night—had been a huge step for her.

A step she'd been forced to retract.

"I am not safe," Elden said as he rested a hand on her cheek. "I am not safe, but I love you."

At this, she pushed away from him and stood. "I need to leave. Please, be careful. Something bad is on the horizon. I'll call you after I leave. We can...talk," she said, her words lame and unpromising. Avalon took that first step away from him with such ease that it killed something inside him.

Elden knew she would not turn back to him. Might avoid looking at him ever again, and, though he knew it was wrong, his heart was breaking and her true name flew from his lips.

"*Ava Golightly, look at me.*"

And she did, her movements jarring and forced. She glared at him, *hating* him for making her do this. For forcing her to do anything.

"*Keep my dagger.*" He held the weapon back out and she

had no choice but to take it. "I know you will want to forget this, to bury me and this place, but I won't forget you, and selfishly, I want you to suffer somewhat. If only when you see that blade."

His enchantment ended and Elden wondered if Avalon would remember she couldn't use that blade against him.

The spell undone, Avalon marched forward, grabbing his face with both hands and with too much pressure to mistake it for anything other than rage. "If you ever use my true name like that again, Elden, I will die hating you."

He placed a hand over each of hers, holding them in place. She dropped her grip and stepped away from him, eyes wide and wet. "Damn you, Elden. You're not making this easy."

"I'm glad it's not easy. I wish it were harder for you."

Her kiss was angry and final, their tongues brushing against one another's before she ended it. "Don't think for a second this isn't killing me, too."

Her confession eased his heart a tad—until she walked out.

Elden could have asked her to stay. Logic, not pride, prevented him from doing so. Pleading would not change her mind, only strengthen her conviction. And he did not *want* to beg her. He wanted her to choose him and temporarily cut this codependent tether to Odele, who, as she had shown rather well with her wails, could more than take care of herself.

What did he want? Did he need her to be safe and far away from him or did he need her to trust him, despite the overwhelming evidence against him, and stay?

What frustrated him most was that Avalon was no coward. She dove into treacherous, naiad-infested waters to save him, despite having no skill with a blade. She had been attacked by his own brother. The second time, her mouth was full of her own blood, and her first concern had been for his dog.

Avalon was not craven. That made her decision all the more painful. If she left now, it would be wiser to never return.

No matter how sincerely he proclaimed it, Elden knew Avalon would not say whether she loved him back.

Perhaps it was better that way.

CHAPTER 37
AVALON

Odele hummed as they did their laundry. The sisters were preparing to leave the Refuge by washing the outfits they wouldn't need for the next two days. And while Odele had been ecstatic to hear Avalon admit she was wrong and that it would be better to rely on their family, namely Valerie, and not the winter warden—Avalon didn't share her sister's relief.

They had the guests' small laundry room to themselves. Odele shook out a tie-dye wrinkled shirt. "Avalon, you *will* get over this. Once you're back to normal, I'll convince Valerie to let us take a trip—on her dime, of course—and you'll forget all about, as you've referred to him, the prince of darkness."

"Normal?" Avalon laughed without humor. "Seems a bit far-fetched for me, don't you think?"

"I mean, we can get back to our routine. You can go back to meal planning months in advance and all that tedious, overbearing stuff you love."

"Right." Avalon folded her shirts, somehow managing to

do it angrily. "Sounds great."

Pausing in her work, Odele said, her tone rather uncertain, "Avalon, I'm sorry this is happening this way. I—I can tell you care about him. But his brother tried to pull out all of your teeth, and we have no idea where he is. What's your grand plan? Stay here forever? I can't keep dreaming about bloody things happening to you. *You'd* never let me be in this amount of danger."

Her sister was right, though Avalon felt no comfort in Odele's logic.

Odele paired a blue sock with a green. "You'll realize this is what's best for us, eventually."

Avalon thought of the premonition Odele had forced her to watch. Remembered the blood dripping down her chest, soaking her clothes. And the inn—covered in flames and Elden nowhere in sight.

The memory caused her to lash out. "I'm not even going to say who you sound like."

Her barb did as she intended—Odele stared after her, dumbstruck, as Avalon gathered her half-folded clothes and left.

The last-minute detailing before an event usually gave Avalon a wild, pulsing energy. Today, after all that had happened, she failed to thrum up that strength. So, she plastered on a fake smile, doing her best not to affect the brides. And Avalon had years of practice hiding her emotions, so she was successful until brunch.

Sabella asked, "Will you be bringing a plus one, Avalon?"

She wiggled her brows playfully as Avalon stuttered for a response. They occupied the tearoom again, Avalon's favorite room in the inn. Avalon tried to ignore the thing she most loved about the cozy setting—a photograph of Elden as a child, brow furrowed and his scowl so like the one he liked to wear now.

Avalon refused to guess at Sabella's meaning. "I'm not sure what you're trying to say."

Maetta scoffed. "Everyone can see how the warden looks at you. If people aren't talking about the wedding, they're talking about you two."

"They're mistaken." Her tone trembled. "Excuse me, I'll be right back." Avalon fought to keep her steps light and slow until she had a shut door between them. Now she ran for the employee bathroom, barely making it to the toilet before she puked.

Avalon reached back with her foot, trying to keep the door closed as she hadn't time to latch it when someone pushed it open from the other side.

"Oh." Lyra stood uncertainly; her eyes were full of sympathy. As Avalon turned away, she could hear the nymph rustle through the bathroom cabinet. A paper cup full of water was presented to her as Lyra helped hold her hair out of her face.

Avalon took the cup, sipping on the contents. "I'm...I'm..."

"If you're trying to say, 'I'm fine,' there's a good reason why you can't." Squatting down next to her, Lyra sighed. "I was determined to hate you forever, Avalon. I wish I hadn't seen you like this. It's hard to hate someone so pathetic."

"Gods, sometimes I wish you feyries could lie."

Lyra refilled the cup and shrugged. "Here's another truth—I'm glad you're miserable. Elden's miserable, too, but he'd welcome you back if you went to him."

"I had to choose. My sister or Elden." Avalon hadn't meant to reveal that, but perhaps Lyra already knew.

"I'm sorry, and I'm probably not the right person to give relationship advice," Lyra warned. "I have no interest in romance at all—it's why I had to leave the feylands. My family tried to have me married off. So, I ran." Lyra helped Avalon stand up, her grip on her elbow light. "I'm telling you that because I know what it means to be vulnerable and to be afraid to reach for what you truly want, despite what your family demands of you."

Avalon's shame was impossible to hide. "I can't." She washed her hands, swallowing the need to puke again. "I can't risk losing Odele. I've earned her love. I—"

"Earned?" Lyra took a step back, shaking her head with a surprised laugh. "You can't think of love as something to be earned. That's not how that works."

No, that wasn't true. The only time Bruce seemed to tolerate her had been when she dragged home some plastic trophy or wrinkled certificate. It helped when she inevitably screwed up, when her temper caused her to act out. And Odele...Avalon had done more for Odele than anyone. Odele *had* to love her.

"Thanks, Lyra. I'm sorry you had to help me."

"Avalon, wait—"

She sped up her exit. She didn't want kindness right now. Lyra was right to hate her. Avalon didn't want to take that deserved emotion away from her.

Avalon spent her afternoon threatening the bridesmaids into behaving. It somewhat worked. The nymphs complained about everything during the over-complicated wedding rehearsal at the lake. They hated the color scheme, the food, and the lack of men to dance with. Avalon didn't care about their poor attitudes, as long as the brides didn't notice.

There was enough to contend with—Avalon's own failing love life and the fact Odele must have screwed up the dates with one of the contractors. A man in a navy jumpsuit and toolbox full of Klein was wandering the inn without any clear purpose. When Avalon questioned him, he only shrugged. "The bossy lady sent me this way."

"Stay out of sight of the party, please." Avalon pinched the bridge of her nose—she was going to murder Odele later. Though it wasn't like her to make a mistake like this. "And before you leave, fix the bell on the front desk. Just add it to the charges."

With the electrician settled, Avalon went to Whimsy to change for the rehearsal dinner. The last thing she wanted to do was to fix her hair and pick out a cute outfit (any other night she would have loved it). All she wanted now was to wear sweatpants and eat Oreos. Which wasn't sad in itself, but she'd *make* it sad.

Tonight, Avalon wore one of her gifted outfits, this time in a dark purple. And, since she rarely had to learn a lesson twice, she strapped her dagger on her hip. Just in case.

The dinner was held outside—the nymphs wanted *everything* to be outdoors. Even if it was a huge pain to maneuver tables to the event area in front of the feyrie mound.

Still, Avalon thought everyone had done a terrific job, and the nymphs had cleared all the snow from the ground, at least around the inn.

The feyrie band burst into a livelier tune after Sabella

passed by with a request. Feyrie music was beginning to sound a little less discordant to Avalon's ears. Soon everyone was dancing—*mostly* everyone. Elden stood away from the party, a royal image in his trademark silver armor, and armed with his short-handled axe and a sword. One of the bridesmaids sidled up to him, gesturing to the dance floor before trying to drag him along.

Elden showed her a mouthful of razor teeth in answer.

Avalon's laughter bubbled up with no chance of stopping it. Elden's head swung, finding her immediately in the crowd. She covered her mouth with a gasp and quickly turned away.

Avalon was a self-serving coward.

Take the risk. Show some weakness. Talk to him, dammit.

She silenced such protests. She was here to do a job, not moon after the man she was contracting for.

Oh, gods. Elden was coming this way. Fine, this was a party. Avalon could be civil and calm without the strain killing her. Throwing herself back into his arms, if Elden would even accept her again, was not an option.

Think of your responsibilities…of your safety…

There was no way she could speak to him without unraveling. There was—

"Avalon." She wished he would say her name like he used to—irritated, like he just caught her with her hand in the cookie jar. Not this polite, inflectionless tone he used now. "You've thrown quite the event."

"With a backdrop like this," she waved to the outdoor area, the inn's landscape blooming in winter and the outside air warm enough—thanks to the Summerlands nymphs—to wander without a coat, "half my work was done for me."

Elden didn't glance away from her. "I wanted you to know

that I told your company that I made the decision to end your contract early. I told Thompson you were both ahead of schedule and could go home early. I didn't...I don't want any bad blood between us."

"Oh. I appreciate that." She wished he wouldn't be so nice to her. All her other exes spent the days after their breakup calling her psycho on the internet.

"If your mother's resources are unable to help you, you'll let me know? You can always ask me for help."

She couldn't say anything in answer, the lie catching in her throat. "Can't you go back to being mean to me?"

"Unfortunately, I don't think so." He considered her a long time before asking, "Will you dance with me tomorrow? At the reception?"

"I think that will hurt too much." *Both of us.*

"If it hurts, perhaps we're doing the wrong thing."

Gods, she wished he could convince her. Once Valerie had vacated her room, and Bruce had bitterly left for Seattle, Avalon had spent every spare minute that day crying in the shower. "Bane is still at large. If he ever found my sister, instead—"

"I know. And she's coming this way to drag you away from me." Quicker than she could see, Elden squeezed her hand once. "I won't dance with anyone else."

"Elden, you wouldn't have danced with anyone else even if you had never met me."

One corner of his mouth tilted upward before Odele snaked an arm around Avalon's shoulders and led her away.

"You're only torturing yourself by talking to him." Odele made a stop at the buffet table, loading up a plate with various snacks. "And you need to eat. I don't take any pleasure in this, Avalon, but you wouldn't let *me* make this mistake."

"You're not sad at all about leaving the inn? Some of these people are your friends."

"Of course, I'm sad! I *was* happy here. Until you got hurt." She pushed the plate at Avalon until she took it. "Sit down for a minute. Eat something. Sabella and Maetta are fine."

Food in hand, Avalon wandered off to be as alone as she could be during a party. She nibbled on a few crackers until her stomach protested even those measly crumbs. The party seemed to be doing well enough on its own—surely no one would miss her if she went to her room for half-an-hour, just to calm down?

She could simply look and see whether her short disappearing act would have any consequences, but she hadn't tried to peer into the future since she announced she was leaving. It went against her nature—Avalon constantly looked ahead to keep her anxiety at bay. But she did not want to experience her last goodbye to Elden twice, and she feared she would see it. Even worse would be glimpsing the possible future where she stayed at his side.

Blind, she dumped her plate in the trash and entered the inn, slowly maneuvering the deserted, familiar halls to reach Whimsy.

It took her far too long to realize her room wasn't empty.

CHAPTER 38
ELDEN

Convincing himself this break would get easier once Avalon was out of his territory helped little. Elden did not run after her, acutely aware of the guests watching their small scene with vicious interest.

It was bad enough that Nora Lee had drifted over, given him a reassuring one-armed hug, and whispered, "She's a changeling, Elden. She doesn't know how to be loved."

He could promise Avalon a lifetime of showing her how, but he couldn't decide if that had a chance of working or would only seem pathetic.

Refusing to further fuel the fey guests' thirst for gossip, Elden instead went back to inspect the mound and rendezvous with the twins.

Tahoma winced at his approach. "You're not going to like this."

"I thought we said we were going to warm him up first." Kenan sighed. "Before we just dropped the bomb."

What *now?* "Explain."

"Your, ah, family is here."

Elden peered around them, squinting into the now open gateway to the feylands. Jin stood within, his toes barely inside the feyland boundary, as if he was still unsure if he wanted to take that next step.

"What are you doing *here?*" Elden could scarcely believe what he was seeing. Jin hated the human realm, not that his animosity was the result of experience. Jin had never left the Winterlands at all.

"The Crown Princess sends her regards to the happy couple." Jin waved, and a few Unseelie warriors came forward, bearing several wrapped gifts. They showed the proper paperwork—something Hia must have pushed the Commission to approve on such short notice. "And the princess wishes for me to attend as well."

"To attend, you'll have to actually come inside the human realm," Elden warned him.

"I am aware."

"Then I welcome you, first son of—"

"Cut that shit out. I'm here because you, like a fool, let Evander into your territory. I don't want to hear you had no choice. Now your actions are affecting *me.*" Jin held his breath and stepped through the gate. "It *stinks.*"

"It doesn't. Well, not this part of the human realm."

Jin was armed to the teeth, meaning Hia believed Evander was up to something and would act soon. Elden appreciated the concern, but he'd been watching Evander's movements around the inn the entire time. Elden had tracked Evander's every step through the inn's cameras, rewatching footage for hours. Evander never paused too long in one place or even acted suspiciously, and he was almost always at the side of the Summerlands warden, Dimitrios. Could he really be that close to the father of the bride? Friendships between Seelie and Unseelie could be formed, but with Evander? It didn't seem likely.

Jin lingered near the gate, casting a glance backwards at the Winterlands on the other side. "Where's your angry lady?"

"I thought you were worried about my uncle, not my lady." Elden held out his hands and brought them together, closing the gate for the night. If anyone else wanted to crash the party, too damn bad.

"Ah, bad news, is it? She came to her senses?"

"I'll kick your ass again, and gladly, Jin."

"*Again*? It doesn't count if you have to use that magic iron of yours."

Elden exhaled sharply through his nose. Could this night get any worse? "Let me show you where the alcohol is. And then I expect to be left alone."

Elden wasn't left alone. He had led Jin to the outdoor bar, something he'd forgotten the inn even had until Avalon discovered it and ordered it cleaned to be used for the wedding. Jin sat at Elden's right, pulling faces at the human liquor but refusing to touch anything the nymphs made. Kenan was on Elden's other side, patting his back.

"Stop touching me."

"Hey, you're having a hard time. And even though we all knew this would happen, we want to help."

"It sounds like you want to die, Kenan. *Stop touching me.*"

"Have you tried getting on your knees and begging her to stay?"

Whiskey wasn't strong enough to withstand this. "Kenan, I'm going to turn your sealskin into a pair of boots."

"Have you tried getting on your knees and eating her—"

Elden pressed his thumb against Kenan's forehead until the selkie yelped. "Brain freeze! I *hate* when you do that!"

Jin drained his glass, paying no mind to Elden's performance of a trick Jin had taught him. "I'm here to watch Evander—not discuss Elden's countless failings with women. Where is he?"

Elden fumbled with his phone, bringing up the app that allowed him to check the security feed. "He's—" He frowned; the application showed every single camera as a black screen, the words "disconnected" blinking at him.

Without warning, Jin shoved Elden off his seat, knocking him to the ground in a loud clatter of armor. A single blade of ice hit the alcohol display behind the bar, shattering glass and spilling liquor.

The brothers looked behind them to see their lost sibling, Bane, who was slowly forming another blade in the air in front of him. Elden thanked Arawn that Bane, unlike Jin, could only form one winter weapon at a time, and leapt to his feet.

An arrow from Jin's quiver flew, speeding past Bane's face, his hair whipping around from the force of it. "My brother or no, that was your only warning," Jin hissed, another arrow already strung in his bow. "Stand down. The next will be aimed to kill."

Bane had clearly finished licking his wounds, but what did he want now? Elden nodded at Jin, heading to the right while his older brother went left. They circled Bane, and Elden thought the thin man looked ill. There was a green tinge to Bane's skin that may have been a sign that his wound wasn't healing well.

The brothers were in the center of the garden party, the

Seelie guests having moved to the outskirts, but no further. The wedding guests seemed to be frozen voluntarily, watching the Unseelie royalty with disturbing interest.

Magic familiar to Elden interrupted their silent standoff. A ring of fire formed around the party, the flames growing to spit ten feet into the air. It had to be Evander, his magic so much like Ashling's, caging them all in.

Most of the guests panicked—the bridal party huddled together in a pastel clump—but a few of the Seelie acted quickly and with purpose.

An arch opened through the flames, allowing enough space for Evander to step inside, *Ember* in his hand.

"What is Evander doing?" Jin demanded. Fear touched the very edges of Jin's voice. "That weapon isn't one of your *mother's*, is it?"

"It is. The last one she ever made." With Ember in his hands, Evander might be unstoppable. Even with Jin present.

Jin swore in the old tongue.

"How'd he find that?" Kenan had followed behind Elden, and tapped the baton at his waist—another one of Ashling's pieces. It quadrupled its length, the point of the spear forming at one end. Tahoma had been gifted a similar weapon before Ashling passed. "Even if Evander got around your feyrie wards somehow, he should have set off the security system."

Bane was more than happy to answer the selkie. "For the latter, any human can unwire a few alarms. And for the former, you have yourself to thank for that, little brother." Bane had finished his bit of magic, an icicle hovering above his head while he held a dagger in each hand. "I've been looking for Ashling's power, her enchanting skill, for a *year* now. Thank you for so kindly demonstrating what your axe can really do, Elden, and what it was *hiding.*"

Elden set his jaw. "How do you even know that my mother's power was unaccounted for?"

"Because the little traitor made a bargain with me," Evander answered with a malicious grin. Bane scowled at the slight. "Nephew," Evander sneered, addressing Elden. "What a waste. You keep such an opportunity—" He lofted the axe. "—locked away in a cage? I suppose, like mother like son."

Elden shouted, "Would you like me to rattle off how many laws you're breaking? A warden should know these things."

Evander's axe, no, *his mother's axe*, swung Elden's way. It was a teasing blow, one Elden was able to parry with the sword on his belt. Elden disengaged, whipping his blade back around for another hit. Evander would have a much longer reach, but his movements would be much slower.

"No!" Bane stalked forward, blocking Elden's path to Evander and raising those daggers up. "Allow me."

Evander shrugged, his gaze moving over to Jin. "It's your funeral, kid."

A duel to the death between siblings was not something Elden had time for. He could feel the energy of the mound rising—it was *excited.* Elden chanced a glance back at the closed feyrie entrance. Black snake-like things burst from the ground. The same twisting things that had appeared when Bane had attacked Avalon that night.

They had buried under the ground, hiding and waiting. The things had even woven themselves into the feyrie gate, hiding among the already existing foliage that covered the gate with leaves and tendrils.

The Seelie sprang forward to beckon the tentacles, controlling and twisting them to their needs. Dammit, they were *vines.*

Vines! Those lying, Seelie bastards!

"Do you like my gift?" Bane mocked, indicating the writhing vines and the Seelie that were now using them to attack the guards Elden had begged from the Winter King. "I've never had a love for landscaping, but the Seelie can certainly accomplish great things with it."

The night Bane had attacked Avalon...it was part of a much larger plan, one that Elden had failed to see as distracted as he had been from Hob and Avalon's wounds.

Jin's second arrow was blocked by Bane's floating ice sword, which shattered on impact, but if it hadn't been interrupted, it would have embedded itself into Bane's pale forehead.

Elden ignored his brothers. More and more writhing vines had burst from the ground, forming a central, octopus-looking mass that reached for anything nearby and flung it into Evander's flaming ring. Each tentacle rose taller than the inn—that thing had certainly grown since Bane had planted it. Elden evaded two vines that flailed his way.

Some of the vines squirmed through the bars of the feyrie gate and slowly began to pry the portal open.

Elden called back to Jin. "Deal with the vines! We can't let them open that portal! *I'll* subdue Bane." With the mound open, who knows what the Seelie might try to bring forth into the world.

"I wouldn't sound so certain of that," Bane jeered. He charged at Elden, spinning and cutting at him with those daggers.

Forced to take a defensive position, Elden blocked and dodged until he was able to disarm one of the twin daggers in his brother's hands. Elden demanded, "What are you trying to accomplish here, Bane?"

Bane's dagger skittered across the ground, but the loss of his weapon only enraged him further. "You have an entire family of warriors and blacksmiths all waiting to put you on the throne, and you squander it! You hide in this filthy place, with mortals and changelings and worse. I am not the heir, nor the general. I have been *waiting* for our father to make use of me, to leave the shadows. Yet, Father continues to call for *you*, to invite you to a court you insult. I have never been given any opportunity, and you spit in the face of yours. Just like your mother."

At the mention of Ashling, Elden ducked Bane's wild strike before backhanding him across the face. "You know *nothing* of my mother or what she protected me from."

"I know she was easy to kill. I know all that armor she crafted did nothing against a tiny, pretty flower."

"*You?*"

Bane seemed to love finally having Elden's full attention. "Yes. Me. Your uncle wanted Ashling's power returned to his family, and I was able to offer a solution. With that axe, and all the magic your mother hid in it, we'll be able to forge and enchant all the weapons we need for *my* new army."

Elden's hands clamped around Bane's throat, and he barely felt the dagger Bane helplessly stabbed into his side, finding a chink in his armor.

For one moment, Elden was aware of how slight his brother was. In the next, Elden jerked his hands and snapped Bane's neck.

Evander laughed as Elden let Bane's limp body slide carefully to the ground. "That's one less bargain I have to worry about. My gratitude, nephew. I was hoping you'd take care of the little prince for me. I promised him the throne, and while I may not be a patriot, even *I* couldn't do that to our lands."

Flame formed in Evander's fist, and he slammed it on the ground. The flame ripped toward Elden, who barely had time to throw up an ice shield. With Ember, the instrument Ashling had poured every last ounce of herself into in order to keep it from her family, Evander's power had more than doubled. "I can't imagine why you'd let this beautiful axe gather dust when it demands blood. Perhaps you and Ashling want to pretend we are not meant to be conquerors, but I won't swallow such lies for the sake of comfort."

Kenan was shouting, straining to be heard over the battle's cacophony. "The gate, Elden! They almost have it open!"

Elden started calling to his gate, grimacing while the mound fought him. It was *loving* this chaos, this opportunity to flood feyrie magic into the human realm. And just when Elden thought he was getting somewhere, an iron shackle appeared around his wrist. Evander yanked him to the ground by that iron piece.

While the two other wardens could not control Elden's entrance, they still had access to their iron manipulation.

The Summerlands warden, Dimitrios, ran into the battle from inside the inn, and under his command, the vines finally wrenched the gate open. More Seelie warriors rushed from inside the tunnel, tossing weapons to a few members of the wedding party who weren't terrified out of their minds. Evander began barking orders to the armed Seelie, something Dimitrios didn't look pleased with.

Jin sprinted over and lifted Elden off the ground while Tahoma held off any attacking Seelie. "We need to get that gate closed. Now!" Jin didn't linger to repeat himself—he charged the gate himself, bow out and ice blades whistling through the air.

The attacking vines twisted around Elden's gate, trying to keep it open. It took time, but he began, after magicking away that iron attached to his wrist, forming a shield of ice around the feyrie entrance. If he could not close the iron gate, he could at least cover the portal in ice and block off any more trespassing feyries that way.

Now Elden understood why the Seelie had insisted the events all be held outside. They wanted an excuse to clear the inn of any snow or ice. Instead of being able to manipulate existing ice, Elden had to create his own—which consumed time and his strength.

Evander was behind this attack, but how did Dimitrios become involved? It was obvious what Evander wanted—the axe, his mother's power. He wanted them so badly that he'd bargained with Bane in order to secure it. But what the hell was Dimitrios and his people attacking him for?

The Seelie must have provided the damned vines, and Bane had planted them on the night he attacked Avalon. The Seelie *could* control Earth's plants, but not as well, and with a family of druids so close it would have been difficult to turn the inn's plant life against them.

"Incoming!" Kenan yelled. He'd been facing off with Evander while Elden tried to deal with the gate.

The axe in his right and sword in his left, Elden re-engaged with his uncle. When he had a half-second to inhale, Elden gave a sharp whistle which ended prematurely as Evander managed to kick him in the chest. Elden had been spoiled, never having to fight against anyone with his same height and reach until now. But Evander and Elden were the same height, and Elden needed to start acting accordingly.

Jin tried to continue sealing the entrance with ice, but he also had to deal with the vines and mentally manage the three ice blades spinning around him.

The twins were battling where they could, and so were the few Unseelie guards Jin had brought along with him, but they would soon be overwhelmed at this rate. Lyra was evacuating anyone who didn't seem part of the coup. And Odele? Elden hadn't spotted the banshee when he had the opportunity to look away from his opponent, but he was sure she'd keep Avalon out of danger.

A howl ripped through the air, rivaling Odele in volume. Bounding into the fray, Hob grabbed the nearest Seelie by the leg and shook him like a rag doll. Evander's movements stuttered at the sight of the black dog, giving Elden the opportunity to hit his uncle in the chest with a backswing of his axe.

Evander stumbled back a few steps and roared. He charged at Elden until white, sharp roots burst out of the ground and blocked his way. One of the roots coiled around Evander's leg, flinging him back across the garden party turned battlefield. The feyrie vines immediately attacked the roots, entangling and knotting together as the opposing plants battled.

A very annoying farmer, and a godsend, headed Elden's way. "Looks like you have a bit of a weed problem, elf."

Elden had never been so happy to see that nosy, bossy farmer. How Abernathy had slipped through the ring of fire, Elden didn't care. *Witches* was all the explanation he needed. "Abernathy, I—"

"I should have brought my harvester," the old witch mused. He watched with Elden as Hob went after the Seelie warriors, circling the twins as their protector. "I have a granddaughter or two with me. We can provide some air support. And help you keep that invasive feyrie shit out of our ecosystem." He jabbed a finger at the offending vines. "But you'll have to deal with the fire your own way." Abernathy left, regrouping with his family and helping them guide down a flock of crows to distract the Seelie warriors.

The farmer's advice echoed—his own way?

"Jin!" Elden barked, using the time Abernathy had bought him to find his half-sibling. "We need to clear the gate!"

"What? I just—" Jin motioned to the ice shield he'd been slowly adding to. One of his flying ice blades switched directions and pinned a nymph to the ground. "You can't be serious."

"The Seelie aren't the only ones who can bring something out of the feylands."

Jin's eyes, as silver as Elden's, brightened.

The general understood.

CHAPTER 39
AVALON

In the middle of Avalon's room stood the Summerlands' Seer, Ilias, and Sabella's mother, Khaira, imperious and terrifying. Warden Dimitrios was hiding behind the bedroom door, and he grabbed Avalon's arms, wrenching them behind her back.

"Check her."

Khaira strode forward, placing a hand against Avalon's stomach. Avalon tried to jerk away. "What the—"

"She's not with child," Khaira announced, stepping back. "Be grateful you're not bearing his heir. That saved you."

"*What* are you talking about?" Now her escape attempts frenzied until those vines that wove around Dimitrios's arms unraveled from his body and started trailing up hers. They bound her arms, thorns cutting into her skin, and Dimitrios shoved her forward.

"I can't believe the prince doesn't have his second chosen. Protecting a mound, heirless. It's insanity."

"It's grief," Khaira determined.

Dimitrios walked around Avalon's body. "The Winter warden may still be without an heir, but she's still a Seer. If Ilias's vision was correct."

"You should have seen what she was sooner, Ilias." Khaira gripped Ilias by the shoulder, pinching into his sallow skin. "If we hadn't given you an extra dose last night, she might have ruined everything."

Avalon rolled over on her back, the vines creeping down to entangle her legs. She tried to scream, but those vines snaked up to her mouth, which she shut quickly, afraid they would try to climb down her throat. She glared at Ilias, who cowered and avoided her gaze, and regretted ever feeling sorry for him.

Ilias's eyes suddenly glazed over, and his whole body racked with tremors. He fell to the floor, Khaira and Dimitrios watching it happen passively. From the ground, Ilias spoke. "Evander found Ashling's power."

Dimitrios's eyes widened. "He needs to wait for the signal."

"He won't," Khaira snapped, pushing him. "And we already took care of the security alarms and cameras." Avalon cursed. That lost electrician hadn't been hired by Odele. Why hadn't she verified that?

Khaira continued, "I'll take care of the Seer. You need to get back down there and assist Evander. But first..." She tugged at one of the vines that held Avalon. "These vines may not be enough. I want her clasped in iron."

The vines retreated, returning to band around the Dimitrios's arm. Iron chains, the mind-numbing burn too familiar, replaced Avalon's former bonds. Her skin sizzled where it made contact with the metal, and she bit her lip as she fought through the pain.

Fucking wardens, Avalon cursed.

"Search her," Dimitrios ordered Ilias before the warden ran out of Whimsy, some of his vines lingering behind and severed from him.

Khaira watched Avalon as she was being patted down. The Seelie were supposed to be representative of life—but all Avalon saw in Khaira was death. Was Sabella a secret traitor as well? Was Avalon that easily fooled?

Ilias was kept blindfolded, but he turned his head in Avalon's direction and she knew he was reading her future. "She's clear," Ilias muttered, sinking down to his knees. Avalon blinked, looking down—for only a second—at the dagger that was now hidden underneath her chains. Was Ilias an ally or simply incompetent?

"Now, dear." Khaira smiled, plucking a mushroom from her hairline and crushing it into her hand. "Would you like a cup of tea?"

On the floor next to Avalon, Ilias trembled.

The mushrooms they powdered into Avalon's tea...they threw her Sight forward and backward until she thought she'd be sick. She watched Ilias dreamily, his face appearing to age and brighten with youth over and over and over.

Laughter encircled her, cruel in its pitch. Only the Summerlands Seer remained silent. How often was *Ilias* drugged? But this thought was swallowed, chewed, and spit back out by the drugs swimming, invading, and pillaging her system.

Her eyes dried up, bulging. Avalon was tearing at the seams. This much power *hurt*. It didn't strengthen her—it made her helpless. It was dizzying, her Sight showing her migraine-inducing snippets of visions until it found one, one in the *past*, and dug its talons in deep.

No, not this. She pushed back, her drug-addled mind ineffectively thrashing against the tidal wave of her own Sight.

The worst night of her and Odele's lives.

And all of it due to Avalon's overreaction.

My fault, my fault, my fault—

Some preppy asshole at school had interrupted Odele's speech to call her a *freaky bitch*. Something the teacher decided to ignore, leaving Odele to stumble through her speech in tears.

And in between classes, when Avalon had found out, there swelled a rage inside her she could not quiet. She made it five minutes into her Calculus test before she stood, oversized textbook in hand, and found Oliver Harm in his Unnatural History class and did what any girl who'd reread *Anne of Green Gables* too many times would do.

With a strength she should not have possessed, she brought that textbook down on his stupid head, cracking his face on the desk. When Oliver screamed and looked up at her, face leaking blood, Avalon had only smiled.

"What the hell is wrong with you?" Her father, he was still her father then, guided her to the "intervention". It was void of any of her peers, Avalon had no friends outside Odele, and the circle was instead stuffed with Bruce's political staff. His Public Relations advisor patted the seat next to her, her warm smile a practiced forgery.

Avalon's mother, Valerie, stared mindlessly into their fireplace.

A low moaning reverberated throughout the over-sized house—Odele's nightmare was ramping up. Avalon tried to break out of the circle. "I need to see to Odele."

Bruce stepped in front of her. "Let her wail. You, sit down."

Her fury returned, the strength that filled her limbs when she attacked Oliver was coursing through her once more. She hurt—her bones ached, particularly the ones in her facial structure, and she struggled to hold whatever this was within.

"I know what's wrong with her."

This did not come from Avalon's therapist, who was also on Bruce's staff, but from a newcomer. One of the bodyguards Bruce had hired upon starting his campaign for governor.

The woman was eerily beautiful, her curled hair ending around her sharp ears and her skin a touch too golden to be human. A feyrie. Few walked around unglamoured and exposed as this one did. Their eyes met while Avalon was sizing her up, and dread filled every square inch of her. This woman did know and knew something that Avalon had only made poor guesses at.

Bruce didn't care for games from those he owned. "What do you know?"

His tone was dangerous and this fed into the feyrie's perverse pleasure. There was the intense feeling of being watched, of being known. Avalon fought back frightened tears, staring down this fey woman with every ounce of her own hatred.

The fey wanted to bathe in Avalon's fear, wanted to lick it from her skin. Feyrie wine could not be imported. Drinking in a mortal's pain was the next best port.

"She's not your daughter." The fey woman savored that sentence. "That's a changeling."

Not an ounce of proof had been offered, and yet, Avalon somehow knew this was true. She had always been skeptical of the old wives' tale that "the fey can't tell lies". But something inside her told Avalon that this horrifying claim was the truth.

Valerie stood, her wine glass falling to the floor and

shattering.

As a teen, Avalon had assumed Valerie's hatred, and the way she screamed, "You ruined our family, you bitch!" had been directed at her.

But now, reliving this as an adult, it was all too clear Valerie had been cursing the fey bodyguard who had spilled her secret. It wasn't a comforting thought, knowing that most fey, including a warden, had been unable to see what Avalon was. So, when Avalon was discovered that night, she must have slipped in her anger and transformed just enough for that damned fey to notice.

In other words, it had been all her fault.

Bruce had once given a talk about the benefits of modern parenting, gentle parenting, and had called for the abandonment of the switch.

The fresh sting of a slap across Avalon's cheekbone proved him a hypocrite.

But, worse than all of that was the small, flickering idea planted in her head that she had deserved it. After all, changelings were monsters.

Avalon slowly returned to the present. Her body was moving, but not by her own ability. While her senses were addled, she was still certain of that. Wind cut against her burning flesh, pain flooding where the iron touched her bare skin. Were they outside? It was difficult to see past the memories wracking her senses. Gods, where was Odele? Perhaps she had foreseen the chaos, the *death*, and was able to get away?

Avalon squinted, trying to shake off the drugs enough to see. Lyra! Her heart soared when she found the familiar face. Lyra and Nora Lee were herding the bridal party out of the gardens while Sabella hoarsely screamed, " *What* is going on?!"

Whoever was leading Avalon guided her away from the chef and the brides. Avalon tried to dig in her heels and found she was floating, just like the Winterlands Seer had during Taliesin's party. Ilias and Khaira walked ahead of her, pulling her along with the iron chain. That must have burned Ilias so— he wore no gloves while he tugged at her bindings.

Avalon gasped—the wedding party was in the midst of a battle, and both sides had spilled so much blood. There were bodies littered throughout the garden. Gore soaked the wedding decorations Avalon had so carefully hung. One of the corpses nearly drove her into a panic, the fallen body of Bane, no longer missing and no longer breathing.

After she stomped her anxiety down, an image struck Avalon violently. *Elden, bloodied and beautiful, and wrapped in iron chains as tight as her own.*

The vision splintered before she could see anything more. *Useless,* she wanted to shout. Avalon tried again, tried to force it.

Evander glared down at her as if she was nothing, one of his eyes swollen, red, and blind.

And it was gone.

Sabella had broken away from Lyra, sprinting back to the party with Maetta at her heels. She wove through a battle, ran between nymphs and Winterlands guards as they fought, getting as close to her father as the fighting allowed her.

"Dad! What are you *doing?*" Sabella lurched for him, Maetta the only thing keeping her on the outskirts.

"Ensuring your future," the Summerlands Warden shouted back, sending one of his vines to tangle around Tahoma's leg.

Sabella swore and took control of the vine, unhanding Tahoma, who distanced herself from the Seelie warden. "You're hurting these people!"

"You're ruining our wedding!" Maetta yelled.

"Wrong energy, love," Sabella snapped, turning back to her father. "What could possibly make you do this?"

"The Pacific Northwest warden has no heir. And our feyrie mound is *dying*. It won't last the year. The Summer Queen already lost the Arizona entrance. Do you know what she'll do to us if we lose Georgia?"

Tears raced down Sabella's cheeks, dropping off at her chin. "So, we're just going to *steal* this one? You'll start a war!"

Maetta pointed out, "I don't think your dad is overly concerned about that."

Avalon felt sick. Khaira had checked her to see if she was pregnant, to make sure Elden had no heir, and if she had been? She would have been killed.

Unfortunately, Avalon had an idea why she hadn't been murdered, anyway. The Seelie, thanks to Ilias, knew she was a Seer. She imagined she'd make a great apology gift to the Summer Queen for causing such mayhem.

Avalon saw fire lick at the inn's foundation, threatening Ashling's legacy. Where was—Elden! He and his brother were at the gate, collapsing the ice shield in front of it and dodging the swinging vines. They moved in tandem, coaxing something out of the feyrie entrance. The summer warmth the Seelie had wrought felt like a distant memory. The harsh, cutting winds of winter blew from the Unseelie lands sitting on the other side of the mound. Snow followed, the flurries rushing inside to form blooms of steam where it impacted with Evander's raging fire.

Elden was so concentrated on preventing the fire from spreading, he didn't seem to notice he had regained Evander's attention. If Evander caught Elden unaware...

Her Sight was fading in and out, but Avalon was certain that, if Evander overpowered Elden, his uncle would unmake him. Everything that Elden was, all that goodness and strength, would be stomped out.

Elden needed her. Avalon had to escape these chains. She—

Oh, thank the gods Elden had psychotically tied her to that tree. Avalon knew exactly what needed to be done.

Remember your humanity, that lack of strength, the vulnerability...

Her mind struggled to see the logic in becoming weak again. Leaning into the constant ringing in her head, Avalon used that to clear her thoughts and to deal with the physical pain that racked her body as she started to change.

She fought against her own mind, that rotted thing that told her, *You can't do this, you'll only ruin everything. Your birth was just the beginning of a blight. You disappoint everyone you—*

No, even if she had been completely human, Bruce's nuclear family ideal was toxic. Unreachable. She could only be what she was—protective, *slightly* overbearing, and loyal, and still able to love with her battered, feral heart.

Avalon, I know you can do this. I need you to do this. I need you.

Her bones hurt, her teeth aching the most, already tender from the damage Bane had inflicted. Though she was putting her body through more agony, the burn of the iron slowly began to lessen. Her feet lowered to the ground, and Avalon threw the chains looped around her body off, the iron hitting the ground with a crash.

Ilias raced forward, tearing the bandage off his eyes. Khaira screamed, "You useless waste! Get her back!"

There was a second when Avalon thought the Seer might disobey his master.

Ilias charged, and she fumbled with her dagger, panicking as she raised it before her. Her defense had an unwanted outcome—Avalon cut into Ilias's tender throat. More blood than she expected spurted from the wound, covering her own chest, and almost bringing her lunch back for a second appearance.

Sorry, Ilias. Should have seen that coming.

Avalon was free—but now what?

Look! Avalon struggled to focus her power, still woozy from the mushroom tea. Only bits and pieces of a vision came to her, like she was reading a book with every other page ripped out.

But she saw enough to *try*. Even if the ending was unclear.

Evander threw an iron chain through the air, wrapping around Elden's legs. Dimitrios, ignoring his daughter's protests, distracted Jin while Evander continued caging Elden in iron.

The Northwest warden was able to magic away some of the chains, but soon Elden was overcome.

The wisp flitted out from Avalon, speeding toward Evander's face and burying, burning, into his left eye. Evander roared, flailing uselessly at his face. The wisp's blue light brightened so intensely it nearly blinded Avalon, before it flickered out to leave a burned-out socket where Evander's eye had been. Avalon made a beeline for his left side, for his off-hand.

Elden was pinned, face down, the iron beginning to wrap around his chest and throat. One hand reached out to her, seeing the intention in her eyes. *Stop!* he wordlessly begged her. *Run!* And when Avalon failed to heed his silent warning, Elden screamed her true name, raw and heartbreaking, "*Ava*

Golightly—"

Her tinnitus was shrill and piercing, blocking out Elden's order. Avalon stuck that dagger in the first vulnerable place in Evander's armor that her inexperience could find. She tried to remove it, to stab him again, but Evander found it first.

Evander ripped the dagger from his side, judging it critically and recognizing its maker. His eyes widened, and he grabbed Avalon by the throat, shaking her, screaming, "How dare you steal this? How dare you even *touch* it!"

It was pointless, clawing at Evander's armored body, but Avalon tried, anyway. She panted, begging for air as her sight faded, until Evander took his sister's dagger and plunged it hard into Avalon's chest. The force of the downward motion was enough to knock her off her feet. When she landed, sprawled out and unmoving on the ground, Elden's screams battled with her tinnitus until Avalon heard nothing at all.

CHAPTER 40
ELDEN

Raw, broken, Elden screamed Avalon's true name over and over, begging her to *stop*, to *hide*, to *run*. With the cacophony of the battle drowning out his desperate pleas, and her terrible hearing, Avalon could not catch a word he said, and still Elden roared.

He crawled forward, each inch he gained only succeeding in strangling him more. Iron squeezed his throat, burning his skin, and vines tangled around his legs to drag him backward. Even as logic left him, Elden was aware that the vines and iron did not seem to be trying to actually kill him, merely restrain him.

Avalon never heard him, and when she fell and remained still at Evander's feet, there was a moment of horrific silence as the reality of it sank in. Evander could not miss his target at that distance, even half-blind. The only solace to be found was in the fact that her death was clean and quick.

Odele's wail cut through it all, stunning Seelie and Unseelie alike. Only Abernathy, his hearing aid ripped out of his ear, was able to move while Odele shrieked.

The witch threw the iron chains off Elden, huffing and swearing with the effort. The farmer said something, something wise, Elden was sure, but he ignored it all. He was on his feet immediately, rushing his uncle.

Vines flew at him, grabbing his legs and dragging him backwards, away from Avalon and Evander. His brother's ice blades severed the vines, freeing him. "Elden, keep moving!" Jin spared one of his three blades to protect Elden in a deadly floating circle.

Elden picked himself up with a shout. Jin's spinning blade shattered, shot down by some Seelie archer. Elden threw his axe, the blade thudding into Evander's chest plate, knocking the wind out of him. The sword his only remaining weapon, Elden met Ember with it, the metal ringing as they collided.

"This place," Evander spat, grinning as his flames began to catch on the inn's roof, "could have been spared all this. *Ashling's secret heir.* We could have made you a *king*, not this pathetic thing she forged you to be. Ashling knew what she was meant to do!"

"You would have made me a puppet," Elden returned, breaking away and attacking with a fury that had Evander backpedaling.

"We would have made you strong. *And we will.*"

Every strike Elden tried, every trick he'd been taught, Evander caught easily. If Elden had another century to train, he might have been able to rival his uncle in swordplay, but today, Elden had to accept that he was the weaker warrior.

"I see Ashling trained you herself. On anyone else..." Evander's grin was hollow, as if the words pained him. "On someone who hadn't trained with your mother for years, you might stand a chance."

Evander almost disarmed him then, but Elden recovered at the last second. "If," Evander said, squinting, "you didn't have those damned eyes, you'd be completely one of us. Nothing of your father at all."

As much as Evander might have wished it, and as much as *Elden* had once wished it, that wasn't true.

Twin blades of ice, the most he could manage, formed faster than ever before. Elden mentally threw the blades Evander's way, sending them spinning around him. With one eye now missing, Evander struggled to keep the swords at bay.

As Evander destroyed the ice blades, cutting them down one after another, Elden used Evander's distraction to his advantage. He summoned a length of iron that he coiled around the axe, stealing it from Evander's grasp. Ember skidded to the ground, out of reach for both of them. His rage dampening his logic, Elden surged forward and grabbed his uncle by the neck, slamming his forehead down on Evander's nose. The sound of breaking bones bordered on musical.

His uncle raged, shoving Elden back and trying to clear his nose of blood. "*You* could have been a conqueror. You could have taken that murderous throne and thrived."

"I'm sure you promised Bane the same thing."

"No," Evander laughed without humor, "making a deal with Bane was a mistake. It was tedious, tricking that damned orator, and for what? He didn't even follow orders. Killing an enchanter of Ashling's skill! I wanted to hack him to pieces for that." Evander's own iron chain caught Ember and pulled the weapon back into his hands.

"Isn't that what you wanted? My mother punished for disobeying the family?"

"Now for that, kid, I really will kill you."

The flames burned wilder and started to consume the garden as well as parts of the inn. A wave of fire licked at Elden's neck, scalding him and certain to leave a scar. *If I can even make it to that point.* There were centuries between them, and Evander's experience was evident with each swing. Elden could barely catch his breath while Evander had no issue *monologuing.*

"Bane told us all about you, Elden, far before our poet-king decided to grace us with the information. What he neglected to say was that Taliesin already stole our family power from you."

"You didn't want my mother's power," Elden realized. "You wanted me."

"It's why you were born. You were Ashling's mission. A way to get our family finally on that throne. But I couldn't tell Bane that! I had to make him believe he'd rule if he helped me. I convinced him what we wanted from you was Ashling's inherited power. That was partially true. And I said that we'd need you brought to us unharmed in order to make use of it. I told him we'd chain you in a smithy—which we would have. It's a good way to break men."

Evander lowered the axe, giving Elden a moment to refocus. "These damned bargains. You can never just be *direct.* I asked Bane for Ashling's legacy to be given back to us, and instead of delivering *you* on our doorstep, the coward *poisoned* my sister."

Because Bane knew what Evander did not—that Elden didn't possess an ounce of Ashling's enchanting skill, thanks to their father. And Bane, desperate for the throne, found his own way to complete the bargain. By killing Ashling, which was far simpler than capturing Elden, Bane thought he was returning her power to her family and therefore still meeting the bargain's terms.

There was a reason Evander was telling Elden all this. He wasn't revealing his master plan just to gloat.

"And after all that needless loss, Ashling's power didn't return to us. Because she hid it away in this axe for her darling, baby boy." Evander had yet to raise Ember again. "Let the Seelie have this damned mound. Their own entrance is dying. I owe them that much for arranging this wedding to give me time and an excuse to find a way to bring you back home. You don't want the mound, anyway. You don't even have an *heir.* You could lose it all just like *that.*"

Evander sharpened his point with a snap of his fingers. "The original plan was just to take you by force, and let Dimitrios inherit your mound's power. But we could go an alternate route, if you'd like. You can be dragged before the Matriarch, before your patient grandmother, or you could act like a man and *walk.*"

Evander dangled the offer before him, letting the flames around the inn die down as if sweetening the deal. Elden shook his head. "It's too late for that."

"Your mother shouldn't have died, but she also shouldn't have betrayed her family. Nephew, we can correct this. With her gifts, we could arm the deadliest army our land has ever seen. The throne could still be yours. Just name Dimitrios as your heir and return to the feylands with me. Your true family has been dying to meet you."

It was sickening, realizing that if Elden had been given the option before all of this, he would have sat on that cursed throne if it meant saving his mother. *If it had meant saving Avalon.* He would have hated every minute of it, but he'd have done it, nonetheless.

But Ashling and Avalon were dead. And, whether it had been deliberate or not, it was Evander's fault.

"No." Elden tried to keep himself from glancing at Avalon's fallen form, but Evander caught the movement, anyway.

Evander stood only a few feet away from his last victim. "*Her*? I'm about to take everything from you and you look at her?" He suddenly kicked Avalon's ribcage, laughing as Elden leapt forward, unable to stop himself. "That lying, changeling bitch. She told me she was nothing to you. *Nothing*."

She was everything, for a short time, and damn Avalon for not ever realizing it.

"You'll have to bring Grandmother a corpse, Uncle."

Evander shrugged off Elden's rejection. "I thought that would be your response. We should have grabbed you ourselves years ago, but Ashling would have sensed us coming." Ember rejoined the battle, its wide swing deadly and controlled.

One of those vines raised ever so slightly off the ground, and it tripped Elden as he maneuvered backwards out of Evander's swing. Elden fell, landing on his back, unable to avoid Ember as Evander brought it directly down on his chest.

Elden twisted as much as he could, but the blade cut into his shoulder, getting through his armor. He saw his own blood splattered on the blade's edge, marring his reflection.

The axe's reaction was instantaneous. It drank in Elden's blood, recognized it as kin, and metal spikes pierced where Evander's grip lay, effectively nailing his hands to the handle.

A failsafe. Even as she was dying, Ashling had saved him.

There was little time to act. With a grunt, Elden pushed the blade out of his flesh, the metal biting into his fingers. He scrambled away, blood dripping into the dirt.

He wanted to stare his uncle in the eye as Ashling's magic

weapon turned on him. Elden instead found Evander was look-ing *past* him, remaining eye wide and afraid as the banshee on the other side of his flames rose. Odele pointed at Evander, ha-tred raising the staticky hair off her shoulders, and *screamed*.

Ember did as it was designed to do and burned.

Dimitrios saw Evander being consumed by the fire radiat-ing off the axe he could not relinquish, and froze, unsure. This gave Sabella the opportunity to wrench control away from her father, taking one of the feyrie vines and wrapping up her father within it.

"As your heir," she intoned, "I deem you unfit to hold the title of warden." When her father dared protest, she covered his mouth with vines as well. Her mother received similar treat-ment.

Maetta complained, "I *knew* we should have eloped."

Jin passed by Elden, placing an uncertain hand on his shoul-der. "Your mongrel handled most of the other warriors, and the rest I encased in ice. I can handle this for now."

Elden understood what Jin was offering—a momentary respite. Elden took it, finding where Avalon had fallen. While he walked dead to the world, Sabella tried healing the wound in his chest. Sabella stammered, "Elden, I am so, so sorry!"

"Sabella." Elden paused long enough for her healing magic to fade. "I understand that you had nothing to do with this, but right now, I have nothing to say to you. I'm...tired."

She moved away, nodding. "I get it, Elden. I'll find a way to help on my own."

Odele seemed eerily calm as he approached. Shock, Elden assumed. She even let him kneel next to her, silent as he cau-tiously reached for her sister.

Blinking away blood and trembling, Elden lifted Avalon's

body into his arms. She was so still and painfully *human*. He didn't inspect her wound—there was too much blood and mess on her chest, anyway—but mostly because he knew Evander would never miss his target.

Elden was empty, simply staring down at Avalon's pale face until Odele reached over and flicked her in the forehead.

Avalon's eyes opened with a start. "Oh," she sighed, blinking at the sudden exposure to light. "I'm alive. I didn't see that coming."

Elden was so startled he nearly dropped her. "You're *alive*?"

Avalon struggled to sit up by her own power. "Don't sound so put out."

Odele shook her head. "Idiot. No one thought to ask the *banshee* if she was dead or alive. And Elden, stop fondling my sister's chest right in front of me, please."

"I'm searching for the *wound*," he sniped, but retracted his hands. "Evander stabbed you. We all saw it."

"Yeah, he did," Avalon agreed, as confused as he was. "And it hurt, like a *punch*, but that was all I felt." Her face flushed. "Gods, I thought that was it." Her hand wrapped around her throat, and she winced. "I couldn't breathe, and I—"

Elden took her hand away, unable to bear the sight of any hand near her throat again. Avalon then touched her chest, probing. "I can't believe it. There's no cut."

He glared at her. "What's the point in being able to read the *future* if you never—" Elden abandoned all thought, opting instead to bring Avalon's face to his own, kissing her thoroughly. She threw her arms around his neck, but only after a few moments of hesitation.

Odele scrambled away from them. "Gods, not right in front of me!"

Elden was interrupted by someone tapping on his shoulder. He let Avalon go, growling, "Who else do I need to *kill* today?"

"Here." Tahoma had retrieved Elden's enchanted dagger and threw it to him, the blade sticking into the ground.

Elden tested the blade's edge, waited for the blade to reappear, and though Odele yelled at him for it, he gently pressed the dagger against Avalon's skin.

The sharp metal portion vanished.

Their eyes met, both wide-eyed at the revelation.

It can't be a weapon against where my heart lies.

Did Avalon remember what he'd said about the dagger? Elden hoped not.

Odele grumbled, "A trick knife, Houdini?"

"Something like that." Elden stepped back, allowing the sisters some room by taking his brutish form out of the way. He couldn't look at Avalon after that kiss, wanting to avoid another rejection from her.

When Elden caught up with his brother, Jin had finished trapping the remaining Seelie warriors with Sabella's help. He spoke, weary and angry. "I'm going to retrieve enough reinforcements to take these usurpers into custody. Can you maintain their ice prisons until I return? I stopped the fire, but there's some damage." Jin sneered. "You can do what you like with the corpses."

"Of course," Elden promised. *But what to do with the axe?*

Abernathy approached, covered in dirt and feathers. "We all survived, in case you were worried, elf."

"I wasn't."

The witch rubbed the back of his neck, complaining that he'd pulled something. "Any ideas on what to do with that axe? I wouldn't recommend keeping it."

"I can't destroy it," Elden mused bitterly. The axe's power would just go back to his mother's side of the family if he tried.

"What if we let the earth take care of it?" Those white, dead roots wriggled under Abernathy's command like worms. "Bury it deep enough and the earth will treat it like a parasite. It will be *consumed*, power and all. Nothing left to crawl back to the feylands."

Elden really should have thought on the solution harder, but as he stared at the burnt corpse of his uncle and the attached blade, he didn't want anything to do with it. Hearing his mother's voice call to him had been a dark comfort, but look at what it had cost him. "Bury it."

Abernathy nodded, removing his bloody cowboy hat and pressing it against his heart. The roots, under his command, pulled Ember into the earth.

Elden had never heard his mother scream, but the axe did a perfect impression of it. Elden covered his ears, doubling over until someone tucked his head under their chin, holding him.

"The roots have it now," Avalon whispered.

Elden raised his head, memorizing those tearing, golden eyes. He hardly noticed that in her human state they'd lost a bit of their shine.

"I can't find the wisp." Her arms moved to settle around his back, keeping his focus on her and away from the burning inn. She couldn't wield a blade to save her life, and still Avalon was constantly protecting him.

"It might have overextended itself," he guessed. "Evander could have been too much for—hey, don't cry." He caught the tear before it could make it down her cheek. "That wisp led to Evander's death. I can't imagine it would want for much else."

Another tear threatened to form. "I couldn't even talk to it, but I loved that stupid thing. It was so vicious and cute."

Sounds like someone I know, Elden was almost able to say before they were interrupted.

"Mom's freaking out. She saw the fire from the cabin, and who knows what else she saw." Odele walked over and pocketed her phone, blinking when she saw how they were entwined. Something like regret flashed across her face, but it was gone in a second. "Let's keep her from having another panic attack."

Avalon hesitated before releasing him and following Odele's exit. And what else could she do? Odele had been *right.* The inn—*he*—was too dangerous to stay around.

Avalon was a madness, and now she was human. His hope that she may need him again in the future was dead.

The mound, open and satisfied, flooded the inn with his father's guards. On a better day, Elden might have made an attempt to care how the new Seelie prisoners were treated or where they were sent.

Today, his inn covered in soot and blood, he turned his back on them.

CHAPTER 41
AVALON

"We're heading to the lake house." Odele finished packing Valerie's car as it sat parked in the inn's gravel lot. Their mother was waiting in the passenger seat for her daughters to say their farewells. Yesterday's battle and fire had convinced Valerie that her vacation was over, and her daughters were escaping with her.

Odele added, huffing, "I suspect when spring rolls around, I'll be busy redecorating all the neighboring summer homes. A lot of farmhouse chic, probably. But I'll overcharge."

Avalon hadn't helped pack, other than stuffing her clothes into her suitcase haphazardly. "You'll be busy. I'd order the *Live, Laugh, Love* signs now."

"Also," Odele continued, looking at Valerie seated in the car, "Valerie agreed to go to family therapy. And *I* get to choose the therapist."

"Smart."

Odele checked her backpack. "I didn't see your luggage in

there. Did you have Kenan pack it in your car?"

"Odele, I know I said I would go with you, but—"

"Oh, shut up." Odele rolled her eyes and actually laughed, a glimmer of her old self. "I know your luggage is still in your room. I was wondering how long it would take for you to confess."

Avalon blinked several times. "You're not angry?"

"No." Odele kicked the tires. "I wasn't going to let you come along, anyway. I've seen how you gaze longingly at each other. And I can't deal with a lovesick adult Avalon. You were angsty enough as a teenager." Odele gave her a quick hug, ending it before they wouldn't be able to let go again. "I do need you to call me—video call me—every single night. And I want to hear absolutely *zero* details about what the two of you get up to."

Her heart lightened. "You're letting me stay?"

"I'm *making* you stay. I'm not letting you in this car, and Tahoma siphoned the gas out of yours."

Avalon threw her arms up around Odele's neck. "*Thank you.* You won't—"

"Oh, I'll regret this. Just make sure that you don't." Odele patted her head. "I'm tired of being the psychotically overprotective one. You can keep that job." Valerie knocked on the window, growing impatient. Odele sighed, as if imagining the therapy work ahead of them. "We could do with some time apart, anyway. You're still expected for Christmas. I suppose you'll be bringing him. That giant better not eat all the apple tarts."

Avalon spotted something else in the car. "You're taking the feyrie cat?"

"Mind your own business."

Elden didn't glance up as Avalon entered the inn's office. He sat in the desk that faced the door, staring at an over-sized, wrapped parcel on his desk. It was clearly an axe, two-sided, and the wrapping was stamped with a silver wax seal that could only belong to the Unseelie royal family.

It can't be a gift from his father? No, it must be from Jin.

Avalon slid a thick sheet of paper across the desk to Elden, forcing him to acknowledge her existence. Those dark brows came together, irritated at someone interrupting him doing nothing, before he raised them in surprise at the sight of her standing in front of him.

Suspicion clouded his features. Elden lifted the paper casually. "What is this? A last-minute bill?"

Her voice was steady and strong. "It's my resume." Avalon pulled out a chair, sitting before his desk patiently.

"Resume?" He straightened, abandoning his former slouch. "Is this for—"

"Head Manager," she clarified. "I have plenty of experience. Not to mention my web skills—"

"Hired. You're hired." Elden reached a hand forward, nearly shaking hers before retracting it. "Actually, *no*. You're not hired. Not until I understand what this really is. If all you want is a pay raise, then no. I won't work next to you *pining* for the rest of our too-long lives."

She caught her resume as he tossed it back at her. Fine, Elden deserved some explanation. "I want us to try—"

"I don't want to *try*, Avalon." He leaned across the desk, dark hair falling on his forehead. "I told you how I felt first, when I'd hoped at best that you tolerated me. If you're going to speak now, I want all of it. Not part. I want all of *you*."

"You may change your mind on that," she whispered. "I'm a lot."

"I don't think I have any room to talk, my feral love."

The odd endearment was encouragement enough to get her started. Avalon drew in a deep, shuddering breath and gripped the armrests of the chair. "My Sight has been a curse. It just feeds into my anxiety. I abuse it whenever I feel an ounce of uncertainty. I spend most days drained from overusing it. But—" Avalon lowered her eyes. "—with you I don't want to look ahead. I don't want to see the next rare smile you flash me, the next kiss, in the haze of a vision. I want to be present with you, not knowing how you're going to drive me crazy next."

He had moved during her speech, and she hadn't noticed until Elden knelt before her, placing his hands on her knees. "What else?"

"What *else*?" Avalon scowled. "I love you, too. That's what else."

He lifted one of her hands, bringing it to his lips. "I accept your offer. I can't wait to work with you."

"How princely." She squeezed his hand hard. "But I'll handle all future interviews. Can't have you kissing all the new employees."

"You'll handle *everything*." He stood, using her hand to pull her to her feet. She ended up pressed to his chest, her other hand between them and flat against his heart. "The only time I want to be in this office is to do things to you that will cause HR to faint dead away."

His closeness chilled and comforted her. "Oh!" Avalon scrunched her nose, blushing. "I did that all wrong."

"You confessed that you love me. Something I was certain

I would have to wrench from your heart. How can that be *wrong?*" Elden frowned. "I won't accept your withdrawal."

"No, that isn't what I meant. I was..." She glanced away. "I was supposed to beg your forgiveness first."

"Beg my forgiveness?! I won't accept that, either. You have endured too much for me already." Elden held the back of her neck still, kissing her fiercely. "Settle your life from before. There will be no begging or retreating from here on out."

When Avalon called Thompson to give him her two weeks' notice, he wasn't surprised. "*It's to be expected.*" Her former boss sighed. "*The man's clearly an incubus.*"

It had been hard to hold in her laughter. Elden was no tempting lust demon, but he was close.

As she ended her call, Elden showed her his phone with a funny look on his face. "I don't recognize the number, but I think your sister texted me."

"Take care of my sister, or else," Avalon read, shaking her head at the ten knife emoticons Odele had included after her message.

"I don't appear to have a choice," he said, but he looked on the verge of laughter.

They cleaned out one of the inn's desks for her use, though Avalon had protested that this could wait until later.

"No," Elden insisted. "If you're going to be running the inn, you need a place to do it from."

Avalon was happy to have Elden throw the inn into her charge. She loved it—all of its problems, too. "Good. I want full control of the place," Avalon demanded of the feyrie prince. "You've no idea how to handle an inn."

"I was always very honest about that." He smiled down at her. "Are you my boss now?"

"Afraid so." And, though she knew it didn't matter, she asked, "Would it be okay if I remain human, just for a little while? The transformation isn't exactly painless."

"As long as you remain with me."

"I have to," she revealed shyly. "I'm *where your heart lies,* remember? At least, the dagger says so."

"That's one enchanted weapon that can't keep its mouth shut," Elden grumped, and they both laughed.

At dinner, Lyra kept piling an overwhelming amount of helpings onto Avalon's plate. Elden held her hand under the table, which did make it a little difficult to eat as Avalon listened to him talk about what the firefighters had said about the damage to the inn. As soon as the battle had been over, Abernathy had gathered volunteers and helped extinguish any remaining flame from Evander's magic. The damage wasn't entirely superficial, but Elden could glamour most of it away until it could be repaired.

Tahoma made a "give me" motion with her hand to her brother. Kenan slapped the cash into her palm, shrugging at Avalon's questioning glance. "Sorry to bet against you, but I didn't think you'd stay. You seem to have a lot of trauma. Remember, I've met your parents."

"Thank you, Avalon," Tahoma sang, fanning herself with the money.

Elden looked as if he wanted to strangle them both. "Avalon, let's go take a walk." He ignored the kissing noises the twins made at their departure.

Avalon and Elden left the inn, pausing only to allow

Avalon time to dress appropriately for the weather. With the axe buried and its power being consumed by Mother Nature, Elden was no longer able to so much as light a match. That was no matter. Avalon kept his cold hand in her warm and nearly human one.

Together, they walked through the forest as Avalon admired the satisfying *crunch* the snow provided underneath their boots. As she was human again, it was harder to see through the inn's glamour. When she mentioned it, Elden placed his free hand over her eyes. After he pulled away, she saw him as he really was and the lovesick relief made her grin.

"Sometimes," Elden began, something out of place in his voice. It took Avalon a moment to identify it—Elden was afraid. He cleared his throat once, continuing. "Sometimes, Avalon, when I look at you, I can't find a single thing to say. I'm empty and yet so full all at once. And other times, I think I could scare you with the words I want to spill." He frowned, studying her open expression carefully. Avalon gave nothing away, simply allowing him time to get what he wanted to say out. "My father's the poet, not I, but sometimes you inspire things in me I'm not used to or comfortable with." She laughed at his furrowed brow, which only made him lower it further. "I'm glad my plight can provide some amusement."

"It's just that I know you're stalling. What you *really* want to say must be truly terrifying indeed, to require this much buildup."

"You gave me your true name, Avalon." Elden took her hands gently, her gloves protecting her skin from his chill. For the inn, winter had arrived a month early and even in her human state she could see the magic ghosting off his skin, shining in his eyes. "One day, Avalon, I'll give you mine."

She stiffened. "Elden, I don't want that power over you—"

"No, no!" He squeezed her hands reassuringly, but gave her a strange half-smile as if there was something she wasn't quite understanding. "Never mind, Avalon. Just tell me what you want and I'll grant it. I may have been a secret prince most of my life, but I imagine I can still get access to the vaults."

Elden's joke calmed her, and she tugged him down to kiss him. "I want *you*. And time with you. Just give me that and I'll be happy."

"No jewels?"

"Nope." Avalon shrugged off the offer.

Elden tried again. "Not even a *crown*? I'd like to see you in one."

"What the hell would I wear with a crown?"

"Preferably? Nothing."

She silenced that ridiculous statement by kissing him again and again until they were both dizzy. Elden ended it, using the weather as an excuse. Weather that was entirely his fault. "We should get you inside. And, Avalon, look."

He turned her head until she caught sight of Hob bounding through the snow, chasing a very familiar blue light.

EPILOGUE
AVALON

The overplayed holiday music coming from her car's speaker was an awkward background to Avalon's rising anxiety. Never had a doorway appeared so foreboding—not even the magic portal into the feyrie realm had filled Avalon with such stomach-clenching anxiety. The only thing tethering her to this earth was the icy hand that gripped hers, squeezing it lightly until she looked at him.

Elden held out her hearing aid with an unsurprised frown that, though it defied all logic, made him all the more handsome. "You left this in the car when you thought I wasn't watching you."

"That's where you're wrong. I know you're always watching me." He scowled at her teasing. "But," Avalon sighed, "I was hoping you'd understand."

Elden opened her car door for her, something he insisted on doing every time. He blocked her view of her parents'—well, now her *mother's* lake house. "I don't understand not using something that helps you."

He was relentless, particularly when it came to her well-being. Avalon gave in to him. "I don't want Odele to see it."

"Ah." He sounded empathetic, but she knew Elden would stand firm on this. "I understand, but she's a banshee. She didn't mean to hurt you. You can't keep protecting her at your own cost." Gently, he began placing the hearing aid in her right ear. "I thought you already learned that lesson."

"I might require a remedial course." Avalon repositioned the aid until it felt comfortable. "There. Happy?"

"More than I thought possible."

The intensity of his words was still startling even after a month of being together. Elden did everything so fiercely, and in love he was no different. "Let's get Hob out of the car before he breaks a window."

Hob had licked a sticky streak across her back window. The car was new, a crossover Elden insisted she needed after her move to the rural, western coast of Washington state. The fey still kept driving the same old, broken truck, but as soon as her old car stalled *once*, she had to have a new one.

Freed from the confines of his rolling prison, Hob followed the scent of cinnamon and apples to Valerie's front door. Avalon let Elden ring the doorbell, swallowing her nervousness at seeing her mother and sister again.

Valerie swung the door open, dressed in a burgundy shawl and several gold bangles. "Ava, I didn't think you'd make it with all that ice on the road!"

"Well, we have some control over that," Avalon admitted. Valerie's embrace felt as awkward as she'd thought it would. But not entirely bad.

"I thought Odele told you this was a casual Christmas party." Valerie examined Avalon's black dress, fingering the skirt.

"And I thought she was kidding."

Valerie didn't hug Elden, and Avalon thought she and Elden both were thankful for the restraint. Instead, her mother eyed the man, and, disappointed, said to her, "Where's his crown?"

"Excuse me?"

Grabbing Elden's sleeve before he could run back to the car, Avalon demanded, "What happened to this being casual?" She was glad she'd popped a few ibuprofens on the way there.

"Princes wear crowns. Is he not a prince?"

"I—I could glamour one, I suppose," Elden offered, his reluctance obvious.

"Yes!" Valerie said.

"No," Avalon said, the final word on the matter.

Avalon pushed into the doorway, letting Hob sniff out the perimeter. Valerie's eyes widened at the size of the dog, but she simply pursed her lips and began introducing Elden to all of her friends as her daughter's *feyrie prince*.

Avalon ignored Elden's silent plea for help and left to find the food. Valerie was in her prime while acting as a hostess, not as meek as her husband had wanted her to be. Avalon muscled her way to the dessert table, shamelessly plucking herself five apple tarts for her plate.

"Glad I stashed some away before you got here." Odele crossed her arms over a tacky holiday sweater. Her cat, Clancy, perched regally on her foot. "I figured if you brought that giant with you, I'd need to be prepared."

Was that a dig against the dog or Elden? Hob was currently dragging away a leg of lamb, ignoring the poor waiter's desperate commands to stop. "We brought food as well. Christmas cookies from Lyra."

Odele brightened, dropping her arms to take up a more relaxed position. "Dad's not coming."

"Good." Avalon bit into the tart—*heaven*. "How's decorating for mom's friends?"

"If I have to install another farmhouse chandelier, I'll puke."

"I'm sure the money's good, though. How's Bruce?"

"Divorce is going quietly, but he's been getting desperate since his PR team crunched the numbers on what this would do to his career. He made Mom a lot of promises."

"Ever the politician."

"She declined every single one. She's covered our medical debt and doesn't want us to mention it again." Odele shrugged, dropping into a whisper. "She wants us to visit of our own volition, I guess."

A few holidays might not hurt. "Not Thanksgiving. You can visit me when that rolls around again. Lyra was absolutely *terrifying* during prep, but the meal was unbelievable."

Faster than Avalon could see, Odele brushed back her hair, revealing the hearing aid hiding beneath it. Odele nodded, as if she'd expected that all along. "I was wondering what happened. You heard everything I said, even when I lowered my voice."

"I'm sorry I didn't—"

"No, I'm glad. It's about time. You wouldn't let me talk about it before." Odele swiped a tart off her sister's plate. "And the inn? Reconstruction finished?"

Avalon allowed the diversion. "Mostly. Have a few items left for when the weather's better. But we're functional."

Odele twitched at her use of "we".

Avalon sighed at her reaction. "Afraid you'll have to accept him, Odd. His father assigned some permanent guards to the inn, disguised as rather unhappy landscapers. Elden's interviewing for a backup warden, which is dragging along but still progressing. We haven't had any issues since that night." Avalon reported all that with some satisfaction.

Though, it wasn't all good news. The Refuge on the Moor was on the Commission's watchlist after all that bloodshed and fire. They had sent Jesse Darling to report on the situation, and she was not as chipper as she'd been the last time.

Elden returned, pressing into Avalon's side to whisper, "Tell your mother that I can't magic ice sculptures at her whim."

Avalon shouldn't have been surprised. "She said this party was casual, and yet she wants *ice sculptures*?"

"No, she wants them for the *wedding*." He glared down at her as if this was all her fault for leaving him for dead. "I hope you'll be happy with a winter theme. I don't think we have any say in the matter. She made me look at invitation examples."

"Congratulations," Odele quipped tonelessly, though she seemed to smile at their agony. "I'm sure Mom's working on a toast as we speak."

Wedding? Evidently, Valerie needed a new therapist, one that specialized in boundaries. "She's being ridiculous. I'll talk to her." Avalon handed her plate to Elden with more force than necessary.

Odele's mood was on an upswing. "Good luck, Princess!"

"Elden, don't let Odele have a single one of those tarts!"

Avalon beelined for Valerie, skidding to a halt as Elden sidestepped in front of her. "Avalon, we're at a party."

"I need to deal with this *now*. She can't just make plans for us like that!"

"It doesn't matter. We can get married whenever you want."

"The point is—" She blinked up at him, stunned. "What did you say?"

He shrugged, as calm as she was panicked. "We can get married whenever you want. Wherever you want." He slyly glanced at her rounded ears. "Though we do have *some* time constraints." He passed his plate to Odele, a big mistake as they'd never see those tarts again, and Elden took both of Avalon's hands. "Just have a little mercy on me and don't make me wait too long. I like the idea of you wearing a symbol that you belong to me. And I to you."

She used to think the only thing a man could ever inspire in her was annoyance. Avalon stammered, "I never considered marriage before."

"You hadn't met me."

His joke sliced through her nerves, making her smile shyly. "Let's stop talking about this with Valerie in the room. We won't be able to discuss anything else if she finds out we're...considering it."

"You mentioned we were staying in a cabin separate from the house?" His grin was as mischievous as Avalon expected a feyrie's to be.

"Why don't I show you?"

Their night ended twisted in blankets, sweaty and happy. Valerie's cabin was almost too warm with the woodstove burning, and Avalon snuggled as close to Elden as she could. Whenever the party ended, they'd return to the main house to grab food to go along with the bottles of liquor they'd stolen on their way out. For now, Avalon was happy to settle herself against Elden, listening to his pros and cons list for marriage.

"And the cons?" She yawned—he'd been talking for a while.

"No cons."

"Oh, shut up." She lightly shoved at his chest. "It's only been a month. We can discuss this after a reasonable amount of time." Avalon sat up, pushing him into the mattress so she could straddle him properly. "You already have my true name. What else could I possibly give you?"

"I didn't ask for *that*." He frowned, the reminder he could control her so completely dulling the mood. "I've made my argument. I can keep silent. For a time." He grinned as she leaned down to kiss him, then turned sober. "I do understand this may be rushing things, but you did break up with me once already."

"That lasted one day, and I didn't want to! I'm not going anywhere, Elden."

"Good. Because you know I'll chain you up if you try. I've done it before."

His joke didn't hide the naked truth underneath it—Elden was afraid she'd try to leave again. Avalon slipped off him, holding out her palm. "Hand," she commanded, and waited until he obliged. She used all of her strength to crush his hand, trying to filter out the immense pain of transforming her muscles, tendons, and bones. The teeth were the worst of it.

"Avalon, you don't—"

She *did*. She did need to do this to prove herself to him. All along the way Elden had acted first, baring his heart to her, who he believed *hated* him. She could not allow him to keep taking the first steps in their relationship. She would show him how committed she was, despite the pain.

Collapsing back onto the bed, Avalon whimpered, "Whiskey, please."

A bottle, no time for glasses, appeared against her lips. She sipped while Elden scowled down at her. He smoothed her hair out of her face as she drank. "Avalon, that wasn't what I was asking for."

"What? Didn't want to be stuck with me for centuries? Too late. I'm not changing back. It *hurts*."

"Does your hearing aid even still fit?" he fussed, checking for himself.

She batted his hands, motioning with the whiskey bottle to get him to take it away. "I love you, Elden. I can't think of a better way to show you than this."

In the distance, they heard someone shout and there was a thud against their door a few moments later. Elden stood to let Hob inside, the dog shaking off snow and mud and carrying in his mouth what was meant to be the Christmas turkey.

Elden whipped the door shut, meeting Avalon's wide eyes until they both laughed.

Christmas with Avalon's family wasn't so terrible. For the first time in her life, Avalon was able to leave Odele behind without having a panic attack. Elden was right—the banshee was capable of taking care of herself, and staying on the lake kept her nightmarish premonitions to a minimum.

Avalon raced through their goodbyes, wanting to return to the inn as soon as possible. The Refuge was a popular holiday destination and Kenan had called, begging for her to return, twice.

"Let him suffer," Elden advised. "He's a grown man."

A grown man who crushed Avalon into a bear hug and raced her to the front desk to deal with the guest currently on hold and demanding an unreasonable, full refund. She dealt with that while simultaneously trying to convince Lyra her mother's apple tarts were, in fact, not better than hers and never would be. Nora Lee watched all this, a satisfied grin on her face. As if she'd had anything to do with Avalon and Elden getting together. Just because Nora Lee had advised Elden not to turn Avalon in and instead watch her every waking moment—

Avalon frowned. She didn't like feeling like someone else had control of her fate.

It was hours of catch-up for them both until Elden was able to steal some time with her. While she ran through the upcoming reservations, Elden told her about his brother's love letters he'd been sending to Tahoma, letters that viscerally described how Jin had seen her disembowel a Seelie during that battle.

"Sounds like something you'd write. Perhaps you're more like your father's side of the family than you like to think," she teased, easing up when Elden glared at her. He handed her a cup of coffee—coffee she had made—and, as she hoped, it was absolutely awful.

"Disgusting. No sugar?"

A sweetener packet bounced off her forehead.

She spent most of her life peering into the future and desperately trying to prevent her visions from coming true. As Elden spun her chair around, pushing her coffee mug down until it clinked down on the desk, she knew exactly what was coming and she could not wait for it another second.

Before Elden could kiss her, Avalon acted first.

CAST OF CHARACTERS

Avalon Golightly: *Blonde, hotheaded, and a Seer, Avalon works as a web designer/manager for Thompson's Hotel Management Solutions.*

Odele Golightly: *Tall and ethereal, Odele is a banshee and interior designer for Thompson's Hotel Management Solutions.*

Miss Pike: *Secretary for Thompson's Hotel Management Solutions.*

Thompson: *Owner and manager of Thompson's Hotel Management Solutions. Thinks everyone he meets could be a magical being.*

Elden Cavanaugh: *The grumpy, tall, dark, and handsome innkeeper of the Refuge on the Moor. His best friend is a dog. He also guards an entrance into the feyrie realm.*

Nora Lee Abernathy: *The kind, head maid of the Refuge on the Moor. Married into the Abernathy family. Former best friend of Elden's mother.*

Lyra: *The passionate and creative chef at the Refuge on the Moor. Self-proclaimed cousin of Elden. Do not be late for this nymph's meals.*

Kenan Little: *Manager-in-training and twin to Tahoma. A quarter fey of the selkie variety. Very friendly until he's not.*

Tahoma Little: *Manager-in-training and twin to Kenan. A quarter fey of the selkie variety. Loves making stupid bets.*

Prince Bane: *Elden's least favorite brother and youngest of his three half-siblings. Vindictive and the perfect example of an orator-type fey.*

Ashling Cavanaugh: *Elden's mother and the one who built the Refuge on the Moor. Reluctantly married to the unseelie king, Ashling is a master forger and enchanter.*

Jerico Abernathy: *Older than he looks, Abernathy is the head of a coven of druids that live next door to the Refuge on the Moor.*

Maetta Bradigan: *The redcap bridezilla preparing to marry Sabella, her nymph bride.*

Maddox Abernathy: *One of Abernathy's granddaughters.*

Evander: *Brother to Ashling, he is the warden of a feyrie entrance set in Scotland.*

Crown Princess Hia: *Elden's eldest sibling and heir to the Unseelie throne. Loves singing and playing pranks.*

Prince Jin: *Elden's favorite sibling and general of the Unseelie army.*

King Taliesin: *Elden's father and ruler of the Unseelie. A poet, Taliesin spends more time writing than serving his people.*

Seer Ilias: *A Seer from the Summerlands.*

Dimitrios: *A Seelie warden of a feyrie mound in Georgia, USA. Father of Sabella.*

Khaira: *A nymph and mother to Sabella.*

Sabella: *The nymph bride of Maetta Bradigan and heir to Dimitrios.*

Bruce Golightly: *Governor of Washington state and father to Avalon and Odele.*

Valeria Golightly: *Mother to Avalon and Odele.*

Nanny Blair: *Fey nanny to Avalon and Odele that was fired at Avalon's twelfth birthday.*

GLOSSARY

Author's Note: *The creatures and places in this book are inspired by known folklore, but some things have been changed to fit the story or just for my preference.*

Feyrie/Fey: *Magical beings that range from pixies to more humanoid courtly feyries. Feyries are split into two kingdoms, Seelie and Unseelie. Neither kingdom has the ability to tell lies, though the Unseelie are skilled at hiding the truth and forming unfair bargains.*

Feylands: *A parallel realm to the mortal world, only accessible through various entrances, known as feyrie mounds, which are guarded by appointed feyrie wardens and the Commission of Magic Management.*

Unseelie/Winterlands: *The darker fey are referred to as Unseelie. They hold their own court in the Winterlands, a world of dark and cold. They are ruled by King Taliesin, an orator of great skill.*

Seelie/Summerlands: *The nature-inclined, lighter fey are the Seelie. They are ruled by their Queen in the Summerlands.*

Feyrie Mound: *A feyrie mound is set into a hillside and allows entrance into the feylands. They are guarded by feyrie wardens and humans are banned from entering.*

Changeling: *Changelings are feyries that are brought to the mortal realm and traded for a human child. They are unhappy after the switch and act out toward their human parents. They undergo a painful physical change to appear human. When they are in their human state, they are able to lie* with only some discomfort and can touch iron. This dark, fey tradition has been criminalized.

Banshee: *An Unseelie, humanoid feyrie that foretells death through their nightly wailing.*

Will-o'-the-wisp: *A glowing orb that misleads travellers off the safe path and into danger.*

Orator: *Feyries that specialize in striking bargains and twisting their words.*

Redcap: *An Unseelie, solitary feyrie that craves violence and bloodshed. Some wear caps that they dip in the blood of their enemies. They have sharp teeth and malevolent tempers compared to other feyries.*

Black Dog: *A supernatural black, hellhound.*

Nymph: *In Greek mythology, these minor feyries are associated with nature.*

Dryad: *A type of nymph that inhabits a forest or a single tree.*

Arawn: *In Welsh mythos, Arawn is king of the Underworld. He was a skilled hunter. When Elden says 'Arawn', he is using it the same way Avalon says 'my gods' or 'gods help me'.*

Gorgon: *Fey women cursed to bear a head of snakes and the ability to turn men to stone if they look upon their face.*

Pixie: *Small, feisty creature capable of flight.*

ACKNOWLEDGMENTS

Self-publishing doesn't sound as if it relies on a multitude of people, but it does. Without encouragement, or people willing to take a look at your mess of a manuscript that was mostly written after the baby finally went to bed, giving up seems like the sane choice.

I have to thank my husband, for letting me talk constantly about my hallucinations of my fictional world, and my son, who was happy (sometimes) to let me write while he chewed on the arm of my computer chair. I want to thank my parents for providing reading material throughout the years, and my sister for listening to me ramble on the phone and letting me send her all the dumb jokes I wrote in this book. And to my dogs, Wiley (who inspired Hob) and Pippin! Thank you two for hanging out during my late-night writing sessions when everyone else went to bed.

Thank you to my beta readers! It still amazes me that anyone was willing to read a stranger's ramblings. Bianca-Rose, thank you so much for being the first person to read this thing. I'm excited to keep reading your work! This was my first novel, so early feedback was invaluable. Sabrina V, Kelly W, Kate K, Sarahbee, Marianna H, and Shalet A, thank you all so much! I hope you can see how much you all changed this book for the better!

Thank you to my illustrators as well! Rashed, I'm so glad I gave you more creative control over the cover. And AB Fominaya, I love how the hotel turned out and the character profiles you created!

With gratitude, Vermilion H Baine

Look out for Vermilion H Baine's next project, the next book in the *Haunted Creatures, Haunted Places* standalone series!

THE ACADEMY
OF THE
DEAD

Maddox Abernathy is the sole necromancer in a family of hedge witches. After attending a special school for necromancers run by the Commission of Magic Management, she returns home to recover from burning out after her finals.

When her rival, Atticus Blackwell, finds her and offers her a chance to return to academia *and* uncover a lost page of the Necronomicon, she knows she can't refuse. Even if she can't stand him. Even if he wants to put their brutal past behind them and become, of all things, *friends*.

But some things are meant to stay in the past, to stay buried. And the Necronomicon may be one of those things...

ABOUT THE AUTHOR

 Vermilion H Baine is an indie fantasy author based in the American Southwest. After a tour as a nuclear electrician's mate in the US Navy, she now works as a field service engineer in the semiconductor industry. She writes fantasy, low and high, and tries to sprinkle in humor between the extreme bouts of angst. If she isn't hyperfocusing on writing, she is hiking, reading, or replaying *Morrowind*. She lives with two very codependent rescue dogs, her grumpy, can-fix-anything husband, and her Viking-sized son.

The Fey Hotel is her debut novel.

instagram.com/author_vermilion_h_baine

tiktok.com/@authorvermilionhbaine

www.authorvermilionhbaine.com

SIGN UP FOR MY AUTHOR NEWSLETTER!

Find me at

www.authorvermilionhbaine.com

Our dog, Wiley, the inspiration for Hob.